SNARED

WHEN NIGHTMARES REIGN (BOOK TWO)

MISU LOY

CONTENTS

Dragon Fangs
Pashun
Historic Dragon Lands
Rokeshin
Chambrin Keep
Sinopel
Hollyhock Forest
Drakkus River
The Hellhole
The Fangwilds
Joltar
Oxlip
Tagetes
Allium
Vesper
Obanth
VALDENIA
N
E
S
W

CHAPTER ONE

From his perch on a half-rotted log, Raine leaned forward and etched another spiral into the dirt. The ground was moist yet firm and yielded nice, clean lines to the stick in his hand. A shadow fell over him, and he paused. Tilting his head slowly upward, Raine expected to see a swath of steel-gray clouds.

It felt as though they were being chased by a perpetual storm—a side effect of the substantial weather system brewing along Valdenia's western flank. It was a foreboding sight that spurred him and Sidian each morning. Eventually, it would catch up with them, but each day they evaded the pending downpour was a win.

The sight that met him wasn't a sea of ominous clouds, however. It was Sidian. His bronze cheeks were flushed a ruddy hue from the chill. In one fist, he clutched two rabbits by their hindquarters. The creatures were limp, dead.

Raine's stomach woke at the sight. It stretched and yawned a low, painful growl.

"Snails in sun hats, huh?" Sidian's head cocked as he surveyed Raine's most recent wallpaper design. He snorted. "You should have put them in scarves and winter caps."

Raine flushed, resisting the urge to scrape out his drawing. He hadn't told Sidian what they were, these images he carved whenever they stopped to make camp for the evening.

How could he? It was too embarrassing. While his mate was out hunting their meals, for their very *survival*, he was dithering on a stump with a stick, creating fanciful patterns on the ground that he hoped would one day decorate sitting rooms and bedchambers.

Oh, Raine did more than that. He helped build their shelters and fires. And he was superior at cooking since the flames couldn't singe his fingers.

But still. He wasn't providing for his mate, and it *galled*.

He'd tried. Many times over the last fortnight. As it turned out, he was a lousy hunter. His mind wandered without permission, spinning mushrooms and winterberries into whimsical wallpaper patterns. Meanwhile, their supper would wander right by without him realizing.

Swallowing his pride was easier when it meant Raine could also swallow the hot, scorched meat of Sidian's kills.

"Here. Let me." Raine took the limp carcasses from Sidian and began to skin them near the fire.

Sidian settled on the log Raine abandoned, his boots careful not to scuff Raine's snails. The fire crackled and whipped against a bitter wind as Raine worked. Blood and viscera painted his hands. It felt deliciously warm, his fingers half-numb.

The days grew ever colder with the earth's unfailing tilt from the sun. Their northward trek only compounded the season's change;

so much so, Raine felt as if they'd been slingshotted from one extreme into the other.

Weeks ago, they had been in the balmy subtropics, scrambling through palmettos and frondy foliage to put as much distance between themselves and Obanth as possible.

Then, green had yielded to amber and gold. Palmettos, to deciduous birch and maples. Darting lizards and whizzy hummingbirds all disappeared. Now, they were firmly in continental territory, camping in a coniferous section of the Fangwilds, where autumn's breath held a promising bite of winter to come.

Another icy gust slurped Raine's body heat like the greedy mouths of frost giants. He shivered. Skewering the rabbits with a stripped branch, he held it over the flames. *What good is a mountain range if it can't be bothered to block the fucking wind?*

"We have to get more supplies before we go any further." Sidian's husky voice was stilted, as if he suppressed chattering teeth.

Raine frowned against the twilight, wishing for the hundredth time that his mate would let them swap coats. Sidian had pilfered their outer layers, along with other basic supplies, while Raine had been insensate from losing his father. Submerged in a grief-logged lake, he'd been too incognizant to realize Sidian gave him the best of everything.

While Raine sported a red cloak, lined with winter ermine, Sidian wore a medium-weight jacket that wouldn't keep anyone warm once darkness fell. Not in this climate. Every time Raine tried swapping coats, Sidian refused. He stubbornly insisted Raine required a hood to conceal his identity should they pass humans.

There were no humans in these woods. They were in true wilderness, a place where rocky earth rejected agriculture. A place where white-capped mountains birthed clear, rushing rivers. But this close to their source, those rivers were mere creeks and streams. They hadn't glimpsed so much as a hunting cabin or hermitage in days.

"How are we g-going to get supplies, exactly?" Raine wasn't as adept at controlling his shivers.

Another heat-slurping gust swept their campsite. Wood clattered and fell, leaving a gap in the slanted wall behind Sidian, where their makeshift shelter stood.

Sidian's frame shuddered. He dug his fingers under his arms, bracing himself against the chill. "We're coming up to Drakkus Valley. Several villages sit near the Fangwilds."

Villages meant humans. And Guardians.

Raine rotated the skewer to cook the backsides of the rabbits. The smoky scent of seared meat wafted enticingly. Almost as enticing as the heat licking his fingers.

"Are you s-sure that's wise?" Raine asked carefully.

"We're well beyond Oxlip," Sidian said, correctly interpreting the reason for Raine's reluctance. "This area is significantly less populated. We'll go someplace quiet to get what we need."

Raine chewed his bottom lip, thinking there *wasn't* any quiet place near Drakkus Valley. Not right now. Winter might be hovering like an eager specter, but it was still peak harvest.

The Drakkus Valley was the tip of a massive swath of fertile land that stretched all the way to Allium. The Pash-Ox Trading Route would be glutted with merchants until the last of this season's grains and hardy vegetables were distributed.

Raine pressed along the rabbits with his forefinger and thumb to test their doneness. Satisfied by the meat's consistency, he snapped the fire-blackened branch in half and passed a skewered rabbit to Sidian. His mate ate delicately, tearing at the outermost meat to release the steam before biting down. Raine scarfed his portion as only a dragon could. The heat didn't blister his mouth, and he fought a moan as he chewed a bulging mouthful.

All too soon, he was down to gristle and bone. He tossed his skewer into the fire and watched Sidian pick apart his own rabbit.

As always, a crushing wave of tenderness enveloped Raine as he surveyed his mate. The most precious being in all the world. It was strange—and frightening—to feel his heart beating inside his chest and know that it was all an illusion. That his heart wholly and completely resided in this man. And that he would never get it back.

Sidian's velvet eyes met his, and Raine's stomach swooped like a flock of starlings.

"I don't know," Raine said softly. "We've m-made it this far without issue only because we've stuck to the Fangwilds. Going into town, any town, f-feels risky."

"All this hunting and foraging slows us down." Sidian paused to take another bite. "Once we have proper supplies and rations, we'll cover ground more quickly. We can reach Moontop inside a week."

Moontop. Raine's blood buzzed at the thought. Sidian still didn't believe Nyx was there. It was one of those things they didn't discuss. Along with Arastus Chambrin's demise, the location of the breeding dragons, and Sidian's defection from the guild.

Those topics weren't off-limits, per se. But they were tricky, like navigating a field of gopher holes in the dark.

Could they really reach Moontop so soon? Raine knew their progress had been hindered by a lack of food, but he hadn't realized just how much. Sidian's idea of grabbing supplies grew more attractive as he considered it.

He couldn't fucking *wait* to see the look on Sidian's face when he was reunited with his long-presumed dead brother. Sidian wore his grief like a mantle. It made him cold and closed off. Wary and distrustful and wounded. Raine longed to rip it off him, to see what Sidian might be like without its weight.

But going into town ...

Raine was eager to get to Moontop. More so than Sidian, considering he was the only one who believed in what—or, rather, *who* awaited them. But Sidian had aided Raine's escape from the guild and was currently on the run with him. Which meant any encounter with Guardians would not only endanger Raine's life ... but Sidian's, as well.

Unacceptable. "We can't. Sidian, the guild will be after you, too. If anything happens to you—"

He broke off as another flush swept his face. Then immediately scolded himself. He was allowed to worry. His concern for Sidian didn't have to mean anything *salacious*. They were friends. It was perfectly normal for him to want to keep Sidian safe.

But he knew it wasn't just friendship that compelled him.

Flustered, he turned and busied himself with smothering the fire. Darkness would be upon them soon, and given their criminal status, they only ever kept a fire long enough to cook.

Thanks to a combination of them sticking to the deeper parts of the Fangwilds and a healthy dose of luck, their smoke had yet to draw any unwanted visitors. But as much as Raine yearned to keep the fire going—last night's cold had damn near frozen his marrow—it was better not to tempt fate.

"I've received considerable training with both stealth and swords," Sidian murmured at his back. There was a wryness to his tone, a gentle amusement. His mate still didn't know how keenly Raine felt for him. That the thought of Sidian in danger made Raine into an animal.

Raine was desperate to keep it that way. The very last thing he wanted was to watch their friendship disintegrate like sun-brittled sand because he couldn't be a friend—and *only* a friend—to the man who housed his heart and shared his soul.

"You are shadow and death," Raine drawled, attempting to ease the intensity of his aborted declaration from earlier. "A m-mighty captain, indeed. But still just a man, and Guardian swords are rather sharp."

Raine's eyes darted to the hilt jutting behind Sidian's shoulder. The Guardians of Vale all possessed glimmering white blades hewn from dragon bone. A macabre necessity, since the only thing that could pierce dragon skin was their bone. And the Guardians of Vale—for all their varying good deeds—were secretly dragon hunters at their core.

And what pierced dragon flesh with the ease of traditional steel also cut through humans like a hot knife through butter. If Raine accidentally touched the wrong side of Sidian's longsword, he'd nick a thumb. But Sidian would lose his.

It was one of the reasons the guild was so well-trained. They had to be, in order to wield their blades effectively while matching dragon-fast reflexes.

"I could take you, couldn't I?" Sidian purred, a gleam in his dark eyes. His lips curled in a manner Raine knew was meant to taunt him. And it did, but not in the way his mate imagined.

Oh, yes. Sidian could take him. *Right here, right now, please.*

Raine grit his teeth against a surge of lust. For the thousand-millionth time, he was grateful for the length and thickness of his coat. He burned for Sidian constantly. A fierce need that never relented.

Somehow, miracle of miracles, he'd grown used to it; being enflamed for his mate. And no matter how great Raine's ardor was, his cock had its limits. His erection would eventually abate, like a kicked puppy that finally understood his master did not want to play.

"I'm man enough to admit when my sword skills are inferior," Raine said primly. And by the Divine, did that sound filthy. He was glad for the cold. His red ears probably just seemed wind-bitten. "But if your ex-comrades are anywhere n-near as good as you" —and they were, regrettably— "then your ability to defeat me won't guarantee your victory against other Guardians."

"How little you think of me." Sidian stood, his rabbit picked clean to the bone. His shoulder brushed against Raine's as he tossed his skewer into the smoldering embers. "I can handle a sword better than any unit we might encounter."

Raine's mind plunged into the gutter. That husky voice, so close to his ear, practically whispering about his sword prowess ... *Fuck.*

He stood there like a tongue-tied simpleton, miming a fish out of water and wishing Sidian would stop looking quite so closely at his countenance, which surely revealed every depraved fantasy he'd ever had about his mate.

A drop of ice struck his nose. Then another. In seconds, a merciless deluge drenched the world. Thousands of heavy raindrops pummeled him. The fire was sodden ash, the ground already gone to mud.

Sidian's face twisted in an echo of Raine's misery as he reached for his hand and tugged. Raine savored the contact as they ran into their shelter. A scruffy lean-to of branches and brush, it was *not* watertight. Frigid drips worked their way through the slanted roof and splashed on his head every few seconds.

"F-Fucking hell," he moaned, yanking his hood overhead.

Dried leaves and pine needles insulated them from the freezing ground, and the branches held back the wind. But their shelter was by no means intended to withstand a torrential downfall.

Raine glanced sideways at Sidian and bit back another curse. His cloak insulated him from the steady trickle above, but Sidian wasn't as fortunate. His black hair was plastered to his head, and water seeped through the thick fabric of his coat.

"No," Sidian said, reaching a hand to stop Raine as he fumbled for the buttons of his cloak.

"You're getting soaked," Raine protested. "Water doesn't get through my c-coat. We can use it as a blanket."

Sidian shook his head. "You'll get too cold if you remove it. My coat's made of wool. It'll be fine."

But for how long? The air only *felt* freezing. As the rain was proving, it wasn't actually cold enough for snow.

Yet.

Raine put his back to one of the tree trunks bracing their shelter and closed his eyes. Defeat welled inside him as he considered their situation.

His mate was *cold*. His mate was cold and wet and exhausted from working so hard to provide.

Vicious claws raked inside Raine's chest, brutal and punishing. He had to do better. His mate deserved more than this. Squatting in the rain, drenched and shivering without enough food. *I will not fail him.*

"Sidian, please take my coat. I don't need it."

Raine reached for the top button of his cloak. Sidian stopped him again. His fingers dug forcefully into Raine's hand. A warning.

"Leave it."

There was a darkness to his mate's command, a note of finality. Raine gnashed his teeth but didn't argue. Truth be told, he was powerless when it came to Sidian. The man could ask him for anything, *anything*, and Raine would give it to him.

If only Sidian would request something selfish for a change. *Give me your rabbit skewer. Switch me coats. Lay in the mud so I may step on your back as I cross this puddle.*

Any one of those would be preferable to Sidian demanding they share food equally. That Raine keep his coat. That whatever they suffered, they suffered together.

It was untenable. *Let me suffer*, he wanted to scream. *Let me bear every burden. Let me* love *you*.

Sidian scooched closer, until their bodies pressed together. Raine's pulse leapt, as it always did when they had to share warmth. But as he glimpsed the blue tinge of Sidian's lips and the bleached white of his damp skin, his burgeoning arousal sank like a stone.

Raine's dragon blood meant he ran hotter than a human. It was a heat Sidian seemed to perpetually crave. His subtropical roots withered in the frost, though he always tried to conceal how affected he was. Probably so that Raine wouldn't rip his cloak off, scattering every button in a great rush to swaddle him with it.

Raine had been proud—so foolishly proud—to be able to provide warmth for his mate. To *be* that warmth, even. He could see now that it wasn't enough. Their conditions were worsening along with the weather.

Sidian was right. Their current gear was too meager to sustain them this far north. The threat of the guild was immaterial to his mate freezing to death.

"We'll f-find better gear tomorrow," Raine said, uncertain of who he was trying to reassure more. "In one of the smaller villages, like you m-mentioned."

Sidian grunted his assent, likely forgoing speech because his teeth really would chatter.

Any supplies scavenging scheme was risky. But it was that, or die out here, exposed to the elements. Something his mate had already realized.

The storm howled and battered their shelter. They huddled together more snugly, their heads and limbs overlapping like littermates seeking warmth and comfort. Raine felt every shudder and breath of his mate, and concentrated on covering as much of Sidian's exposed skin as he could.

That Sidian didn't try to deter him said more than anything just how chilled he was.

In the pattering darkness, they slept.

CHAPTER TWO

They stood before a lone cabin. It sat on the outskirts of a village bordering Drakkus Valley, a sweeping stretch of plains that folded into the young Drakkus river. A watchtower was perched miles away, on the highest knoll of a distant field.

This village was small, boasting a single road—which they stood at the very end of. The reeking stench of a tanning hut wafted on the breeze, explaining why so few hamlets occupied this side of town.

"This is a bad idea. Who even lives here?" Raine hissed.

Sidian pointed out a discreet metal pendant dangling behind a dusty windowpane. It was the guild's emblem, three shadow warriors crouched protectively before a backdrop of nine mountains.

"Servicemen and women sometimes offer their homes for guild use during their terms. This is Captain Lyka Vithier's cottage. She's away on duty and has reserve gear we can use."

Raine blinked in surprise. He *knew* Lyka Vithier. She was the svelte female captain who had attacked Evin's thunder outside Sinopel.

He recalled the bald hatred in her eyes, the way she'd chased his death as if he were a diseased rat. It was definitely a good thing Lyka was away.

Sidian searched the withering rose bushes near the front door and produced a false stone. The guild enjoyed their hollow rock cases and sure enough, it opened to reveal a house key.

The door hinges squeaked open, revealing a simple yet feminine dwelling. Lyka the Hellcat enjoyed frilly pillows and furniture patterned with dainty pink and white phlox.

Sidian slung his ratty, stolen pack onto a floral sofa cushion and beelined for a closed door. His was the stride of a man who had been here before and knew where he was going. Raine's insides twisted as he wondered just how closely acquainted Sidian was with Lyka.

Lyka, who was built like Rosa, with hips and breasts that beckoned most men's hands like braziers on a cold night. Had her curves beckoned Sidian? Was that why his mate knew this residence?

Shutting the entrance behind him, Raine moved more slowly through the space. The cabin's pine board walls were incapable of masking the fetid miasma of animal skins curing to the east. Any carnal delights partaken in Lyka's home would have been inundated in the foul odor. The thought flooded him with petulant satisfaction, bordering on smug.

Sidian is a grown man, entitled to his pursuits, Raine reminded himself.

Even so, his hands formed fists as he trailed Sidian into a bedchamber. A bed large enough for two sat against the far wall, trimmed with a garish fuchsia comforter. His heart winced, both for its crime of taste and his brief mental image of Sidian and Lyka intertwined beneath it.

His mate knelt upon the floor and rummaged beneath Lyka's elevated mattress. One after another, he extracted sacks of gear and weapons. Several rolled sleeping bags, a tent condensed into a carrier, rucksacks, coats and boots, bundles of sheathed daggers and swords ... Soon, a heap of supplies dominated the floor.

Sidian stood and faced the pile, hands on hips as he surveyed their loot. "This should get us to Moontop."

Raine opened one of the backpacks: a fire striker, flint, spare guild hose and socks, empty canteens. He extracted a small pouch. It was full, but he couldn't tell what was inside. Undoing the twine, he found cracked yellow corn. Birdfeed? An oddly fanciful item amid the necessities.

Apparently, Captain Lyka's enmity for winged creatures stopped at dragons.

"Put it back," Sidian said when Raine cast it aside as useless. At Raine's puzzled frown, he added, "Crushed maize is lightweight and full of calories. There'll be a small pot in the bag for boiling."

Ah. Well, that explained it. Lyka hadn't struck Raine as a tender-hearted feeder of birds or any other creature.

Cracked corn was an ingredient, not a meal. Raine obediently replaced the grain sack, then slid the bulging backpack toward Sidian before going to search for other provisions. It wasn't like Sidian required his assistance sorting through gear he was already familiar with. A little *too* familiar.

Lyka's larder yielded more shelf-stable goods. Dry oatmeal, cured meats, and salted walnuts. Everything was lightweight, high energy, and easily packed. Raine lined the countertop with his bounty, pursing his lips. They had food and gear. But there was one necessity blatantly absent.

Crossing his fingers, he opened the last unexplored room. *Yes.* Raine struck gold. Captain Lyka's bathing room possessed a round wooden tub, fed by a pump on the wall. The towel shelf beside the tub was laden with soaps and oils that sang to the depths of his soul.

He stripped without conscious decision and clamored into the washtub, then worked the pump until his shoulder burned and water swallowed his thighs. It was uncomfortably cold, but nowhere near as brisk as the mountain streams.

A long-suffering sigh came from the doorway. "You realize we need to leave promptly, yes?"

"Nope," Raine chirped, working a cake of oat soap into a milky lather. "You're the one who said Lyka is away, and this house is ours to use."

"No." Sidian stepped through the doorframe and hovered near the basin, peering down at him with a puckered brow. "This house is for the *guild* to use. We were fortunate enough to discover it vacant, but traveling Guardians can stop here at any time. Did you not see the watchtower?"

Raine dunked a nearby clay pitcher into his bathwater and wet his hair. Massaging his mane with a peony-scented shampoo bar, he said, "Yes, I saw the watchtower. But last I checked, Lyka can't be more than thirty summers old. That watchtower has been around for a century, at least, so the sky watchers must stay someplace else."

Sidian's brows rose sharply, making him resemble Nyx so strongly, Raine's breath caught. He really was a numbskull for not marking their relation sooner.

"Lyka joined the Guardians of Vale the same year I did. We went through training together. You know her?"

Leaving the shampoo to marinate, Raine began scrubbing his frame a second time. "Not as well as you," he muttered, lathering his arms. "She attacked me on the road a while back." Sidian's eyes widened. That mild display of alarm snapped Raine's temper. "Don't worry. Your precious girlfriend is alive and unharmed, probably gallivanting across Valdenia in search of innocent dragons to slaughter."

"Lyka is skilled. My concern was for you," Sidian said rigidly. "And there is no arrangement between us. Our association was purely physical." Sidian frowned at Raine's expression, which felt pinched tight. "Unlike dragons, humans do not mate for life. I don't appreciate your judgment. I've neither sired bastards nor broken hearts."

Raine averted his gaze, shame welling. Sidian thought he looked down on him. Raine couldn't correct him, either. He couldn't admit that it had been jealousy marring his features, and not some inflated sense of moral superiority. Not without revealing things better left secret.

Sidian's footsteps clipped out of the room. Shoulders sagging, Raine rushed through his bath and emerged on a dripping trail, one of Lyka's too-small towels wrapped around his waist.

Sidian was in the kitchen packing up the rations Raine had set out. He paused to throw Raine a bundle of clothes without looking. Fleece-lined tights and a cream sweater hit Raine square in the chest.

He dressed in an awkward shuffle, the damp skin of his legs sticking inside the tights.

Sidian resumed packing their provisions with short, angry motions. His mate was mad. At him. Truth welled in Raine's mouth, words that would damn him more than this minor tiff. He turned away from the kitchen, horrified at the powerful urge to divulge all.

He needed distance. A moment alone to ground himself and suppress his bleeding dragon heart. His gaze caught on the towel shelf, reminding him of his original purpose in seeking the bathroom. He ducked inside and gathered as many bathing products as he could carry.

Muffled voices permeated the cottage.

Raine froze at the threshold, an array of soaps and oils clutched to his chest. Sidian stood across the way, similarly arrested in the kitchen archway. Their eyes met in shared panic.

Sidian recovered first. He rushed the cabin entrance and threw the bolt as the doorknob turned.

"It's locked," a man complained, jiggling the handle to no avail. He began knocking. "Hello. Who's here?"

Sidian held a finger to his lips as he crept from the door. They swiftly collected the gear Sidian had separated for their journey. Sidian strapped two extra swords to his back before pulling on a gray winter coat and rucksack. The tent carrier was strapped beneath his pack like a bedroll.

Raine crammed soaps and vials into his pack. Sidian gave him an exasperated look, but Raine just shrugged. "You have your priorities, and I have mine."

They were fully outfitted in under a minute. Sidian yanked Raine's hood over his damp hair before leading them to Lyka's bedroom window. Sidian drew the curtains, and two Guardians gaped at them from the other side.

"Run," Sidian yelled.

They dashed through the living room, drew back the bolt, and sprang out the front door. There was a shout of pain as the door smacked into something solid. A Guardian sprawled to the ground, clutching his forehead.

"Sorry," Raine called over his shoulder, wincing as blood dripped down the man's face.

"Not that way," Sidian barked without slowing. Raine had begun angling for the Fangwilds. He corrected course, falling in line behind Sidian, who added, "We don't want them to know where we're going. We have to lose them first."

Lose them? Raine chanced another backward glance. *Shit.* All three Guardians were hot on their heels. He kicked up his pace to match Sidian's as they speared deeper into town.

"How are we going to lose them? We're in the middle of fucking nowhere."

An elderly couple rocked in wicker chairs beneath a porch awning. They were bundled in patchwork blankets, enviably relaxed and unthreatened as they sipped steaming mugs. The street was otherwise empty, the villagers preoccupied with the endless chores that came before winter.

"They don't know who we are," Sidian panted. "Probably think we're squatters or thieves. Keep running. They'll tire eventually. Decide we're more trouble than we're worth."

Just then, a gust of wind grabbed Raine's hood like a fist and ripped it from his head. The cool air felt like ice against his wet hair.

One of their pursuers shouted, "It's him! It's Raine Chambrin."

Fuck. Raine craned his neck and winced. Sidian's supposition lost all merit as the Guardian unit redoubled their efforts to catch them.

"Now would be a good time to transform," Sidian gasped. "We can escape on your wings."

"I don't know how." Sidian flashed him an incredulous look over his shoulder. "Dragons are taught by their parents or some shit. I don't know," Raine snapped, embarrassed and frustrated he couldn't oblige his mate.

They had to think of something soon. The road ran to open sky and valley. Scant trees formed windrows between farm fields, where villagers steadily plowed the post-harvest soil. A watchtower loomed beyond.

Nowhere to run. Nowhere to hide. Danger behind and ahead. *We have to fight*.

Sidian reached the same conclusion, breakneck gait slowing as he dug for the blades on his back. Raine was ready and caught the sword tossed at him. White dragon bone shimmered, a razor-sharp gladius.

They were in the thick of town, humble hamlets lining either side of the uneven road.

"We need to engage them here, without drawing the watch-tower's attention," Sidian said, lurching left.

Raine followed him down a stone garden path between houses. It dead-ended at a copse of fruit trees. *Good.* The trees provided cover from the watchtower.

They spun around. Branches, heavy with apples and pears, scratched at their backs as three Guardians appeared. The captain charged ahead of his unit—the man they'd knocked down with Lyka's door. He looked absolutely savage. The whites of his eyes popped against smears of scarlet blood as he snarled.

Raising a longsword, the captain swiped at Raine's stomach.

The sword arced downward, but Raine made no move to dodge or parry. His eyes were caught on the glint of gold banding the hunter's bicep. Paralyzed by revelation.

These are good men.

Unlike the corrupt Guardians who had kidnapped Rosa, this captain and his unit were simply following orders. Orders that, in their minds, protected Valdenia. Protected their families. Raine couldn't just cut them down like wild dogs. Doubt and indecision turned his body to stone. His gladius hung limp at his side.

Sidian leapt in front of Raine and blocked the captain's blow. Muscles strained against the shoulders of his coat as he shoved the man back with the edge of his longsword. Then, Sidian was on him.

No hesitancy. No compunction. Just kill or be killed.

The sight should have galvanized Raine. It should have turned his stone limbs back to useful bone and sinew and life. Instead, he stood there like a dumb statue as the other two Guardians reached him. One fisted a short sword and the other, a rapier. Both blades were pale and shimmery in the dappled light.

One of the journeymen lunged at Raine, his rapier drawn back for a lethal plunge. A half-rotted apple tripped the journeyman mid-stride. As the hunter pitched forward, his rapier bit through the fur lining of Raine's cloak and sliced his side.

That slice of pain was an awakening. Sidian's words of only weeks ago echoed through Raine's mind. *The only atonement a dragon can offer is their throat to a knife.* His mate no longer believed those words, but these journeymen did.

It was either them or Raine. Needless death either way, but he'd be damned if it was his own.

Raine's gladius met and blocked the hunter's next thrust. As the other journeyman joined their fray, Raine found himself in a two-against-one skirmish. The mixed weapons of his opponents gave the duo an edge. While the rapier performed long strikes that kept Raine on the defensive, the short sword ducked low and close, aiming for the arteries exposed by his upraised arms.

He retreated through the trees, butting against a woodshed as he dodged and struck. Swordplay was a familiar activity for Raine, emphasis on the word *play*. He was used to dull steel, not razor-sharp bone. Used to parrying his ruthless yet doting father, not two vicious strangers who were blinded by lies and eager to spill his blood as if he was their worst enemy.

This was not swordplay, but a fight to the death.

As Raine struggled to adjust his fighting style accordingly, the two journeymen pinned him against the shed. Busy thwarting a rapier to the face, Raine reacted a second too late to evade the swinging short sword. There was a shock of pain as the blade glanced off his ribcage. It continued forward and sank through the shed wall at Raine's back.

Elsewhere in the yard, Sidian cursed. His voice sounded gruff with pain.

Raine's restraint snapped. His mate needed him.

Preoccupied with working his short sword from the shed, the journeyman didn't have time to register his end. Raine's gladius cut through the hunter's neck like softened butter, severing his head from his shoulders.

Whipping around before the man's head hit the ground, Raine deflected an incoming rapier thrust and buried his gladius into the other journeyman's abdomen. The man coughed red as his rapier thudded against the earth. Raine wrenched his blade from the dying man's chest with an impatient twist, then went to help his mate.

Only, Raine's assistance wasn't needed. Death stained the grass as the hostile captain's throat emptied across the lawn. Sidian stood over him, wiping a handkerchief down his longsword to remove the blood.

Adrenaline drained from Raine faster than an uncorked bath, leaving him shaken.

Justifying the hunters' deaths in the heat of battle was one thing. In the ringing silence that followed, the deaths of good men weighed him like anchors. His knees wavered at the grisly corpses around them.

These men had families. Hopes and dreams and countless breaths, all stolen for eternity. They'd just been doing their *job*.

Once he was satisfied with his sword's cleanliness, Sidian sheathed it. Their gazes met and held.

A well of emotion burgeoned behind those fawn eyes, darkening them to black.

Fuck. Did Sidian believe his honor was now tarnished? As soiled with blood as the rag fisted at his side?

Raine's heart bled with pain. "Sidian." His voice cracked.

Sidian's countenance shuttered to inscrutability, until Raine couldn't begin to guess at his thoughts. He dropped the bloody handkerchief onto the slain captain's cooling corpse, then glanced at the watchtower.

"We need to leave."

CHAPTER THREE

Wind howled through the forest, battering their tent. Outside, evergreens thrashed so violently, it sounded as if the mountain itself was shaking apart. Raine cracked an eyelid, just enough to make sure the earth held firm and there was no immediate danger. A gray dawn peered at him through the slit of their tent flap. Satisfied, he closed his eye and snuggled deeper into the bundle of silken warmth at his side.

There was something about the cold, harsh conditions beyond their thin tent that made him feel that much cozier. Raine could spend eternity just like this. Here. With his mate. Safe and warm, alone together and deliciously comfortable.

Sidian's voice, extra raspy from sleep, shattered Raine's fantasy. "It's time to get up."

"No, it isn't."

Sidian shifted, as if to stand. Raine clung like a limpet, tightening his arms and legs around his mate's frame to keep him still.

Camping halfway up a mountain had its perks. Last night had been practically polar, forcing them to cleave more closely than ever to share body heat. And if Raine enjoyed it far more than a platonic traveling companion should have? Well, that was his business.

"We slept in," Sidian said, prying Raine's arms with enough determined strength that Raine released him.

"It's barely dawn," Raine protested. He sat up and accepted a handful of walnuts.

"It's ten thousand feet to the summit from here. We need to reach ..." Sidian faltered and Raine winced.

From the start of their journey, Sidian had made it abundantly clear he did not believe his brother was alive. Nothing Raine said changed this. Nothing. With Sidian, seeing was believing. Period.

"... our destination by nightfall," Sidian finished at length. "It'll be too cold to make camp."

Sidian said the word "cold" like it was a swear word, causing a brief smile to flit across Raine's face. In the sweltering south, his mate couldn't handle the heat. In the mountains, he couldn't handle the cold, though he did his best to mask his discomfiture. Sidian was one persnickety flower, and for some ridiculous reason, that made Raine melt with fondness. If he could, he would dedicate his life to regulating Sidian's atmosphere, always ensuring his mate's supreme comfort.

Sidian was more than persnickety. He was also right. They had begun their steep, relentless climb two days ago. First, traversing over the foothills leading up to Moontop. Then, scaling the first half of the towering volcanic mountain they presently perched upon. Moontop's midsection was sprawling and pleasant. The wildlife, gentle and varied. They'd seen marmots and bobcats and reindeer and more. Dozens of streams trickled over the rocks, splashing into thundering cataracts that fed the rivers throughout Valdenia. Fragrant pines and balsam firs sheltered them from the biting wind.

Last night, they made camp at the tree line. From here on out, no more forest. Just slick rocks and jutting cliffs. And snow. So much snow. They had until tonight to locate Nyx's mysterious hideaway. And if they didn't? If Raine was wrong?

They would die.

We won't die. If Raine believed nothing else, he knew his father had loved him. And he would have never directed them here if there was any chance of failure.

He swallowed against the foreign mass in his throat. Thoughts of his father always made it swell. It felt so frighteningly physical, he once made Sidian check inside his throat, convinced there was a melon-sized stone crammed beneath his collarbone. His mate swore there was nothing there.

But there was. Raine knew there was. Sometimes, like now, it swelled so large he couldn't breathe.

Sidian knelt in front of him. Warm fingers cupped his forehead as if feeling for a fever. "Are you okay?"

Raine closed his eyes and reveled in the contact. The mass in his throat eased like a bear retreating inside its cave. It wasn't gone. It never was. But for now, a reprieve. "Yeah. Sorry. Want me to help take down the tent?"

His mate's hand dropped as he shook his head. "There's no point in bringing it. It won't be of any use to us, and we need to pack as light as possible."

Fawn eyes flicked meaningfully to Raine's backpack, which was weighed down with soaps and scented oils.

Raine grabbed his pack and cradled it protectively. "Necessities," he said firmly.

Sidian's eyes rolled heavenward, but he didn't argue.

They had each slept in their coats and they were leaving the tent behind, so it wasn't long before they were prepared to depart. Which was fortunate since, as Sidian already pointed out, they were late to start.

He climbed out of the tent after Sidian and stood in a misty white world. Sidian was gone, vanished in the fog. Raine held a hand in front of his face and saw nothing but white. It was the thickest fog he'd ever experienced. And the deadliest, considering they were about to climb a damned mountain. The steepest, most dangerous section of it, with no trees or level ground to stop an accidental plunge.

What were they going to do now?

"It's a cloud." Sidian's voice was further away than Raine expected. "Walk towards me. You're almost through it."

Raine smiled at the mist. A cloud. He was in a cloud and he wasn't even flying. The fog didn't seem so bad now. More like a friend. Throwing out his hands, he walked forward blindly. After ten careful steps or so, he wondered if he was heading in the right direction. As he opened his mouth to call for Sidian, a hand grasped his wrist and tugged. Raine's stomach jolted with alarm as he was pulled through space and lifted onto a boulder. His feet fumbled against uneven rock.

Strong arms steadied him as Sidian's features came into sharp focus. By the Divine, he was handsome. It struck Raine out of nowhere sometimes, how gorgeous his mate was. Like a sucker punch to the gut, it left him gasping.

Sidian's smirk was fiendish with the mercenary triumph of a successful scare. Raine huffed and stepped away from his mate before he did something insane. Like, try to kiss the smugness from Sidian's lips.

The sky was a pale, watery blue with only a few straggling clouds. He looked down where one of those stragglers swallowed their feet. It wrapped the mountain like a milky sea, so thick he could drag his fingers through it. When he turned back around, Sidian just stood there, watching him. His expression was perfectly masked, as impassive as the clouds. It made Raine twitchy.

He shifted his weight, adjusting his backpack. "Ready?"

Sidian's soft mouth thinned with displeasure. "As I'll ever be."

Raine snorted a laugh, both at his tone and demeanor. "What's the matter? Is the big, bad mountain too tall for you?"

Sidian grabbed the top of Raine's pack and yanked him forward so that Raine was in the lead. "It's an active volcano with a climb so perilous, it's illegal. And there's snow on its peak."

He said that last part as though it was a crime against nature. Raine snickered into his hand but let Sidian prod him along without further teasing.

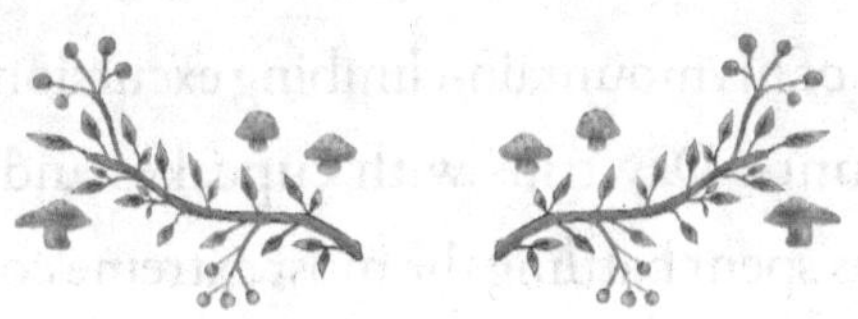

He lost his mirth after about six thousand feet of climbing. "How much further?" he whined, holding his knees.

Raine was as strapping a lad as any, but after ascending sheer rock walls and cliff edges for ages, his limbs ached in protest. A dragon's unmatched stamina had nothing on Moontop. Its terrain was steep and impossibly rugged. Sometimes, the rocky ground beneath them disappeared at a cliff's edge and they had to get creative to press onward.

What they lacked in appropriate tools and gear, they made up for with bodies in peak physical form. They had their strength, and they had each other. More than once, they had navigated an unpassable section of mountain with acrobatic handholding and sheer grit.

"How should I know?" Sidian shrugged. He stood tall and undaunted, having adapted almost magically to Moontop's demands. As if their climb was a stirring challenge for his guild-honed physique.

"You're a freak of nature," Raine accused, his own posture slouchy and very much daunted. "Aren't you sore, even a little?"

"All Guardians are required to hike the eastern Fangs. It's part of our onboarding, the first task assigned after a unit is organized. Afterwards, we're subject to regular climbs to ensure we remain in shape. I've hiked the ridge between Snaggletooth and Draggair six times now."

Sidian spoke of his mountain-climbing excursions as if they were quick, little jaunts. Day trips with cupcakes and picnic baskets instead of weeks spent battling the most extreme conditions on the planet. As he spoke, his breathing was so perfectly normal, Raine wanted to push him. Only a little. Nothing dangerous. Maybe just shove his back up against that craggy mountain wall and then slam their mouths together and—

And, what? Raine wasn't sure. His knowledge of sex was vague on purpose, considering he'd avoided the subject like a disease most of his life. But the longer he was around Sidian, the more difficult it was to resist his desire—this fierce, primal urge to possess and be possessed. It pulsated from his core and permeated every fiber of his being.

"That's really special," he drawled, hoping his wind-chafed cheeks camouflaged the hot flush enveloping him. "Just so you know, I've hiked zero mountains, ever. And if we have to climb another six thousand feet, I'm done. Just leave me here to die."

Raine slumped upon a boulder. Half its rocky surface glistened as if wet. Nothing was wet this high up. It was ice. Black ice. It seeped from a thousand wrinkles along the mountain walls and encased their path, making every step treacherous. The higher they went, the harder it was to find dry patches to place their feet so the crooked rocks wouldn't spill them over the edge.

"Moontop's peak is not six thousand feet up," Sidian said with deliberate patience. "And considering the summit doubles as the mouth of a volcano, I assume our destination lies lower." He turned, looking outward at the horizon and distant mountains. "We need to reach it soon."

We need to reach it soon. It was true. The watery sky had turned a richer shade of blue over the last couple hours. Richer ... and darker. Day was tumbling into dusk right before their eyes. Moontop's climate was already forbiddingly glacial in full sun. After dark, it would frost them over the same way it had frozen cascading streams mid-splash.

"Alright," Raine said, pushing himself up. "Let's do it."

For the next hour, Sidian pushed them arduously, keeping their bodies warm with exertion. Death hovered over them; a ticking clockface with a hoarfrost mouth, spurring them faster and further and always *up*. They made it another two thousand feet before the sun began to set.

There was no sign of Nyx. Or a hideaway. Or even the slightest evidence that anyone had ever traversed this gleamingly gelid terrain prior to them. Raine exhaled a stream of frosted breath as he surveyed the rapid onset of night. Already, blue shifted to purple. A sickle moon brightened against the deepening twilight.

It was done. They were done. It would be pitch black in a handful of minutes. They could neither press forward nor descend to safety. It would be impossible to avoid the slick swatches of black ice in the dark. Death beckoned from all sides.

"So much for the fifth spine," Sidian said dully, sitting on the flat edge of a jutting black rock. Raine hopped up next to him and pulled his cloak tight, suppressing a shiver.

When he was sure his teeth wouldn't chatter, he said, "We have to be close. Nyx wouldn't stay that much higher up. It'd be unlivable."

It is already unlivable, a quiet voice whispered.

"How cold are you?" Sidian asked, sounding suspicious.

"As cold as you, pro-ba-bly." His teeth rattled together. Sidian looked more closely at him and cursed.

"Your lips are turning blue, idiot." Raine winced as Sidian viciously massaged his fingers.

"Hurts," he said, shivering harder. Sidian pulled Raine's hands inside his coat, tucking an icy palm beneath each of his armpits. He then huddled Raine closer, sealing their bodies for warmth.

"We're really high up," Raine murmured into Sidian's chest.

"No shit. That's the problem. We should have turned back sooner," he whispered darkly. His chin rested atop Raine's hooded head like a reassuring weight.

Raine shook his head, jostling Sidian. "Nyx doesn't know we're here, and he can't see us. Maybe he can hear us. We're high enough up, only someone on this mountain will be able to."

Sidian pulled away and seemed to consider Raine's suggestion. Then, he tilted his head back and bellowed, "NYX!"

A vise clamped Raine's heart at his mate's cry. Sidian's determined skepticism was more formidable than iron. That he trusted Raine enough to suspend his disbelief, even for an instant ... It shattered Raine. He was humbled and awed and terrified. Especially terrified. Because if Nyx didn't come through, Sidian would never recover from the pain of losing his brother twice.

Please hear him, Nyx.

But Sidian yelled and yelled, his brother's name echoing in the darkness. Nobody came.

Sidian lapsed into bleak silence after screaming himself hoarse. His fingers dug painfully into Raine's back beneath his cloak as he sought to keep his extremities from dying.

And they would die. The black of night encompassed them. Wind cut through their coats like razor blades. Raine's shivers slowed as his mind grew sluggish.

It was strange being here. Raine had viewed this mountain his whole life, never once imagining it was where he would die.

The mass in his throat swelled with his sorrow, and an early memory teased the edges of his mind; the first time the Cavern dragons shook the land with their combined roars. Raine had been sunning himself on the lawn with Clover and Yip when it happened. His fear had been all-consuming as he gripped the grass, waiting for the world to break into pieces.

The mass in Raine's throat grew larger still, constricting his lungs. He struggled to breathe as his thoughts kept spiraling. He recalled each roaring earthquake in rapid succession. There'd been seven altogether, spread over ten years. Raine had been convinced they were the result of the Cavern dragons' fury. That something or someone had angered them each time.

The mass in Raine's throat was bigger than it had ever been. It throbbed and raged as if he swallowed a storm. If he opened his mouth, it would pour out of him like a steaming kettle. Like a bereaved dragon's roar.

A bereaved dragon's roar.

He swung his head up sharply, knocking Sidian's jaw with a harsh clack. "Sorry," Raine gasped. He met Sidian's slitted glare as his mate cupped his chin and mouth. "I have an idea, but you need to plug your ears."

Raine must have sounded as urgent as he felt because Sidian didn't hesitate. He moved his hands to his ears, the motion uncovering his mouth. A thin line of red escaped the corner of Sidian's lip, trailing down his chin.

Raine froze, fixated on its progress. In a blink, he was back in Silvan Dredge. He saw his father's waxen face, smeared with prison grime. A ruby bead had pooled in that same spot as he died.

"Fuck, I'm sorry," Raine whispered, losing sense of who he was speaking to. His tremulous fingers escaped his mate's underarm to wipe away the crimson line.

Sidian captured his hand and replaced it in his coat, tucking it beneath his armpit once more. "Stop. I bit my lip. It's nothing."

Raine drew a shuddering breath and nodded. Once both of Sidian's ears were firmly plugged, he faced the crescent moon. Certain in a way that defied explanation that this is what the force in his throat demanded. He opened his mouth and gave into his broken heart at last. He roared.

The sound pierced sky and vale. It thundered from his core, shaking his frame as Sidian steadied him. On the brink of ice death, on the side of a dark, lonely mountain and cradled in his mate's arms, Raine didn't just know he was a dragon. He felt it, marrow and soul.

As the keening cry projected from his diaphragm, emptying the swollen mass from his throat, Raine marveled that he'd ever mistaken the meaning of the sound. It wasn't anger. It was anguish. The dragons had never raged, as he'd once believed. They had mourned, powerfully and expressively through this innate channel of grief that was solely dragon.

Raine's lament was long and loud and choked with heartache. It was an overdue expression of loss for his late father, and he suddenly understood why he had remained insensate for so long after escaping the prison. Because he had failed to grieve as he was meant to. As he was now.

Raine shook the mountain with his sorrow, not stopping until the crushing weight in his chest was gone completely.

Sidian's thumbs unerringly smoothed the tears from his face in the darkness. The need for his mate overcame Raine, visceral and immediate. And too powerful to be denied for a minute longer.

He was going to kiss Sidian. And probably get thrown off a volcano. It would be worth it. Raine would die a thousand times to experience the feel of his mate's lips just once.

He leaned forward. Their puffs of breath mingled.

A sudden gust of unnatural wind pulled their gazes upward. The hulking, shadowy figure of a dragon descended.

CHAPTER FOUR

Raine jolted awake clutching his chest. He looked down, expecting to find a bloody gash. There was nothing. Just smooth, unmarred skin. But that wasn't right. He ached. No, he *hurt*.

He sat up with a groan. It wasn't just his chest. His entire body felt cleaved, as if angry spirits had been at him with phantom axes all night.

Blankets pooled at his waist. Genuine blankets. He was in a bed. For the first time in forever, he had slept in a bed. Used to piles of withered leaves for a mattress and waking curled around a full-bodied mate for warmth and comfort, he gazed around blearily, confused. Gradually, the events preceding his rest caught up with his sleep-addled brain.

Ascending Moontop with Sidian. Nearly freezing to death. His lamenting roar, which had drawn a dragon to rescue them. Not Nyx, but a *dragon*.

Try as he might, Raine could recall nothing afterward. Just a vague impression of Sidian lifting him onto the dragon's back, then heat. Blissful, heavenly heat. And now he was here, wherever this was, and his body felt like a gaping wound. He scrubbed his eyes with the sides of his fists and inspected his surroundings.

A bedchamber, cave edition. The ceiling and walls were roughly hewn rock. An oil lamp burned next to the bed. Formed of copper with an S-shaped handle, it sat on a makeshift nightstand that was really just a perfectly flat boulder positioned against the mattress. He pushed the white sheets aside and stood.

Coarse, hard stone met soft bare feet. Raine was naked. He scratched his head, surveying his proud morning wood with a frown. Why the hell was he naked? And where was Sidian? His foggy mind snapped clear at the thought of his mate. Sidian was gone. The realization sliced through him, drawing fresh blood from invisible wounds.

He needed to find Sidian.

Nobody had ever told Raine he would experience physical pain if separated from his mate, but he knew it anyway. A body couldn't survive without its heart, and Sidian was his.

Raine scanned the room, enlivened with purpose. His rucksack and all his clothes were gone, too. Not sure what else to do, Raine fashioned a flat sheet from the bed into a rudimentary frock that tied at his shoulder. Gripping the oil lamp, he exited the doorless cave-slash-bedchamber. It opened to a narrow, rocky corridor. It was roughly hewn but not by men, he realized, raising his lamp to a pockmarked wall. By magma.

Divine Father, he was *inside* Moontop. Centuries or eons ago, molten rock had flowed through this tunnel. Just how far below ground was he?

He gripped the oil lamp tighter. Its wick was tiny but mighty. Without it, he could get lost forever in the vast darkness. He progressed slowly, taking care not to trip on the uneven floor. An occasional opening led to other narrow veins in the volcanic cave system, but he instinctively stuck to the broader fissure angling upward.

Just as Raine began to wonder if he would ever find his way to the surface, a pinprick of light appeared. As he reached it, the tunnel widened like the inside of a mouth before abruptly spitting him into a humongous, disc-shaped chamber. It looked like something colossal had taken a bite out of Moontop itself, as if it were an apple instead of a volcano. The chamber was vast and dry, with a jagged ceiling that stretched to shadows. Mountainous walls encased all sides except one, which overlooked the ocean.

Raine's eyes fixed on the sea. Grayish blue in the clouded dawn, it was wrinkled and alive. It went on forever, as endless as the sky. He tore his gaze away from the ocean to inspect the chamber itself. The air was warm despite its gaping exposure to the elements. Neatly stacked rocks sat at the chamber's center. The mound was about the size of a carriage and glowed like a heap of embers.

Driftwood benches were situated around the rockpile as if it was a campfire. The occupants of said benches were all female and, although they occupied their human forms, they were all indisputably dragon. As one, they stared at Raine. Disappointment lanced him as he reviewed their faces. Sidian was not among them.

A blue female stood, her hair loose and wavy down her back. She wore a tight indigo sheath with matching slippers that made him feel as underdressed as he was.

"Good morning, Raine," she said, approaching him. Her heartfelt smile would have eased him if he wasn't so intent on his missing mate. "You look much better than you did last night."

He shifted awkwardly. "I'm sorry. I don't recall the evening well. Or your name, if you've given it."

"It's Naiah," she said easily. "And I'm not surprised. You were fairly out of it. Too long in the cold does that to a dragon. To be brief, we heard your Requiem." A somber weight touched her features, and Raine realized she referred to his mournful roars. "I flew down to investigate, and brought you and your companion back here."

Her explanation left Raine with more questions than answers. The entire evening after his rescue was a blank memory. These female dragons were an incredible, wondrous mystery ... but one he could unravel later. First, he needed to find Sidian. Raine felt his mate's absence like a severed limb; the pain and blood loss wouldn't abate until he rejoined him.

"Do you know where my companion is?"

"Of course. Sidian went off with Nyx. They were still gabbing like geese when I passed Nyx's bedchamber earlier. I don't think they've slept at all. Not that I blame them. It's so wonderful that you're here." Naiah reached out and grasped Raine's hand, squeezing. Her eyes were shiny. "Nyx's brother and Arastus's son. It's like receiving a gift from the Dreaming Mother directly. We are so, so glad to see you."

Raine's thoughts spun like a vortex. *Nyx is here. This is his hideaway. This is his big, secret mission.* All along, Nyx and his father had been hiding dragons. Raine couldn't believe they kept it from him. *What pricks.*

And Naiah said Sidian was with Nyx. Which meant Raine had missed the look on Sidian's face when he saw his brother for the first time. Raine had to see him. He had to know what Sidian's eyes looked like, unhaunted by grief and sorrow for the first time in a decade.

He blinked rapidly, his own eyes going shiny. "I will go check on them, if you'll point the way."

Naiah's answering smile was dazzling. "The tunnels can be confusing if you aren't used to them. Allow me to escort you."

The vast, ocean-facing chamber anchored five separate tunnels. Raine hadn't noticed them when he surfaced, as they lined the basalt wall at his back. He'd emerged from the second tunnel to the left. Naiah borrowed Raine's lamp and directed them down the center passage. He trailed his fingers over grooved rock in her shadowy wake. This tunnel was less narrow than the one he had traversed earlier, but it was just as dark and far steeper.

They turned twice at intersecting passages before Naiah paused outside a rocky opening. Bright yellow light shone from within. A male voice was speaking, too softly for Raine to understand.

"I'll leave you to it," Naiah whispered. A parting wink and she was gone.

A different voice sounded from the room, quiet and husky. Raine's belly zinged with recognition. *Sidian.*

The Wade brothers' conversation was low and seemed deeply personal. Raine hovered outside Nyx's chamber, reluctant to intrude. The brothers deserved time to become reacquainted without some interloper barging in.

Raine's separation pangs had already abated, his soul as lax and content as a fed cat with his mate near. And perhaps now that he knew where Sidian was, the pain would be lesser while he awaited him from the main cavern.

But Naiah had taken the lantern with her. And the last thing Raine wanted was to be found camped outside Nyx's doorway like a creep. His mouth went dry as he stepped through the threshold.

There they were. Sidian and Nyx Wade. Darkly handsome and so alike in appearance. They were on a bed much like the one Raine had slept in. They sat shoulder-to-shoulder, backs against the cave wall at the head of the bed.

The smudges beneath Sidian's eyes were darker than ever, but he exuded a soul-deep contentedness that lit him up from within. The corners of his lips quirked upward as he spied Raine. His velvety eyes were hooded with exhaustion and pleasure—like someone who had just scaled the highest mountain in the world and found a heap of treasure awaiting him.

"Kid," Nyx choked. Lines creased his face like crumpled paper. "Oh, kid."

Tears fell as Nyx stood. Raine's eyes pricked in response. He didn't know who moved first. In an instant, Nyx's arms were wrapped around Raine as fast and firm as his father's, enveloping him in a crushing embrace. They collapsed into each other and fell to their knees in the center of the chamber.

Raine lost it. Tears spilled down his face. His nose burned and ran with snot. Sobs shook him as he clung to the only other person in the world who grieved his father as he did. Nyx rocked him like a small child and murmured an endless stream of consoling nonsense that permeated Raine's skin, steeping his heart in pure solace.

If Raine had thought his Requiem would put his grief to gentle rest, he was sorely mistaken. His Requiem had been an expression and a release, but not an end. Grief had no ending, he was starting to realize. He would never think of his father without missing him desperately.

Sharing sorrow with Nyx hurt, like peeling back a scab and digging a finger into it.

But it also soothed. Just knowing he wasn't alone, that someone else bore the same wound, helped. Raine's eyes were swollen but dry when they drew apart an indeterminate time later.

Nyx smoothed back Raine's hair the way he used to when Raine was little. "I'm so sorry, kid."

Unable to speak for fear of a fresh round of tears, Raine nodded. With a final, tight squeeze around his middle, Nyx stood. He offered a hand, pulling Raine to his feet, then wrapped an arm around his shoulders and faced the bed. Sidian sat cross-legged on top of the mattress, his expression shuttered as he watched them.

"I can't believe you brought my brother here," Nyx crowed, his voice hoarse from crying. "It's crazy."

Raine gratefully seized the subject change. "What's crazy is that a gaggle of fucking dragons are hiding out in a volcano. Who are they? Where did they come from? What have you been doing here?"

Nyx shot him a tired smile that was pure Sidian. He truly was an older, leaner version of Raine's mate. His nose was shorter, his eyes lighter. But there was no denying the Wade brothers had been snipped from the same branch.

"Oh, kid. We've got so much to talk about." A yawn nearly split Nyx's face in half.

Raine shook his head. He wanted answers, but Nyx could barely keep his bloodshot eyes open. "It can wait. You both look beat. Naiah said you two stayed up all night."

Another yawn cracked Nyx's jaw. "We got a little carried away catching up." He grinned lazily at Sidian. "Want me to show you to a room, stinkbug?"

A burst of surprised laughter bent Raine forward. *Stinkbug* shot him an irritated glance, then glared daggers at his older brother.

"I am an elite warrior and a man," Sidian said with rigid severity.

Nyx raised his hands defensively. "Alright, alright. Cut me some slack. The last time I saw you, you still wet the bed. No more stinkbug." He said that last part regretfully.

Sidian's eye twitched violently. Raine did a poor job stifling his chortles. As Sidian's murderous glare swung on him, Raine wheezed, "I'm sorry. I'm sorry. I'm not making fun of you, I swear. You just look so pissed."

Sidian did not look appeased, at all. If anything, his visage darkened. "Forgive me if I fail to find the same humor as you."

Raine's laughter stopped as his stomach cinched with remorse. Hoping to mollify Sidian by taking the attention off of him, Raine plucked at the sheet covering his frame and said, "Does anyone know why I'm naked?"

Nyx's arm tightened around Raine's shoulder as he laughed. "Do you want to tell him, or should I?"

Sidian sighed as if put upon, but his expression was lighter when he answered. "As soon as Naiah brought us here, you stumbled off her back, curled up on their burning rockpile, and fell asleep. Your cloak and clothes caught fire, but we were able to get your boots and pack off before they were ruined."

Sidian stood from Nyx's bed and showed him their supplies, which were tucked against the opposite wall. Two rucksacks, one bearing scorch marks. Only one jacket, the gray coat Sidian was using—which made sense if Raine's cloak was now ashes in the wind. Raine's beautiful buckskin boots stood next to Sidian's sturdier, black leather boots. They were partially melted in certain places, probably where they had contacted the firestones, but were otherwise serviceable. When Sidian threw on his rucksack and boots, Raine copied him.

"Just go to sleep," Sidian said to Nyx, bundling his coat under one arm. "Raine can take me to his room."

The wings of a thousand butterflies tickled Raine's stomach. Sidian wanted to share his room. He'd been offered one of his own and turned it down.

Yeah, because he knows you just woke up and won't be sleeping in the bed with him, a voice snarked in his head.

"Alright," Nyx said through another sleepy yawn as he climbed into bed. He was squirming beneath his coverlet when he paused to grab something from his bedside. "Don't forget this. And a lamp."

Sidian crossed the chamber to accept a leather-bound book from his brother, then took one of the two lamps burning on the nightstand, which was made of actual wood and not a large, flat boulder like the one in Raine's bedchamber. Nyx extinguished the other lamp and waved them off, mumbling "Good night" into his pillow.

"I don't actually remember how to get to my room," Raine admitted after they exited Nyx's bedchamber. He had tried to learn the route as Naiah guided him, but they'd taken one turn too many for him to keep track of.

"I do." Sidian smirked at Raine's expression. "Who do you think carried you there?"

Sidian had carried him to bed … while he was *naked?* Raine's face burned so fiercely, it nearly caught fire. "You could have woken me up."

"Believe me, I tried. A corpse would have been easier to rouse."

Sidian stepped ahead and raised his lamp as they walked. Raine trailed after him, thankful his mate knew where he was going. Even if Raine could recall the way back to his room, he would have been useless. His mind was gone, trapped in an erotic stupor. He scarcely registered where his feet went.

Sidian was going to sleep in his bed. *In his bed.*

Raine's blood surged south. His skin was tight and jumpy everywhere, but especially over his groin. The image of Sidian and him sharing a bed—not a tent or hastily erected shanty in the middle of the wilderness, but an actual *bed*, with sheets and blankets and pillows—made his cock twitch against the sheet draping him.

All of Raine's illicit dreams took place in an imaginary bed. All of them.

He stumbled to a halt when Sidian ducked through a dark, craggy opening. The chamber beyond glowed with the light of Sidian's lamp. He followed and discovered it was the bedchamber he had slept in. Raine couldn't recall them passing through the main cavern to reach this tunnel, but they must have.

He needed to stop imagining Sidian in his bed. It led to perverse thoughts that made him as witless and observant as a stone.

And as hard as stone, too. He fluffed his sheet to disguise his erection while Sidian placed the book and oil lamp on the boulder-turned-nightstand, then shucked his backpack and boots. Raine expected him to stop there and sleep in his clothes. For weeks, they had slept bundled in coats and multiple sweaters. And earlier, prior to Obanth, Sidian had kept his Guardian uniform on, even in sleep, at all the inns they had stayed at.

Raine's mouth went dry as Sidian reached for the hem of his sweater and pulled it over his head. Another shirt followed. Raine stopped breathing as Sidian peeled away his Guardian uniform. The tight, black bodystocking unwrapped Sidian like a gift. Soft light played along broad shoulders and a taut chest as Sidian bent to tug his legs from the clingy lotus silk.

Raine devoured the display of skin he'd only glimpsed sparingly. Thankfully, Sidian was too focused on his task to notice Raine's drooling. He stripped down to a pair of drab underpants they had plucked from a blind hermit's clothesline. Raine still felt wretched about it. The old man's hands had shaken as he pinned his wash. Temperatures had fallen faster than they could survive, however, and that hermit's penchant for Tagetesian wool had saved their lives.

Sidian's back and shoulders rippled in a wall of satin muscles as he climbed over the mattress. He settled beneath the blanket, in the exact spot Raine had so recently vacated. It took every ounce of Raine's concentration to stay perfectly still so that his improvised robe didn't shift and betray his condition.

Sidian's head rested on the pillow. Their eyes met and held.

"Thank you for bringing me here." Sidian's husky voice was thin with exhaustion. "I didn't deserve the trust you placed in me. Maybe now," he amended when Raine opened his mouth to protest, "but not in the beginning. I know it was you who gave me a chance first. And after I attacked you, then took you prisoner and treated you like an inferior. I don't know how you endured it all and still found something worth redeeming inside me. But you did. Now, I have my brother back and I have a best friend. I just need you to know how grateful I am."

Best friend. Warm, glittering light flooded Raine's veins like fizzy wine. His mate considered them friends. Best friends, even. In less than a season, Sidian had gone from loathing his existence to cherishing Raine as his closest friend.

He couldn't prevent a tender smile as he surveyed his sleep-deprived mate. Sidian's fawn eyes were heavy-lidded drops of velvet. His mouth looked soft and sweet. Raven black hair feathered over his brow, as if begging for a lover to smooth it back. Raine's stomach flipped at his mate's unconscious sensuality.

"You don't owe me gratitude, Sidian. Not for anything."

Sidian frowned, but he was fading fast, his sleepless night catching up to him as his eyes closed. "Yes, I do. You changed my life." His syllables slurred.

Raine reached down and tucked the blanket around his mate's shoulders. "You changed mine," he whispered.

His gaze landed on the book at Sidian's side. He hesitated, staring down at the innocuous volume bound in chestnut leather. The silhouette of a dragon in flight, black on tan, was stamped into its cover in place of a title. "What's up with the book?"

Sidian's eyes cracked open, then closed just as quickly. He was half-asleep as he murmured, "Nyx wrote it. A study on dragons. History and culture."

If Sidian's eyes hadn't been shut, he would have seen Raine's peachy complexion blanch whiter than the sheet he wore.

CHAPTER FIVE

Raine's mind was in a tailspin. *A study on dragons*. Of all the things Nyx could have been up to, why did it have to be that? The words repeated over and over in his mind, a hellish and damning reprisal.

He hovered near Sidian's bedside, staring at Nyx's book for ages. He wanted to hide it. Burn it. Throw it into the ocean.

His fingers reached out, gently brushing its tanned leather cover, and Raine knew he couldn't do any of those things. This book was a piece of Sidian's brother. Raine could never deny his mate any connection to Nyx. Not after witnessing how deeply Nyx's loss had affected him, the untold suffering it had put him through.

As for what Raine was going to do once Sidian read the accursed book? He had no idea. None whatsoever. He had better ideas on how to reach the moon.

Sidian was never supposed to learn that they were mates. It wasn't like anything good would come of it. He already knew Sidian's stance on mating with him. It was obvious he wasn't interested.

Fact: Sidian wasn't reserved about sex. He had enjoyed casual affairs with two women that Raine knew of, and probably a dozen more that he didn't.

Fact: Sidian hadn't looked at Raine with so much as a glimmer of desire or lustful appreciation for his appearance.

Fact: Raine was essentially a walking erection around his mate, so there had been plenty of opportunities for Sidian to express some sort of carnal interest. He had expressed *none*. Not once. Not ever.

Conclusion: Sidian did not want to mate with Raine. Sidian would not welcome Raine as a mate. Telling Sidian they were mates would only make Sidian uncomfortable or worse.

This was a nightmare. A clusterfuck of divine proportions. Raine had half a mind to find a shovel and dig through the earth's crust until he hit scales. That way, the Dreaming Mother herself could explain why she'd bound his soul to a man more interested in eating mud than sampling Raine's charms.

Sidian's breath relaxed into deep slumber, filling the chamber with slow, rhythmic exhales. Raine sighed as he traced the handsome lines of Sidian's face.

The Dreaming Mother couldn't have matched Raine with a more gorgeous specimen. Raine would grant her that much. Sidian looked softer, almost vulnerable, in his sleep. Raine could watch him for hours and never grow bored. He considered doing just that. The pain he'd awoken to wasn't something he was eager to reexperience, which further cemented that plan in his mind.

Were those dragonesses still in that huge chamber? Naiah and the rest? Raine wondered who they were and what they were doing here with Nyx. Whatever it was, it had to do with Raine's late father, as well. Arastus Chambrin and Nyx Wade had been in cahoots all these years, working in secret. Not for the guild, but against it. Raine could parse that much on his own, but all his theories had more holes than a sea sponge.

Holes that could be filled in by Naiah or the other dragonesses.

He took a long, lingering look at Sidian and decided a quick visit up-tunnel would be fine. At the first sign of separation pain, he could simply pop back down here. One glimpse of Sidian and his pain would wash away like it was never there.

He removed his rucksack and grimaced as he caught a whiff of it. The pack smelled burnt and bitter. There were holes in the canvas where fire had eaten through. He placed it next to Sidian's pack, hoping the damage wasn't as bad as it appeared.

As he went to grab the oil lamp, his gaze snagged on Nyx's book again. It didn't appear harmless and innocent, the way a book sitting on a rock near a bedside should. Instead, it seemed to taunt him. Raine imagined the air around it was darker, malformed by a sinister presence.

It would be so easy to make it disappear, then pretend he had no idea where it had gone.

No. It wasn't an option, damn it.

Maybe it wouldn't be so bad. A study on dragons didn't *have* to include mating specifics. What would Nyx know about sparking, anyway? It probably only included bits about dragon morphology and other things Nyx could observe directly.

Okay, Sidian *had* mentioned history and culture. But that could refer to *anything*. Like details about the Dreaming Mother, perhaps. Or a mind-numbing genealogy of every dragon born, ever.

Feeling marginally reassured, he took the lamp and hurried from the chamber. His passage through the dark, uneven fissure felt much faster this time. Before he knew it, he was entering Moontop's main chamber, which was replete with fresh air and natural light. Raine inhaled deeply, savoring the primordial essence of wind and sea. He opened his eyes, which he didn't recall closing, and spied the dragonesses still perched around the firestones.

Like earlier, Naiah hopped from her seat and met him halfway. Her fair features were set in a perfect oval, her eyes the wintry blue of a snow wolf. "Hello again, young one. Did you find Nyx and Sidian well?"

"I did. They're asleep, finally."

"We probably won't see them before supper," she said with a fondly exasperated smile. "Would you like to sit with us? There's tea," she added, as if to entice him.

"I would love to," he said, meaning it.

Mystery had brought him there, but the kindred pull of dragons, of others like him, compelled him even more. It felt like years had passed since he was amongst his own kind.

As Naiah escorted him to the firestones, the dragonesses blinked at him with wide, gemstone eyes. One female possessed garnet irises and loose, crimson hair. He was reminded so fiercely of Aly, it felt like a fist had reached into his chest and squeezed.

The radiant warmth of the firestones was deliciously palpable as they drew near. Raine kept a respectful distance from their promising heat. For all he knew, every female in this chamber had already received an unfiltered view of his privates when his clothes burnt off. Whether that was the case or not, he wasn't after a repeat.

There were five benches total, each wide enough to seat four. At Naiah's encouraging nod, he claimed the nearest empty bench.

A pair of identical purple dragonesses shared the next bench over, dressed in similar butter-yellow gowns. "I'm Amari," the one on the right said. Her lavender hair was unbound and flowed to her waist.

"And I'm Amara." The one on the left waved at him with a smile, her hair braided into a halo atop her head. "We're twins," she added, somewhat unnecessarily.

Naiah stood at his side and smiled approvingly as the other females introduced themselves in rapid succession. Two green dragonesses, Carissyne and Eva. Two red dragonesses, Tejayla and Sarsana. The two purples, Amari and Amara. Naiah was the odd blue out.

Raine's brow furrowed with puzzlement as he surveyed the all-female thunder. "Do lady dragons eat the males and nobody told me?"

Naiah's laughter was as high and bright as windchimes. "Our lack of males is just a coincidence," she assured him. "There was only one unmatched male below Chambrin Keep."

Raine felt his eyes pop. "You're from the Cavern?"

Naiah patted his shoulder. "Let me pour us tea before I explain."

"I'll get it, Mother. Please, sit." Amara stood, her yellow dress loose around her shoulders as she poured several steaming mugs of tea from a bronze kettle balanced on the firestones. She passed steamy mugs to everyone, starting with Naiah and serving herself last.

Raine's fingers ignored the handle, curling directly around the body of his flared bronze mug. It would have been blistering hot to human fingers but felt exquisitely right to him.

"We all came from the Cavern," Naiah said. She sat beside Raine, cradling her tea in her lap. "Arastus, your father, is the reason we're here. He and Nyx worked together to save us from being killed."

Raine glanced first at Naiah's profile, then at the other dragonesses. "I don't understand," he said slowly. "Why would you have been killed in the Cavern?"

Naiah stared straight ahead, as if the firestones' glow held the answer. "Because we weren't breeding."

Tejayla, seated on the bench to their left, flicked her fiery hair, as reddish orange as the heated rocks, and said, "The Nine audited their breeding program and learned several dragons weren't producing eggs. Arastus claimed he didn't know which dragons weren't contributing."

"Which was total tripe," Eva said, leaning forward to speak past Tejayla, who otherwise blocked her from view. "Arastus knew precisely which of us weren't breeding. Had the Nine actually taken the time to learn how their breeding program worked, they never would have bought his lies."

"But they didn't," Tejayla said, jabbing a slender elbow into her green companion's ribs as she took over again. "Have a clue, that is. So, the Nine ordered Arastus to identify and eliminate the non-breeders."

"Only he didn't," Eva said, chiming in again. She neatly dodged Tejayla's next elbow shove. "Instead, Arastus faked our deaths so thoroughly, even the other dragons thought he and Nyx carted away corpses instead of rescues."

Raine gawked at Eva, whose eyes were as green as spring peas. "My father and Nyx faked your deaths and brought you here?"

Tejayla said, "Yup," while Eva nodded.

Wind whistled sharply through the cave opening, its bitter chill neutralized by the firestones. Outside, the ocean churned, muttering secrets that broke into the mountain far below. The stark scenery added to the cozy feel of the cave, its shelter and warmth amplified by comparison.

Beside him, Naiah sighed. "I can still hear their Requiem after Arastus told me to lie limp. It broke my heart, leaving my friends trapped in that terrible place while I was set free."

Raine picked through his memories with new eyes. Those periodic, thundering cries from the Cavern ... Had each occurrence truly been precluded by a visit from Nyx? The more Raine thought, the more he recalled. And yes. Each time the Cavern roared, Nyx had visited just prior. Raine had never connected the two.

"They're trapped no longer," a red female, Sarsana, said. She stood from her seat and shook out her damask floral skirt. Her eyes, the same deep crimson as Aly's, pinned Raine to his seat. "Nyx's brother said they have been freed from the Cavern. That you were there and might know how to find them."

Guilt speared Raine at his mate's uncertain knowledge. He had come close to divulging the Hellhole's secrets, its whereabouts and occupants, to Sidian numerous times. But as frustrating as it was, not all secrets were Raine's to share.

Sidian was blatantly curious about Raine's role in the breeding dragons' abscondence, which made keeping it from him that much harder. Sidian had never pressed for answers, though. And as time passed and their distance from Obanth grew, the subject was broached less and less until it became a nonissue.

Sarsana's beseeching stare didn't waver. Soon, all the females were focused on him. Their hope was so thick in the air, he could taste it.

"I know where they are," he admitted. Elated gasps echoed around him. "It's a hike, though. Practically the other side of the country."

"I don't care." Carissyne stood. Her vivid green eyes flashed, as if facing a challenger. "This is a sign from the Dreaming Mother. I can feel her wings on my back, guiding me outward. It's time to leave this cave and find our friends."

Sarsana clasped Carissyne's palm. Her red eyes lit with defiance as she stared down Naiah. "I agree with Cari. We've waited forever for the others to escape the Cavern. They're out there, right now. We need to go to them."

A wave of approval sounded from the other dragonesses. Naiah surveyed them with earnest affection in her pale blue eyes. "We cannot act incautiously. We've survived this long due to seclusion and secrecy."

While Naiah sipped her tea, frowns coated the dragonesses' features like battle paint. Carissyne stepped forward, tugging Sarsana along with her.

"Mother," Carissyne began in a slow, measured voice that conveyed she was right and intended to make Naiah realize the same. "Divided, we are weak. Why do you think the humans are so successful at oppressing us?" She paused, but not long enough for anyone to respond. "Because they understand there's strength in numbers. They're organized and they stick together while we spread ourselves thin. We've reduced ourselves from a mighty storm to a weak drizzle."

"Cari is right. It is past time we band together," Sarsana said. Her fiery gaze throbbed with anger and something else, something vulnerable, as she implored her audience. "We went from rotting in cages to cowering in this overgrown rabbit warren. Now our friends are out there. Right now, they're out there and they need us. I won't let them down."

"Me, neither. We're dragons, not rabbits," Tejayla said, pumping her fist.

Amari and Amara pumped theirs, echoing her. The females turned to Eva, as if waiting for her fist pump.

"I like rabbits," Eva said, widening her pea-green eyes innocently. Carissyne placed her hands on her hips, glaring. "I'm kidding, Cari. Relax. We're dragons, not rabbits."

Eva gave a fist pump for good measure, which must have satisfied Sarsana because she turned to Naiah. They all turned to Naiah. And Raine, being the paragon of observation that he was, realized Naiah was their den mother.

Naiah hid a smile with the rim of her mug. Raine only saw it because he was sitting right next to her, at exactly the right angle. "When Nyx awakens, we will communicate our wishes to him and develop a plan to achieve our goals."

"Truly?" Sarsana gasped, as if she couldn't believe what her den mother said.

"I have my reservations," Naiah said somberly. "But like you, I grow weary of hiding. And the white dragon of rebirth can only be a message from the Dreaming Mother herself."

Raine flushed as all eyes settled on him. "The what, now?"

Naiah angled herself on their bench to face him more directly. "White dragons are incredibly rare. I've never encountered one in all my three hundred years. My mother used to recount dragon lore every night before I went to bed. One of her stories depicted the white dragon of rebirth. Essentially, whenever a white dragon is born, a great change will occur. It means an ending of one era and the ushering in of another."

"That's one of the stories in Nyx's book, isn't it?" Amari asked.

Raine's attention sharpened at the mention of Nyx's book. Was it a collection of bedtime stories, then? The white dragon of rebirth sounded harmless enough, if a little far-fetched. More like a fanciful children's tale than real history. He felt himself relax. Chil-

dren's tales were hardly going to discuss the intricacies of dragon sexuality.

"I think it's the story about all our colors and their mean-
ings," Eva said. "I don't know how much I believe that particular story, though. Doesn't it teach that purple dragons are
creative? Amari and Amara are the least imaginative dragons I
know. No offense," she added as an aside to the twins.

"Oh, none taken," Amara said airily. "I agree, in fact. That
story is nonsense. It also teaches that green dragons are wise,
and the opposite is true, in my experience."

Eva rolled her eyes. "There's a difference between wisdom
and intelligence, so you didn't call me stupid, if that's what
you're aiming for."

"Wow, what a wise thing to say," Amara simpered, fluttering
her lashes. "The story must be true after all."

"Enough," Naiah said mildly. She glanced between the bickering dragonesses on either side of her bench. "You are mixing
up our lore. I was referring to *The White Wings of Rebirth*. It is
the tale of Pryssine. She was the first white dragon to ever hatch.
It was said that on her hatching day, great sheets of ice cracked
and thawed. Frozen land grew green and fertile. A whole world
was reborn."

"Then what was I thinking of?" Eva asked with a frown.

"*Lazula's Many-Hued Brood*," Naiah said in academic
tones. "Lazula was the only dragon to ever produce a hatchling
of every color."

"That's right," Eva said, as if remembering. "Her oldest was a
green male. It was said that even storm mothers flocked to him
for advice, so Lazula called him her wise egg."

"Her purple hatchling painted murals all over the country," Amari added. "Famous scenes like Myrrah saving Darrok from the river, and the banishing of the ichneumons."

"And neither of their accomplishments are meant to imply anything about you," Naiah said firmly. "Our talents are unique to our hearts, not our scales."

"Yes, Mother," Eva and the twins chorused in unison, looking suitably admonished.

Carissyne and Sarsana retook their seats. Conversation lulled as everyone sipped their tea. Raine fiddled with his mug, his stomach knotted with uncertainty.

"About Nyx's book," he began tentatively. Even as his lips formed the question, he wasn't sure he was ready for the answer. "What's in it, exactly?"

"Nyx recorded all of our lore in a single volume," Naiah said, beaming proudly. "Dragons possess no written history. We pass the tales of our ancestors down verbally, through stories. Nyx believes the guild would not have been so successful in their persecution of dragons if humans knew more about us. He wants to find a way to distribute his work throughout Valdenia and educate the masses."

It was such a noble and selfless plan that Raine immediately felt like a villain. To think that he'd been a hairsbreadth away from trashing something so pure and good ... He hadn't gone through with it, no. But his temptation had been so extreme, he was sticky with shame as if he had.

"That's incredible," he said sincerely. "Nyx is right. The Nine rely on public ignorance. They don't want anyone outside the Guardians of Vale to know that dragons are people, too. It's this huge secret. So, if the public learns dragons possess human forms and intelligence, it could change everything."

"The rocks are getting low," Tejayla announced.

Amara stood, grinning. With a deft tug, her loose dress pooled at her feet. Raine blushed, looking away. Dragons might not regard nudity the same way humans did, but he'd been raised human and it was just weird. Crackling pops sounded like a bonfire and when Raine next looked, Amara was longer than a horse from snout to rear. Her massive wings were tucked tightly to her sides and her lavender scales gleamed like stained glass.

Everyone stood and moved away from the rocks. Not sure what it was about, Raine stood and moved away with them.

Amara opened her dragon's maw and released a stream of blazing fire over the rockpile, blowing until the glossy black stones seemed to lock the flames within. The firestones soon radiated intense heat, glowing the red-hot orange of a true fire.

In a blink, Amara was human and nude. She threw her dress back on and smiled smugly at Raine. "My fire is the hottest, so I'm in charge of refreshing the rocks."

Instead of sitting back down, the dragonesses began filing out of the main cavern, as if responding to a signal. He watched them disappear, splitting off between two of the tunnels, then turned to Naiah. "Did I miss something?"

"They have chores to do. Laundry, cooking, cleaning. Simple tasks we all share." Naiah gestured at the kettle, which rumbled with freshly boiling water. "More tea?"

He nodded, then asked, "Am I going to get chores?"

"If you remain long enough." Her back was to him, blocking the firestones as she poured their mugs. "But it sounds like we'll be departing soon, so don't count on it." She turned and handed him a deliciously scalding mug.

They sat in comfortable silence, listening to the howling wind outside. A thought niggled him, too wispy and insubstantial to identify. It twirled around the edges of his consciousness, drawing his gaze to Naiah. *Nai-ah.* He dragged out the syllables in his mind.

"I've heard your name before," he groused, frustrated after raking his mind only to come up empty again. "But for the life of me, I can't recall where I've heard it."

"You may have heard it when you were very young," she said after sipping her tea. "I was named after a human legend often shared with children. The story of Naiah is about a snow wolf born barren; she raised fox kits as her own when their mother perished."

Raine shook his head. "I've never heard that story." He sipped his tea. The fragrant water was wonderfully hot, like silken fire on his tongue.

Again, he dragged her name out in his mind. *Nai-ah. Nai-ah.*

It hit him then. Like a chunk of basalt breaking from the ceiling and smacking him over the head. *None of the Cavern dragons died.*

Lukor's mate hadn't died.

Lukor's mate was sitting right fucking beside him.

"*You.*" He thrust a finger at her, his mouth hanging open like a drawn bow. "You're Lukor's mate!"

Naiah paled. Her delicate face pinched into a pained expression. "Lukor was my mate, yes. He was killed during the invasion, when the human army attacked us. How do you know of him?"

"Lukor is not dead," he protested. Her expression was a pale blue echo of Sidian's when Raine had first tried explaining about Nyx.

Once again, Raine was in the anomalous position of conveying the continued existence of a loved one to a broken-hearted skeptic. "I promise I'm not lying. Look." Raine wracked his brain for a way to convince her. "Big, dark purple dragon? As mannerless as a coonhound? Mega asshole to everyone?"

"How?" she whispered.

Raine almost laughed at Naiah's ready acceptance of Lukor's description, but the intensity in her gaze kept him serious. "I didn't break the dragons out of the Cavern by myself. There was a thunder hiding out in Sinopel. They took me in when I had nowhere to go. Lukor is one of their members."

Naiah's chin dipped to her chest, eyes downcast. Her sudden gloom caught Raine off-guard. He swirled his mug and tried to give her a moment, in case she needed it. When her spine curved, deepening her slump, he figured she'd had enough time. His tone was tentative as he asked, "What's wrong?"

She gave him a tight, wobbly smile. "Nothing." At Raine's plainly disbelieving stare, she sighed, facing the firestones. "I'm overjoyed, really. But ... why didn't he come for me?" Tears welled in her eyes, and she jabbed at them impatiently with one hand. "Had our positions been reversed, nothing in this world would have prevented me from getting to him, Raine. Nothing. Two hundred years. He never came. Two hundred years." Her voice cracked. "He never came."

Ah, fuck. Raine grimaced. Lukor was far from his favorite dragon, but he would call the bastard a prince if it helped ease Naiah's despair. Her distress made him feel itchy all over, as if his skin was too small for his skeleton.

"Lukor was desperate to reach you. No, seriously. It's because of Lukor that we rescued those dragons in the first place." Her back straightened, just a little. "He loved you too much to risk his rescue being in vain. So, he waited until he thought there wouldn't be a better chance. And we went. He's the reason the Cavern is empty right now. He came for you."

Naiah exhaled shakily. "I will try to withhold judgment and see what he has to say," she said at length. "Our bond is so powerful. I was convinced he had died, knowing he would have come if he'd been alive."

She fished a square scrap of cloth from her skirt pocket and blew her nose. It was pink and raw when she faced him, smiling weakly.

"What do you mean by your bond?" Raine asked, desperate to draw Naiah's attention to a safer topic, one that wouldn't brook more tears. He relaxed as her smile reached her eyes.

"Our mating bond. When a dragon meets their mate, they spark." Raine nodded to show his familiarity with the concept. "The mating bond forms during consummation. Through it, Lukor and I can sense each other. Our emotions and ... other things. It is almost impossible to explain." She sucked in a breath, her hand flying to her mouth as if shocked. "Our bond has been in so much *pain*. I've lived in agony since the day I thought he died. I assumed it was the enduring heartache of a broken bond, but if Lukor is alive..."

Raine's eyes widened. "You're feeling his pain," he finished for her.

She nodded, blinking rapidly against the moisture shining in her eyes. "I can't believe I didn't realize it sooner. I must see him. I've missed him so much. More and more each day. That's how it goes with a mate. You think you couldn't love them more than you already do, but every day it grows anyway."

Raine thought of Sidian and privately agreed. "Naiah, um. I have maybe a weird question."

She tilted her head encouragingly.

"Is it possible for a dragon's mate to be human?" Raine felt foolish asking. He knew it was possible. Sidian's status as his other half was a truth carved into his soul. But none of the other dragons seemed to have a human mate, and he wanted to know how odd his situation might be, or if she had any information on his type of mating bond specifically.

Naiah leaned forward. "You found your mate." Her puffy eyes danced.

Cautiously, he nodded. "What gave it away?"

"You did, by asking." She smiled at his puzzlement. "Our mates are so deeply ingrained in our hearts, it begins in the shell. If your mate was a dragon, you'd have hatched as one. But we all know you hatched human, which is why Arastus took you in. While unusual, it simply signifies your mate is human. Nothing more. I assumed you found your mate because you wouldn't have thought to ask about it otherwise."

"Huh," was all he could say. Naiah had cleared up two mysteries by answering one question. It was odd that he'd been born in his human form when all the other dragons of his acquaintance were born with wings and tails.

That meant they'd all have dragon mates, then.

"You should read Nyx's book," Naiah added. "Those stories will answer just about any question you can think up about dragons."

"Oh?" Raine's stomach dropped. "Does his book get into much detail about dragon mates, then?"

"Of course," she said, lowering her cup without taking a sip. "Mates are the core of our culture and the heart of our lore. More than half of the tales mention the mating bond to some degree."

Raine closed his eyes and contemplated throwing himself into Moontop's caldera. "Awesome."

CHAPTER SIX

Tejayla and Carissyne grinned like they won a prize when Na-iah asked them to give Raine a quick tour of their volcanic den. Carissyne skipped over to an oblong boulder resting against the wall of tunnel openings. Copper lamps with thick, tufty wicks and glass bottles of oil lined its surface. She filled and lit two of the lamps, passing one to Raine as he and Tejayla reached her.

"This way's the kitchen," Carissyne said over her shoulder as she spearheaded them down the nearest tunnel.

Unlike the two tunnels Raine had previously been down, this one was filled with natural light. It skirted Moontop's surface like a vein budging beneath skin. On their right, the wall was webbed with holes that functioned like windows, offering a view of open, endless sea. Gusts of frosty air whistled through the openings. The wicks in his and Carissyne's lamps sputtered wildly, and they shielded them with their palms as they walked.

With the layout of the tunnel being what it was, Raine expected the kitchen to be on their left—a hollow space hewn from the volcano's central mass. But to his amazement, the seaward wall beveled to form a covered outcropping. It was like an ancient, open-air gallery. On all sides, the kitchen's walls were wide-open and propped by natural columns. An ocean breeze flooded the space, salt-scented and bracingly cold.

A long, wooden countertop was placed like an island in the middle of the room. Sarsana sat on a stool, bundled in a fur-lined robe. Her nose and cheeks were windblown as she hunkered over a lumpy, misshapen seashell. She glanced up as they entered, then stabbed the shell with a knife. A bucket of similar ugly shells sat at her elbow. She extracted a slimy, silvery piece of something from the shell and slapped it into a wooden bowl already half full of the things.

"Yay, oysters. Again," Tejayla said dully, standing over Sarsana's shoulder to watch.

"Yay, you found a way out of helping me shuck them. Again," Sarsana shot back, stabbing another shell with more force than necessary.

"Hey, don't be mad at me. Mother asked me to help show Raine around. Was I supposed to refuse?"

"Whatever, Jayla. It's always something. Don't worry, I've got it. I've *always* got it."

"Seriously? You know what, just give me the knife. I'll shuck the rest."

"Oh, you mean now that I'm almost done? So you can take all the credit while doing less than half the work? I don't think so."

Tejayla went to grab the knife. Sarsana held firm. The red dragonesses began grappling for the instrument. Tejayla twisted her torso to wrench it out of Sarsana's grip. Sarsana sprang from her stool for better purchase, nearly toppling the oyster bucket.

"Thank the Dreaming Mother you're here," Carissyne said, standing beside him as they watched the scuffle unfold. "I don't think we can last another week trapped in these caves, let alone years."

Sarsana dropped her knife to the floor and pulled Tejayla's hair. Tejayla grasped Sarsana's wrists and tugged while kicking her shins, screaming with pained rage.

"How long have you all been here?" Raine asked.

"Mother came first. Nearly ten years ago. Sars was next, about eight years ago. I came after her. Jayla arrived after me. Then, Amari and Amara arrived nearly two years apart. Eva is our newest addition, after you. She arrived only this past summer."

"I don't care," Tejayla suddenly yelled, drawing their attention. Her chest heaved where she stood, facing Sarsana on the opposite side of the open kitchen. Her hair was a wildfire of tangles, her cheeks flushed with flame-red fury. "I'm sick of oysters. I'm sick of seafood. I'm sick of this stupid fucking mountain and I'm sick of you!"

Tejayla stormed from the kitchen without a backward glance. There was a long pause where nobody moved or said anything. Then, Sarsana calmly corrected her skewed stool's position and resumed shucking oysters. The silence was as brittle as overbaked clay. As brittle as Sarsana's composure. The red female's movements were as unnaturally stiff as her upper lip. She looked a breath away from tears.

Raine took an unconscious step back. He *hated* tears. Nothing made him feel more powerless.

"Hey, it's fine," Carissyne said softly. "You heard Mother. We're getting out of here. Those are the last oysters we ever have to eat. *Ever*," she stressed as Sarsana looked at her.

"Do you promise?" Sarsana asked. Raine thought she referred to the oysters, but then her gaze transferred to him. "Do you promise to take us to the other dragons, no matter what? Even if Mother decides against it?"

His refusal would shatter her. He could see it as plainly as if she were a ceramic vase splintered with cracks. "I promise," he said. "I will escort you to them personally, along with anyone else who wishes to accompany us."

After his conversation with Naiah, Raine was certain they would be leaving Moontop, and soon. Lukor was out there, drowning in grief and pain. Naiah would stop at nothing to reach him. Raine knew, because nothing would stop him from reaching Sidian, were he in her position.

"Thank you," Sarsana mouthed silently. He caught a glimmer of tears before she looked down at the oyster in her hands. Her hair fell forward in a crimson curtain, closing her face from view.

Carissyne gently pulled his bicep, and he followed her back to the tunnel. "Sorry about all that," she said as they walked back to the main chamber. "Dreaming Mother, that was so embarrassing. I swear, we don't usually act like a bunch of berserk, gravid dragons competing over the best nesting hollow."

"It's okay," Raine assured her. "I don't think any of you are acting like, um ... whatever that is?"

She muffled a giggle. "Sorry. I forgot you were raised by humans. We learn these things as hatchlings, so your confusion makes you seem really young. A gravid dragon is like a pregnant human. It just means they're going to lay an egg."

Raine blinked, still not accustomed to thinking of himself as a creature who procreated like a chicken. A sudden, horrible image assailed him—of a rooster, wearing his face. A fat, floppy wattle dangled from its—*his*—chin as it pecked at crickets. Suppressing a shudder, he pushed the image away. Just because dragons laid eggs didn't mean they were anything like chickens.

"Yeah, no," Carissyne said. "We're nothing like chickens."

Had he said that aloud? Raine shook his head, trying to focus. "Good to know. So, pregnant dragons are gravid. And being gravid makes them berserk?"

"Kind of," she said distractedly as they reached the main chamber. The firestones glowed the vivid red-orange that meant Amara had recently reheated them. There was no sign of Tejayla. Carissyne moved to the next tunnel and pointed with her lamp. "Our bedchambers are that way, along with some storage areas. It's nothing too interesting, but I'll show you if you want."

Raine declined. He didn't wish to prolong their tour with unnecessary stops. It had only been a couple of hours since he left Sidian sleeping in his room, but he wanted to return before his mate awoke. For starters, Raine had left him without a lamp. There was also the fact that crippling pain could grip him at any moment, his body seeming to reject any prolonged absence from Sidian's side.

"Alright," Carissyne said with an easy smile. She gestured at the next tunnel. "This one leads to Nyx's room. There are more storage areas, too. You've got to be careful, because some of those tunnels keep going forever. They make for fabulous games of hide-and-seek."

They walked past Nyx's tunnel and came up to the passage leading to Raine's room, where Sidian slept. "That's the smallest tunnel. Nothing much down there. It dead-ends near the bedchamber Mother gave you. It was originally meant for Zane. Nyx was supposed to rescue him from the Cavern in the spring, but obviously that won't be happening now."

Raine mocked a gasp. "You mean you were actually going to welcome a male dragon into your midst?"

"Stuff it," she said with a laugh. "I can't believe you thought we ate the males."

"It was a valid question," he interjected.

"What makes you think we would admit it, if it was true?" Carissyne waggled her eyebrows, making them resemble a pair of green jay wings in flight. "And now for the fifth and final tunnel." She flung out her arm dramatically. "It leads to the butchering room, where we dismember male dragons and make roasts out of their juicy butts."

"I think that was a joke," Raine said slowly, peering into the tunnel in question. "But now, I'm terrified of going anywhere alone with you. Just in case."

"Oh, you'll go down that tunnel, pretty boy. And do you want to know why?" she asked, leaning in to whisper. "Because that tunnel leads to the hot springs."

She was right. With an ecstatic gasp, Raine bolted down the tunnel. He was more than willing to risk dismemberment and cannibalization for a hot bath. Carissyne's laughter echoed as she chased him.

"Not so fast," she called out. "There are a lot of twisty turns before you reach them. You'll get lost."

He skidded to a halt seconds later and raised his lamp. The tunnel branched in three directions. Carissyne came up beside him and pointed as she spoke. "Laundry. Toilet. Hot springs. Come on."

He was absolutely jubilant as he trailed her down the far-left branch. As jubilant as that time his father had taken him into the woods to forage mushrooms. They had discovered a cluster of pink and blue mushrooms beneath some mulberry bushes and sampled a few.

Wylan had discovered them hours later. His father's underwear had been wrapped around his head like a bonnet as he serenaded a petrified wood mouse. Raine had purportedly stared into a mudpuddle for several hours without blinking. He couldn't recall any mudpuddle, though. No, all he remembered was a mind-bending elation. It had lifted a veil from his eyes, revealing the radiant spirits of a sparkling realm.

He felt a similar elation now. His steps were light, as if aided by wings. "Is the water hot? Not, like, human hot. Please, *please* tell me it's dragon hot," he moaned, already fantasizing about boiling water that was neck deep.

"Both." Carissyne grinned smugly. "There are two separate hot springs. One of them is too hot for Nyx but perfect for us. The other is lukewarm and smells terrible. It's like bathing inside an old, boiled egg."

Raine tried to feel sorry for Nyx and his smelly hot spring. He really did. But it was impossible to feel bad about anything just then. He was about to take a piping hot bath in water heated by veins of molten rock. It was a dream.

"You never explained why gravid dragons are berserk," Raine reminded her as they progressed.

"It's not being gravid that makes them berserk. It's when they're gravid and more than one wants the same nesting hollow. Sites where dragons choose to brood," she added at his confused frown. "When two or more dragons want the same nesting hollow, it leads to all sorts of conflict. It was a nesting hollow feud that created the first storms. Not rainstorms. *Dragon* storms. We all lived together in a great, big community once. That was when Myrrah was still around, long before now. Myrrah's great-great-whatever dragons got into it over a nesting hollow. The next thing you know, everyone took sides and split off. Instead of one community with one leader, there were many."

Huh. "It's strange to think of dragons feuding with dragons," Raine mused aloud. For whatever reason, he had assumed dragons didn't war with each other. Evin and Naiah were both so thoughtful and wise. Feuds required the sort of rash, violent acts he didn't think either den mother capable of.

"Oh, we feud like mad," Carissyne said cheerily. "Some think it's because our vanity makes us easily offended. Others say it's because our fire makes us quick-tempered. Who knows?" Her shrug was as carefree as her tone. "You should check out Nyx's book," she added with a teasing grin. "It mentions all our major feuds, plus it'll teach you the things you should have learned as a nestling. You probably don't even know what sparking is."

Raine's stomach sank. Of all the things Nyx could have included in that damned book, he had to explain sparking? What *didn't*

Nyx's book have in it, at this point? Given the breadth of its contents, the infernal thing should have been as thick as Raine was tall. As thick as Moontop itself.

He wished, fervently and not for the first time, that Nyx had taken up knitting or hand-rearing baby wolverines. Or pretty much anything other than painstakingly recording every damning scrap of dragon-mating minutiae, then passing it all to Sidian the second he saw him after a decade of pretending to be dead.

"Tada," Carissyne sang as they stepped through a sudden tightening in the tunnel. "Welcome to the source of my sanity."

His thoughts scattered like marbles as he gaped. Hot, humid air enveloped him more exquisitely than the Divine Father's embrace. High overhead, the rocky ceiling formed an aperture, venting the steam like a chimney. The opening was wide, splashing sunlight throughout the space. A vast pool of water sat beneath it, rippling in the light. Rushing water thrummed in the background, splashing into the pool near the wall.

Raine sat his lamp on a rock shelf and stripped his sheet and boots in a daze. Deliciously hot water encased him as he melted into the spring. He closed his eyes and sighed as his bottom rested against an underwater ledge. His muscles turned to pudding and his neck arched backwards, pointing his face to the sunlight above. The most profound, serene calm perfused him. When he opened his eyes, twin orbs of popinjay green twinkled down at him.

"Bathing supplies are to your left, near the waterfall. I'll go ahead and take your, um, sheet to the laundry and bring you a towel and clean clothes."

A massive wooden chest sat next to the waterfall, soaked on one side from the overspray. When Raine opened it, a grin stretched his mouth so wide, his cheeks ached. Dragons were his people.

Inside was a dizzying array of oils, soaps, and shampoos. He smelled all of them before choosing vanilla soap and shampoo to match. After a thorough scrub from mane to toe, he massaged scented oils into his skin and closed his eyes, floating in the deep side of the spring.

Steam wafted from the water, steeping him with peace and relaxation. He thought of his father. Arastus Chambrin. Unfalteringly brave and compassionate. All this time, his father had been working with Nyx to liberate the Cavern. It was incredible, the magnitude of his father's undertaking. All of it inspired by love for his son. Raine was beyond humbled. He was awed. And would give anything to look his father in the eye one more time, with no secrets between them, and tell him how very much he loved him. Fiercely and forever.

His mind flashed a hazy silhouette. Two indistinct figures. A mother and father. He grimaced, his mind shying away from the mysterious biological parents awaiting him at the Hellhole. Too much baggage accompanied thoughts of them. Guilt. Fear. Shame. Too much. It was all too much. He couldn't avoid it forever, but he could avoid it. For now.

CHAPTER SEVEN

Without a dying fire to cool his bath, Raine lost track of time, dozing between thoughts. After a slightly longer nap that left him hugging a rock against his cheek, he climbed out of the spring and found a neatly folded pile next to his lamp. A fluffy cotton towel, wool socks, and a scrap of dark, slippery fabric that made him groan. A Guardian uniform, probably one of Nyx's spares. Raine would have preferred the damn sheet he'd been wearing, but Carissyne had taken it.

The silken black fabric stretched over his body, clinging to every sculpted inch, just as he feared. Raine was not ignorant of his physical appeal. In fact, he took pride in it. But in this jumpsuit, there was nowhere to hide the bulge snugly outlined between his legs.

While Sidian already knew Raine was ... excitable, he remained ignorant of the vast majority of Raine's erections thanks to his modest shirts and winter layers. This tight, black bodystocking, on the other hand, would advertise the precise dimensions of his turgid cock every time it swelled, which was pathetically frequent. Raine would appreciate keeping the exact frequency to himself.

Heaving a resigned sigh, he grabbed his lamp. Then frowned at its weight. The oil lamp was light; less than an hour of fuel sloshed in its belly. He started the steep trek back to the main cavern, glad he had decided to leave when he did. Otherwise, he might have been stuck in the dark.

Oh, no. Sidian. Raine kicked up his pace and ran. He had been in the hot spring for hours, which meant Sidian might be awake. If Raine had accidentally trapped his mate in a dark cave for a whole day, he was never going to forgive himself. Cold evening air hit him as he emerged from the tunnel. Goosebumps prickled his flesh, steam billowing off his skin.

The sky had darkened to night. *Fuck.*

He started toward the next tunnel to find Sidian. A head of dark hair caught his eye. Raine's gaze snapped to the firestones. They glowed orange with fresh heat, illuminating the chamber. He scanned the benches, where the dragonesses leaned forward, absorbing the heat of the firestones as they chatted.

And there he was. Sidian. His head was bent, looking down. He must have felt Raine's eyes on him, because he glanced up and locked on Raine immediately. Heat unfurled through Raine's belly, trailing lower.

No. No, no, no. Not now. Raine clipped past Amara, Eva, and Carissyne—all of whom scooched to make room for him—and threw himself next to Sidian before his cock fully hardened.

Sidian's dark eyes raked over him. "I have never seen anyone make Guardian hose look as indecent as you do," he murmured, shutting the book in his lap.

"I'm a fantasy brought to life. It's my burden to bear," Raine said with mock solemnity, trying to disguise the secret thrill darting through him. It was all he could do not to puff out his chest like a damned peacock.

That wasn't a compliment, he chided himself, but his inner scolding fell on a deaf dragon heart. It was too busy doing gleeful somersaults to listen to reason.

Sidian snorted softly, but his reply was drowned out by a whistling kettle. Eva hopped up to grab it. As the piercing whistle died, she poured steaming water into a row of familiar bronze mugs. She carefully kept the lacy edge of her skirt from brushing the firestones as she passed them around the benches.

Raine's stomach growled as he accepted a mug. Eva chuckled. Handing a mug to Sidian, she said, "Mother and Nyx are making dinner. It'll be out soon."

Raine arched a brow, surprised their den mother assisted with meal preparation. It wasn't how Evin's thunder operated, but he supposed everyone had their own leadership style. He sipped his tea while Sidian blew on his, and his gaze dropped to the book in his mate's lap. The shape of a dragon was stamped on its cover. He stiffened, then forced his shoulders to relax.

"Already started reading that?" he asked as nonchalantly as possible. "I figured you and Nyx have so much to catch up on, you'd have to read his book some other time."

Sidian traced a finger over the embossed dragon. When he spoke, his voice was low and rough with emotion. "I didn't just spend a decade believing my brother was dead. I spent a decade thinking the worst of your entire species. This book brings me closer to Nyx while teaching me the truth about you. I started reading it as soon as I woke up."

His mate's response was so earnest and caring that Raine felt lower than dirt. At Sidian's mention of waking, even more guilt pricked him.

"I'm sorry," he blurted. "I didn't mean to leave you for so long. I knew you didn't have a lamp and wanted to be back before you woke up, but I lost track of time in the bath."

His excuse was lame, even to his own ears, but Sidian shook his head. "Don't worry about it. Nyx woke me up an hour ago and brought me out here. Carissyne told us you were at the hot springs. If you weren't back by dinner, I was going to retrieve you."

Relief swept through him. He hadn't left his mate in the dark. "Well, I'm still sorry for leaving you, even if it worked out."

Raine sat his mug on the cavern floor and began combing his fingers through the damp snarls in his hair. His mane was long enough to graze his buttocks and the tangles were a bitch.

"We have extra brushes, Raine. Want me to get you one?" Tejayla asked from the bench on their right.

Her smile was easy and genuine. There wasn't a trace of the distraught, angry dragon from earlier who had fought with Sarsana and stormed out of the kitchen. In fact ... Raine leaned forward and saw that Sarsana sat with Tejayla. The two must have resolved their spat.

Raine brightened at her offer. "Please," he said eagerly. Some days, he felt like all he needed was a proper hairbrush and every-thing would be okay again. There was a comb in his rucksack, but it had dull, wide teeth and was terrible to work with.

Tejayla flitted from her seat in a swirl of dark skirts and darted down the center passageway. Moments later, she emerged and offered him a boar-bristle brush and some hair ties. He thanked her effusively and got to work on his snarls. His hair felt more matted than when he'd gone to Sinopel with his braid caked in soot and chimney filth. Others might have simply cut the tangles out. Not Raine. Scissors were sacrilege.

"Come here," Sidian ordered. He plucked the brush from Raine's hand. Raine scooched closer and Sidian began to brush out his hair. "You need to move closer," Sidian murmured into the shell of his ear. A frisson of desire snaked Raine's spine, tightening his stomach.

He slid to the floor, folding his calves beneath his rear as he settled between Sidian's spread knees. Sidian brought his legs together, cradling Raine's sides between his thighs.

Raine's entire world narrowed to the hard muscles snug against him. He clenched his jaw as his prick hardened further. The damn Guardian uniform did fuck all to conceal his condition. As discreetly as possible, he tucked his hands in front of the blunt protrusion between his legs, which was currently saluting the firestones.

Sidian brushed his hair with slow, deliberate movements. Raine had always enjoyed being brushed, but it had never been an erotic pleasure. Until now. The brush rasped his skull, and he tingled. His body enlivened further with every stroke, primed for something raw and sensual.

The warmth from the firestones was more direct on the floor. He closed his eyes, reveling in the dual heat of fire and desire. Outside, the wind and sea roared like primordial gods trying to outdo each other. Around them, the dragonesses spoke quietly as they relaxed with their tea. It was such a comfortable, warm place. His soul purred at the domesticity, the feelings of safety and belonging that flooded him. His raging hard-on was the only thing that prevented him from being lulled into a puddle of tingly goo on the ground.

His hair dried quickly due to his proximity to the firestones. All too soon, it was a tangle-free, gleaming mass of white, with glints of color like crushed jewels shimmering in the light. Yet Sidian continued to brush him, combing his fingers through Raine's hair after each brushstroke. The touches seemed reverent, as though Sidian gained as much pleasure with his actions as Raine did. It couldn't be true, but joy welled within Raine nonetheless.

Nyx and Naiah emerged from the kitchen tunnel, each balancing wide platters of steamy dishes. Sidian set the brush down to take a bowl, and Raine swallowed a whimper at the loss of contact. As Naiah offered him a bowl, he belatedly realized he would have to lift his hands to accept. The hands currently occupied with cupping his arousal from view. He quickly shifted position, bending his knees to block his erection before accepting the bowl from Naiah. She flashed him a brief smile before sweeping past to serve Tejayla and Sarsana.

Raine remained on the floor between Sidian and the firestones, tucking his bowl into his chest to eat. While he would have liked to sit next to Sidian, he wasn't sure how to accomplish it without flashing his condition to the entire room. Envy filled him for females and their ability to be aroused discreetly. A woman could be on the verge of climax, and so long as she schooled her features, who would know? Thanks to the soft, form-fitting jumpsuit Carissyne had brought him, Raine's erection might as well have been uncovered. The clingy, black fabric left no room for imagination.

His bowl brimmed with a briny stew. It was deliciously seasoned, a balance of salt and heat, with herbs to brighten each bite. Nyx passed out loaves of freshly baked bread, offering one to Raine and Sidian to share. The center of the loaf was slathered with creamy butter. Raine used the last of his crust to clean his bowl so that not a drop of broth remained.

Amari collected their bowls with a smile. All of the dragons had facilitated their meal in one way or another except Raine, and he was starting to feel like a useless lump. "Can I help clean up?"

She tucked a lavender curl behind her ear with one hand, balancing a stack of now-empty bowls in the other. "You're a guest. You don't have to do anything." He was ready to protest, and she cut him off. "It's really sweet of you to try, but Mother would be upset if I let you do anything. If you're with us long enough, you'll be put to task. Until then, just enjoy it." She gave him a parting smile as she moved to collect Tejayla and Sarsana's bowls.

His arousal now sufficiently reined, Raine stood and sat next to his mate. "Thank you," he said, carding his fingers through his silken, untangled hair.

His mate was silent. Raine turned to see if something was wrong. Sidian stared at him with such stark intensity, Raine's eyes widened. Was Sidian angry about something?

"You're welcome," Sidian whispered, his husky voice more hoarse than normal.

"Do you have a headache?" His father had sometimes gotten that look when he suffered a migraine. If Sidian's head hurt, Raine knew how to massage his crown and temples to alleviate the pain. In fact, thanks to Wylan, he also knew a couple of herbal remedies. He began assembling a mental list of ingredients. Most were pretty common.

Sidian parted his lips to respond.

"May I have everyone's attention?" Naiah stood with her back to the seascape, away from the firestones so everyone could see her clearly. It was full night, the ocean and sky blending into a single sheet of darkest blue, nearly black, behind her.

The room turned as one to face her. "Now that we're all gathered—"

"And conscious," Eva chimed. Everyone glanced at Raine, most laughing.

"And conscious," Naiah agreed with a smile. "There are things I would like to address. Raine Chambrin, son of Arastus, and Sidian Wade, brother of Nyx, have brought news that profoundly affects us all. Together, we grieve the loss of Arastus. The man who saved our lives and single-handedly altered the destiny of every dragon alive today. Any hope we have of reclaiming our autonomy can be traced directly to Arastus Chambrin. I want to take a moment to say to you, Raine." She looked at him. "Your father was our hero, and there are no words to express how deeply we will miss him."

Raine's nostrils burned. He dug his nails ruthlessly into his palms, determined not to cry. His grief was too unpredictable. Sometimes, it took the form of a few neat crystalline droplets. Other times, blubbering sobs made his nose run all over the place. This wasn't the time to gamble on which faucet Naiah's speech had twisted. Muffled sniffles sounded around him, but Raine stared at the firestones, clutching his composure with both hands.

After a pause, Naiah continued. "Raine and Sidian have brought other news. That hellish Cavern has finally been emptied. Our friends are free. And I believe, as many of you do, that it is time to reunite with them. They're in a safehouse which Raine has agreed to lead us to."

Nyx went to stand with Naiah. "Does anyone wish to stay behind?" He looked intently from one dragoness to the next. "Don't be ashamed if you do. Reaching the other dragons will be perilous. If we are discovered, we will be slain. You have safety here. Your odds of survival are significantly higher."

"We have wings and talons and fire." Tejayla stood, her hands forming fists at her sides. "If you think we're going to cower in this mountain like a bunch of bunnies at the bottom of the food chain, you've got another thing coming."

"We're dragons, not rabbits," Sarsana yelled, standing in solidarity with Tejayla. It ignited into a chant that swept the chamber. In seconds, every dragoness bar Naiah was pumping a fist and shouting, "We're dragons, not rabbits."

Nyx raised his hands in a placating gesture. "Understood, ladies. Please, don't take my head off. I had to ask." He clapped his hands together and blew out a breath. "Okay, listen. It's going to be hell carting you across the country in secret. You all sparkle like precious jewels. Amethysts, emeralds, rubies. Dragons have been called the true treasure of Valdenia, and it's easy to see why. But it makes it impossible for you to blend in with the humans. Every Guardian of Vale is out there voraciously hunting for Raine and the Cavern escapees. You aren't going to be able to cover your heads with cloaks and sunbonnets this time around. My best idea is to shave the lot of you bald—"

"Over my dead body," Tejayla shrieked.

Objections rang through the chamber, bouncing off the stone walls in a calamitous uproar. Raine was more circumspect in his refusal, but he did pull his precious hair close and stroke it as if to reassure himself. When Sidian rolled his eyes, he pretended not to see.

Naiah interceded, quieting her thunder with a stern look so that Nyx could continue.

"I knew you wouldn't go for that, and obviously I can't force you." Nyx sounded put out, as if they had refused to try his new crumpet recipe as opposed to shaving off their jeweled crowns of glory. "But that means we need ideas. We could soak your hair in ink—"

"No," Raine cried, clutching his hair reflexively. "What is with you people and ink? It's for paper, not hair, you monster."

Nyx closed his eyes very slowly, then opened them as if to make sure this was his real life. "What about the rest of you, then? Raine refuses to use ink, but if everyone else does ..."

"If you take one step towards me with a bottle of ink, I'll make you drink it," Carissyne said bluntly.

Amari and Amara crossed their arms. "Same," they chorused.

Observing the other dragons' reactions, Raine felt vindicated for all the fits he used to throw at having to powder his hair. Dragon vanity was real and serious. He hadn't been acting like a brat. It was his *nature*.

A heart-ripping pang followed that thought. Raine would never be able to say as much to his father, inciting a back-and-forth session of playful barbs and insults—their language of love.

Nyx must have realized the anti-ink sentiment was unanimous. He buried his face in his hands and groaned through his fingers. "Fine. What do you suggest?"

Eva stood and threw out her hands. "Why don't we fly?"

Around her, the other dragonesses chimed their agreement.

Nyx shook his head. "There are sky watchers, remember? They'll track where we land."

"We can land someplace away from the safehouse and then run there on foot," Sarsana said as if this was obvious.

"I can see why you'd think that, but it will not work," Nyx replied patiently. "Why do you think we didn't fly when I brought any of you here from the Cavern?"

"Because you don't have wings?" Eva said, half-questioningly.

"No," Nyx said slowly. "Because sky watchers are trained to arrive late at a landing site. They are expert trackers. It doesn't matter how careful you are. There are always signs of passage. It wasn't worth the risk when I brought you here. And now, with the size of our group? It's not a risk. It's a guarantee. They will find us if we fly no matter what."

Eva's shoulders sagged as Nyx detailed his objection. The others sat with visible pouts.

"How did you get around undetected?" Amara, the fire-stone-heating twin, asked.

Raine shifted on his bench as the group collectively regarded him. He hadn't had to hide his hair in forever. There'd been no need as Sidian's captive. And then, on their way to Moontop, he and Sidian had been so deep in the wilderness that there hadn't been many humans to hide his hair from. A simple hood had sufficed.

He had, however, experienced a long, undercover journey before his capture. Raine smiled in recollection. "My friend Aly and I used wigs to hide our hair when we traveled from Pashun to the safehouse." Pashun also happened to be the closest city to Moontop. From the volcano's base, it would only take a day to reach the city. Raine looked at Nyx. "You can sneak over to Pashun and buy a bunch of wigs for us."

"It's settled," Carissyne announced, pouncing on this solution. To Nyx, she said, "If you travel through the night, you can arrive just as the shops are opening."

"I'll get your cloak." Sarsana jumped up and sprinted away without giving Nyx any chance to protest.

Nyx turned to Naiah, his features slack and bewildered. Her winter blue eyes danced, though her tone was tranquil as she said, "It's a good thing your sleep schedule was so recently flipped. Being up all night should be no trouble."

Sarsana flew back into the chamber and shoved a dark woolen cloak and backpack into Nyx's face. He rolled his eyes but took the proffered articles.

Once Nyx was cloaked and prepared to leave, he bid his farewells to the dragonesses. Each of them hugged him tightly, murmuring demands of safe travel and expediency. Sidian and Raine stood as Nyx reached them. Raine embraced him first. Then Sidian, who whispered something private into Nyx's ear. As they drew apart, Sidian produced a handful of silvans and deposited them into his brother's palm.

"Consider it done," Nyx said, pocketing the coins. To Raine, he asked, "Which store has the wigs?"

"Oh. Um, it's called ... Love Play." His cheeks burned hotter than the firestones as the brothers regarded him with identically arched brows. "I didn't choose to shop there. It's a long story," he said defensively.

Nyx grinned and ruffled his hair. "My little baby is growing up."

CHAPTER EIGHT

Naiah removed her dress in one fluid motion. Raine flushed and turned away while she transformed. From his peripheral, he noticed Sidian turn, as well.

Eva leaned against Raine's side, laughing as she patted his chest. "You're so shy. Why is that adorable?"

"Leave him alone," Carissyne said, bumping Eva's shoulder. "He was raised by humans, remember? He didn't even know what gravid meant."

Naiah's scales shone like sparkling ice, even in the dim glow of the cavern. Nyx climbed upon her back, as she was his ride to the sprawling foothills many thousands of feet below, on the opposite side of the mountain. He nearly lost his perch, his entire body jerking sideways, as Naiah dove into the roaring night.

"Wait, wait, wait. That's right." Eva peered at Raine as if he was a fascinating new specimen. "You're so *little*. You practically hatched yesterday."

Sidian smirked, wicked amusement dancing across his features. Humiliation scorched Raine's ears. He locked stares with Eva, attempting to silently communicate something along the lines of, *Please stop denigrating my size in front of my mate.*

"I'm not little. *Anywhere*," he stressed, hoping to quell any comments to the contrary.

"You're a big, strapping dragon," Tejayla assured Raine in the same tone he once heard Wylan use when his father discovered gray in his hair. *The gray gives you a mature, distinguished look. Women love it.*

"A big, strapping *baby* dragon," Eva said, sending herself and Tejayla into paroxysms of laughter.

Sidian clapped a hand over his mouth. Raine narrowed his eyes. Was Sidian laughing? His shoulders shook once, twice. And then, Sidian's smoky laugh rang out, too. Raine's face was hot enough to put the kettle on, even as his belly fluttered at the sound.

"Dreaming Mother, can you even shift forms yet?" Eva asked, wiping a tear from her eye.

"Oh, please say you can." Amari clasped her hands, as if in prayer. "I've never seen a white dragon. Everyone goes on about how beautiful Myrrah was. I want to see for myself."

"Myrrah was a white dragon?" Raine asked. Why had no one shared that sooner?

"Oh, yes," Amari said, looking surprised at his ignorance. "I thought everyone knew."

"You definitely need to read Nyx's book," Tejayla said.

She meant well, Raine knew. But at that moment, he wanted to chuck Nyx's book at her head. He was sick of hearing about it, and really, his mate did not need any more incentive to read it than he already had.

"I will, thank you," he ground out. "And no, I can't shift forms."

Amari slumped, crestfallen. Amara came over and hooked elbows with her twin. "Perk up, Mari. That just means we can teach him."

Amari grew ten inches taller, gripping her sister's arm with delight. "Do you think so?"

Amara's response was lost as the dragonesses all chattered excitedly. They drew into a tight cluster and began discussing the best ways to teach Raine—as though he'd already agreed to be their student.

Sidian watched them for a moment, then snorted. "Good luck with that."

He began to walk away.

"Where are you going?" Raine called after him.

"To bathe."

Before Raine could stop it, a vivid image of Sidian's sculpted body, slick with hot, soapy water, assailed him. A touch breathless, he asked, "Do you need me to show you where the hot springs are?"

"Nyx already showed him last night," Carissyne said, startling Raine as she appeared at his side out of nowhere. She waved Sidian off, then turned on him. Her smile was wolfish. "It's time for your first lesson."

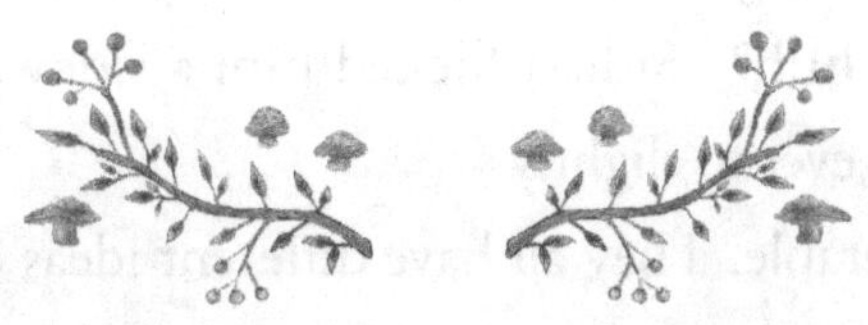

Raine hurried down the tunnel to his room, wondering if he would find Sidian there. It was late, after midnight. His "lesson" had dragged on for hours, much longer than he expected.

Even worse, it had been pointless. He was no closer to shifting into a dragon than he had been that morning. Probably because his lesson had lacked any actual teaching. Instead, it included lots of squabbling, conflicting instructions that made no sense, and at one point, a three-way brawl that Raine hadn't been involved in, yet somehow his hair ended up getting pulled.

Light emanated from his bedchamber ahead, making it glow like a beacon in the pitch-dark tunnel. Raine's stomach clenched hotly. He had thought Sidian might choose to stay in Nyx's room, especially since his brother was away. Raine ducked through the entrance and froze.

Sidian sprawled atop the mattress, one powerful leg draped carelessly over the edge. Both pillows were tucked behind his head as he read Nyx's book, balancing it on a bent thigh. His face was clean-shaven, showcasing his wide, dusky mouth and angular jaw. He was encased in pristine black hose that traced every dip and valley of his musculature. Another of Nyx's spare uniforms; one way or another, they were going to be the death of Raine.

"You're back," Sidian murmured, without looking away from his current page. "How was the lesson?"

"Splendid," Raine deadpanned, depositing his lamp next to the one already burning on the rock stand.

"That well, huh?" Sidian flicked him a sideways glance, his mouth curling ever so slightly.

"It was miserable. They all have different ideas on how to unlock my dragon form and wouldn't stop fighting about it. Tejayla and the twins think I need to meditate. They claim I can con-tact the Dreaming Mother in a trance, and she will show me directly. Then, there's Sarsana. She says I need to be struck by lightning. *Lightning.* She tried getting me to craft a metal pole for the next big thunderstorm. Winter is quickly arriving, so she was very ... urgent about it. And if you think that is deranged, Carissyne believes I need to hunt and kill a mountain lion. With my bare hands. Then *eat* its still-beating heart. If this bedchamber had a door, we would be locking it."

Sidian's shoulders shook with a silent laugh. Raine feasted on the sight. His mate was warm and safe and laughing. No moment in his life had ever been this perfect. It took him a moment to recall what they'd been talking about.

"And Eva thinks I have to be in extreme duress," he added, picking his words with care. "As if I'm going to deliberately traumatize myself just to shapeshift."

What she'd actually said was, an immediate threat to a drag-on's mate overrode their biology and forced the shift, but Raine's belly quivered at the thought of mentioning mates to Sidian.

Flustered, he spun around and headed for their rucksacks. He couldn't remain in a Guardian uniform and be around Sidian. Not without making things very awkward for them both. As he knelt, the pungency of scorched wool and cotton saturated the air. He opened the flap with an uneasy feeling. A foul smell plumed, watering his eyes.

"They're ruined," Sidian said from the bed. "Nyx gave us a stack of clothes. Those need thrown away."

Raine stood and scanned the room for a clothes pile. Other than a leaning stack of folded black near their bags, there was nothing. "Did he give us anything other than Guardian uniforms?"

"No."

"Oh. Well, do you have any spare clothes I can use?"

He was already inching towards the other rucksack when Sidian said, "No."

Raine eyed the plump lines of Sidian's pack, where spare clothing plainly bulged. His mate was lying. But, why? He stood and turned to find Sidian's stare narrowed on him.

"I know the Guardians of Vale are a corrupt organization," Sidian said. "The Nine have a lot to answer for. But wearing that uniform doesn't make you anything like them."

"It's not that." Did Sidian think Raine was judging him for wearing one, too? "I don't have a problem with the uniforms because of where they came from," he insisted, willing Sidian to believe him.

"Then what is it?"

"They're just ... too tight," he said lamely.

Sidian sat up. Placing Nyx's book on the mattress, he walked over to Raine. Stopping in front of him, Sidian pinched the fabric covering Raine's left shoulder. It was the precise spot where Sidian had run a sword through Raine on the first night they met. Sidian's mouth hardened, and Raine wondered if he was recalling it, as well.

"It's not too tight. The uniforms are designed to accommodate any size without restriction." Raine opened his mouth. To say what, he didn't know. Sidian cut him off. "Furthermore, the fabric is interwoven with lotus silk. It acts as a type of chainmail. It will protect you."

"Not from the guild." Raine didn't need to say why. They both knew dragon bone blades shredded Guardian jumpsuits like tissue paper.

"Leave that part to me."

Raine's breath hitched at the quiet intensity lacing Sidian's words. They were more than an assurance. They were a promise. Sidian blinked slowly and waited, as if daring Raine to issue more protests.

Raine wouldn't. He *couldn't*. Sidian had just sworn to protect him, to be his armor. Raine felt faint, as if he might swoon.

"I'll wear the uniform," he managed at last, his voice thinner than he liked.

"Good." With that, Sidian returned to bed.

Raine's pulse ticked faster as he watched Sidian get situated on the mattress. His mate separated the pillows and laid them side by side. Then, he leaned back against the wall, stretching his frame across the far side of the bed. The other side was plainly meant for Raine.

The bed wasn't narrow. But it wasn't wide, either. Their bodies would be squeezed together, practically on top of each other. Raine's pulse became a wild thrum, and he concentrated on slowing it. This wasn't a big deal. He'd been sleeping against Sidian for weeks.

Yeah, for survival, an unhelpful voice interjected. *In the freezing cold. With both of us wearing so many layers, it was like two sleeping bags cuddling together instead of two men.*

Of course, that had never stopped Raine from becoming … stimulated. But it *had* prevented Sidian from detecting his condition. Between their coats and multiple layers of pants and sweaters, his erections had been cushioned to obscurity.

There was no such cushioning now.

Sidian grabbed Nyx's book and glanced at him. "You coming to bed?"

There was nowhere else to go. The dragonesses had all retired, as well. The firestones were black and cold in the dark, whistling cavern above.

Raine's soul beamed ecstatically even as his feet trudged toward the bed with the weary gait of a prisoner hooked to an iron ball. There was no way in hell this scenario ended with his dignity intact. As he reached the bedside, another problem reared its hideous head. Right there, protruding from the pages of Nyx's book, was a greyish-brown osprey feather.

It wasn't the feather itself that perturbed Raine. It was its position. If Sidian was using it as a bookmark, that meant he was already twenty percent through Nyx's book. The pages were as fine as onion skin, which made twenty percent a damning amount of dragon lore.

A bubble of panic rose in Raine's throat. He struggled to draw breath around it as he stared at the feather. Sidian cracked the book open and resumed reading.

Sickly dread coursed through Raine. His head streamed a constant, *What do I do? What do I do? What do I do?*

But he couldn't do anything. The amount of shame and self-loathing he experienced any time he tried to come between Sidian and that cursed tome made interference impossible.

Flip. Raine's stomach churned like a sinking ship at the crinkling turn of a page.

"Something the matter?" Sidian asked, without looking up.

"N-No. Why do you ask?" Blood roared in his ears.

"Because you are frozen like a startled deer and clearly fighting a panic attack," his mate said blandly.

Flip.

It was true. On top of which, he must have looked weird hovering next to the bed without getting in. Raine concentrated on his wooden legs, willing the muscles to relax so he could resume motion.

He tried speaking and a horrible croaking sound emerged. He cleared his throat and tried again. "You know, I think those stories are more fiction than fact."

Flip.

"Funny. That's not what Nyx said."

"Yeah?" Raine managed a staggering step. The soft edge of a mattress pressed against his thighs.

"He said dragon history is recorded verbally, through stories. Naiah's mother was a storm mother." Sidian's dark eyes glanced at Raine. "Do you know what that means?"

Raine's brows creased in thought. "They rule dragon communities. A den mother governs her family, which is a thunder. And a storm mother governs a community of thunders."

Sidian nodded like a satisfied instructor who'd already possessed the answer. Anxiety wrenched Raine's stomach. Dragon lore was more edifying than he feared if Sidian already had a practical understanding of their social structure.

"Storm mothers have a secondary duty," Sidian said, his eyes returning to the open pages near his lap. "They are keepers of lore. Naiah has heard the tales more than anyone. Her biological mother was also a storm mother and recited dragon lore in place of bedtime stories. Naiah corroborated with Nyx, and he created the first ever written record of dragon history. This book" —Sidian raised it with a small shake— "is one of a kind and more valuable than any quantity of silvans can purchase."

Pride lit Sidian's features with such fervor, Raine winced and looked away. He mentally added *discrediting* to the increasingly long list of things he couldn't do to Nyx's book. The damn thing was like a demigod, as inviolate as the Divine Father himself. And Raine just ... gave up.

He gave up. He might as well tell Sidian the truth now. It would give him a chance to control the narrative; to explain that, although they were mates, he expected nothing. That he knew nothing would happen between them.

Flip.

"Sidian."

"Hm?"

"There's something I need you to—" Raine stopped and drew in a breath. Then another, and another. But no matter how much he inflated his lungs, the words wouldn't come. His courage had abandoned him. "Whatever you read, it doesn't have to change anything," he managed at last.

There was an agonizing silence. *Flip.* "Doesn't have to change anything?"

"Yeah. I mean, yeah," he said lamely. Sidian looked up at him and arched a brow, silently letting him know how ridiculous he sounded. Raine huffed, feeling defensive and foolish and more vulnerable than a baby bird fallen too soon from its nest. "I'm just trying to tell you that I'm happy to be your best friend. I don't want your regard for me to diminish."

Sidian stared hard, unblinking as he searched Raine's expression. "Is there something in this book that would change that?"

"No. Yes." He sighed, lowering his head. "Maybe?"

"Raine," Sidian said, commanding his attention. Raine's stomach felt like it was skipping rope. Reluctantly, he looked up. "I promised to tell you what you say in your sleep once we made it out of Obanth."

"You did," Raine said weakly.

He remembered. Of course, he remembered the teasing promise Sidian had made before marching Raine through the gates of Silvan Dredge Prison. Sidian's attitude had been playful, leading Raine to believe his sleep talk wasn't too incriminating.

And yet, Raine was all too aware of the perversity of his dreams and who starred in them. It was difficult to imagine he'd mumbled something innocent.

Contemplating the possibilities gave him hives, so he hadn't reminded Sidian about it. In fact, he'd hoped his mate had forgotten all about the matter.

No such luck.

Sidian snapped Nyx's book shut. Raine's skin jumped an inch off his frame at the sudden clap. He felt more on edge than if he was standing on a cliff.

"My name," Sidian said. "That's what you say in your sleep. Over and over, usually while dry-humping me. Do you think I haven't noticed how your cock gets hard whenever I'm near you?"

Raine was too mortified to speak. His entire body flushed so hot, he wasn't sure how the stone floor didn't melt beneath his feet. He didn't know precisely what dry-humping meant, but he knew the word *dry* and he knew the word *hump*, and he knew he would never recover from the humiliation of this moment.

"I don't know what sort of oversexed dragon pubescence you're suffering through," Sidian continued in a calm, reassuring tone that did nothing to ease Raine's desire to spontaneously combust and die. "But if it bothered me, I wouldn't be here. And since none of that has driven me away, I'm not sure what's in this book that you think will turn me against you."

Sidian's jaw ticked as he sat back. Giving Raine his profile, he glared into space. "It is not your fault you think so little of me. I hated you without reason only weeks ago. But I hope, in time, you will understand that I've changed."

Fuck. Raine hadn't meant to imply a lack of faith in Sidian. He knew the man's feelings had changed. Hell, he'd called Raine his best friend just that morning.

"I do not think little of you," he protested. "Sidian, your honor and integrity have been apparent since day one. There is no one I respect or admire more."

Sidian continued staring into space. It was like he wasn't even listening.

Raine fisted his hair and fought a scream. "I'm not worried about you being an *inconstant friend*. I'm worrying because ... I've kind of been keeping some stuff from you."

Sidian's eyes sharpened to knifepoints as his gaze swung back to Raine, who threw up his hands as if to block real daggers.

"Nothing like that, *yeesh*. I don't want to burden you or make you uncomfortable—that's all. If the book reveals anything that makes you feel that way, please know I will be the best fucking friend ever, okay? Whatever you need."

Sidian gave a slow nod. "That was vague, though I suppose you meant it to be. Suffice to say, I have every certainty I will remain your true friend upon learning this dreaded secret," he said wryly.

Raine stretched his lips into what he hoped was a believing smile. Of the two of them, it wasn't Sidian who needed to prove his steadfast friendship. No, after Sidian was through with that book, it would be up to Raine to prove himself as a genuine friend. As someone who required nothing of Sidian beyond his continued good health and happiness.

In fact, it would be a good idea to get a head start on demonstrating his platonic intentions. That way, by the time Sidian learned they were mates, he could look back and see how Raine was an excellent friend, and that there was no need to distance himself or feel uncomfortable.

"I know my sleep can be a bit restless." His face burned as he recalled Sidian's blunt words from earlier. *My name. That's what you say in your sleep. Over and over, usually while dry-humping me.* "If you want to sleep in Nyx's room while he's away, or ask for a bed of your own ..." He trailed off awkwardly.

Sidian's face was a mask of impassivity. "The first few nights after escaping Silvan Dredge, we didn't sleep against each other. Our surroundings were tropical. There was no tent or cold weather to force our proximity."

Raine shivered as Sidian's husky syllables wrapped around him like velvet smoke. His mate's gaze turned inward and darkened, as if reliving a bad memory.

"You had nightmares. Real ones, not the made-up bullshit you said in Vesper to conceal your wet dreams. I discovered you would calm down if I laid beside you. By the fourth night, I started bedding down with you as a matter of course. Your unconscious frottage is easy to endure compared to those nightmares."

Raine didn't like the shadows veiling his mate's expression. It reminded him of the perpetual melancholy that had clung to Sidian like a second skin until recently. Sidian was quiet and guarded by nature, but he'd lost the haunted look in his eyes since coming to Moontop. Raine preferred to keep it that way, so he girded himself and climbed onto the mattress.

The bed was too narrow to accommodate them unless they were fused together. As Raine's side pressed snugly against Sidian's, his abdomen clenched with heat. He inhaled deeply, trying to cool his ardor. It backfired immediately as Sidian's scent flooded him. Beneath the sweet-clean smell of sagebrush soap were notes of smoke and sea and something uniquely Sidian. Raine's blood surged south.

He squeezed his eyes shut, as if plunging this one sense into darkness could limit the others. It didn't work. The strong lines of Sidian's body were silken steel against his side and more tempting than a mountain of firestones. His scent was everywhere, thicker than if Raine buried his nose into his mate's bare skin.

Raine forced himself to take slow, measured breaths. It was that, or pant like a dog in midsummer sun.

Dread funneled through him as the full ramifications of their exchange penetrated. Sidian believed Raine's hardness was a generic affliction caused by dragon puberty—a belief Raine had cultivated on purpose. But now, Sidian also knew that Raine's arousal was linked to him specifically.

Oh, what did it even matter? Hopelessness bore down on Raine like the crushing weight of a dragon. Soon, Sidian would know everything. He would know the precise extent that Raine's hardness was linked to him. He would know they were mates.

Flip.

CHAPTER NINE

Moontop's cave system was as intricate as it was nonsensical. Like someone had handed an inked quill to a toddler and let them scribble for an hour; the result being hundreds of ropey, interconnected passages. Raine was down one now. So far and deep into the black belly of the mountain, he felt a twinge in his chest. The same twinge which had awoken him the previous morning.

His fingers massaged the area over his heart, right where it ached. As he took another step down and away from the main cavern, the pain sharpened.

Epiphany bloomed. He had thought the aches were the result of not seeing or touching his mate after too long. But that wasn't the case. It was a tether. An invisible string that only permitted Raine to travel so far from Sidian before slicing into him.

Well, then. Raine reversed direction, upholding his lantern as he climbed back the way he had come. The pain in his chest alleviated almost instantly.

A faint giggle echoed in the dark. Then, a shriek.

"You're out," he heard Sarsana call gleefully. She was close, but he couldn't tell if she was further up his passage or along a nearby branch. He tucked his lantern behind his back and sidled along the wall.

"No fair," Eva cried, sounding somewhere up and to his left. "Amari gave my spot away."

"I did not," Amari said. "All I was trying to do was hide before Sars found me. How was I supposed to know you were down here?"

"You and Eva make five," Sarsana said, dripping smugness. "I just have to tag Raine to win. Did anyone see where he went?"

Raine couldn't make out Eva or Amari's reply. Gritting his teeth, he kept edging forward. His strange tie to Sidian had chosen the most inconvenient time to needle him. It was going to be tricky, if not impossible, to sneak past Sarsana. He wanted to extinguish his lantern, but that was a dangerous ploy this far down the tunnels. It might spare him detection while costing his life, if he got lost.

Hiding the lantern behind his back concealed its light from Sarsana's seeking eyes, but it also hid the loose rocks littering the tunnel floor. The toe of his boot caught one. It skittered along the passageway in a damning clatter. A chorus of excited whispers rushed at him. Muffling a curse, he crouched against a shallow cranny. His palm cradled the wick of his lantern. It licked his skin like a hot tongue as three flickering globes of lamplight floated down the black corridor.

He held his breath. If he was lucky, they would pass right by him.

The leading lantern slowed, bobbing with Sarsana's stalking gait. Raine curled tighter into himself, cursing his hair. It practically beamed the instant light touched him. He'd already lost a dozen games. To be the seeker, one had to win the previous game. Raine had yet to be the seeker and at this rate, he never would.

Sarsana's lantern splashed the tunnel walls. Left and right, back and forth. As her figure aligned with his hiding place, the lantern swung to the opposite wall. She took two more steps before swinging it back. By then, the beveled edge of the cranny blocked Raine from view. She kept walking.

Eva and Amari followed more slowly, moving side by side. Their combined lanterns lit the entire area around them. He saw the exact moment they noticed him. Eva's grin was nothing short of villainous.

"What's a pretty little thing like you doing in a place like this?" she asked, darting a glance where Sarsana had gone.

Raine imparted as much silent venom into his glare as he could. His face said what his mouth didn't dare. *Shut up.*

Amari snickered. "Come on, Eva. We should give him a chance to actually win a round. It's getting pathetic."

"Best I can do is a head start," Eva said with mock regret, as if her hands were tied by a higher authority. It was bullshit, and Raine would have said so if she hadn't kept talking. "You've got to the count of five. One. Two."

Raine shot out and ran, their laughter echoing behind him. Eva must have reached five, because he heard her sing, "Oh, Sars. You're going the wrong way."

He flung himself down the second intersection he reached. His heart pumped furiously, driving his legs faster. Haste made him loud and easy to track. Sarsana and the others made the correct turn and chased after him.

There was nowhere to hide. He had to outrun them. What was the rule? If he made it to 'safety' before Sarsana tagged him, he won.

Safety was the firestones. They were hell to reach. There was only one route back to the glowing hot rocks in the main cavern, and Sarsana liked to camp in the long stretch of tunnel before the surface, waiting to tag them out.

But Sarsana wasn't there now. If he was fast, he could make it.

The thought gave him an extra burst of speed. But the damn passages were too tangled. Unlike the dragonesses, Raine hadn't been exploring them for years. He got turned around easily, always finding the dead ends that the others were smart enough to avoid. His heart slammed against his ribcage as a solid rock wall appeared before him. *No. Not again.*

He wanted to scream as Sarsana chortled obnoxiously in his ear. "Got you. I win!"

"Who's up for another round?" Amari asked, not sounding at all winded.

"Not me," he groused. "You all cheat."

"We do not," Eva cried. "I just gave you an advantage. If anything, I cheated in your favor."

Raine crossed his arms and glowered. "You're not supposed to help her look."

"He's just being a sore loser." Amari shook her head, as if disappointed in him.

"Who's being a sore loser?" Tejayla asked, approaching.

"Raine," Amari said. "He's mad because he lost again."

"Again?" Tejayla tsked. "You're terrible at this game."

"No, I'm not." Raine scowled at their mock pitying looks. "It's this stupid hair. I practically glow in the dark."

"That you do," Eva purred, then laughed at his expression.

"We can't play any more rounds anyways," Sarsana said. "Mother will get cross if we don't start packing. Nyx will be back tonight."

"Are we leaving as soon as he gets here?" Tejayla asked, bubbling with anticipation.

Sarsana shook her head. "No, Nyx will be exhausted. Mother wants to give him a chance to sleep first. We leave first thing tomorrow."

Even Raine's sullen mood wasn't immune to their exultation as they began chattering about their upcoming adventure. He was smiling by the time they encountered Amara and Carissyne. The two sat in a tunnel closer to the main cavern, lamps on the floor as they played a handclapping game.

"We're going to pack," Sarsana told them, then looked at Raine. "Do you need a new backpack and things? Your bag looked a bit burnt up and we've got plenty of extra supplies."

He thought of his charred rucksack and melted soaps. "Please," he said gratefully.

Contrary to the hefty weight of his pack, Raine felt light as he walked back to his room. It was crammed with soaps and oils, a hairbrush as lovely as the one he'd lost at Olan's entrance exams, and a few precious pairs of tights and fine-spun tunics that Nyx apparently never wore. Thank the Divine Father for that particular discovery. The guild's uniforms were comfortable but too immodest for his excitable manhood.

He found Sidian splayed across their mattress, arms behind his head with a distant gaze. His movements were lazy, indolent, as he turned to face Raine. "Who won your little game?"

Contrary to his casual demeanor, Sidian's eyes burned, as penetrating as fire irons. Was Sidian that invested in Raine's success? If so, he was bound to be disappointed.

Raine pouted, setting his new backpack on the floor. "Not me. I was found first in almost every round."

Sidian smirked. "Maybe you're just terrible at picking hiding places."

Raine rolled his eyes. "There were *rules*. We couldn't hide inside of things or in certain rooms. My hair kept giving me away," he grumbled, setting his lantern on the table beside Sidian's.

His hair was mostly dry from the steamy bath he'd taken after supper. Extracting his new brush from the pack, he braided it with quick, efficient movements and tied it with one of the ribbons Amara had given him while packing. Sidian watched him quietly, arms still folded behind his head.

"Did I interrupt your brooding silence?" Raine teased.

His mate snorted. "I don't brood. I think. Though I'm not surprised at your failure to discern the two."

Raine shrugged, unperturbed. "My father always said I'm lucky I'm so pretty since I'm as dense as a boulder."

Sidian frowned. "You're not stupid, and I seriously doubt your father thought so, either."

"You're in a mood," Raine noted lightly. The troubled expression didn't fade from his mate's features. Raine gentled his tone further. "It's okay, Sidian. I know how highly my father esteemed me. It was a joke."

Sidian's furrowed brows smoothed. "I know. I was making sure you knew." He waved a hand at Raine's backpack. "When do we leave?"

"Naiah's flying down to pick up Nyx at midnight, but we won't leave until morning."

Sidian fished an object from the mattress near his hip and set Nyx's book on the nightstand. Raine's knees turned to jelly as Sidian deliberately placed the osprey feather bookmark on top of its closed cover. His velveteen eyes fixed on Raine, steady and sharp. Raine's haunches quivered as he suppressed the urge to flee, feeling more hunted than he had in any round of hide-and-seek.

"You don't know much about dragons, do you? Come here."

Raine shivered at the smoky command. It sounded sensual. His desperate libido was probably twisting Sidian's words and tone, but that didn't stop his cock from hardening. Raine moved to the bed, sitting gingerly on the edge furthest from Sidian.

He was in the middle of folding his legs in a manner that would shield his erection as they talked when Sidian leaned forward and grasped his ankle. With a rough yank, Sidian slid him across the bed. Raine fell onto his back, blinking dazedly at the craggy ceiling.

Before he could gather his wits, Sidian straddled his stomach and glared down at him.

"Tell me what you know about your *puberty*. Then, I will fill in any blanks."

Desire assaulted Raine. An onslaught of lust so powerful, he swore he felt the earth move. "Um, it's hard to think with you sitting on me," he protested thinly. Sidian arched a brow, then leaned back into Raine's hardness, grinding against it. The pressure was hot and delicious and, "*Oh*."

His mate leaned forward, removing that awe-inspiring friction and heat. "You're always hard when I'm around. Tell me what you know," he whispered darkly.

Fuck. "Alright. Alright." Raine squeezed his eyes shut, struggling to draw blood back to his brain to think. He was too frazzled, too ignited. The truth left him in a clumsy rush. "I know that dragons remain sexually latent until we encounter our mates. My body sprang to life the instant I laid eyes on you. I burn with need, constantly. Sometimes, it feels like I'll die from it."

His eyes opened. Sidian's features were twisted with an indecipherable emotion that made his heart stutter. "I'm happy to be your friend, Sidian," he choked through his constricting throat. "Your friend and nothing more. I swear it."

"You expect me to reject you." Sidian's dark eyes flashed. "Do you know what happens when a dragon's mate rejects them?"

Raine had a guess but didn't want to say it. Mutely, he shook his head. Sidian leaned forward, bracing his arms on each side of Raine's shoulders.

"They die," he said bluntly, his eyes shadowed by the blue-black fringe falling into them. "Heartsickness consumes them from the inside out. It's something that only ever occurs when a dragon is matched with a human, since two dragons never reject each other."

Raine swallowed around the dragon egg lodged in his throat and nodded, albeit jerkily. "I'll be fine," he whispered. "Thank you for preparing me."

Sidian's eyes slitted dangerously. "You think I'm going to let you die."

Raine saw it then. The sheer determination in the set of Sidian's shoulders. The iron resolve lining his jaw. "Sidian, no," he protested, horrified. "I will let myself die before I allow you to sacrifice your future to save my life."

Sidian's gaze narrowed further. "I don't see how it's going to be your choice." His words were satin and steel. "You're desperate for me." He straightened, still straddling Raine, and reached a hand behind his back. Strong, deft fingers gripped Raine's cock and stroked him firmly through his silken hose.

Raine moaned. His eyes rolled to the back of his head as Sidian's clever, wicked hand massaged his shaft. One flick of Sidian's wrist had Raine arching off the mattress, his lips parted, eyes glazed. The pleasure was too much to endure. His soul was going to tear out of his skin. He was panting harder than he ever had in his life, sucking huge gulps of oxygen as Sidian released him.

Raine whimpered at the loss, staring into fathomless fawn eyes. Sidian's face was tightly drawn, warped as if in pain. As if that simple touch had been abhorrent.

"No," Raine gasped, hurt and misery slicing so deep, his arousal wilted. "Sidian, I will not let you do this. You deserve to choose who you share your body and life with. Not be forced into it because of some soul bond you never asked for."

Sidian's jaw flexed. "As you've just pointed out, the choice is mine to make. And we are consummating the bond. Tonight."

"What?" Raine squeaked. "I just said—"

"Once we leave here, anything could happen," Sidian snapped harshly. He fisted the stretchy material covering Raine's chest and lifted his torso several inches, lining their gazes as he spoke. "If I die before we establish the bond, your body could interpret our lack of consummation as my rejection. It's better to do it now and not take chances."

"Look, I understand your ... urgency." Raine's mind floundered like a fish on dry land as he tried to think of a way to put Sidian off.

He was terrified that Sidian was correct. That he wouldn't be capable of refusing his mate if Sidian pressed his suit. But it would shatter Raine, heart and soul, if Sidian sacrificed himself that way. Sidian didn't love him. Not as a mate.

But Sidian's gaze was darkly determined. He thrummed with tension, his body taut and braced for battle. He was prepared to throw away his life, his future, so that Raine could live.

Raine would have been awestruck and profoundly humbled that Sidian cared so much for him, if he wasn't so busy panicking. His mind raced for a reason that would succeed in putting Sidian off. In preventing his mate from making such a monumental mistake.

"This is too sudden," he said abruptly. "And-And overwhelming. I've never even been kissed. I'm not ready for all of this."

Raine would *never* be ready. Not if it meant ruining Sidian's life. Somehow, he had to find a way to keep Sidian's cock in his pants, tonight and every night after. It was the last thing Raine thought he'd ever try to do, but here he was. The Dreaming Mother had a twisted sense of humor.

Sidian tilted his head, his bangs falling sideways. "You've never been kissed?"

Raine stiffened at his tone. "I was sexually latent until you tried to kill me in Pashun. And the only one I will ever grant such permissions with my body is you, so how could I have—"

Lips, warm and soft and certain, covered his. Raine gasped, and his mate's tongue slid into his mouth. Sidian's silken tongue stoked a fire in his belly. His cock throbbed as Sidian's hands dug into his hair, pulling his braid. Raine moaned, and Sidian slanted their mouths, ravishing him with smooth, hot strokes, sucking his tongue.

When Sidian pulled back, his lips were shiny and swollen. His dark brown eyes looked black. They were both panting.

"I always thought kissing looked stupid," Raine said, exhaling roughly. Sidian was silent. "Not that I'm saying I still think that," he added hastily. "It's precisely the opposite, I assure you. I never knew there were all these lines in my body connected to my cock. My mouth feels like it has several. Um, you're really good at finding them."

Sidian didn't answer with words. He leaned down and eagerly captured Raine's mouth once more. They kissed hard and fast, then deep and slow. He didn't know how long. His cock wept, a damp patch blossoming where the tip strained against his hose. His hips were thrusting, seeking.

"I'm so hot," he moaned into Sidian's mouth. His blood was molten in his veins, feeding his volcanic lust. Pressure kept building, and it *ached*. His body trembled in its need to erupt. What would it feel like? In all of his dreams, he never got to that moment. Always waking on the verge of a precipice.

Sidian grabbed the hidden zipper of his jumpsuit and yanked it down. Raine slipped his arms out and his mate stood, tugging it swiftly off his body. The cave air felt cool against his heated skin.

He watched Sidian remove his own jumpsuit next, and sucked in a breath as his mate's cock sprang free. It was dusky like his mouth, and gorgeous. Thick and heavily engorged, upturned in its excitement. Moisture gleamed at its flared head, which was slightly pinker than his shaft. Raine felt a primal tightening in his lower belly as he eyed Sidian.

"I didn't think you liked men," he whispered, dragging his eyes up to his mate's face.

Sidian climbed over him again, this time straddling him so their cocks met and rubbed between their bodies. "I don't," he said, clasping their cocks together and stroking them as one.

Raine nearly fainted at the erotic image alone. His balls tightened, feeling heavy. Sidian flicked his thumb over his own cock, collecting precum. Then, he massaged Raine's crown with slick, firm fingers. Raine exploded in a white-hot eruption. His back arched savagely, and he cried out, distantly registering a choked moan from above.

Their spend splashed over Raine's abdomen and slicked between Sidian's fingers. Their cocks slipped together exquisitely. Wave after wave of ecstasy crashed through his veins, until Raine was sure he had died. This pleasure was too intense, too heavenly, to be found in an earthly body.

Aftershocks wracked his frame as he panted for lost breath. He peeled his eyes open and saw Sidian, heavy-lidded and gasping as he braced himself with one hand against Raine's chest. His other hand cradled their spent cocks, knuckles digging into Raine's stomach.

"That. Was not. My plan," Sidian panted. He climbed off Raine and grabbed one of their discarded jumpsuits to dab the cooling wetness from Raine's skin. His motions were tender, his eyes soft.

"What was your plan?" Raine felt like a lazy log, letting his mate tend to him, but he didn't trust his legs to support him to help.

Sidian tossed the soiled garment, lamplight shadowing his features. "To consummate our bond."

Raine jolted upright. "Dreaming Mother, I'm an asshole. Sidian, I'm so sorry. That shouldn't have happened."

He was pathetically lacking in self-control where his mate was concerned. One touch to his dick, and all his altruism flew out the cave. He grimaced, disgusted at himself. "You are more kind and generous than I ever expected, but I can't let you do that, Sidian. It would kill me," he insisted.

His entreaty might have seemed more sincere if his rebellious eyes weren't hungrily tracing the defined planes of Sidian's chest and abdomen. Though Raine's body was objectively beautiful, he felt like a cold, wan statue compared to Sidian's delicious warmth.

There was a knowing gleam in his mate's eyes as he said, "We'll see about that. Did you load up your backpack with vials of oil again?"

Raine blinked at the non sequitur. "Is that a real question?" Of course, he had.

"That's a yes, then." Sidian looked smug.

"You don't even use the oils. I don't think." He frowned, thinking back. "Whenever you're done bathing, you only smell like soap."

Sidian climbed into bed. They were both still naked. Raine hummed his approval as Sidian's arm wrapped around him, half-pulling him onto his chest.

"I think I will use them now," Sidian said, a hint of amusement in his voice, as though he'd spoken with a smile.

"You like that sagebrush soap. I think there's some sage and eucalyptus oils that you'd enjoy," Raine murmured sleepily. Sidian's free hand carded through the hair on Raine's crown, and he purred. His body was a puddle of languid warmth and light, swirling him into oblivion.

Sidian's chuckle rocked him gently. "I'm sure I will enjoy them very much."

CHAPTER TEN

Raine wrestled to consciousness, feeling as slumberous as a cave bear mid-hibernation. His thoughts were slow and scattered. Like the confetti paper tossed at newlyweds, they wafted between the grasping fingers of his mind. He stretched, arching his back as his arms reached overhead.

"It's about time," Sidian said from somewhere nearby.

Raine cracked an eyelid. His mate was awake and dressed for travel, gray coat unbuttoned to reveal a Guardian jumpsuit beneath. His hair was damp, his skin flushed. A rucksack was strapped to his back.

All at once, events of the previous evening caught up with Raine. He looked down and found himself nude, tangled in sheets.

"Nyx arrived late last night. It's morning now. Everyone is getting ready to leave." Sidian tossed him a clean jumpsuit.

Raine caught it reflexively and dressed, sensing the silent urge for haste. Equipping his pack and boots, he rushed into the dark tunnel after Sidian.

Rough basalt walls steadied Raine as he tripped along the passage, his head spinning too wildly to mind his feet.

All this time, he had stewed in anxious dread over Sidian's reaction should he ever discover they were mates. He'd been so afraid of Sidian's disgust, of his contempt, that it never once occurred to him that his mate might take the news well.

Better than well. Sidian wasn't contemptuous or repulsed, at all. In fact, he *wanted* to consummate their bond. It was insane. A dream come true, except ...

I didn't think you liked men.

I don't.

Raine flinched as he recalled their exchange. He'd been so gone with lust at that point, Sidian's words hadn't really penetrated.

They were penetrating now.

Sidian liked women. He only wanted to mate with Raine to save his life.

Raine couldn't allow it. His mate's happiness was infinitely more precious than padding his lifespan. He had slipped up last night, but it couldn't happen again. Passion, desire, lust? They were the enemy, and they would not win.

He would not let Sidian down.

"Perfect timing," Nyx crowed as they entered the main chamber.

Everyone was awake, seated around the firestones as they tucked into wooden bowls of hot porridge.

Raine's face heated as their eyes fell on him. For a heart-stopping second, he thought they knew what he and Sidian had been up to last night. But the dragonesses gave him easy smiles and returned to their breakfast. The only awkwardness was his own paranoia. Raine forced himself to relax as he joined them.

The buzz of many conversations engulfed him. The atmosphere was energized, the dragonesses festive. Cheeks flushed and eyes glittering, they openly chomped at the bit for adventure.

Amara handed Raine and Sidian each a full, steaming bowl of hot oats. Raine almost didn't recognize her. Not a trace of her lavender hair was visible beneath her flat brown wig.

"These are genius," Amari said, petting the wig in her lap like a cat.

Next to her, Eva tried securing her hair beneath a dark, curly-haired wig that reached the center of her back. Pea-green tendrils escaped the sides no matter how she positioned it.

"You should wear your hair plaited to your scalp to keep your natural hair from spilling through." Raine indicated Amara as an example.

It was something he and Aly had learned together at the Sleepy Bear Inn. His lips curved as he recalled how perfectly ridiculous they'd been, prancing around their suite, play-acting with lopsided wigs.

The dragonesses got to work at once, forming a line where each female braided the head before her. Raine declined to join them, reaching for a second helping of porridge instead. The crock was warm upon the firestones. He filled his bowl and replaced the lid. When he turned, Sidian was scraping his bowl clean.

Without a word, Raine swapped bowls with his mate, giving Sidian the full one and filling the empty bowl for himself.

He sat next to Sidian and watched as his mate's dusky mouth blew on his spoon. Raine's cock went wooden. He crossed his legs, alarmed at his reaction. Sidian eyed him wickedly and licked his spoon. Raine swallowed a groan. His body should be sated, right? Wasn't that the point of climax? But that brief sip of ecstasy seemed to have only deepened his yearning.

He shifted on the bench and tried to focus on his oats. Sidian's smoky laughter tickled his ear.

"Greedy," he whispered into Raine's sensitive shell.

He shivered, partly from pleasure. And partly from fear. He had known Sidian's pursuit of their consummation would be earnest, but that knowledge hadn't prepared him for *this*. Loaded glances and sexually charged teasing.

Raine couldn't resist his mate when he was plunging a sword through him. How the fuck was he going to resist him while he was actively seducing him?

Because I have no choice, he thought grimly. *The only way I can be a worthy mate for Sidian is by not being his mate at all.*

"Alright, everyone," Nyx called, addressing the chamber at large. "We can leave after breakfast, as soon as every dragon has their wig on straight."

Delighted whoops echoed through the chamber. The dragonesses scrambled to grab their cloaks and packs. Raine shifted in his seat, wishing he had a coat to shield his condition. The movement drew Sidian's gaze, which fell onto the erection snugged between his thighs.

His lips twitched. "I'll get your wig."

He took Raine's empty bowl and deposited it with the dirty dishes before receiving a wig from Nyx. Raine quickly braided his hair, then held his breath as Sidian gently fixed the wig on his head. His scalp prickled with pleasure as Sidian tucked his flyaways.

"It's going to be dangerous, even with your wigs," Nyx announced once everyone was ready. "The Guardians of Vale are swarming across Valdenia like a plague of hornets. They treat everyone with suspicion. We will strive to avoid them, keeping off the main roads and cutting through woods and fields along the way. Make sure you have everything you need. Not just soap," he chided, looking sternly at Tejayla. "You should each possess a canteen, a bedroll, and plenty of spare socks. If your feet get wet, it will be miserable without dry socks to change into."

Tejayla and Carissyne wore sheepish grins as they went to grab canteens and socks. The bedrolls were the same thin, padded mats the guild supplied to their units. Nyx brought a couple to Raine and Sidian, who rolled them into tight logs and fastened them beneath their rucksacks, where thin straps dangled for that express purpose.

"Here, you'll need this," Nyx said, coming back. He held out a mid-length shearling coat with a floppy hood.

"Thank you!" Raine snatched the jacket with a joyous gasp and shrugged it on. It was a little snug around his shoulders, but the toggle buttons fastened without issue. He equipped his backpack, then faced the inner wall of the cavern while Naiah undressed.

Naiah was the only dragon not wearing a wig. Her winter-blue hair was plaited, but she couldn't adorn her wig until they were on the ground. She transformed, then quickly flew the dragonesses down in two trips of three.

Raine, Sidian, and Nyx went last. Raine mounted first, carefully settling between her wing joints. Sidian wrapped his powerful legs around his waist. Raine's blood zinged with awareness, and he focused on the smooth scales beneath his hands. He was not going to get hard while straddling Naiah's back. The mortification would end him.

Nyx climbed up behind Sidian, and Naiah was off. Her lithe dragon form descended in a rippling ribbon of sinewy grace, swooping down the backside of the volcano where no sky watchers could sight them. The breeze caressed Raine's skin like a frigid kiss. His belly danced as she flew, a grin splitting his face as he stared at the blue-on-blue horizon of ocean and sky. He still couldn't believe he possessed wings of his own. That one day, he would soar into the vast oasis above—not as a passenger, but as a living, breathing jewel on the very crown of heaven.

Once below the tree line, Naiah circled the mountain. Her wingtips were a whisper of wind, then a rustle of leaves as she landed deftly in the middle of the upper Fangwilds. In moments, Naiah was wigged and dressed, a bulging rucksack at her back.

"The trees are orange and yellow," Sarsana announced incredulously, flinging her arms.

"Yeah, they do that every year, Sars. It's called autumn," Eva deadpanned.

"Shut it. I haven't seen a tree in ages. I'm allowed to be excited." Sarsana hopped on her heels. "Which way do we go?"

As one, they looked at Raine. He blinked, thinking hard. Without his father's map, Raine could still find the safehouse, but picking a direct path that eschewed major roadways would be impossible without it.

"The safehouse is near Campion. It's a small village in Holly-hock Forest, closer to Joltar. Once we hit Joltar Trail, it's a straight shot."

"We can't travel on Joltar Trail," Nyx said. "It's the harvest."

"It's the only way I know how to get there, but the stretch near Campion is really quiet. Not a lot of thru traffic."

"Reaching that section without taking any main roads won't be simple." Nyx frowned, considering. "The Pash-Ox Trading Route is a nightmare this time of year. I think we should head directly east, almost like we're going to Rokeshin. We can turn south before we hit the eastern Fangs. That should line us up with the trail outside Joltar while keeping us in backcountry."

Raine wasn't familiar enough with that route to lead them to Campion with confidence, but he nodded. They didn't have much of a choice, since the guild's search for him had intensified. The Nine wanted the breeding dragons back, and he was their shiny, opal ticket straight to them.

"Let's get a move on," Amari said, adjusting her pack. "We can figure out the exact route once we reach the road."

"The whole point is to avoid roads." Nyx rolled his eyes but began walking.

They shuffled into a loose formation behind him. The air was cold, but not too wintery with the forest insulating them from the more powerful gusts. Their boots crunched leaves and snapped brushy twigs as they picked their way through the untrodden wilderness.

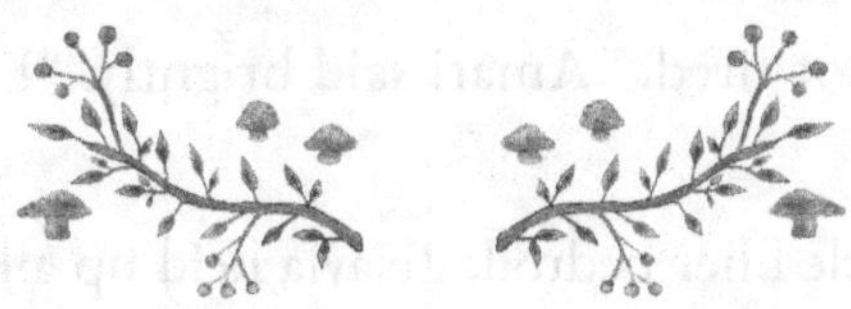

By nightfall, they reached the northern branch of the Pash-Ox Trading Route.

"Let's camp here," Nyx said, routing them back into the Fang-wilds and away from the roadside.

"Thank the Dreaming Mother." Tejayla dropped her pack, then collapsed on top of it. "My feet are killing me."

Raine's lips twitched, though he sympathized. It had taken days for him to adjust to lengthy foot travel. He held his bedroll and glanced around for a good spot.

Sidian took it with a smoldering look that made his ears burn, then spread it on the ground beside his own.

"Dragons aren't meant to walk," Eva said. She frowned severely at Nyx, as though this was all his doing, then collapsed beside Tejayla.

"Oh, really?" Nyx drawled. "I suppose your legs are just ornamentation, then?"

Nyx missed his brother's pinched expression as he spread his bedroll next to theirs.

Raine sighed with relief. His resolve to remain unmated might shatter if Sidian started plying his body with bone-melting pleasure like he had the night before. But amid seven dragonesses, with an older brother sleeping beside them, Sidian would be hard-pressed to try anything tonight. It was a reprieve. A much-needed one, given how hot and fluttery Raine's stomach was.

"Well, I'm not tired," Amari said brightly. "I could walk all night."

As she unfurled her bedroll, Tejayla held up a hand. "Oh, no. You go sleep by someone else. I can't deal with your energy right now."

Eva nodded. "At least have the decency to act like your feet are sore."

Amari rolled her eyes but dragged her bedroll a few feet away. "What do we do now?"

"Um, sleep?" Tejayla said, eyeing her like she was mad.

"I can't just sleep. I feel so buzzy. It's like my legs need to keep going until we arrive."

By the looks on Tejayla and Eva's faces, strangulation was imminent. Amara must have sensed her twin's jeopardy. She grabbed Amari's arm and tugged her down to her bedroll.

"How about a story?" Naiah asked, smiling fondly at Amari's pout. "That should wind us down."

"Good idea," Carissyne said, sitting upright. "Raine hasn't heard most of them."

Raine sat between the Wade brothers. His bedroll was cold beneath his bare palms, but he couldn't feel it against his bottom thanks to the thick coat Nyx had given him. Naiah waited until everyone was settled, then rubbed her chin thoughtfully, as if searching for the right story.

"I want to hear the one about Vesspira," Amari chimed.

"No." Tejayla groaned. "We've heard that one a million times."

"Raine hasn't," she shot back. To him, she said, "Vesspira was my great-grandmother. She lived over a thousand years ago and was a total legend."

"Very well." Naiah inclined her head. As she spoke, her voice grew soft and dreamy, as if laced with magic. "Vesspira was a very opinionated dragoness. She thought it wasn't fair that dragons held such a small amount of land while humans got the bulk of it. Her idea was a swap. The humans could have the dragons' territory and the dragons could take over the humans' land."

"Really?" Raine's eyes widened. "How would that even work? I always thought the dragons' territory was a super small section up north. The humans wouldn't all fit."

"A thousand years ago, Valdenia wasn't even a glimmer of a country. It was wild and sparsely populated, with only a few settlements," Naiah explained. "Suffice to say, they would have fit. But it was terrible timing on Vesspira's part. The nomadic tribes had begun to settle. Humans were sowing crops and erecting permanent homesteads. Vesspira, and many like-minded dragons, grew obsessed with lands they never cared about before. Something about the humans staking a fixed claim upon the land drove them mad."

Raine frowned. People always wanted what they couldn't have. It was why children squabbled over a single doll when there was a whole chest filled with other toys available. But a population of wise, gentle dragons should have been better at sharing, he would think.

And why should they, when humans are just as bad? He winced at his own invasive thought. Their present circumstances were proof enough that it was true, and yet …

"What happened?" he asked, hoping her tale didn't end with dragons as the original tyrannizers. Was Valdenia's ancient history a twisted, back-and-forth struggle for dominance between humans and dragons?

"Vesspira gathered a following. Her words were passionate and made sense to many dragons. They decided to seize the southernmost human settlement and work their way up, gradually herding the humans north as they overtook the land they felt was rightfully theirs."

Amari appeared titillated in the shadowy twilight. She caught Raine's gaze and mouthed, "Total legend."

He looked away uncomfortably. A warm hand closed around his own and squeezed.

"Relax," Sidian murmured. "It isn't what you think."

"When Vesspira and her contingent reached the southernmost human settlement, they decided to strike at dawn. Their goal was to be as civilized about it as possible. They hoped to frighten the humans away without bloodshed. But Vesspira was impatient. She didn't care to wait. So, while her followers slept, she crept away to accomplish it alone."

Amari was practically squirming out of her skin. "Let me tell the next part. Please, please."

"Chill out, Amari. She was my great-grandmother, too. We can let Naiah tell it," Amara said, swatting her.

"It's fine," Naiah said, a smile in her voice. "Go ahead, Amari. You tell it better."

"Well," Amari said importantly, with zero abashment. "Like Naiah said, Vesspira decided she was going to herd the humans all by herself. Only, she wasn't used to flying so far. She over-exerted herself on her flight to the settlement and sprained a wing."

"Sprained wings are super painful," Carissyne said, interrupting Amari's narrative to inform Raine. "You can't fly at all once it happens."

Amari resumed her tale as if Carissyne hadn't spoken. "Vesspira was overtop the human settlement when her wing gave out. All these humans were relaxing around this great big fire, enjoying a peaceful night when this hulking dragon landed in their midst, roaring like crazy. The humans should have been terrified. Vesspira was ready for it. She acted aggressively on purpose to frighten them off.

"So, imagine her shock when they didn't run." Amari's voice filled with relish. "The human chief had a thing for hawks. He trained them to hunt and deliver messages. Straight away, he saw that her wing was injured. He thought she was acting a brute because of the pain. He calmed everybody down and approached her with empathy. Vesspira was confused and didn't know what to do. She didn't want to hurt the humans. She only wanted to scare them away, but it wasn't working. The humans brought her fish and meat, even though they were too thin and clearly needed the food for themselves. The chief then insisted on checking over her wing and even knew how to bind it so it would stop hurting.

"Vesspira felt so ashamed of her plan in the face of their kindness that she couldn't go through with it. While she was at the settlement, she noticed the humans were struggling in certain areas. The way they were filtering sea water was making them sick. Their tools were really crude and inefficient, leading to poor harvests and hunger.

"Vesspira walked the whole night through to reach her followers before sunrise. She told them what happened and used her charisma to persuade them to help the humans instead. They arrived at the settlement in their human forms and showed them better ways of doing things. When they returned north, she told all the dragons to leave humans be. That the land was big enough to share."

"There's a reason my home city is called Vesper," Sidian added. He sounded almost as proud as Amari.

Raine blinked as realization dawned. "They named their settlement after Vesspira?"

"They sure did," Amari said smugly, as if it had been named after her instead. "She kept an eye on Vesper for the rest of her life. When a massive typhoon wiped away all of their homes, she went back and helped them rebuild, showing them how to make their structures stronger so they could withstand future storms."

"Vesspira's story is close to my heart, too," Nyx said quietly. "It's one of many that I hope will alter human perception of dragons and put a stop to the madness we're living in."

The twilight was fading fast, the dragonesses all but shadows beneath the canopy. One by one, they slid back onto their bedrolls, preparing for sleep. Raine imitated them, curling onto his side. His rucksack made a poor pillow. It was too hard and lumpy from all his bathing supplies, so he gave up.

Tugging his shearling hood up for a cushion, he caught sight of Sidian's dark outline. His mate was on his side, facing Raine. Though it was dark, Raine felt his eyes on him. A warm hand snaked under his coat and laid over his heart, which leapt like an eager puppy.

Raine covered Sidian's hand with his own and wedged it snugly at his center. He shouldn't. He really shouldn't. Holding Sidian's hand like this felt like a lot more than the stolid friendship he had resigned himself to.

Raine ordered his hand to let go, but the signal became lost or confused before it could reach his fingers. His grip tightened, instead.

The feel of his mate was spellbinding. It soothed him down to his marrow, where his soul whispered, *Mine.*

CHAPTER ELEVEN

The following morning, they broke their fast with nuts and dried fruit. Light weight and energy dense was the perpetual motto of guild fare, something which had obviously stuck with the Wade brothers. Nyx had personally selected their rations, ensuring there was enough to last them to the Hellhole.

The dragonesses drifted away to answer nature's call. Something Raine had taken care of immediately upon awakening, so he packed up his bedroll and fixed his wig, which had gone wonky in sleep, before meandering towards the road.

It was a crisp morning with a blanketed sky, the clouds a watery gray that didn't appear too foreboding. At most, it would sprinkle.

The clouds dimmed the sun enough that Raine didn't see the spiderweb until he was practically on top of it. It was enormous, stretched between two ash trees. He halted in his tracks, riveted by the web's perfectly repeating fractals.

His mind imploded with wallpaper designs, all triggered by the spiderweb. Some designs possessed the exquisite delicacy of lace; others were sharp angles and sweeping lines. Muted colors, bold colors. Textured, flat. Glossy, matte. Raine struggled to assimilate his avalanche of ideas. It happened this way sometimes; he would get especially inspired by some random object or scenery, and his imagination would take off like a bolting horse.

Sidian nudged their shoulders together. "You're doing it again." His voice was amused. "Creating patterns in your head."

Raine blushed but didn't bother denying it. There was no point. Over the course of their journey from Obanth to Moontop, Raine had been brought to a standstill by sights as mundane as withered grapevines, firethorn clusters, and hollowed trees filled with sleeping snails. Usually, once they stopped hiking for the day, Raine would etch the designs he'd imagined into the forest floor with a sharp stick—his method of carving them deeper into memory.

"You might want to get your inspiration elsewhere. I don't think anyone's going to want spiderwebs decorating their dining room walls."

"What did you say?" Raine's head snapped sideways, mouth agape.

Sidian was already looking at him. His smoky laughter seeped out in a foggy ribbon at Raine's horror-struck reaction. "I know your dirt drawings are more than idle scribbles. They're designs for wallpapers."

Raine had never told anybody about his love for wallpaper, let alone that he wanted to design his own. He felt so open, so exposed, that he didn't know what to do with himself. His eyes dropped like stones to the ground. His face burned.

"Raine, hey. Look at me," Sidian said quietly.

That husky command was like the steady pressure of a palm beneath his chin. Raine raised his head, his blush deepening to crimson. As he met Sidian's stare, liquid fawn eyes dragged him into a bottomless world. A place where all he could see or feel or breathe was Sidian.

Sidian's brows slashed downward as he grasped Raine's shoulders, jerking him back to awareness.

"Raine," he repeated. Their boots touched as he stepped closer. "You find beauty and humor everywhere, in a way that fills me with wonder over and over again. Someday, we will have a home adorned with your designs, and I can't fucking wait. Don't be embarrassed. Be proud of your talent and the joy it will bring to others, myself included."

Raine couldn't speak. A giant's fist had clamped around his throat and squeezed. He blinked furiously, just in case his damn eyes decided to do something totally contemptible like cry.

Sidian made him sound so ... so *special*. He said Raine filled him with wonder. *Over and over*, even. His knees felt weak, which made no sense because the rest of him had never been lighter.

The rustling crunch of many footfalls drew his attention. The dragonesses and Nyx hiked towards them, Carissyne in the lead. She bounded ahead of the group, and Raine thought she meant to tackle him.

He braced himself, preparing to take her down mercilessly even as gratitude swept through him at her timely interruption. He had been seconds away from blubbering all over his mate, which was the last thing Sidian deserved after sharing such profoundly kind sentiments.

Carissyne raced faster and faster. The wavy brown locks of her wig whipped behind her like a cape. Her color was high, her grin dazzling as she adjusted her angle. Too late, Raine realized Carissyne didn't plan to tackle him, at all. She was running for the road, on a trajectory that would spear her directly between the ash trees.

Before he could call out a warning, she went face-first through the orb weaver's web. The *occupied* orb weaver's web. The spider was as fat as a plum and solid black with bands of gold along its legs. It was also right in the center of Carissyne's face, scrambling for purchase on the bridge of her nose.

Carissyne pierced the world with her shriek, arms wild as she ran blindly into the street.

"Fuck," Nyx shouted, but like the rest of them, he was too far away to stop her.

A team of four bay geldings brayed and reared, violently rocking the coach they were fixed to. The driver's whip cracked frantically as he attempted to control the horses before they toppled the carriage.

Nyx caught up to Carissyne and dragged her from the street. Her wig was a mess on her head but miraculously, still in place.

The carriage door flung open. The edges of Raine's vision blurred as a man emerged. Not just any man. He was middle-aged with flat, dark hair and a pointed chin. He wore a black robe and a scowl. And his eyes were a brownish yellow that raised all the fine hairs on Raine's arms.

"What is the meaning of this disturbance?" he barked, spraying spittle.

Six dark shapes poured out of the carriage and pooled around him. Guardians.

Nyx averted his gaze and began ushering Carissyne out of the road.

"You, there. Stop right now and explain yourself." Nyx froze but kept his head down and turned away. "I am Chieftain Morseth, traveling on urgent Valdenian business which you've just delayed."

Too late, Raine realized Nyx's situation. His human eyes and hair were a perfect mask for blending in, but not if he was confronted by someone who knew him and very much thought he was dead.

The road congested with halted traffic. Few travelers were on foot, but as Raine's gaze darted desperately, his eyes snagged on cloudy silver orbs. The woman was ancient and gnarled, her hair a scraggle of white about her shoulders. Time seemed to freeze.

"I'm so sorry, Chieftain Morseth," the old woman said. She moved forward, blocking the chieftain's view of Nyx and Carissyne. "My granddaughter Esba was born simple. She fears horses. We don't usually take the main roads, but we got a late start to Vesper. We're trying to make it there before my joints seize up from the cold."

There was a long, heart-palpitating silence. Sidian was as stiff as marble against Raine's side, poised to intervene. But the chieftains knew him, too. It would be a disaster. Raine's hand felt numb as he clamped his mate's arm, wordlessly telling him to *stay put*.

Morseth uttered something that sounded like, "Fucking snowbirds." Louder, he said, "Control your granddaughter, ma'am. Perhaps a late arrival is best, all things considered."

The old woman bowed low. "I agree. This was a mistake that shan't be repeated. It is a privilege to make your acquaintance. I'm so sorry it wasn't under better circumstances."

The chieftain nodded once, sharply. Without another word, he reentered his carriage. There was a breathless moment where the Guardians wavered. "Come on," Morseth snapped from within. "I don't have time for this."

The Guardians vanished back into the carriage, and the door slammed shut. Nyx dragged a slightly stunned Carissyne to the roadside as the driver cracked his whip. The knot in Raine's stomach didn't ease as the carriage rumbled out of sight.

Too close. That had been too close. And it wasn't over.

The old woman approached them with two companions in tow. She grinned at Raine, revealing all gums and no teeth. "We meet again. Allow me to introduce myself. Idesta Layvish. These are my granddaughters, Esba and Kemmy."

The two young women framing her offered Raine friendly smiles. Recognition jolted him. They were the sisters he had danced with in Pashun. And Idesta, well. He had recognized her at once. She was the crone who had spoken with him at the bar in Debauched. Her strange words from so long ago whispered through him. *You will fly again.*

"I'm not simple, by the by," Esba said with an exasperated look at her grandmother. "Why did you use *my* name for that ruse? Kemmy is the flighty one."

"Excuse me," Kemmy squawked. "You're the one who failed your math final."

"I'm Carissyne," Carissyne said, joining them. She looked pale but otherwise recovered from her near-trampling. "I'm not simple, either," she added cheerfully.

Nyx snorted behind her. "Could have fooled me, the way you just acted."

Naiah stepped forward. "Thank you so much for your help with that situation," she said to Idesta. "I don't believe Chieftain Morseth would have been as accommodating of our mishap without your intervention."

"It was no trouble," Idesta said. "Now, why don't you tell me why a group of dragons think this is a good time to go traipsing around the country? Don't you know what's going on? You should be in hiding."

Naiah's jaw unhinged. She looked so caught out and unprepared, it was almost comical. Nyx's features hardened. He reached near his hip, where he kept a knife.

"Whoa," Raine said. "It's fine, guys."

He actually wasn't sure of this. He scarcely knew Idesta or her granddaughters. It wasn't knowledge that fueled his assertion, but a gut feeling. He couldn't get Idesta's long-ago words out of his head. *You will fly again.*

"How did you know?" Naiah whispered, clutching at her breast without looking away from the crone.

"Please." Idesta gave her an arch look that stacked her forehead in a dozen wrinkles. "I know a dragon when I see one. I'm not blind. Yet."

"For the last time, you're not going blind, Grams." Esba rolled her eyes. To Naiah, she said, "We know what you are because of our family's history. Don't you notice anything odd about me and my sister?"

The other dragonesses had crowded around them by this point, and Tejayla gasped. "Dreaming Mother, are you dragons, too?"

It was Raine who answered. "No." He knew at once what Esba referred to. She and Kemmy possessed certain traits that would jump out at anyone familiar enough with Valdenian folk. "They're foreigners."

"Are not," Kemmy said, affronted. "We were born here, thank you. And so were our parents and their parents."

Idesta clucked her tongue. "You know what he meant, girlie. And yes, our ancestors were Garganthan."

Esba and Kemmy blinked their matching gray-blue eyes. They wore cowls to ward off the chill, so he couldn't see their hair, but their eyebrows were a shade of brown much lighter than the norm.

"Where are you headed?" Idesta asked abruptly. "My joints ache ferociously from this weather. That part wasn't a ruse. We're bound for Vesper, where we'll stay with my son's family until spring. I'd like to make it there before snow starts falling."

She shuddered, as if snow was the equivalent of maggots. The thought made Raine shudder, too. Sidian reached out and tugged up Raine's hood. He did it casually, as if the action required no thought. Raine's heart swelled, but when he went to beam a smile of thanks at his mate, Sidian's eyes were trained on Idesta. Like Nyx, he was tensely alert, not yet willing to trust these strangers.

"We are going south, as well," Nyx said smoothly. That was a lie. They had planned to head east first. "But if you know so much about dragons, you know we can't take a road filled with horses."

"Yet here you are," Idesta said, thick with reproval. "Begging for a carriage accident, at that."

Nyx scowled and took a step toward her, as if he was about to impart a few choice judgments of his own.

"We were only going to cross Pash-Ox," Raine hurried to explain. "Then continue on a smaller road. It was bad timing."

"Well then." Idesta glanced up and down the road, which was interspersed with carts and wagons hitched to all manners of equines and bovines; a lumbering assortment of beasts with full stampede potential. From the oxen to the donkeys, all of them would react poorly to a single dragon's scent, let alone eight. "It'll slow us down a little, but we can take Corkstaff Road with you for a spell before hopping back onto the trade route."

Idesta turned and, as if the matter was settled, began walking south. Her granddaughters framed her. One on either side, they stuck close as they followed. Raine watched them progress for a few seconds, then glanced at Nyx. Naiah and her thunder did the same. It was as if they were all yelling the same silent question. *What the hell are you scheming, you great, big liar?*

Nyx shrugged, still half-scowling from Idesta's censure. "We need to follow them. They know what you are. We have to make sure they're not a threat."

His stride was clipped as he caught up with Idesta and her granddaughters. Sidian kept pace with Raine, but he positively radiated his urge to catch up with Nyx, to be able to step in and contain any potential threats. It was as if he and Nyx expected Idesta to pull a fistful of dragon bone daggers from beneath her fleece-lined skirt and fling them at any moment.

Raine walked faster, half-jogging to reach Nyx and the women before Sidian came out of his skin. Without discussing it, Idesta kept to their left, insulating them from the nearest conveyances and their dragon-skittish beasts.

"So," Nyx said tightly. "You said your ancestry has to do with your knowledge?"

"Normund Layvish was my ancestor," Idesta said curtly, blowing on her hands as she walked.

Sidian frowned. "You expect us to believe you're Garganthan royalty?"

"Believe what you want, young man. I think I know my family tree better than you."

"Then why are you here?" Nyx pressed. "If you're related to the late king of Gargantha, you're a princess. All three of you are."

"Shows how much you know of history." Idesta sniffed.

"I know more history than most," Nyx said in a tone that reminded Raine he'd dedicated years to writing a meticulous historical chronology. It had been about dragon history, to be fair, but his passion for the past was evident.

"Then you should know that when King Normund invaded, it was against the royal council's edict. When his army was vanquished, Gargantha revoked the crown. The Fulgars hold the throne now. We Layvishes are nothing but peasantry."

Raine hadn't known that. Not any of it. King Normund had always been referred to as, well, King Normund. The affairs of Gargantha were not a focal point of Valdenian historical record, not the least because Valdenia had remained completely and deliberately isolated from the northern continent for the last two centuries.

"Fine. You're still descendants of a king." Nyx voiced it like an accusation. "What are you doing here, and what does it have to do with dragons?"

"Oh, it has everything to do with dragons," she said darkly. They grew silent as they passed a group of pedestrians heading north. "Do you really think now is the best time to discuss it?"

Idesta darted a meaningful glance around them. The Pash-Ox Trading Route was glutted with travelers. Many elderly Valdenians traveled south for the winter, their migration as regular as morning doves. It was harvest season, on top of it. Raine had never seen so many wagons bursting with ripened vegetables. It created a nonstop cacophony of clicking hoofs and clattering wheels. Even with Idesta and her granddaughters masking their group's scent, they needed to leave the main road as soon as possible.

A protest formed on Nyx's lips. He was in strict protection mode for the dragons he'd spent years harboring from danger, unrelenting in his mistrust.

"She's right," Raine cut in. "Now isn't the time. I'll vouch for them in the meantime. If you can't trust them, trust me."

"How are you acquainted, exactly?" Amari asked, sidling up on Raine's other side.

Esba threw him a wide grin, brimming with mischief. "Oh, we used to dance the nights away together. From sunset 'til sunrise. It was amazing."

Sidian's inquiring stare seared the side of his head, and he flushed. "It wasn't like that. We met at a nightclub in Pashun."

If Nyx's brows arched any higher, they'd fly off his face. "A nightclub? In Pashun?"

He made it sound like a bawdy house, and Raine's flush deepened. "There was a band. We just danced. It was perfectly respectable."

Nyx's skepticism grew. "There is nothing respectable about the nightclubs in Pashun's pleasure district."

"Oh, for the love of ... Tell them," he implored the sisters, who kept stealing glances and giggling at his distress.

"It's true," Kemmy said, taking pity on him. "We knew he was a dra—um, you know, straight away. There was no other possibility, with eyes like his. I approached him to see if we'd spark."

"No, I approached him to see if we'd spark," Esba said, leaning across Idesta's back to shoot a glare at her sister. "You can't ever let me have something for myself, so you inserted yourself in my business."

"Whatever, Esba." Raine could practically see Kemmy's eyeroll even though she faced forward. "The point is, we didn't spark. Even so, it was incredible meeting one of your kind in real life. And you were the best dancer there, so of course I stuck by you anyway."

"It was a treat while it lasted." Esba sighed wistfully. "You were the only guy there who didn't try to slip a hand beneath my skirt."

Gradually, Sidian relaxed. It was almost like he'd been ... jealous. A thrill swept through Raine at the thought, but he ignored it. Sidian couldn't be jealous. There was only one reason he wanted to mate with Raine, and it had nothing to do with romantic interest.

The Corkstaff junction finally appeared. It took ages for a gap in traffic long enough to cross the Pash-Ox Trading Route safely. They required a lot of clearance so that no animals would be spooked.

The dragonesses were hooked on the concept of nightclubs, particularly Carissyne and Tejayla. Hours passed as Esba and Kemmy extolled the virtues of seedier human entertainment to a rapt and curious dragon audience.

CHAPTER TWELVE

I desta and her granddaughters could camp with them for a single night before they had to part ways at the next junction. Travelling east with the dragons any longer would put them too far behind schedule.

The boon of accompanying three suspicious women who claimed to be descendants of a king became wonderfully apparent as they built a roaring campfire in a clearing off of Corkstaff Road. Fire was a luxury they couldn't afford on their own; not when they were well beyond the seclusion of the Fangwilds, and the only two humans in their group were recognizable to the guild.

Raine sat as close to the flames as he dared, inching back only when the heat threatened to melt his boots.

"I don't have any more spare coats," Nyx warned from above, skirting the fire to find a place.

Sidian tucked his fingers into the neck of Raine's coat and yanked him back a few more inches. "Better," he murmured, sitting next to him.

His side pressed into Raine's, their folded knees overlapping. It wasn't necessary with their coats and the fire's warmth, but Raine was unable to move away. The contoured strength of his mate's body was addicting. Raine's flesh hummed with awareness at each contact point, every fiber reaching for more. How the fuck was he ever going to find the strength to refuse Sidian?

His fists clenched, and he buried them in his lap. He would find a way. For Sidian, he would do anything.

"You guys are adorable," Kemmy cooed, plopping down on Raine's other side. She wedged herself against him as tightly as Sidian had. "You must be really close friends."

On Raine's opposite side, a hand grabbed the underside of his thigh and squeezed. It felt like an order. Or a warning. Raine's cock pulsed, interpreting Sidian's punishing grip in an entirely different way.

He couldn't shove Kemmy away without making everyone wonder why it was okay for Sidian to be this close and not her. Raine agonized with indecision as Sidian's grip tightened. His cock swelled harder. Then, Kemmy's head snuggled against his shoulder.

He jerked away, his ardor wilting as if he'd been doused in ice water.

"What's the matter?" Kemmy asked as Raine leapt to his feet.

He made a show of batting at himself, his face as hot as the fire. "I think I sat on an anthill. Sorry. I'll just ..."

He went and sat between Amari and Amara, the latter crying, "Don't bring your ants over here."

Sidian's stare burned holes through him, but Raine was committed to the coward's way out and avoided his gaze.

"Alright," Nyx said, once everyone was settled. "This is as much privacy as we can expect. Why don't you tell us what being long-lost Garganthan royalty has to do with dragons?"

His tone was firm, an order phrased as a question. Idesta pulled a thin, checkered blanket over her shoulders, almost as close to the fire as Raine had been. Flames danced in her cloudy eyes like mirrors. "Very well. It's a tale passed down through my family for generations. The story of how King Normund went mad and attacked the dragons."

The dragonesses shifted to attention. The wind's quiet breath buffeted dead leaves as the fire crackled. All else was silent.

"Attacked the dragons?" Nyx leaned forward from his perch on a decaying log. "You make it sound as if he intentionally set out to do so."

"Because he did," Idesta said matter-of-factly.

Nyx was already shaking his head. "No. Gargantha invaded for the vale's riches. Their army took a wrong turn and ended up in dragon territory by mistake."

"Oh, is that so? You mean to tell me that they couldn't follow the broadly marked roads to the tribe settlements? That they somehow fought through a tangled wilderness for weeks, wading deeper and deeper into the Dragon Lands because they were seeking the famed treasures of the Rokes and Strowa?"

"You have to remember—while the vale wasn't yet a country, it was still a popular territory," Esba said from her grandmother's side. "Merchants and travelers came from all over. The routes were established and known. How do you think Gargantha even knew about the gold and jewels to begin with?"

For this, Nyx seemed to have no comment. Idesta took his silence as permission to continue. "Gargantha was in a time of peace and complacency. They had enough wealth and resources of their own. They didn't need to plunder the vale. One day, King Normund went mad, like a man possessed. Overnight, his sole ambition became stripping the tribal lands of their riches."

"Exactly," Nyx said, nodding like she'd finally gotten it right.

Idesta smiled, but it was a sad smile. "The royal council rejected Normund's petition for war, so he overruled them. Within a fortnight, he assembled the bulk of Gargantha's army for his campaign to pick the pocket."

The phrase resonated, plucked straight out of history. It was hard to believe events centuries prior bore so much relevance to their lives. Raine caught the transfixed expressions of the dragonesses and was forced to reassess his perspective. This was no history lesson for them. It was personal. They had lived it.

"Go on," Naiah said gently.

"My great-grandmother, Queen Penella, had a terrible feeling and insisted on accompanying Normund to the tribal lands. She didn't know she was with child at the time, or she wouldn't have gone. Normund's forces marched through Rokeshin's Pass without resistance. When tribesmen spotted the army, they fled to alert their chieftains. Normund did not pursue them."

Idesta gave weight to those words. *Normund did not pursue them.* Raine would have thought it was a good thing Normund hadn't pursued them, as it meant the locals had gotten away unslain and with the opportunity to warn their people of the invasion. Idesta's ominous tone suggested otherwise.

"Penella and most of the soldiers grew more and more confounded as they progressed. The Rokes were the first tribe they would lay siege to. Or so they thought. But Normund didn't even seem interested. He steered his forces west. Not towards the gold-rich Roke tribe or the jewel-laden Strowa tribe, but into a stretch of vast wilderness. A place that, rumor claimed, was the territory of dragons."

Naiah cupped a hand over her mouth, her eyes hazy with memory. "The day they arrived was unlike anything. We were confused, then alarmed once they began attacking. It was chaos. There wasn't time to grab our eggs and flee."

"Most wouldn't have, even with proper warning," Eva said solemnly. "It was our land, our territory. It is not a dragon's nature to run."

"We're dragons, not rabbits," Tejayla said with a brittle smile, evoking several weak chuckles.

"I always thought that the humans' attack was too organized, too brutal, for happenstance," Naiah admitted. Her gaze was apologetic when it landed on Nyx. "I know what human history claims, and I never wanted to argue. Besides, I have no proof."

"Neither do they," Nyx said grimly, but he looked away, as if his convictions couldn't withstand the atrocities gleaming like fresh nightmares in Naiah's winter blue eyes.

"You're correct. I can't prove any of this," Idesta said. "But it's true, nonetheless. Picking the pocket was a guise. A convenient ruse. Normund was never after riches. He sought the total annihilation of dragons. He all but succeeded. It was—"

"A massacre," Idesta and Naiah and several other dragonesses chimed. The words seemed to infect the fire. It whooshed and roared, lashing furiously at the night sky.

"Just so," Idesta whispered. "Penella wasn't in the thick of it. Normund had enough presence of mind to keep his wife back at the camps during his death march. Two days passed before she realized something had gone wrong. She arrived in the wake of destruction. The forest was in cinders. Blackened armor and charred remains piled the ground a hundred men deep. She had to climb their corpses to reach the heart of the battle, where the only lives she found were a handful of crippled and bleeding dragons. Most were unconscious, on the brink of dying. She tended to them as best she could, knowing nothing of their bodies or how to care for them."

"I remember that," Sarsana burst. "Penella, of course. She called herself Pen, though. My leg was twisted, and she helped set it so that it would heal properly. Damn, that hurt."

Sarsana massaged her leg where it must have broken. Carissyne straightened beside her. "Yes, Pen. Gosh, we were so out of it. If she hadn't brought us food and water, we would have died. Don't you remember, Mother? You told her so much of our lore, to pass the time and take our minds off our injuries."

Naiah nodded, tears shining as she looked at Idesta. "Your ancestor saved all of us. We never knew who she was or where she came from. One day, she was there. The next, it was the chieftains, carting us into their wagons and trapping us in an underground cave."

"When the chieftains arrived with their company of warriors, Penella was forced to abandon you." Idesta's features lined with remorse. "She wanted to stay, but as queen of the invading country, it was too dangerous. If she had known what they would do to you, she would have remained regardless. It was her greatest regret."

Naiah waved her words away. "Please, don't be sorry. As I said, Pen saved us. Without her kindness, none of us would be alive today. You have our gratitude, now and always."

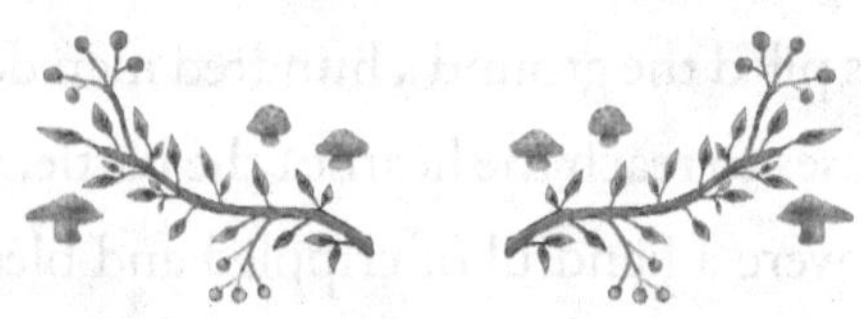

Once yawns started cracking in earnest, Sidian practically dragged Raine away from the others.

"Where are we going?" Raine's stomach jumped at the firm pressure of Sidian's hand in his. Sidian walked like he was on a mission, striding into the trees away from the clearing.

"To find a place to sleep that isn't right next to my brother," he answered without slowing.

The reason they would require such privacy made Raine's mouth dry. His head felt dizzy, and he tripped over a tree root. Sidian kept him upright effortlessly, tugging him onward before halting at a spot he deemed satisfactory. Raine watched in a lust-fogged stupor as his mate spread their bedrolls at the broad base of a gnarled oak. It had lost most of its leaves, creating a soft, fragrant cushion for them to sleep upon.

Sidian's velvet eyes were molten in the starlight. "Come here."

"Sidian," Raine said, plea and protest. He scarcely heard his words over his own thundering heartbeat. "We can't do anything. I won't."

There. That sounded firm. Unyielding. Sort of like his cock was now, at full mast beneath his coat. He modified Tejayla's mantra in his mind and clung to it like a liferaft. *I'm a dragon, not a beast. I'm a dragon, not a beast.*

He would rise above his baser urges if it killed him. The fact that it might didn't faze him. Death was a sweet and beautiful alternative to ruining Sidian's life.

Besides, Sidian wasn't technically rejecting him. Theirs could be a dragon tale yet unheard of. Not a rejection, not a consummation. Something in between, equally precious. A pure and lasting friendship. It didn't feel like it would kill him, though he knew Sidian was convinced. That was the problem.

Sidian stood before him, as broad and powerful as their shelter. Raine's chin inched up ever so slightly to meet his gaze. He tried to emanate the iron resolve of his father whenever he had asked to eat pudding for dinner.

It was almost too dark to discern the curve of Sidian's smile, as if he was humored by Raine's adamance.

He reached out and tugged Raine's wig off. The cold night air intensified around his exposed crown. He held his breath as Sidian grasped the base of his braid. His hold was tight, almost cruel, as he pulled Raine forward for a kiss.

The repetitive crunch of approaching footsteps stalled the action. Raine wasn't sure if he was grateful or disappointed when Sidian released him and stepped back.

"Hey, guys." Nyx clasped each of their shoulders in greeting. "Nice spot." He was little more than a shadow in the darkness as he shrugged off his rucksack and unfurled his bedroll, butting it against Sidian's, which rested alongside Raine's.

Raine's prick was ramrod stiff and leaking, but his shoulders shook in silent, helpless laughter at Sidian's twitching irritation. With Nyx sleeping beside them, Sidian couldn't try to consummate their bond.

This was a sign. Fate was on his side, also not wishing for Sidian to make a rash decision he would come to regret.

Sidian brushed against him and felt his amusement. He growled low, the sound wrapping around Raine's dick.

Nyx yawned noisily. "Try to get some sleep. We hit the road at sunrise."

"Sounds good," Raine said, injecting his tone with false cheer. "Goodnight."

His bedroll was thin but felt softer with the leaves underneath. Sidian jostled him gently as he situated himself, resting between Raine and his brother.

Without warning, a pair of sinewy arms latched around Raine's midsection and dragged him forward, until Raine was flush against Sidian's chest in the dark. Hot breath tickled his neck before a warm, wet mouth closed around the flesh where his ear met his nape. Raine bit into the thick arm of his jacket to muffle a moan.

"What are you doing?" he breathed. He kept his voice hushed to the barest whisper, mindful of Nyx's proximity mere inches from them.

"Be quiet or he'll hear you," Sidian whispered into his ear, making his words a caress as he nibbled and kissed the sensitive skin of Raine's lobe.

"No, Sidian." Raine tried wriggling out of his mate's grasp, but Sidian's arms were iron bands. Unless he was prepared to wrestle his mate for freedom, Raine was stuck.

He tensed as questing fingers wedged beneath his coat and massaged the globes of his buttocks through the thin, stretchy material of his hose. Raine's breath came faster as Sidian's hand traced the crease of his ass, grazing his heavy sack before finding the hidden pocket at his groin. It was intended for easy access to relieve his bladder, but Sidian used the opening for another purpose entirely. Slipping his fingers around Raine's aching shaft, Sidian stroked him from base to tip.

Raine swallowed his cry of pleasure too late. Sidian's sinful ministrations halted as a sleepy voice interrupted. "You okay, kid?"

Sidian's teeth sank into Raine's shoulder, biting him with equal parts passion and frustration. Raine savored the pain, letting it ground him enough to reply evenly. "Something crawled on me."

Nyx's husky laughter floated to him, almost identical to Sidian's. "Since when are you afraid of bugs?"

It was a fair question. Raine had been the epitome of a rough-and-tumble youth. Eager for swords, mischief, and mayhem. No doubt, Nyx recalled when he used to hide snakes and grasshoppers beneath bedlinens to startle the keep's chambermaids.

Sidian laved at the skin he'd bit. The hot wet swipes of his tongue made Raine's brain go muzzy.

"Um, it's dark," he answered feebly, stifling a moan as Sidian's mouth trailed higher, nearing the sensitive flesh of his ear. Raine swiftly jabbed his mate with his elbow. Sidian's mouth fell away with a muffled grunt. "I think I killed it," he added sweetly, holding back a snicker when Sidian pinched his side in retaliation.

Sidian was more determined than Raine had realized if the presence of his brother wasn't enough to put him off. Raine stewed in quiet dread, wondering where the fuck his willpower went the second Sidian touched him.

Fortunately, they had a week's travel ahead of them. With Nyx blithely joining them for sleep every night, Raine would be safe. More importantly, *Sidian* would be safe. And the Hellhole offered no privacy anywhere, affording Raine even more time. Weeks, or perhaps months, would pass before his mate found the seclusion necessary for a full seduction effort.

Raine started to extricate himself from his mate's arms, knowing he should return to his own bedroll to sleep. Sidian tensed, his biceps locking so that Raine couldn't move away. A soft mouth nuzzled his ear. "Where do you think you're going?"

Fuck. Raine's hips flexed involuntarily as his cock throbbed. Resigned, he cuddled closer, hoping Sidian couldn't feel his hardness through the combined bulk of their coats.

Perhaps this was a good thing. Prolonged exposure to Sidian's body might help build his tolerance. Eyes closing, Raine savored the warmth that bloomed where their bodies met and warded off the chill as they slept.

CHAPTER THIRTEEN

Kemmy lunged at Raine, jumping high with her arms outstretched. Raine was too startled to do anything more than stand there like a frozen tree as she latched onto him. The chit was heavier than she appeared. He fought to keep his spine from bending as she clung around his neck, her feet lifting off the road.

"I'm going to miss you so much. Please come back to Pashun next year. We're always there for the summer months, at the very least."

"Let him go, Kemmy. By the Divine, you are so obnoxious." Esba snatched the back of Kemmy's coat and yanked her off with a grunt.

Raine tried not to look too relieved as he was unburdened. He was fond of Kemmy, and Esba for that matter, but he hardly wanted to wear them like door wreaths. His gaze locked with Sidian's as Esba sprang at him next. Raine stumbled as he caught her, then patted her back awkwardly beneath his mate's narrow-eyed stare.

"That's enough, you two," Idesta said. "We've tarried enough as it is." To Naiah and her thunder, she said, "Not that I regret our meeting. I've dreamed of this my entire life—encountering those who my grandmother aided so long ago."

"It was an honor to make your acquaintance," Naiah said, dipping her head slightly. "I wish you a safe and swift journey south."

Raine sucked in a grateful breath as Esba released him. She flicked Kemmy a taunting smile as she approached Idesta.

"Seriously, Esba?" Kemmy trailed her with a scoff. "You *always* have to have the last hug. Or word. Or biscuit. You never let anyone else ..."

The sisters continued to squabble as Idesta led them in the opposite direction, back towards the Pash-Ox Trading Route and the road to Vesper.

"Well, that was interesting," Raine said to no one in particular.

"That's one word for it," Nyx said darkly. His air turned brooding, and Raine knew Nyx was dwelling on Idesta's dissenting version of history. It was a foundational truth, that Gargantha had invaded the vale out of greed.

Nothing had felt certain to Raine since the day he discovered he was a dragon, so he could well sympathize with Nyx's world being turned on its axis. He could almost read the turmoil in the man's eyes. The uncertainty. The, *What else is a lie?*

"I can't wait to see the other dragons," Eva said as they continued east. "I wonder if they'll remember Pen, too."

"So many of us were out of it. I doubt all of them will," Amari said, skipping ahead. The chit was so full of energy, she made Raine feel tired. And he'd just woken up.

"I'm excited to see Nesslyn and Aldred," Tejayla said brightly. Her smile slipped a little as she added, "They didn't do so hot in the

Cavern. I wanted Nyx to take them instead of me, but he explained that they had to liberate the unmated dragons first."

Nesslyn and Aldred. Two names out of twenty that Raine didn't know. Guilt coursed through him as he realized he hadn't tried to learn anything about the ex-breeding dragons. Or his parents.

"I'm looking forward to seeing Tassil," Sarsana chimed. "That hatchling always thinks he can best me. *Psch*. It's been way too long since I wiped the floor with him."

Naiah's lips twitched. "I, myself, am eager to meet with Betony and Lorrivare. There's much for us to discuss."

"You have fun with that," Amara said with a shudder. To Raine, she said, "Betony is the only surviving storm mother. And she's the most domineering. Thankfully, my old thunder wasn't under her purview. I don't think any of ours were."

"No," Naiah confirmed. "Betony lost her entire storm. All except her mate, Lorrivare."

"What a coincidence," Amara muttered. She shrank beneath Naiah's quelling glare.

"Betony's storm died with honor, to an unjust enemy that should have been too powerful for us to defeat."

"We know," Eva said hurriedly. "Amara didn't mean it like that."

Raine rather thought she had, but Amara quickly nodded, her expression chastened.

Naiah huffed and faced forward. "You may think Betony domineering, but remember that it was she who kept us going in the Cavern. Betony pushed through her anguish and found the strength to knit a new storm out of us. It enabled her resonance to develop, and we might not have survived without it."

"Wait just a minute," Sarsana said, looking alarmed. "I know Betony became our ... *emergency* storm mother in the Cavern, but we're out now. Don't we have the right to not join her storm?"

Naiah pursed her lips, though the gesture seemed more thoughtful than angry. "There's always a choice," she said at length. Sarsana's shoulders drooped with relief. "That being said, I intend to follow Betony's leadership. If you do not care for her as your storm mother, you will have to find a new thunder, as well."

Sarsana's crimson brows drew tight, her features resigned. "I won't leave you, Mother. Whatever you choose, I will follow."

The other dragonesses chimed mutual sentiments, and Naiah's wintry blue eyes glistened. "And I will do everything within my power to ensure your trust is not misplaced."

A twig snapped behind Raine. He whirled, his heart in his throat.

Sidian's smirk was a slow, sensual taunt. "What are you doing that has you so jumpy?"

"Hiding from Carissyne," Raine admitted shamelessly. "She's a menace."

Sidian arched a raven black brow, wordlessly requesting an expanded explanation.

Raine glanced around them, but all he could see were trees, their branches mostly bare. Autumn's final vestiges of red and gold leaves clung to them with admirable tenacity, but every whistling gust sent more gliding to the dense carpet surrounding them.

Satisfied that the dragonesses weren't onto his hiding place, Raine blew out a breath. "Carissyne is obsessed with unlocking my dragon form. She said, if we're caught out by hunters, we'll need all the fire we can muster to get away."

"Ah." Sidian nodded, looking serious. "And she's the one who wants you to get struck by lightning?"

Raine scowled. "No. That's Sarsana. Carissyne wants my help finding a mountain lion. She and the twins are searching for one right now. They honestly think I'm going to rip out its heart and eat it. *While it's still beating.*"

Raine couldn't curb the scandalized edge of his voice. Seriously, what was wrong with those females? No wonder dragon society was matriarchal. Dragonesses were pure savages. The lot of them. Who knew what sort of vicious cunning Evin's mild disposition concealed? And Naiah probably bathed in the blood of her enemies and made bracelets out of their teeth. He wouldn't be surprised.

Sidian's lips twitched. "We're on the periphery of Hollyhock Forest. There are wolves and coyotes. But no mountain lions, I assure you."

"Good." Raine relaxed slightly. "How's the road look? Any better?"

They'd been enroute to the Hellhole for days without issue. Then, just as they'd been about to reach Joltar Trail, their little dirt-packed sideroad had glutted with travelers. An endless parade of families and merchants. And Guardians. All headed in the same direction.

The presence of so many Guardians had caused Nyx to halt their travels. Until the lumbering progression ceased, they would remain tucked in the woods, secure from the suspicious eyes of dragon hunters.

"Yes and no. The bulk of the crowd has passed, but there remain too many stragglers to reconvene on the road as of yet. Nyx wants to give it another hour."

Wonderful. Another hour of cowering in the woods, hiding from bloodthirsty females who delighted in Raine's torment like barn cats with a juicy rat.

The faintest giggle reached his ears, followed by a sharp shushing sound. Raine's gut tensed with fear. He whipped his head around but saw nothing except vacant forest.

His eyes were wide and frantic as they latched onto Sidian like a lifeline. "Help me."

"They can't make you do anything you don't want to," Sidian pointed out reasonably.

Raine's skin leapt off his skeleton at the sound of rapidly approaching footsteps. His neck swiveled wildly, but he couldn't see either Carissyne or the twins.

"Hide me, Sidian. Please," he implored. "They're coming. Please, Sidian. *Please.*"

Sidian's brown eyes turned black. His jaw ticked as his face pulled into a taut, almost pained expression. Before Raine could breathe another desperate plea, a callused hand banded his wrist and wrenched him forward.

Raine trailed after Sidian like a kite string, his wrist clamped tight in his mate's grasp. If they lost their pursuers, he couldn't say. It took every ounce of concentration to keep his footing as they flew across jutting roots and patches of rot-slicked leaves. Sidian moved like wildfire as he darted through tree gaps and lunged up the quick, sharp inclines that crinkled the forest floor like a scrunched blanket.

After what felt like miles—but must have been only minutes—Sidian skidded to a stop. Raine stumbled, his momentum projecting him into Sidian's broad back like a cannonball. They both went down, Raine landing like a lump on top of his mate. "*Oof.*"

He scrambled to get off Sidian, mindful of how heavy he was. But the instant Raine's bodyweight left Sidian's back, his mate flipped over and tugged Raine to the ground. Raine's wits scattered as Sidian straddled his waist. Sidian's forearms were like cage bars as they braced the ground on either side of Raine's head.

Butterflies rioted in Raine's stomach as he blinked up at eyes more decadent than melted chocolate. Sidian's face was so close, he could feel his mate's breath as he exhaled.

"Sidian? What are you—"

Warm, soft lips covered his. Raine gasped. Sidian deepened their kiss, sweeping his silken tongue inside Raine's mouth. Rough hands tangled through his hair and pulled as Sidian devoured him.

Raine forgot everything. Their surroundings. His resolve to resist his mate's overtures. Fuck, he forgot his own name.

All that he knew was heat and desire. The hard lines of Sidian's body. The punishing grip of his mate's hands in his hair. And that mouth. That soft, wicked mouth that plundered and took and turned Raine's blood into fire.

Sidian's lips tore away, leaving them both panting as they stared at each other.

"Fuck," Sidian rasped. One of his hands slid from Raine's mane to caress the side of his face. His thumb brushed Raine's mouth. "Fuck."

"You already said that," Raine said weakly. His voice was thin with need.

"It bears repeating." Sidian made no move to get off him. Instead, his hand continued down Raine's chest, as though trying to feel him through his coat. His dark eyes were intent, swimming with emotions Raine couldn't decipher. "I'm going to go mad if I don't fuck you soon."

A wave of cold apprehension washed through Raine's veins. His molten lust turned to ash and stone, and he shoved against Sidian. It was like pushing a boulder. Sidian didn't budge.

"Sidian, no." Raine shoved at him twice more before falling back with a groan. "Why am I so fucking pathetic?" He raked his hands over his face, biting back a scream of frustration. At himself. His weakness. His selfishness.

Was Raine's love for his mate so shallow that he would allow Sidian to ruin his own life? Raine thought the answer was no.

The only way he could ever be worthy of Sidian was if the answer was no.

Sidian's eyes narrowed. "You're still on that bullshit, aren't you? That we aren't going to consummate the bond."

"Yes," Raine hissed. "Sorry," he added more gently, realizing how harsh he had sounded. "I'm upset at myself, not you."

Sidian drew back. Not so much that Raine could stand, but enough that his mate's torso was ramrod straight. Raine struggled valiantly not to notice how this new angle lined their groins. The winter-thick material of their coats cushioned them too much for their position to be compromising, but knowing that a few scraps of fleece were all that separated his cock from Sidian's wreaked havoc on his lust.

"Because you wish to spare me from being forced into a future with you?"

There was an edge to Sidian's question. Raine swallowed, feeling the phantom press of a blade at his neck.

"Yes," he answered firmly, sounding calmer than he felt.

Sidian huffed a humorless laugh. His mouth twisted, but it wasn't a smile. "Cute. And how will you manage that, when you can't even leave my side?"

Shame coated Raine's insides like sickly slime. "I didn't mean to presume upon your companionship. Shit, Sidian. I'm sorry. You don't have to accompany us to the Hellhole. Or, if you'd rather I leave, then—"

"Idiot." Sidian shook his head, then sighed. "That's not it, at all. My words were quite literal. You cannot leave my side. I thought it strange that you didn't try to escape my unit when I first captured you. Nyx's book cleared up that mystery, among others."

Raine winced, feeling unaccountably exposed. "It didn't occur to me to try until we reached Joltar. My mind was too preoccupied with ... well ..." He flushed, unable to finish.

"With me," Sidian said bluntly. "Sparking is a complex and pow-erful process. Your instincts must have ruled you for days. Weeks. They rule you even now, compelling you to protect me. To care for me. To provide for my every need." His voice dipped low, turning to a smoke-laden drawl as he added, "To fuck me."

Raine's breath stuck in his throat as heat speared him. Sidian's gaze roamed over him, taking in his reaction. He snorted. "Just so.

And after a dragon sparks, a courtship tie forms. Essentially, you cannot leave my side until our bond is consummated."

Raine frowned, recalling not only the way his legs had seized when he considered escaping Sidian's unit in Joltar, but also the awful ache in his chest when he'd awoken inside Moontop with his mate nowhere to be found.

"We aren't glued together," Sidian said, as if following his thoughts. "There is a certain leeway. But even if your soul doesn't interpret the lack of consummation as rejection, we will never be able to live separate lives."

"I'll find a way," Raine swore. "Your future should be one of your choosing. It isn't *fair*."

"You'll what?" Sidian sneered, at once appearing as he used to; an embittered Guardian captain with a heart more frozen than ice. "Set up a cottage next to mine and encourage me to build a life with another? Do you expect to listen through the walls as I fuck my wife? Be Pretty Uncle Raine to my children?"

Raine shut his eyes against the images that gouged him like iron spikes. His soul howled, a keening desolate cry of pain too great to endure.

"If I must," he gritted.

Those words cost him everything, but when he opened his eyes, Sidian's sneer was gone. In its place was a lethal intensity that scored Raine's flesh to the bone and left his soul naked and glittering where it wept.

"Our bond might be fated, but it is my *choice* to be with you," Sidian breathed, leaning down until their mouths nearly touched. "Fight this all you want. But in the end, you and me? We're inevitable."

Raine didn't know what to say to that. Not the least of which because … he was afraid Sidian was right.

Sidian's frame stiffened. At the same time, Raine detected several voices approaching. Leaves crunched to their left as Sidian deftly stood.

The voices grew steadily closer. Raine could make out their words.

"—can't wait to let my hair down for a week. It's going to be incredible. I hear the whole thing's being catered." A woman, one Raine didn't know. A corkscrew formed in his gut.

"No. Really? But there will be thousands of people attending." Another woman, another stranger. The corkscrew twisted.

"Tell me about it. I'm glad for the break, but this traffic is murder," a third unidentifiable voice said. Raine's insides cinched tighter than a wrung mop.

Sidian's palm shook impatiently, almost batting Raine's nose. He suspected his mate had been offering it to him for a while. A tremor wracked his hand as he placed it in Sidian's. Unlike Raine, his mate was cool and collected. There wasn't a whisper of sound as he smoothly pulled Raine to his feet.

"My parents met the night of Chieftain Willamyr's pyre," the first woman said, a note of wistfulness in her tone. "My father was a sheep herder from Tagetes, and my mother dyed cloth in Sinopel. I don't think they ever would have met if—"

The woman broke off mid-sentence, spying Raine and Sidian where they hovered not ten paces away. She was older but still lovely. Fine lines fanned the corners of her eyes like remnants of laughter.

She wasn't laughing now.

Raine's stomach plunged.

First, at her expression, which was an unholy combination of wrath and glee.

Then, because he glimpsed a patch of brown fur in the leaves near his boots. Which wasn't fur, at all. It was his fucking wig. Raine became suddenly, acutely aware of the cold air teasing his crown.

In a flash, all three women held milk-white blades. A captain and her two journeywomen, he realized as his stomach finally bottomed out in pure panic.

"Well, well, well," one of the journeywomen said, flourishing her short sword. "If it isn't the dragon we're all so eager to find."

The older woman, who Raine presumed to be the captain, grinned. Her eyes crinkled fetchingly. "You say dragon. I say promotion." Her features were lit with excitement. "I'm about to be the first female master in the guild."

"Wait. Our orders are to take it alive," the other journeywoman said.

"I'm aware of my own orders, Krisha," the captain said sharply. "But once our commanders have what they require, I'll be the one honored with slaying it."

"Uh, Sidian," Raine squeaked. "Should we be running now?"

"No," Sidian muttered, keeping his voice too low for them to hear. "They'll just follow us. And if they find out about the others, they'll flee."

The grimness of his mate's tone conveyed what his words didn't. If the women discovered that there were even more dragons tucked in these woods, they'd leave for reinforcements—then return to either capture or kill every dragon they found. Which would most likely be all of them. Dragons referred to Guardians as hunters for a reason. They were expert trackers. All they required was a starting point, and they'd chase their quarry down like a pack of bloodhounds.

Deadly, bone-wielding bloodhounds with bilious hatred and the fervency of a noble cause.

This was nothing Raine and Sidian hadn't done before—fighting Guardians to the death. Raine could still feel the echo of flesh and bone severing as he sliced a man's head from his body. The satiny give of another man's belly when he'd run a dragon-bone gladius through his abdomen.

He could still see the stark, troubled look in his mate's eyes as he stood over the third Guardian's corpse—a fellow captain and comrade right up until Sidian had defected from the guild. Those deaths had weighed heavily on Raine in the aftermath. For all their violence and commitment to kill, those men had been innocent in a way. Following orders they believed were just.

And these three women were the same. They believed in the Nine. They believed in their covert mission to eliminate dragons—the monstrous scourge threatening the safety of their homes and loved ones.

These women were good at their core. Tools too ignorant to know any different.

And now, they would die for it. They had to, because lifting a sword against Sidian was a death sentence. That was the law of Raine's breath and blood.

The first journeywoman said, "What about the man? The human."

The captain's smile warped into a malignant thing. "He's with the dragon, isn't he? So, he's a traitor. And traitors die. We have no orders to bring any men back alive."

Sidian unsheathed his longsword, the quiet whisper of bone masked by swaying branches.

The captain hissed like a startled cat. "Twice the traitor. I thought you looked familiar. You serve the guild."

"I've undergone a career change," Sidian said, his voice as soft as downy snow. "I no longer follow the orders of crooked men who lie and kill without remorse."

"With the company you keep, I'm sure you manage just fine by your own volition," the journeywoman—Krisha—jeered.

The three hunters edged closer, spreading out to prevent their escape. If Raine and Sidian wanted to flee, back the way they had come was their only option. Except, it was no option with Naiah's thunder tucked deeper into the forest.

"I don't know who is more despicable," the captain said through her teeth. "The traitor or the beast."

She raised her longsword but kept her motions slow and purposeful as she crept nearer. The forest sounds grew ominous, as if charged by the hunters' malevolence. Branches slashed the slate sky as leaves whipped and skittered across the ground, creating eddies of amber and gold.

"The traitor," Krisha spat. Her nut-brown eyes latched onto Sidian as tendrils of dark hair escaped her topknot. "Even the beast knows how to be loyal to its own kind."

Sidian angled his sword in front of his chest. His features were taut, his knees bent for a fight. Raine's silver eyes rolled like marbles as he took in the many weapons brandished around him. His own hands were excruciatingly empty.

Sweat dampened his palms as he took a measured step backward. Then another, until he was shoulder-to-shoulder with Sidian. Like Jaska, his mate kept a dagger in his boot. If Raine didn't want to face these women unarmed, he would have to draw it.

"They're both scum," the other journeywoman said. "Neither can be worse than the other when they're already as low as it gets."

The hunters took another step closer, their motions almost choreographed as they pinned their prey. In a few more steps, they'd be close enough to strike.

Whips of indecision lashed at Raine. Did he grab Sidian's dagger in a rush, then bury it into one of the hunters in a single movement? Or did he reach with deliberate care, so as not to provoke the hunters into a rapid assault?

"Too true, Corawyn," the captain said. "I do so rely upon your logic."

Her eyes were avid black beetles against Raine's throat. Her orders were to keep him alive, but her preference was clear. She wanted to spill every last drop of his blood until the forest floor was soaked with him, the leaves painted red.

The hunters took another step, and Raine didn't let himself ponder the matter further. Not with a mate to protect and an entire thunder of vulnerable dragons relying upon him.

His body was a blur. Swifter than the wind, he yanked the dagger from Sidian's boot sheath and threw. The milky blade wasn't airborne long enough to glint before it disappeared.

Krisha clutched her chest. Her dainty features pinched with pained disbelief as she observed the weathered steel handle protruding between her breasts. Her Guardian-black coat disguised the blood soaking through fleece and wool and lotus silk.

She collapsed like an accordion, her body folding smaller and smaller until she was a limp shadow, face-down in the leaves.

Raine was so preoccupied with Krisha's death throes, and the helpless despair scraping his conscience for what he had done, that he almost failed to dodge the captain's furious thrust as she charged him.

Corawyn and Sidian's blades met with a resounding clash that wasn't metallic like steel or dull like regular bone. It was crystalline and piercing, a sound that raised goose bumps down Raine's arms.

He knew from experience that his duty was to focus on his own opponent and trust in Sidian to handle his. His instincts were deaf to logic, rampaging in his chest to protect his mate even as he distanced himself from the pair. The captain followed him, her longsword whizzing endless arcs as it sought his flesh like an angry scorpion's stinger.

The captain gained the high ground and leaped. Raine twisted and ducked. Her sword bit into a tree, right where his head would have been if not for his speed. The dragon bone's edge was so sharp, it sliced halfway through the mature oak's trunk. And got stuck there. The crushing weight of the oak tree pressed down on the blade, keeping it firmly lodged.

The drawback of wielding such preternaturally sharp weapons was that they really could cut through almost anything. But after, they could be rather difficult to withdraw.

The captain tugged futilely to free her sword, but there wasn't sufficient give to maneuver the blade. Without any momentum to power her weapon, she would have to slowly serrate it loose.

Her elbow jerked harshly as she worked her blade free. Her sense of time must have been skewed. Battle did that to a mind, warping reality so that an hour felt like seconds.

... Or seconds seemed an hour.

Lost in her task, the captain was incognizant of the time that had passed. She didn't glance once over her shoulder, perhaps thinking Raine was still sprawled on his knees and had yet to stand or regain his breath.

But Raine had already done both of those things. And now he was death at her back. His hands clamped around her head like a foot snare. He felt more than heard the crack of her neck. One short, sharp twist was all it took to make her fall like a lifeless sack.

She had wished him dead. Despised his very existence. He didn't even know her *name*. But none of that mattered as he looked down at her crumpled figure. The unnatural angle of her neck.

This woman had known Sidian. She had probably known his father, too. They were of an age. Had they trained together? Shared meals and laughter between missions?

Raine's fists clenched as he imagined this captain and his father, holed up in one of the guild's many rustic cottages as they traded shifts at a nearby watchtower in their early service days.

It was all so fucking *fucked* and wrong, he didn't know where to start. He stood frozen while a vortex of grief and confusion spun him down to the murkiest depths of his soul. Until he was entrenched in all the hideous thoughts he kept buried like corpses.

At what point did the guild's mission transition from polished gold to fetid rot? And how was Raine any better? Dragons were supposedly creatures of dreams, but he felt like a night terror. A killer of men and women who strove to protect and serve Valdenia.

It had been Raine's ambition for so very long, to be precisely what this broken woman had been. What his father had been. What Sidian had been.

Sidian.

Alarm blossomed in his chest, a splash of dark ink that snaked through his pores and infected every inch of him with feral urgency. He twirled, his stomach a hard knot. His limbs were featherlight and thrumming to seize any threat to his mate. To rip and gouge and destroy.

His eyes lit upon Sidian, who was crouched and waiting, sword raised as he faced off against Corawyn. She snapped forward like a rubber band, hoisting her blade for a killing blow.

Corawyn's right boot slipped against the forest floor mid-lunge, as if she caught a patch of ice. Time slowed as she tripped into Sidian's sword. The angle left her midsection wide open and unguarded. Sidian's arm jerked as she fell, cleaving her body in half.

Never had Raine seen as much blood as what poured out of her in a thick, viscous splash. Her torso, arms, and head were all attached as they landed at Sidian's feet. Her legs and lower abdomen skewed towards Raine as they fell sideways. He grimaced as pinkish intestines spilled over bloody leaves like bloated worms.

There, resting near the tip of her right boot, was a brown, short-haired wig.

CHAPTER FOURTEEN

A cross piles of rustling leaves and steaming gore, Raine's gaze met Sidian's and held.

Sidian's eyes narrowed to slits. "Knock it off."

"Knock what off?" Raine asked, looking down to ensure his limbs hadn't taken on a life of their own. His boots, half-swallowed by leaves, were completely still. His arms hung motionless at his sides.

Sidian stepped over Corawyn's upper body without a glance, the slain journeywoman already forgotten. All his focus was on Raine, pinning him like a dried moth to a specimen board.

"Feeling guilty," Sidian said in his husky captain's whisper. "If it was up to them, they'd be standing over our corpses right now. And I assure you, there would be no remorse."

Sidian's voice rasped Raine's skin like a wicked caress. He shivered, certain he would go to the dragon equivalent of hell if he got hard right now, with three dead hunters practically underfoot.

"I don't feel guilty, exactly," Raine hedged. "But I can't help thinking about how unfair it is. The guild is filled with people like my father. Like you. Men and women who are only trying to do good. And I know I was defending myself. That this wasn't outright murder, but ... They didn't deserve this. It isn't *right*."

"It isn't wrong, either." Sidian walked around Corawyn's lower half and scooped up Raine's wig. He dusted the detritus from the hairpiece, then passed it to Raine. "They tried to kill you. Simply for existing."

"Because they didn't know any better—"

"*I don't care*," Sidian snarled. He closed his eyes and blew out a slow, controlled breath. Calmer, he said, "I don't care. They attacked you. That's more than enough reason for me. I told you I would protect you from the guild. I said to leave that part to me."

"I remember," Raine murmured, still awed by how ardent his mate had been. The quiet intensity as he said it, like a solemn vow.

"For two centuries, the Guardians of Vale have been nothing more than glorified butchers." Sidian's black brows slashed downward. "I was hunting you when I should have been defending you. The past is the past. I can't change it. But you better fucking believe I will protect you, now and forever after. From anything and everything."

His mate didn't say, *including yourself.* But Raine heard it anyway. He swallowed, hard.

"I want to protect you, too," he said softly.

Sidian's sinew corded with ferrous determination. Raine saw the argument brewing in his mate's dark eyes. Knew they were both thinking about the mating bond and Raine's resolve to save him from it.

Blood dripped from the tip of Sidian's sword. A soft *pat, pat, pat* that struck the earth. Tiny red rivulets slipped beneath withered leaves to iron the soil. Raine's heart flinched. Thus far, he'd succeeded in protecting his mate from an embittered cage of consummation. But he was failing Sidian in so many other ways.

"I'm so sorry," Raine croaked.

"So help me, if you're apologizing for defending your *life*—"

"I'm not. I'm apologizing because you did," Raine burst. His eyes were trained on the blood as if hypnotized. He felt each soft drip like acid on a wound. "You should have never had to raise your sword against your fellow Guardians. I'm so afraid that you'll think your honor has been besmirched by it. That one day, you'll regret—"

"*No.*" Raine's words crumbled and died at the force of his mate's outburst. Sidian's free hand gripped his chin and dragged his gaze up. Eyes, burning like black brands, razed the breath from Raine's lungs. "These women weren't my fellow anything. Make no mistake. My honor lies in *you*," Sidian hissed. His fingers dug almost cruelly into Raine's jaw. Sidian looked like he wanted to shake him. "My only regret? Is that I didn't kill all three of them."

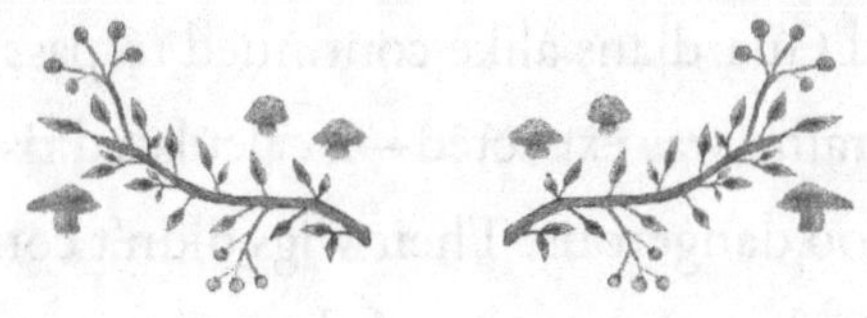

Raine and Sidian decided not to divulge their run-in with a Guardian unit to the others. The matter was moot since all three hunters were dead, their bodies littering the forest like acorns.

It hadn't felt decent, leaving them like that. There hadn't been any opportunity to cremate the unit they encountered in Drakkus

Valley, since they'd been in the middle of a civilian's backyard with a watchtower hovering on a nearby hill. But this time was different. There had been no immediate need to run. They could have figured out a pyre.

But when Raine suggested as much, Sidian had objected. Cleaning his sword on a bit of torn cloth, he said, "If we burn them, their families will never receive closure."

"We should at least move their bodies closer to the road," Raine said, already stooping to lift Krisha's corpse.

"Stop. Leave them be." Sidian's tone had been so severe, it shocked Raine to stillness mid-crouch.

"I just want to expedite their discovery. If we leave them here, wild animals will be all over them before they're found."

"If you expedite their discovery, we'll have more hunters on our backs. Better for them to be found days from now, when we're long gone and our trail is cold."

And so, reluctantly, Raine had left the bodies where they lay.

As they rejoined Nyx and the dragonesses, it was only to receive more bad news: the traffic was unending.

Civilians and Guardians alike continued to pass in trickles and droves. Some traffic was expected—a calculated risk. But the current level was too dangerous. Their wigs didn't conceal their eyes. If just one Guardian unit stopped them for questioning, it was over with.

"It's fine. We'll just walk the woods along Joltar Trail instead of the road itself," Nyx assured them. "They both go to the same place."

"But taking the woods will slow us down so much," Sarsana whined, falling dramatically against a bent basswood tree. Staring up at its naked canopy, she said, "It's going to take for*ever* to reach the others."

"Based on what Raine has said, it will delay us by a single day," Nyx said. Exasperation lined his words. "Provided you all move at a steady clip, we have two days until we reach the hideout instead of one. Think you can manage that?"

"I can," Amari chimed, even though nobody asked her. And they wouldn't, either. Amari was always eager for exertion. Of course she was down for an intense, two-day hike through dense forest. "Come on, Cari. This is going to be awesome."

"Speak for yourself," Carissyne said. "I hate the woods. I'm scarred for life after running into that massive spider's web. I can still feel its feet on my face."

"I've heard that, sometimes, spiders crawl inside your *ears*," Tejayla said, her scarlet eyes as round as an owl's. "While you *sleep*."

"*Excuse me?*" Sarsana shrieked, already patting her neck and face as if she felt something crawling. "That's it. I'm out."

Nyx grasped her elbow, stalling her retreat to the roadside. His tone was cajoling as he deftly maneuvered her back toward the center of their group. Naiah watched nearby, a fond smile tracing her lips at her thunder's dramatics.

Raine's gaze wandered to Sidian, whose rich brown eyes were fixed upon him and dancing with humor.

"What's so funny?" Raine asked, as though he wasn't half-breathless from Sidian's sucker punch smile.

"Nothing much," Sidian murmured. His lips curved wickedly, belying his statement. "Just recalling a certain dragon's reaction to a simple, harmless insect."

"If you're talking about that *thing* outside of Vesper, you're insane. I still don't think it was a cockroach." Silent laughter wracked Sidian's frame and Raine scowled. "It wasn't, was it? I knew it. I knew it was some sort of venomous hell bug. They probably paralyze you with dozens of sharp, tiny teeth and then eat you slowly while you can't even scream."

"What are you talking about?" Sarsana demanded. Her legs pranced like a skittish horse as she looked around in horror. "There are bugs that do that?"

"No," Sidian said. At the same time, Raine said, "Yes."

Nyx threw up his hands as Sarsana darted for the road. "Thanks a lot," he snapped at Raine. "You can go get her this time."

Raine took in the lines of irritation bulging Nyx's neck and jawline, and nodded. As he dashed after the waving curtain of Sarsana's glossy brunette wig, he heard Nyx addressing the other dragonesses.

"Yes, there are *bugs* in the *woods*. No, they will not *kill* you. But I might if you don't ..."

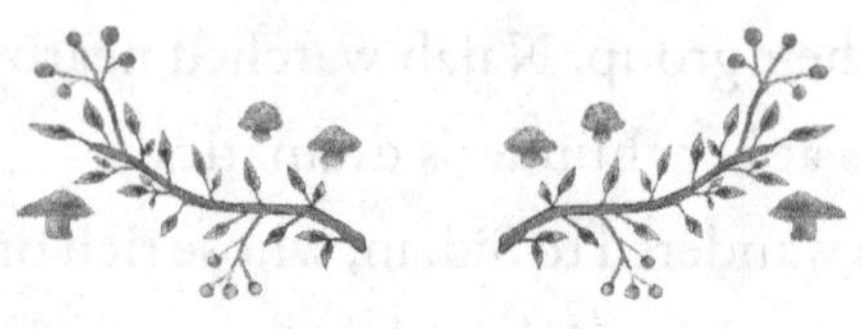

Raine attempted to channel the shadowlike stealth of Nyx and Sidian as he led their group for the final hours of their journey. Every so often, a branch snapped beneath his boots, and he pouted.

It wasn't that stealth was necessary right now. They were far enough from Joltar Trail—and its constant stream of travelers—to avoid notice even if he shouted.

But that wasn't *really* the point.

Earlier, Sidian teased him for being louder than a passel of wild hogs as he hiked. Raine had bristled like a boar. Even if he was loud, did he really deserve to be compared to a bunch of dirty, grunting pigs?

No. No, he did not. So, he'd undertaken a private mission to prove Sidian wrong. He could be quiet. And stealthy. And as light on his feet as a butterfly.

Thus far, his progress was ... mixed. He hadn't realized quite how much noise he made as he walked, but now that he was paying attention, the truth was inescapable.

Raine was about as stealthy as the sun on a cloudless day.

Even so, he was determined to improve until he possessed enough stealth to wipe that gloating smirk off his mate's face. It didn't matter that Sidian's smirk made his belly hot and his blood sing. Or that his heart could fly right out of his ribcage with exuberant glee at the sight of his mate being carefree and playful.

It was the principle of the thing. Whenever someone—anyone—told Raine he couldn't do something, he was immediately compelled to make it happen. He would train his lummox feet to be as silent as stalking fox paws if it was the last thing he did.

Another twig snapped beneath his boot. Raine growled down at his feet and very deliberately did not look at Sidian, who followed two paces behind him. He already knew the sight that would greet him. An incendiary smirk and shaking shoulders, because his mate could even *laugh* stealthily.

"How much further?" Sarsana asked plaintively. For the third time in as many hours.

All the dragonesses wanted out of the woods, but none more than Sarsana. Thanks to Tejayla and Raine, she thought razor-mouthed insects were going to crawl inside her brain while she slept and eat her from the inside out.

He turned and found Sarsana sagging beneath the weight of her pack, her face lax with exhaustion. The other dragonesses trudged behind her, each as bent and weary as the next. Even Amari had lost her spirit of adventure—right after they had resumed hiking at dawn, and she discovered the blisters on her feet.

Raine gave them an encouraging smile. "Believe it or not, we're almost there. We should arrive within the hour."

They brightened at his announcement, passing the news backward on a chain of excited gossip. It was mid-afternoon and the weather held beautifully, a final hurrah of mildness before winter crept in.

"If we're almost there, I must have picked you up right outside the door," Sidian mused, moving forward to walk alongside him as the game trail broadened.

"You did," he admitted sheepishly. "I'd just snuck out and planned on going to Chambrin Keep to retrieve my father when you brained me with your dagger hilt." His nose scrunched at the memory, and he massaged the echoing pain at the back of his head.

Sidian smiled smugly, not an ounce of contrition in his expression. "You barreled out of the woods, completely oblivious with your hood down. You're lucky it was me you ran into."

Raine rolled his eyes. "I didn't feel very lucky at the time."

"And now?" Sidian's gaze torched his skin.

The rapid crunch of Nyx and Naiah's approaching footfalls spared Raine from embarrassing himself. Because the only answer he could think of was the truth. The mushy, gushy, love-laden truth that was guaranteed to freak Sidian out. Sure, his mate acted calm enough after reading a dry book of dragon facts.

But the abstract knowledge that Raine was head-over-heels obsessed with him wasn't the same thing as having it passionately monologued to his face.

The less Raine said of his feelings, the better. Particularly when they weren't reciprocated and he was never going to act on them anyway.

"Not to sound like Sars," Nyx drawled, "but how far away is the safehouse, exactly?"

"It's across the road and hidden in the woods, maybe a mile down the street." They were very close, probably a half-hour's walk.

Nyx nodded. "We should look at recrossing the street soon."

They'd been putting it off because of all the traffic, but Nyx was right. They needed to start scanning Joltar Trail for an opening.

"We have to get closer to the road's edge to scout for a safe opportunity to cross," Sidian said.

"Right." Nyx frowned, his dark eyes darting toward the dragonesses. "We'll have to remain quiet to avoid detection that near the road."

"I'll relay our objective to my thunder, as well as the need for silence," Naiah murmured before moving back toward the dragonesses, who flocked around her to listen.

"And I'll carry Raine on my back, so his clodhopping heels don't give us away," Sidian quipped.

Nyx snickered at Raine's expression and put a hand on his shoulder. "You'll get the hang of it eventually. And you aren't so bad that you need a piggyback ride," he added, casting a chiding look at his younger brother.

Sidian merely arched a brow. The expression somehow conveyed both his own superiority as well as his dubiousness of Raine's abilities.

Raine stuck out his tongue.

Five minutes later, their group was making its way painstakingly through the thorny, tangled understory of Hollyhock Forest. Sidian and Nyx had taken the lead since they truly were as stealthy as ghosts. It was creepy. And annoying.

But even Raine could appreciate the benefits of having two full-bodied shadow assassins at their disposal to sneak ahead and ensure their passage was clear.

More and more weedy burrs grabbed at his coat. He picked at them, his fingers finding prickly clusters along his sides and even under his arms. So preoccupied was Raine, with grooming his coat, that he didn't notice the Wade brothers had gone motionless until he plowed into their backs. Sidian's hand darted back to steady him.

"Shh," Nyx whispered, sounding urgent.

Their group went still, straining to hear.

"Wait here," Nyx mouthed to Raine and the dragonesses, who nodded.

Sidian and Nyx ducked through a wall of rust-red foliage. How they did that without the branches rustling was positively unnatural. Raine made a note to pester them about it later.

There was a long, tense silence while the dragons waited, darting uneasy glances at the shadowed woods around them. An eternity later, Sidian and Nyx reappeared. Their movements were even more phantasmic, if possible. Raine swore the leaves didn't flatten beneath their feet as they beckoned the dragons to retreat deeper into the forest.

Raine wanted to ask what they had heard, why they were being so cautious, but he knew better than to utter a sound. Their faces were pale and tense with worry.

Once their group was further from the road, Naiah paused and held up a hand. "What did you see?"

The brothers exchanged grim-mouthed looks.

"This area is being patrolled," Nyx explained in a hushed whisper.

Sidian nodded. "Two Guardian units are walking the wood line along Joltar Trail."

"They aren't moving like they're traveling. They're moving like they're searching," Nyx added.

A thousand horrible thoughts assailed Raine. He forced himself not to conclude the worst. If they were searching, that had to be a good sign. The guild didn't know where the Hellhole was, but somehow, they knew it was around here.

But, *how?*

"The map," Raine blurted, suddenly remembering.

He inwardly lambasted himself for ever thinking it was a good idea to mark Campion on his father's map. Sidian had kept the map in his backpack. But when they fled Silvan Dredge, Sidian hadn't had his pack on him. The guild must have found it.

Sidian wouldn't meet Raine's eyes as he said, "I left my pack in Master Kollus's office when I stopped to make my official report."

Raine squeezed his mate's shoulder until Sidian looked at him. His gaze was flat and shuttered. "It doesn't matter. The map marked Campion, not the Hellhole," Raine said, trying to reassure him.

"It matters if we want to reach the hideout undetected," Nyx said bluntly. "We'll have to double back and cross Joltar Trail from further away."

It was a simple, elegant solution. Except, "I saw Guardians entering the woods opposite," Sidian said. "Crossing the trail unseen won't matter if we encounter them in the forest."

"We need to get closer and try to determine how deeply they're searching the other side," Nyx whispered. "Or if there are any blind spots in their patrol."

How could there be, with Guardians swarming the woods around the safehouse? Raine caught himself just as he was about to tug his wig in frustration. Fear stamped the dragonesses' delicate features as they huddled together, far enough away from the roadside to avoid detection.

But it was the figure of Sidian, fists balled and eyes downcast, that had Raine feigning an optimism he didn't feel.

"Right. The guild's only human. They're bound to make an error," he said rousingly.

"Wait here," Nyx said, addressing the dragonesses. Naiah stepped forward defiantly. "Fine," he muttered. "The rest of you, wait here."

Raine, Sidian, Nyx, and Naiah left the dragonesses sequestered in dense foliage and moved closer to inspect the Guardians' activities. Nyx silently directed them to fan out, and they each chose a covert vantage to observe the hunters.

The bush Raine selected kept threatening to rustle. When another twig tried removing his eye, he backed away with a huff. Glancing around, he spotted a towering birch that would offer a sweeping view for miles. Most of Hollyhock's trees were winter bare, but the birch still possessed a few clusters of stubborn leaves. They were withered and brown, but dense enough to conceal him while he scouted.

Decision made, he nimbly climbed it, sticking close to its trunk so the branches wouldn't waver with his weight.

Up high, his stomach sank as he observed the Guardians. They searched the inner forest, skirting a perimeter that broadly outlined the atmos stump. It was their worst-case scenario: the hunters had the Hellhole surrounded.

The only silver lining was that they definitely didn't know where it was. They moved slowly, poking at every foxhole and crevice. Most of them seemed tired, their movements halfhearted as if they'd been at it awhile and hadn't gotten any closer to their goal.

Raine noticed Sidian's black crown beneath his perch and sidled down. Naiah and Nyx joined them, and they gathered near a low-lying brook. Its clear, trickling water split the difference between the waiting dragonesses and the roadside.

"They don't know where the safehouse is," Raine said softly. "But it's obvious they have an idea. They're all over the area. I didn't see any blind spots."

"They're tightening their perimeter," Nyx said grimly.

The severity of Sidian's frown indicated he still held himself responsible for current events. Raine elbowed his side. "The map didn't necessarily have to lead them here." He rubbed his chin, considering. "It could have been any number of things. They might have run into a dragon on watch duty. Or saw them bathing or even out hunting. We won't know what drew the guild's attention until we reach the Hellhole and talk to the dragons there."

"This place is crawling with Guardians. I don't see how we can reach the hideout," Nyx said, shifting his gaze to scan the woods.

Naiah stepped forward. "I do. We need a distraction. If I transform and take flight, they'll give chase. That'll give you all time to reach the safehouse unseen."

Raine began to protest but Nyx waved him silent. "No, she's right. We aren't getting in unless we lure the Guardians away."

"We can wait until nightfall. See if they leave," Raine sputtered.

"Waiting is pointless. Fresh units will take their place for the night shift," Sidian said.

Nyx nodded. "The guild has definitely picked up the safehouse's scent. They won't let up until they find it."

"So, we're just going to let Naiah risk her *life*—"

"Youngling." Naiah touched his shoulder. "I can fly. I will be alright."

"They launch bone spears and arrows. They will track where you land. They'll—"

"Are you volunteering?" Nyx cut him off.

"The fuck he is," Sidian snarled, then glowered at Raine, as if daring him to argue.

"Raine will not be volunteering," Naiah said placidly. "I am a skilled flyer and will evade them. Trust me. Please. While I trust *you* to get my thunder to safety." Her ice-blue eyes were wide and imploring.

"Fucking fine," Raine hissed, hating this plan.

His father had risked everything to ensure the safety of these dragons, yet here Raine was, using one as bait. There was a bitter taste in his mouth as he quickly described the precise location of the Hellhole, including how to operate the hidden switch in the stump.

Nyx said, "If you lead them far enough away, you can fly right back and get inside before they catch up. Even if they track you back here, they will only know as much as they already do. The entrance will still be unknown to them."

Naiah nodded, looking determined, her face already tilting to the sky.

CHAPTER FIFTEEN

A branch snapped, the wood dry and crisp from many days of fair weather. Raine's heart pumped furiously at the sound, priming his body to fight or flee. Voices drifted to them from downstream, as if several people were following the small brook.

Nyx blanched, the whites of his eyes huge in their sockets. An answering horror pebbled the flesh down Raine's arms. If Guardians saw them, their plan was doomed before it could be implemented.

Naiah ripped off her coat and gown, not giving any of them a chance to preserve her modesty. She shoved the dark, wadded fabric into Raine's chest. He clutched it reflexively as Nyx scooped her backpack and fallen wig out of the leaves. He promptly dropped them again as her huge, leathery wings knocked them all on their asses. She shot into the air like a bottle rocket, gusting them with a downdraft so powerful, it would have toppled them had they been standing.

A man's voice shouted. Then another. With riotous excitement, the nearing footfalls began to pound in the opposite direction, away from them as they chased after Naiah's soaring figure. Her scales dazzled in the late afternoon light, as if pieces of the sun and sky had merged and come to life.

A hand nudged Raine's chest. "Come on," Sidian said impatiently. Raine grasped his mate's palm and let the man pull him up.

Nyx was racing toward the dragonesses. Raine and Sidian followed swiftly, breaking through a tangle of brambles as Nyx said, "Come on. We have to run. Now."

The dragonesses had grown weary of waiting. They splayed indolently amid the leaves, using their rucksacks as props for comfort.

Nyx's urgency couldn't be denied. They lurched into action, donning their rucksacks without pausing to brush away the leaves that clung to their skirts and bags.

In seconds, they were hurtling through the woods like a pack of fleet-footed deer, Raine at the lead. The Guardians were a solid black mass on the road, sprinting after Naiah as if they had any chance of catching her. They remained none-the-wiser as Raine's legs propelled him over Joltar Trail at a bound. He leapt the broad stretch of cobbles and continued into the woods beyond without looking to see if the others kept pace.

There was no telling how much time Naiah had bought them. Each second of exposure felt like a century, as if an executioner's axe would descend at any moment. In minutes, he reached the densest part of the woods. The foliage was wild and thick, cluttered with thorns and snagging branches.

Raine didn't slow as he waded the unforgiving understory. Instead, he sped up. He angled his arms as if he were diving and speared his body through a mass of barberry bushes. Heels digging into the brush, he skidded to a halt on the other side, directly before the Hellhole. A hard body thudded against his back. Raine pitched forward. A steely arm reached around to steady him. Raine didn't have to turn to know it was his mate. Sidian's scent always held a special sweetness, as if Raine could detect the essence of his soul.

It was an excellent thing all the Guardians were far and away. Amari and Sarsana shrieked as they pushed through the bushes, and Carissyne screamed at a spider that crawled on her arm, announcing their location to all and sundry.

Raine tamped down his impulse to shush them. There was no point. Any damage was already done. They needed to get below ground, *now*. He felt around the base of the huge, knotted atmos stump and pressed the switch to unlock the Hellhole's disguised entrance.

"Whoa," he shouted, falling backward as Jaska's fierce, sharp countenance greeted him, a white dagger raised to impale his head.

Midnight pond eyes widened in shock. "Raine!" He scrambled out of the tunnel and threw himself at Raine, crushing him to his chest. "Where have you been? Aly's going to *kill* you." Jaska jerked back, slack-jawed as he stared over Raine's shoulder. "How ..."

Raine interrupted him. "What the hell happened? Why are there Guardians swarming around the Hellhole like ants at a fucking picnic?"

Jaska stepped back with a grimace. "They arrived a week ago. They used to be more spread out, but an unlucky sighting helped them narrow their search. They know we're close but can't figure out where."

Fuck. "Let's get inside before any of them wander back."

Jaska nodded, stepping aside. Raine motioned the dragonesses down first. Nyx followed, then Sidian and Raine. Jaska sealed and locked the entrance behind them as they descended the steep ladder to the Hellhole, with its musty air and damp walls.

Home sweet home. *Not.*

The dragonesses clustered against the wall below, waiting in the shadows. The crush of bodies swallowed Jaska like displaced water as he dismounted the ladder. Raine pressed his back against the swell, giving the green dragon space to pluck his lantern and guide them through the tunnel.

Raine brought up the rear with Sidian behind him. A hand smoothed over his ass, squeezing a cheek suggestively in the dark.

"Not. Now," he gritted, swatting blindly behind him to stop Sidian before his cock stirred.

His mate's sly laughter tickled his ear, and Raine gritted his teeth. If he had an erection when Evin embraced him, he was going to stab his mate, instincts be damned.

They spilled into the large, communal den. Straw mattresses were spaced along the right side of the chamber. At least twenty dragons occupied them. Lanterns revealed some to be sleeping while others amused themselves with various small pursuits. Brushing and braiding their hair. Talking quietly. Several pairs were engaged in board games, likely carved by Savere.

The room erupted as Naiah's thunder cried out, recognizing their comrades-in-cages. The other dragons immediately ceased their activities, spilling game pieces and blankets as they jumped to their feet. It seemed as if the entire room embraced, one way or another. Joyful exclamations bounced off the walls, and many eyes shone with tears.

A few of the dragons stared at Raine, as if trying to place him in their memory. They wouldn't be able to, since he was a stranger. He hovered awkwardly before edging out of the crowd. This was a heartfelt reunion of old friends, not a time for new introductions.

Discreetly nearing the next tunnel, Raine shivered as a warm, callused hand slipped under his coat to rest at the base of his spine. Sidian walked beside him, keeping his palm against Raine's back. Raine's stomach spiraled hotly at the pressure, but he tried to seem unaffected. Sidian did *not* need that encouragement. He was already touching Raine more and more each day without it.

Escalation was inevitable, a molten road that led to a single destination: consummation. And Raine still had no fucking clue how he was going to deny Sidian his body. He had hoped to develop a tolerance to his mate's touch, so he could be resolute when the time came. What a joke that idea had been. Raine was being courted by the other half of his heart. The perfect match to his soul. Radiant pleasure exploded through him at the merest whisper of Sidian's touch. There was no getting used to that.

At least the Hellhole was packed beyond capacity. It didn't matter how determined Sidian was to consummate the bond. Or how concerned Raine was that he might not be able to resist. Nobody was going to have sex in this overcrowded pit.

The tunnel branched ahead and Raine veered left, entering the chamber that boasted a massive, round table sliced from the very atmos tree the stumped entrance had come from. Savere had been busy. The old, roughly hewn seats were now actual chairs, their numbers increased to fourteen seats total.

Before Raine could identify the jewel-toned dragons occupying the table, a blur of red hair and brown woolen skirts barreled into him. "*Oof.*"

He stumbled backward, automatically clutching the female's shoulders as he fell. Sidian steadied Raine from behind, pulling him back against a lean, hard chest.

Aly drew away and snatched Raine by the front of his coat. "You stupid, selfish, idiotic bonehead." She punctuated her insults by shaking him. "Give me one good reason not to skin you alive. We're short on blankets, princess, and you'd make a real fucking pretty one."

"Aly," Evin said firmly, in her den mother voice. "Give Raine some space and a chance to explain his absence."

Aly curled her red lips back in a silent snarl, garnet eyes flashing. "Fine. Explain yourself," she hissed, releasing him with a small shove.

Footsteps approached from the tunnel. Sidian still had his arms around Raine's waist and directed him physically to the side of the tunnel as Jaska and Nyx emerged.

Raine looked around, noting Lukor, Oka, and Savere at the table. Savere continued carving a hunk of wood into some sort of figurine, unruffled by the chaos. Lukor was tight-lipped and flushed with anger. Oka leaned forward on his elbows, simply taking it all in.

Three strangers were seated at the table, as well. A blue male with high cheekbones and wideset cerulean eyes, his hair shorn short. And an obviously mated pair who sat with their bodies flush against each other, the female a pale purple, her eyes and hair almost—but not quite—silvery gray. The male possessed wine-colored hair and eyes, the deepest red he'd seen on a dragon.

Oka gestured for Raine to join him. Raine grabbed a chair and moved around the table. There was already one empty seat next to Oka. Raine made room for another and positioned the extra chair between himself and Savere. He indicated for Sidian to sit as Oka snatched his wig off his head.

"This one is way better than that other one you had," Oka declared, inspecting the wig from all angles.

Aly sat next to the blue male dragon, her gaze letting Raine know she hadn't forgotten that he owed her an explanation for taking off on them.

Evin cried out suddenly, clutching her chest in shock. Tears poured down her face as she skirted the chamber. Raine had never seen such a display from the reserved den mother. He followed her trajectory and spied Eva, her pea-green eyes equally misty. The dragonesses met and embraced with such tearful emotion that Raine looked away. When his gaze met Oka's, the mallard green dragon looked as confused as Raine.

"Everyone." Evin's smile wobbled. "I'd like to introduce you to my daughter, Eva."

"No shit." Oka grinned.

The rest of Evin's thunder greeted Eva like the miracle she was. With choked salutations and genuine awe. Evin's grief for her mate and children had kept her locked in her room; isolated and consumed by pain so palpable, it left her thunder aching. Eva's arrival was a balm for them all, their first hope that Evin might heal and start living again.

Evin kept looking at Eva as if her daughter might disappear. Eva must have sensed something similar. As she sat beside her mother, she held her hand and whispered, "I'm here. I'm really here, Mom."

At Aly's curious glance, Raine introduced Sidian and Nyx, keeping it brief. "Nyx worked with my dad to free the dragons we brought with us. Without him, they would have still been in the Cavern. Sidian is, um. He's Nyx's brother, and he's helping us, too."

"It's nice to meet you both." Jaska nodded to Nyx, then to Sidian. "I've got to resume guard duty. We keep watch at the mouth of the tunnel now," he explained at Raine's questioning look. "There's no way to keep a lookout aboveground with the hunters everywhere."

"You're lucky you showed up when you did," Oka said as Jaska departed. "If you guys came one day later, you would have found this place empty."

"It must be impossible to stay here with Guardians flooding the forest," Nyx said.

"And flooding our den," Lukor growled. Raine turned sharply at his menacing tone. Lukor bared his teeth and continued. "You put us all in danger when you disappeared like a skulking criminal. We had no way of knowing if you were going to betray our location. Evin refused to suspect you and forced us to wait, even after the hunters arrived."

Lukor stood and smacked the table with his fist. "Then, you drag two of those swine down here, parading them before us, and expect me to think this isn't a fucking set-up?"

"Lukor," Evin said, inserting sharpness into her normally serene voice. "Sit down, now."

Lukor sat, though he pulsated with rage, boring holes into Raine's head with a baleful glower. Raine typically tried to empathize with Lukor's hostility. Not this time. He barely refrained from leaping across the table and wrapping his hands around Lukor's thick throat.

Sidian placed a restraining hand on Raine's bicep, as if sensing how close to losing it he was. Somehow, Raine located a sliver of calm in the ferocious storm brewing inside his chest. He clung to it, white-knuckled.

"Lukor." Raine's voice was pure ice. "Never insult them again." His mercury stare drilled into the purple dragon, filled with deathly promise.

Aly inhaled audibly, then outstretched her arm and pointed directly at Sidian. "He's your mate!"

Raine blinked, refocusing his gaze on his best friend. How the ever-loving fuck had she logicked that one? The scarlet female began bouncing in her chair, her eyes bright with excitement. "What's your name, again?"

If Sidian was similarly shocked by Aly's shrewd observation, he didn't show it. Instead, regarded her coolly, his expression schooled. "Sidian. And you?"

"I'm Aly, and that's my best friend you're shacking up with. Welcome to the family." She looked at Raine. "How crazy is it we found our mates back-to-back? This is Zane." She put her arm around the blue male's frame, squeezing him affectionately while resting her cheek on his shoulder.

Raine felt his eyes widen. He hadn't recognized Zane, who looked significantly different from when he'd seen him last. Aly's mate was well-groomed and seemed healthy. Still a whiff too thin, but he looked fit. Zane met his gaze confidently and nodded a greeting.

Raine grinned back. "My condolences, Zane. Not sure how you pissed off the Dreaming Mother enough to get saddled with Aly. That's a hell of a life sentence."

Aly gasped, outraged. "Zane is blessed beyond measure, you bone-headed, cabbage-brained ninny. He can't do better than me."

Raine inspected his fingernails. "Sure, Aly," he said unconvincingly. "It was my mistake."

She lunged across the table and tackled Raine out of his chair. His breath whooshed out of him as his back collided with the floor. Digging her fingers into his sides, she tickled him mercilessly.

Laughter pealed out of him until he was writhing and crying beneath her relentless hands. "Please," he cried. "Mercy!"

Aly finally relented, grinning like a demented fox. "You were right, Raine. It *was* your mistake."

He could only pant in response, wrecked from torture. Sidian eyed him from his chair, a calculating gleam in his eyes. "You're very ticklish," he observed, his voice darkly musing.

Aly stood and beamed at him. "You bet your sweet ass he's ticklish. If you ever need to wrestle him into submission, it's the only way. He fights dirty, so you have to fight dirtier."

Sidian smiled at Aly. It brimmed with mischief and made Raine's stomach clench. "You sound like you know Raine well."

She looked positively devious. "Oh, yes. There are lots of things I can tell you about your little princess here."

Raine scowled at them as he retook his seat.

"Can we get back on track?" The wine-red dragon swept them with a stern look, his burgundy brows pinched in a protruding arrow above his nose. "Time is running short and there are matters to discuss."

"Sorry, Lorrivare," Aly said, sounding genuinely abashed. She skirted the table and resumed seating.

"We cannot remain here another night," Lukor said. He refused to face Raine or the Wade brothers, which was just as well. Raine would hate to ruin everyone's joyful reunion with bloodshed. "The hunters are right on top of us. We're out of time."

Evin looked at Raine. "We decided, with great reluctance, that we could not continue to await you. I admit I put off our leaving as long as I could. Now that you're here, I agree with Lukor. We must depart at the earliest opportunity."

"To Chambrin," Lorrivare said firmly. The pale purple female beside him nodded her agreement, her chin resolute.

"We already agreed we leave for Rokeshin," Lukor protested.

The pale purple dragoness's eyes flashed. "No, *you* agreed. I see your priority to save us from the Cavern does not extend to our children. You only cared about your mate, and since she's gone, you want to tuck your tail between your legs and hide. Well, I hate to break it to you, but we still have loved ones at the humans' mercy. We are going to save our children, with or without your support."

Lorrivare rested a hand on her shoulder. "Easy, Betony."

Jaska entered the room, his face ashen. "Lukor," he said hoarsely.

Lukor stiffened at Jaska's strangled tone. Raine sucked in a breath, feeling like a complete bastard. No matter how shitty Lukor's attitude was, Raine should have told him the instant they arrived. He hadn't withheld the information out of spite. He'd been genuinely sidetracked by the commotion. Between the guild swarming Hollyhock forest and Eva being Evin's long-lost daughter, it had slipped his mind.

He watched Lukor turn in his chair, moving slowly, as if in a dream. Naiah emerged from the tunnel behind Jaska at the precise moment Lukor faced them. She was nude but for a threadbare blanket tucked under her arms.

All hell broke loose.

CHAPTER SIXTEEN

Raine sat next to Sidian on a corner mattress, their backs against the rough dirt wall. Aly and Zane faced them, along with Nyx, who wore a mildly stunned expression as he looked between Raine and Sidian and back again.

"When the hell were you two going to tell me? I feel like an idiot."

"Oh." Raine suddenly found it hard to focus on Nyx's face. He glanced at the ceiling, fidgeting his thumbs. "Well, it's pretty new," he prevaricated. "We're still working it out ourselves."

Sidian snorted. "It's no one's business but ours. We would have told you when we wanted you to know."

"Sorry about that," Aly said, not sounding sorry at all. "I didn't know you guys were playing at secret mates or I wouldn't have said anything."

No, Aly wouldn't have said anything, but she'd have held it over Raine's head and teased him incessantly. Blackmail would have inevitably been involved, so being outed was probably for the best.

There was a distant clamor and then a noise that sounded distinctly like a moan. Raine screwed his eyes shut, wishing rather fervently he was anywhere but here—up against a wall where, some feet away on the other side, Lukor and Naiah were experiencing a ... heartfelt reunion. It sounded indecent, to say the least.

About the time Lukor had torn off Naiah's blanket, his mouth mauling hers, everyone had made themselves scarce.

"What if they're doing it on the table?" Aly asked, aghast. "I eat in there."

"Shut up, Aly. Just shut up." Raine groaned. There was another distant moan, then something like a chair falling over. "I know I'm supposed to be happy for them, but seriously, I'd be fine if the ceiling caved in."

Raine looked up, almost hopefully, but the ceiling appeared as intact as ever. A sheet of dark, petrified rock and dirt with thousands of roots protruding like clumps of wiry hair.

Zane clucked his tongue. "The both of you are acting childish." This accusation was punctuated by another long, loud moan that could only be Lukor. Raine and Aly's eyes met, and they shuddered in mutual abhorrence. "I grant you, they could be a little more circumspect in their timing, but think of their emotional states. I can't fathom the pain of losing Aly, let alone the uncontrollable elation of meeting her afterward."

"Yeah, well Evin just had some uncontrollable elation of her own, but I didn't see her swaddling Eva in a nappy and forcing a bottle down her throat," Raine groused.

Sidian chuckled. Raine slanted a suspicious glance at him, as if to ask, *What's so funny?* His fawn eyes glinted devilishly. "I don't require a prolonged separation to spread you on a table."

"Ugh, no." Nyx flailed his arms, scandalized. "I take back any offense at not being told sooner. Just don't say anything like that again where I can hear you. *Please*."

Raine blushed so hotly, he thought it might damage his skin. Frostbite, only blushbite. The more Sidian touched him and made these comments, the harder it was not to believe Sidian was genuinely interested in him. As if he burned for Raine the same way Raine burned for him.

But Raine knew better. Sidian didn't desire *him*. As relentless a martyr as he was a captain, Sidian was simply using every tool in his seductive repertoire to chip away at Raine's resistance. It was unsettling, how good an actor Sidian was. It was more unsettling that Raine couldn't stop himself from responding, even though he was aware of his mate's true feelings.

More moans sounded from down the tunnel, where Lukor and Naiah continued ... whatever the hell they were doing. The other dragons had assembled in the communal sleeping area to grant the pair some privacy. Only, their privacy was an illusion. Every single grunt and moan carried like a trumpet down the too-short tunnel on Raine's left. What was worse, Raine's group had gotten stuck with the mattresses nearest the table room.

"I'm as happy for them as anyone else," Aly said, sounding just the opposite. "But honestly, how long is this going to go on for? What if there were children here?"

"You practically are children," Savere drawled, approaching them with Oka, who cast a disgusted glance in the direction of the tunnel as Lukor roared. Actually roared. What the hell was that?

"See?" Aly gestured sharply at Raine, then herself. "We're precious dragon babies and we don't deserve this kind of abuse. Make them stop."

"Not even if the forest was on fire," Savere said blandly. "Me and Lukor are close. Not that close."

"It won't go on forever." Nyx assumed the crisp tones of a lecturer. "Grinnich and Eldessa, a mated pair, were separated for a century when the great ice rift trapped Eldessa below the world, and Grinnich above. It is said they coupled profusely upon reuniting but were able to control themselves after a few rounds."

"Lukor has roared twice now. If that's his *sound of completion*"—Aly drew out the words with a grimace— "then maybe they're nearly done."

"Thank the Divine Father for that." Raine rubbed his aching head. Each time Lukor made any discernable noise, it was like a shaft of jagged ore being driven straight into his skull. He never, ever wanted to be in this position again.

"The Divine Father?" a waspish voice parroted. "You're a dragon, not a human. How dare you come in here uttering their curses."

"It's not a curse," he snapped, meeting the pale lavender eyes of Betony. "And I'll utter whatever I like, Strange Dragon Lady I Barely Know."

Her mouth hung open, as if shocked. It only made Raine more irate. Who the fuck was this female who thought she had any say in how he spoke? She gathered herself, the beginnings of a snide putdown twisting her features.

Bring it on, he thought viciously. A shouting match with a stranger might drown out the final throes of Lukor's fuckfest.

The wine-red dragon, Lorrivare, placed a steadying hand on her. "Now, Betony." Quieter, as if so no one else would hear, he said, "The youngling's mate is human, if you recall."

His words didn't quite mollify her, but they did hold her tongue. With a disdainful *hmph*, she moved towards the tunnel.

"Um, I don't think you want to go in there," Nyx said, pointing delicately.

"They've been at each other long enough," Betony announced, sweeping out of view. Lorrivare was a better dragon than Raine, because he dutifully followed his mate, though his expression was grimly resigned.

"What a lovely couple," Raine deadpanned in their wake.

"You don't know the half of it," Oka said. When Raine looked at him, Oka shook his head. "You'll see for yourself soon enough. It doesn't take much exposure to Betony to figure her out."

While the Hellhole's acoustics had seen fit to broadcast Lukor's moans pitch-perfectly, Betony's tirade was a discordant garble of overlapping syllables. He caught phrases like, "off her, now," and "not the time."

She emerged with Lorrivare in tow, dusting her hands as if she'd performed a menial chore. "The disruption has ended," she called in a carrying, authoritative voice. "Evin, if you'd care to resume?"

It wasn't really a question. Evin stood and nodded graciously. "Of course, Grandmother."

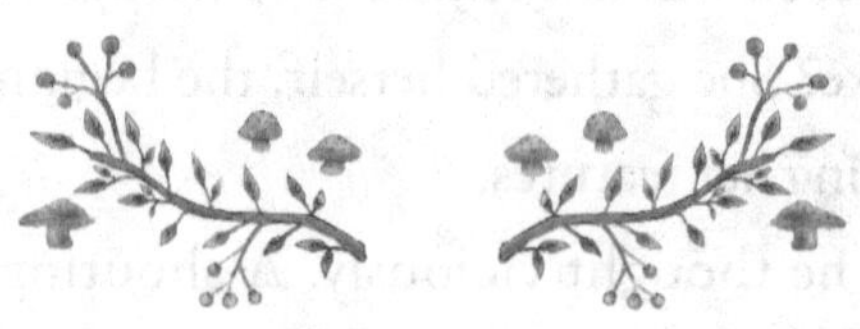

He glowed. Honestly, genuinely glowed. And when his deep amethyst eyes met Raine's, he smiled. It was a handsome, glowing smile. As if every drop of love and happiness ever felt in the history of the world lit him up from the inside.

Raine was, frankly, disturbed. He kept exchanging silent *what the fuck* glances with Oka and Aly, who were equally freaked out by Lukor's extreme personality shift. Sidian observed their silent interactions but didn't comment; though his velveteen gaze wandered to Lukor and Naiah, as if he, too, understood how bizarre and out of character the antagonistic dragon was behaving.

Lukor all but placed Naiah in his lap, draping himself over her. His gaze brimmed with awe whenever it fell on her, as if he still couldn't believe this was real and not the sweetest dream. Raine would have been touched if Lukor hadn't just confiscated the table room to bang his mate's brains out. The purple male showed no shame for it, either. Dragons didn't possess the same principles of modesty as humans, but that entire episode was beyond Raine's limit. The next time two dragons needed to get down and dirty, either they were going outside or he was, Guardians or no Guardians.

Betony wasted no time resuming where she'd left off, squaring herself as she faced Evin. "We will not leave our children to be used and abused by those humans while we roam free. Although it is selfish of me, I must ask, if only for the sake of our children. Will you help us?"

"I want to," Evin said gently. Her features etched with pained reluctance. "But I fear the consequences of hasty action. We have only recently rescued you all. You're still weak. If you can wait a while longer, until you're stronger—"

"I am strong enough to save my children," Betony cut her off. "And I will not wait. My mind—our minds—are made. My question is if you will help us or not."

As Evin and Betony parried, Sidian slid his hand beneath the table and grasped Raine's thigh. Raine stiffened at the unexpected touch. Sidian gave him a smoldering side-eye as he dragged his palm further upward. Heat coiled through Raine. His cock began to lengthen. Right there. At the table. Inches away from Evin's thunder.

Raine's stomach pitted with horror. Quicker than a serpent strike, he reached down and halted Sidian's questing fingers. He met his mate's smolder with a warning glare. Someone cleared their throat.

"I will help you," Aly declared. Her garnet eyes clashed with Evin's blue. "Zane and I discussed it this morning. We're in."

"I am your den mother, and I have spoken." There was uncharacteristic steel in Evin's tone. "I want to help reclaim the children, too, but it is not the right time. We go to Rokeshin."

Aly reared back like a mare bucking in protest. "You might be our den mother, but Betony is a storm mother. She outranks you. I don't even know why she's asking us for help when she has the right to demand it."

Raine bristled on Evin's behalf, belatedly recognizing the irony of his reaction. He'd had misgivings about Evin's leadership since the beginning. Her depression had sealed her like a tomb—as if she wasn't truly a part of this world, her spirit dwelling in the land of the dead with her mate and children. She hadn't seemed invested enough in her own life to be in charge of others.

But as Raine looked from Evin to Betony, he knew who he would follow unquestioningly, and it wasn't the pallid stranger angrily accusing Evin of apathy after she risked everything to free the breeding dragons.

Sidian's hand remained too close to his groin. Raine struggled to concentrate on the conversation, his errant prick straining for his mate's touch. He shifted in his seat as his mate's hand slid inward. Just another inch ...

No. He clutched Sidian's hand, torn between pulling it higher and pushing it away. He was too aroused to think straight.

"I will not demand the obedience of any dragon in this task," Betony said, eyeing Evin pointedly. "You risked everything for us once already, and my gratitude is sincere. However, Lorrivare and I leave for Chambrin Keep tonight. The other parents' hearts are set, as well. I implore you to join us. However, I wish you a safe journey to Rokeshin if you will not."

"Me and Zane are in," Aly repeated on the heels of Betony's speech. She peered at Raine. "Are you coming?"

As many eyes shifted to regard him, a searing flush climbed Raine's neck. He shoved Sidian's hand off his lap.

"We'll have a hell of a better chance at success if he comes," Oka announced. "And yeah, that means I'm in."

Raine rolled his eyes. "The last time I went, you assholes put me in charge when everything was going wrong."

"And we made it out just fine."

Raine grabbed his wig, which now rested on Oka's verdant crown, and dragged it forward, covering the dragon's eyes. Oka pulled it back up with a laugh and they began wrestling, each trying to shove the other off their seat.

"Why will our odds of success be so greatly improved with *his* aid?"

Lorrivare's derisive drawl implied they'd be better off asking a feather duster for help. Raine graced the burgundy dragon with a scowl. Unfortunately, it was the distraction Oka needed to win their tussle. Raine's chair toppled sideways as he fell into Sidian, who caught him effortlessly.

Raine's cock swelled harder at his mate's casual strength. He sat back in his seat and glared at his lap, betrayed. It was official. He couldn't win. Between Sidian and his dick, dignity was nothing more than a memory.

"Because Raine knows Chambrin Keep like the back of his hand. He was raised as Arastus's son," Aly said for him, an unmistakable bite in her reply.

"He was human-hatched," Oka added.

Betony threw a hand to her breast. "You-You're one of the children?"

Raine's body slid lower in his chair. Betony's gaze searched him for any sign he might be her child. It felt like spiders crawling over his skin. He stared down at the table, as if enrapt by its concentric rings.

"Three of the children are ours," she whispered. "You could be ours."

Betony was pale, the palest dragon he'd ever seen beside himself. For a wild second, he was petrified she would decide he was hers.

Then, rationality prevailed. Dragons couldn't recognize their offspring by their coloring. The hue of every dragon was random, their scales painted at the Dreaming Mother's whim. He felt cowardly at the relief that flooded him. But the loss of his father was so painfully raw, Raine couldn't endure welcoming a fresh set of parents into his life. Not now. Maybe not ever.

He sucked in a breath and forced himself to meet her longing stare. "There's no way to tell. A puzzle to be solved later." His effort to mask his rising panic made his voice curt to the point of rudeness.

"Of course," Betony murmured, looking embarrassed.

Raine glanced away, feeling like an ass. "The war dragons are not mistreated," he said, trying to make up for his standoffishness. "They aren't even kept prisoner. They fly freely and live in that enormous spire you can see from miles off."

"They were stolen from their parents before they even hatched. They have been mistreated," Betony snapped, outraged that he suggested otherwise.

Lorrivare nodded, his eyes narrowed on Raine. "They are being raised as animals, used to perform military service for the very humans who butcher and enslave us."

Raine glared, irritated at their offense. "I was merely trying to offer you comfort," he said brusquely. "Your children have been raised in peacetime. While they've received extensive military training, they are essentially spoiled pets. Their lives have been downright luxurious compared to your own."

The table *thunk*'d as Savere sat down his woodcarving, a half-formed crow. "I agree with Raine. The war dragons endure no current hardship. However, there is a different reason we should consider liberating them expediently."

Raine's brows furrowed as the other dragons leaned forward, eyeing Savere curiously.

"They are leverage. The perfect tools for manipulating us. What's to stop the Nine from torturing the war dragons or taking their lives if their parents fail to surrender themselves?"

The dragons absorbed Savere's statement with mute horror. Multiple hands flung up to smother gasps. Betony's eyes brightened with a sheen of stricken moisture. She appeared on the verge of transforming and flying to the keep straightaway.

Raine shook his head and withheld his objections. They would fall on deaf ears; it was easy to see. Savere's words had roused them more urgently than anything else thus far.

Oka looked at his brother. "So, you're in?"

Savere nodded. "I'm in." He looked at Evin. "It is going to be risky, but it's more risky to leave the war dragons in the Nine's custody. They can use the war dragons against us in more ways than one."

Betony's temper flared. "Are you suggesting our own children would harm us?"

Instead of answering her, Savere looked at Raine.

He sighed. "The war dragons love their humans. I think they would be easily convinced we're the villains, particularly if we threaten their loved ones. Which are not *you*," he said, pinning Betony and Lorrivare with a glare.

It was churlish, but they needed a strong dose of reality.

Betony's eyes flashed, her expression half-feral. "Don't you dare presume to speak for them. My children will know my love, and damn whatever you think. I will not leave them there."

Raine's hands smacked the table. "You're not listening. It's not up to you. It's up to them. We can rescue dragons all day long, but taking them against their will is beyond our abilities. The war dragons aren't caged or chained in any way. They could fly here tonight, right this minute if they chose to. They're more likely to help capture you and put you back in the Cavern than they are to leave."

"Not the mated ones," Nyx interjected.

Raine nearly broke his neck as his gaze swiveled to the elder Wade brother.

Nyx met the inquiring looks around the table with the easy confidence of a warrior and leader—a bearing instilled in him by his late mentor. "There are twenty-three war dragons at Chambrin Keep. All of them are of age to be mated. I'm willing to bet a handful of them will find their matches among the unattached dragons here."

"They will leave with their mates, no question," Aly said excitedly. "And they might even convince some of the others to come, too."

Raine shook his head. Their idea was brash and ill-fated—closer to wishful thinking than an actual plan. It was a fucking miracle they'd succeeded the last time. And look what it had cost him. His heart winced and bled at the too-high price he'd paid.

Sidian's hand cupped Raine's clenched fist beneath the table. Raine let his mate uncurl his hand and link their palms together. A comforting squeeze soothed his turmoil, reminding Raine of what he had to live for. Not just to honor his late father's memory, but to love and protect his flesh-and-blood mate beside him. He turned and met Sidian's rich, dark eyes. For a heartbeat, everything faded from existence, leaving only Raine and his mate.

"You don't like this idea," Sidian observed.

Raine wanted to lap the husky sound of Sidian's voice from the air like crystalized honey. He'd suffered a week of his mate's incessant flirting and covert touches. Nothing in this world could have prepared him for a Sidian determined to consummate their mating bond. What was worse, it was working. Sidian had him on a knife's edge of need. The smallest things sent him spiraling with desire.

Slowly, Sidian's words penetrated his lust. "No." He blinked and realized the others at the table were listening in. "My father's aid was pivotal to our past success. He was executed by the Nine and cannot help us this time."

Saying the words aloud felt like a lie. Like something so hellishly awful couldn't possibly be true.

"Oh, Raine." Evin's sky-blue eyes shone like glass. "Your father was a good man. I'm so sorry."

"He was the best of anyone," Aly agreed softly.

Raine squashed the grief rising in his chest and cleared his throat. "Furthermore," he said, willing them to drop the subject, "the Nine will have increased their security measures. I guarantee Chambrin Keep is crawling with more hunters than the forest above us. They're counting on you to come. They have the perfect bait. We'd be fools not to anticipate a trap."

Oka removed his pilfered wig and set it on the table. He looked as serious as Raine had ever seen him. "You're right, but the Nine are ignorant of our culture, for all that they persecute us. It's like Nyx said. Some of the war dragons are bound to be our mates. And that bond will supersede any lies they've been fed. Whatever trap the Nine springs might be their downfall."

"Or it will be ours," Raine was forced to point out. "How do you even expect to get near them?"

"Unlike the widdlest dwagon here, we can fly," Aly cooed. Contrary to her tone, her eyes were wells of pain, clearly still affected by the news of his father. Seeing his grief mirrored made his throat ache, so Raine plucked the wig from the table and launched it at her face.

"The Roost," Naiah said. Thus far, she'd been content to cuddle against Lukor in a blissful, post-sex stupor. Raine hadn't thought she was paying them any attention until she spoke. "I've seen the spire. It's outside the battlements. We can fly directly into the war dragons' roost and explain our situation."

"We wouldn't have much time," Nyx remarked. "The curtain guards' arrows can't strike us from that angle, but they'll reposition themselves and surround the Roost the moment they spot us."

"We'll be fucked afterward," Raine argued. "Even if we get in and out before we're surrounded, the sky watchers will get a lock on us. With a group as large as ours, they'll track us easily."

"Not if they're dead," Lukor said smoothly.

Raine tensed, but it was Savere who said, "That would leave a perfect trail of ash and death for the hunters to follow."

The whole table fell to squabbling. A dragon would produce an idea, only to be shot down by the neighbor at their elbow.

It was an impossible situation. The Guardians of Vale had been decimating the dragon population for centuries—until all that remained was a ragtag handful of rebellious leftovers. And although they had recently grown in numbers, Betony's storm was still weak from their confinement in the Cavern. They weren't fit to rescue their children.

Not only that, but the Nine had to expect them to come for the war dragons next. Going to Chambrin Keep would play right into their hands, Raine was sure of it.

Jaska came running in. His dark eyes were wild as he threw out his arms. "They're gone."

"Explain," Evin said evenly, as though the generally staid dragon before her wasn't behaving like he'd drank a keg of ale.

"The hunters," Jaska shouted. "They're gone. The forest is deserted."

CHAPTER SEVENTEEN

Jaska's pronouncement roused every dragon in the Hellhole. One after another, they squeezed into the too-small table room, until each breath Raine drew was warm and humid—the only air to be found on the exhale of someone else.

"Everyone, please remain calm," Evin said, standing to address them. "There is no reason to act alarmed." She turned to Jaska. "Are you certain?"

"Yes," he said firmly. "The hunters are gone. All of them. Hollyhock is empty."

"They went for reinforcements," Betony cried. "They saw Naiah fly this way. They've narrowed our location. If we don't leave now, we will all die."

A green dragoness started pushing and shoving at the crowd, escape written in the panicked lines of her body. Her sudden bolt incited a chaotic storm, the entire throng of dragons turning as one to flee. The narrow tunnel couldn't accommodate but three abreast, and they bottlenecked in a tangle of fighting limbs, each scrambling to leave first.

There was a disturbance in the tide. An arm popped through the solid line of retreating backs, followed by Sarsana's head. She elbowed her way through the surge and spilled out the other side, face flushed and wig askew. The rest of Naiah's thunder wedged through on her heels.

Carissyne gave Raine a cheeky grin. "Was it something you said?"

"Try her," Raine said dryly, pointing at Betony.

Evin came as close to a filthy look as Raine had ever seen, practically glowering at Betony. "You need to subdue them before anyone gets hurt."

Betony's pinched lips could have spit nails, but if Evin's command violated dragon hierarchy, the storm mother decided this wasn't the time to address it. Instead, Betony hurried after the stampeding dragons—presumably to instill order before they all flung themselves into the sky and a quiver of bone arrows.

"The Guardians didn't leave for reinforcements," Sidian said in the ensuing silence. "Not if all of them are gone. They would have kept most of their units here while sending one for backup."

"What would make them leave like that?" Evin asked. Her shoulders sagged, as if squaring up to Betony had cost a day's energy.

"I don't know," Sidian muttered ominously. "Nothing good. After sighting Naiah, nothing should have been able to draw them away."

"She's right, then," Aly said. "Betony. We need to leave."

Sidian nodded slowly. "I think that would be best."

"To Chambrin Keep," Aly said, throwing her words like a gauntlet.

Evin looked at her for a long moment, then sighed. "To Chambrin Keep." She looked at Raine. "You'll lead us, won't you?"

"Whoa, whoa, whoa." Raine waved his hands as if batting a swarm of flies. The way Evin was looking at him, he wanted to make like Betony's storm and run, too. "My vote's for Rokeshin."

No way was he going to oversee another botched rescue mission. Going after the war dragons was asinine. The Nine weren't going to compromise the unflinching loyalty of twenty-three war dragons by torturing them in order to draw their parents.

No, the war dragons were in no danger. Unlike these dragons, who seemed hellbent on rushing into death, disaster, and cages.

"You know the keep. You know the dragons," Oka wheedled.

"I don't know *these* dragons," Raine flung back. "I don't have the first clue how we'd pull this thing off, even if the parents were all level-headed and reasonable. Which they're *not*." He gestured needlessly at the tunnel, where they had just witnessed the extent of Betony's storm's mania. "Nobody could lead them on anything."

"Betony is a storm mother. They will heed her, and she will heed you once we discuss it." Evin glanced towards the tunnel as Betony and Lorrivare emerged. Betony must have heard some of their conversation in the tunnel. She gave Evin a tight, affirming nod.

"We cannot afford a rift," Evin continued. "If we have any chance of overcoming the guild's persecution, it must be together. Since the parents will not be swayed from their goal, we have no choice but to help them or lose everything."

Raine felt like a clock hand, only he was ticking bright gemstone gazes instead of minutes. They either implored or challenged him, all demanding too much. They would go with or without him, that much was clear. Which left him with only one possible answer.

"Fine, I'll do my best to get us to the war dragons. But that's it," he said, already regretting this. "And I make no promises this won't end in disaster."

Raine's jaw clenched hard enough to crack bone as they trekked Joltar Trail. Openly. Brazenly. As if thousands of elite shadow warriors weren't out hunting them to extinction.

At least it was dark. The road was a broad strip of black in the night, overshadowed by Hollyhock's canopy. Luckily, the endless throngs of travelers had vanished with the sun.

It also helped that Raine had come this way before, to get back home. They had taken this exact path to Chambrin Keep after their fateful decision to rescue the breeding dragons. He knew how to avoid the sky watchers, as well as which forest trails would bring them closer to the keep while avoiding human settlements.

These advantages were slight compared to the enormous disadvantage loudly griping behind him.

Thirty-three dragons. Was that really how many there were? Raine did the math twice. Then again for good measure. Between Evin's thunder, Naiah's thunder, and Betony's storm—yup. Sure enough, thirty-three dragons trailed his wake. Twenty of them, loudmouthed and stupid.

Fly. They wanted to *fly.* As if the sky watchers were as lethal as gnats. The parents hadn't lived outside the Cavern in two centuries and were boldly unintimidated; arrogant to the point of conceit. Raine wanted to scream at them.

"Soft-bellied humans in tree stands are no threat to me," a dragon grumbled. Raine didn't know the voice. Didn't turn to see who. It was dark. They were all indistinct shadows on the road. "I'd roast them and their puny stands to nothing in a single breath."

"It's not so simple," Jaska said, for the umpteenth time. "The sky watchers track where we land. They send signals to each other and coordinate attacks. It's very organized and always deadly."

Repetition wasn't the only thing making Jaska's voice stiff. Raine ground his teeth, fuming that Jaska had to listen to their ignorance after witnessing the slaughter of an entire thunder first-hand, brought about by their same insistence to fly. Raine recalled Jaska's stare—gaunt with ghosts and the wretchedness of surviving unscathed—when he'd shared that tale; how he had to choose between hiding for his life or dying with his friends. A decision that haunted him to this day.

"*We're* organized and deadly," the other dragon insisted.

Sidian scoffed at Raine's side. He didn't turn, but his voice carried deliberately as he said, "I'm not proud of what the guild does, but you'd be a fool to dismiss their abilities."

"Big words for a human," another dragon spat. "Your kind always thinks so highly of themselves. You forget, boy. Humans have knives, but we have claws. Humans make fire and we *are* fire."

A wave of hot fury crashed through Raine. No one was going to disrespect Sidian.

Before he could tear into the blustering idiot with a death wish, Sidian said, "A dragon's strength is superior to a human's, you're right. One human pitted against one dragon is a foregone conclusion. But you've seen what humans can do when they unite for a common cause. There are thousands of human warriors out there, trained specifically to fight your kind and win. Our best way forward relies on discretion."

No one had anything to say to that. *Good.* Perhaps the parents possessed some semblance of self-preservation, after all.

Then again, perhaps not, considering they were willfully marching back into their cages.

Every instinct inside Raine told him this was a doomed mission. A trap. The Guardians' abrupt retreat was not a stroke of the Dreaming Mother's intervention, or whatever Betony's storm believed. Raine knew they didn't have all the facts, and his gut churned with foreboding.

How the fuck were they going to pull this off?

Aly walked up beside him and whispered, "How the fuck are we going to pull this off?"

Good question. He glanced around and found Nyx walking slightly behind Sidian, with Carissyne and Tejayla framing him. "Nyx, how did you constantly sneak in?"

"I would send a coded message to Arastus regarding the date of my arrival, and he'd arrange for a Garganthan moose to get set loose on the grounds."

Raine was grateful his back was to the others. He had to look an absolute dimwit with his jaw scraping the road. "Are you kidding me?"

"No? The guards are obsessed with moose meat. It never fails to distract them."

Raine recalled the handful of times a mountain moose was caught on the grounds; the jovial atmosphere as the curtain guards spit-roasted the beast, turning it into an all-day cookout. His father had been particularly indulgent those days, the men serving partial shifts and leaving gaps in the guard coverage.

"It will fail now," he said glumly. "That's how I lured them away from their stations during our first rescue."

Nyx sputtered a laugh. "You are your father's son."

"They would have to be brain-dead not to realize it was a trick for us to get past the guards last time." His father had been successful in employing the moose ruse largely because Nyx's presence and subsequent dragon liberations had remained secret. Unlike Raine's last break-in, which the whole damn country knew about.

"I say we storm the place," another unknown dragon said.

Raine bit his tongue on an acidic reply. *Nobody fucking asked you.*

"If we all attack at once, we can take out the humans before they gather their defenses," another said in approval.

"If we stand any chance of convincing the war dragons to leave with us, we have to be more diplomatic than launching a full-scale assault on their home and loved ones," Raine snapped, his patience as thin as a frog's hair.

Several dragons began issuing ideas, all yammering over each other. They sounded like a bunch of drunken sots itching for a pub brawl, as if their suggestions weren't the equivalent of a massacre.

Raine tuned them out. It was Betony's job to contain their idiocy, not his.

He wracked his mind for ways to get past the guards. Unlike last time, they didn't have to go miles below ground and break dragons out of diamond cages. Which was a shame since they now knew where the hidden entrance to the Cavern was. Too little too late, it did them no good now. Their destination was high above ground instead of underneath. Somehow, they had to figure out a way into the Roost without being sighted.

Then, it was a small matter of convincing the war dragons that their entire lives were a lie. And somehow get them to abandon their loving, happy home to be criminals on the run with a bunch of crackpot dragons that oozed an off-putting desperation to coddle their hatchlings.

Raine grimaced. Perhaps the parents were only off-putting to him, but he doubted it. Betony's storm sought to rescue their stolen infants; not the grown, confident dragons that those infants had become. It made things awkward. He suspected the war dragons would balk.

"I don't know a way to sneak into the Roost," Nyx murmured, apparently mulling over the same problem as Raine. "Not with this many dragons, at any rate. Maybe we can get a few to serve as a distraction, like how Naiah did so we could reach the Hellhole."

Raine nodded thoughtfully. Nyx's idea abandoned the hope of stealth, but it was better than a catastrophic siege that would end with the very targets of their rescue efforts beating the piss out of them.

Betony's storm could serve as the distraction. Raine felt a pang of guilt, at using more dragons as bait, but if Naiah could do it, so could Betony's storm. Besides, if the parents wanted their children freed so badly, they ought to be willing to do anything to help.

Behind him, the parents grew louder. Almost feverish. Raine couldn't make out their words, but they sounded as rallied as any mob.

"Control your dragons before they mutiny," Sidian intoned to Betony, who marched not too far behind.

Betony's reply was as sharp and brittle as dry, cracked bones. "Humans do not command me or my storm."

The din of objections increased. A female voice from the back yelled, "Enough is enough. I demand we fly. If you think I'm going to walk like some clod-footed human while my children are imprisoned, waiting to be rescued—"

The female's outburst was like a struck match in an arid hay-barn. The dragons revolted entirely. A billion knuckles snapped and cracked in the darkness as they transformed, shredding their patched coats and garments. Tumultuous air currents rioted the naked branches overhead as nearly twenty dragons rocketed into the starry sky.

With a savage, frustrated shout, Betony tore out of her own coat and followed. Lorrivare was only seconds behind her. Amid the tattered scraps of fabric where Betony's storm once stood, Evin and Naiah's thunders stared at him, nonplussed.

Raine blinked at Sidian. "I don't know if that could have gone worse," he said conversationally.

"It will get a lot worse if we don't stop them." Sidian's gaze flickered toward the sky of diminishing dragons. Betony's storm had already gained a dizzying amount of ground.

Evin reached them first, Lukor and Naiah close on her heels. "What should we do?"

Raine closed his eyes and inhaled deeply. "Call this a loss and hightail it to Rokeshin?"

Aly raised a hand. "I second that." At Raine's arch look, she drew herself up. "What? I'm allowed to change my mind. They abandoned us. We abandon them. Fair's fair."

Zane looked at Aly with strained patience. Very tenderly, he said, "We need to stop them."

Raine shook his head. "Betony's storm is going to ruin any chance of a positive reunion with their children. The war dragons will be piledriving them into the dirt before we get there."

Evin placed a hand on his shoulder. "Raine, we cannot leave them to suffer defeat and recapture. We only just saved them."

He huffed. "Yeah, and they were so grateful, they immediately went to launch a haphazard assault against the most well-guarded keep in the country. Don't you think whatever happens next is their own fault?"

"A great leader takes full responsibility for the actions of their unit," Nyx admonished in a haughty tone.

Sidian smirked at Raine's disbelieving stare. "A great leader would've been able to control their unit in the first place."

"Unbelievable. Then you assholes go lead them. I agreed to get us to the war dragons, not play babysitter to their grown-ass parents."

"You failed to lead them because you are apprehensive of connecting with your birth parents," Lukor said, choosing now of all moments to become emotionally insightful. "This has caused you to distance yourself from them. Your avoidance has resulted in poor communication and the inability to contain their unruliness."

"*Wow*. Is it my turn to vomit your emotional baggage to the group?"

The purple male narrowed his eyes. "If you could not overcome your 'emotional baggage,' you should have refused to lead."

"I did!" Raine threw up his hands. "Did even a single person hear me say that I'd direct us to the war dragons, and that's it?"

Nyx made a sweeping gesture. "What's done is done. The best thing to do now is get there and try to salvage the situation as best we can."

"If the war dragons attack, it's game over," Raine said. "Our priority should be to reach them as quickly as possible and explain the situation. It's unlikely we'll get them to join our side, but maybe, *maybe* they'll agree to let their parents go instead of recapturing them."

"Let's go," Sidian said.

Evin and her thunder dropped their rucksacks and shifted, choosing to tear their clothing over wasting any more time stripping. Naiah's thunder was more reluctant, noticeably pouting as they fingered their finer coats. Their dresses were nicer, too. A benefit of having Nyx as their caretaker, since he had been able to frequent Pashun's dressmakers to outfit them. When Naiah transformed, ripping her cobalt dress and matching coat to smithereens, her thunder followed suit with the contorted features of humans being burned at the stake.

Nyx climbed onto Naiah, but Raine hesitated. It was a long flight, and her frame was too slight to carry three for such a distance. Oka chuffed at him, waving his tail in a *get-on* motion. Raine climbed onto Oka's back, pulling Sidian up behind him.

The ground fell away as Oka soared like a missile. In four powerful propulsions of his leathery wings, they were on top of the world. It was freezing, both this high up and moving as fast as they were.

Sidian shivered against his back. Reaching behind, Raine tucked his mate's hands beneath his coat. It was like shoving two blocks of ice against his sides. He hissed but was glad he did it. Sidian risked falling off if his hands went numb. That was the logical excuse, but the truth was that Raine would give anything, do anything, for his mate's slightest comfort. No imminent danger required.

"Look," Sidian said, his lips pressed against the back of Raine's ear.

Raine shivered, not from cold, and turned in the direction he thought Sidian's chin was nudging. It was a watchtower. A vacant watchtower. Raine frowned. He'd passed dozens, maybe hundreds, since the day his life turned upside-down and he became the most hunted dragon in Valdenia.

None of them had ever been empty.

CHAPTER EIGHTEEN

They saw Chambrin Keep miles before arriving. It blazed orange against the inky sky, like a gigantic torch. Raine's stomach clenched sickeningly. His grip around Oka's wings loosened for a precarious second, and black spots threatened his vision.

Sidian's arms squeezed him hard enough to crack ribs, had he been human. The pain grounded him. With his lungs crushed beneath his mate's iron strength, Raine breathed.

His home was on fire. *What have they done?*

Despair threatened, but rage won. His body turned to steel as Oka propelled them faster.

The scene that greeted them was chaos. Oka's back offered an aerial view as Betony's storm unleashed hell upon the keep. The smaller, weaker humans were reduced to prey as the dragons chased and burnt them like fire-breathing falcons.

Some fought valiantly, but they were outmatched. Fallen men littered the grounds. Dead or injured, it was impossible to tell.

Two men split his eardrums with their agony as they rolled on the ground, desperately attempting to quell the flames cooking them alive.

Raine's teeth gnashed, his blood flashing hot and cold as he watched humans getting massacred for doing nothing more than defending their home. *His home.*

Half a glance told him interfering was useless. Battle fever rode the parents hard. It would be like trying to reason with wildfire.

"Oka, the spire," Raine shouted against the wind. He couldn't witness a moment more of this fire-blooded slaughter that proved dragons were monsters. His heart crumpled painfully as he imagined what Sidian must think.

Oka soared upward, heeding Raine's request. His mallard green scales glowed molten as he dodged a rogue blast of dragon fire. Whipping across the sky, they passed Chambrin Keep and all its violent pandemonium in a blur.

The spire was the epitome of serenity by comparison, its white stones lucent against star-dappled sky. A broad archway opened high upon the tower, allowing the war dragons to swoop in and out of the upper levels where they lived and roosted.

Oka surged through the opening, which was wide enough that his wingtips didn't brush stone. The noise outside became muted, like a scream underwater. The battle now sounded softly distant, almost dreamlike.

Raine looked around the Roost, dumbfounded. The round stone chamber was vacant, the rushes musty and old. Cobwebs hung overhead where the everyday movement of dragons should have inhibited their formation.

"They're gone," Raine breathed.

"Did we miss them in the fight?"

At Sidian's question, Oka turned to face the opening just as Naiah soared through. Nyx slipped off her back, then came up to the opening alongside Sidian and Raine. As one, they gazed outward, scanning the grounds where Betony's dragons continued to decimate the human guards.

"The war dragons aren't down there or up here," Nyx said, sounding perplexed. "Where else would they be?"

"The Roost has been empty for a while, by the looks of it," Raine said, frowning as he watched the chaos below.

The force that had met Betony's storm was much smaller than it should have been. If Raine had to guess, there were a hundred men dead or injured scattered throughout the bailey. Only a handful remained standing. Several had their backs in a circle as dragons surrounded them.

They were locked in a stalemate. The guards wielded long, bone-tipped spears that kept the dragons from rushing them. And the dragons' fire couldn't reach the humans without bringing them within range of the lethally sharp spears.

"Not just the war dragons are missing," Nyx said, voicing Raine's thoughts. "The entire brigade is gone. Over two thousand men-at-arms. It's like Chambrin Keep has been reduced to bare-bones staffing."

"This isn't a trap," Sidian said grimly. "It's a decoy."

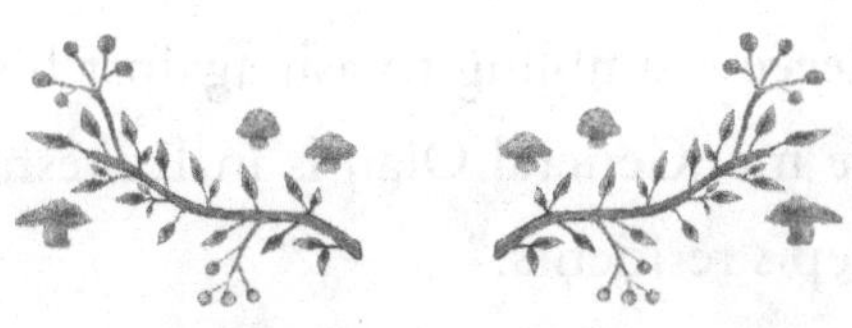

"Get the fuck away from him," Raine snarled, leaping off Oka's back before the dragon fully descended.

A purple female with hard, reptilian eyes blew fire at him. Raine hissed through his teeth, near feral with rage at his mate's proximity to the fire stream. Oka immediately reversed his descent, gusting Raine with each powerful beat of his wings as he carried Sidian out of danger.

The purple female hesitated. Raine could see the debate in her stare, on whether or not to lunge at the human cowering nearby. Raine bared his teeth and stepped deliberately between the dragoness and her target, silently daring her to attack. Black smoke puffed from her nostrils in a show of temper, but she darted off, in search of easier quarry.

The man whose life he'd intervened to save fell upon Raine's burning coat, batting the flames as he sobbed. "Young Master, you're on fire."

The man tugged at Raine's backpack and slid it off him. It hit the grass with a tinkling thud. When he tried removing Raine's coat next, Raine firmly clasped the knobby, earth-stained hands of Wylan before the old man burnt himself.

Wylan was neither Guardian nor soldier, but the keep's steward and one of the kindest men of Raine's acquaintance. "I'm fine, Wylan. Where is everyone?"

Wylan's aging face lined with worry as he scanned the material of Raine's coat. Patches on his side and chest smoldered black and red, the fleece crumbling to ash against his skin. "Young Master, forgive me. General Olan is in Rokeshin, along with most of the keep's residents."

Raine's heart stopped. His mind was a whirlwind of confused horror. A powerful gust brought Oka and Sidian to the ground beside him. The cold breeze of Oka's landing blew away the tunneling darkness of his vision. Raine's wobbling knees held.

He heard himself speak as if from a great distance. "General Olan?"

Wylan's shoulders hunched, his face downcast. "Aye. When the Nine took General Arastus into custody, Olan was appointed head of Chambrin Keep and its forces. It isn't right, considering that you are Arastus's next of kin, but Chieftain Eddic was adamant in his decision. He said you were a traitor, Young Master. That we are to report any sighting of you."

Raine forced a smile at the steward's anxious frown. "We both know I'm no traitor," he said lightly, wanting to reassure Wylan that his loyalty was not misplaced. "And neither was my father."

Wylan closed his eyes in an anguished expression. "I'm so sorry, Young Master. Your father was my dearest friend. His palace rest is well earned."

Raine swallowed against a too-tight throat and nodded. Later, they would have plenty of time to grieve and reminisce. But now—

A cry of distress, shrill and feminine, warbled on an acrid breeze. Raine cursed and darted toward the sound, the others following behind him. Rounding the corner, he found two dragons caging a maid against the keep's walls in the garden.

Raine squinted in the dimness. "Lissy," he shouted, recognizing her. A woven basket was upturned at her feet, spilling onions and beets across the flagstone walkway. Lissy looked at him, her eyes white with fear, before facing the two dragons. They pressed closer. A male opened his mouth, preparing to breathe fire.

The glint of a pale blade peeked through the grass ahead. A deceased guard, his body charred beyond recognition, was several paces from the sword, face-up on scorched earth. Raine snatched the sword without slowing, without thinking. In a burst of inhuman speed, he pitched himself between Lissy and the dragons, brandishing the sword.

But it was too late. The dragon began to blow. Flames, foul and fierce, engulfed Raine. Lissy threw out her arms to protect her face and screamed. A hellish shout of unspeakable pain.

As the flames dispersed, she slumped to the ground, her legs splayed amid the strewn vegetables she'd been harvesting when the dragons attacked. Weak, mewling cries poured from her mouth as she cradled her arms. From her hands to her elbows, the skin was raw and grotesquely melted.

With a ferocious snarl, Raine lunged for the dragons. The dragoness shot into the air, but she wasn't who Raine was after. The other dragon, the male who had tried to burn Lissy's face off, issued a challenging roar.

Raine pushed every drop of his fury into his muscles and charged. The dragon retreated, his wings spreading as if to join his companion in the air, but Raine was fast. His blade slid into the scales below the dragon's breastbone, biting deep.

The dragon thrashed and roared, belching fire. Blinded by the flames, Raine held tight and dug the blade deeper. Then cursed, realizing he had missed the dragon's heart by inches.

Raine withdrew the sword to try again. His next thrust met only air as the male scurried out of reach. Broad, leathery wings beat the dragon above the keep and out of sight.

Raine stood motionless in the shadowed garden, gazing blankly where the dragon had been. His breath sawed out of him, loud and hoarse. Lissy whimpered in the background. Lost in pain, she made no move to stand.

"Oka," he growled. The silhouetted dragon straightened. "Tell the others it's over. Anyone who refuses to curtail their savagery will answer to me."

Oka roared his assent and took to the sky, flitting over the keep in a thick, serpentine ribbon. Wylan ran over to Lissy and helped her up. She folded into his side, weak and sobbing as he tried not to touch her ruined arms.

Raine gave Wylan a short, grateful nod and headed for the keep.

Someone grabbed his elbow and held firm when Raine tried to shake them. He whirled, teeth flashing, and encountered the last face he wanted to see.

The warm glow of the exterior sconces made Sidian's handsome features both sinister and ethereal, a masterpiece of light and shadow. His velvet eyes were veiled, unreadable.

Raine wanted to curdle in shame. Sidian had just witnessed firsthand how despicable dragons could be. That his earliest impressions of them were not false, at all.

Callous. Monstrous. Dishonorable.

He felt each aspersion as if it were carved into his skin, felt his mate's soft brown eyes trace over them like disfiguring scars.

When Sidian's lips parted, he said the last thing Raine expected.

"You're naked."

CHAPTER NINETEEN

Raine was glad he'd taken the brunt of the dragon's fire. It was the only reason Lissy was alive, after all. But the heroic cause of his nudity didn't make it any more pleasant. Even his boots had burnt away, leaving his toes bare against the icy flagstone path.

He became excruciatingly aware of the frigid night breeze against his cock. His testes climbed inside his body like two small, frightened voles.

Sidian tugged off his pack and coat, extending the latter towards Raine.

Raine dropped his scavenged sword to snatch the heavy wool garment from Sidian's fingers. Drawing it on with alacrity, he snapped the most prudent buttons shut to shield his nakedness before his prick froze off.

A sudden wind gusted his braid, announcing Naiah's arrival as he fastened the last button. She landed hard in her urgency, spraying sod with her claws. Nyx rolled off her back and ran over to them, his face ashen.

"This is a nightmare. What do we do?"

"Oka went to stop Betony's storm." Raine indicated the direction Oka had flown. "He'll need help."

Naiah nodded at his unasked question. Chuffing a brief flame, she speared the sky after Oka. Nyx started away, as if he was going to round the keep and join the fray.

"Nyx, no," Raine called before he went too far. "It's not a fight. It's a fucking barbeque, and you're flammable. We need to get inside the keep and barricade the entrances."

He prayed that most of the servants were inside and unscathed.

"Barricading the keep is impossible. There are too many ways inside, and all the doors are wood," Nyx said grimly.

Raine looked around, searching for a solution. But his thoughts unraveled as he surveyed his home. Flames as tall as mountains blazed in all directions. Hollow, blackened stone would be all that remained in the coming dawn. His father would have been devastated.

Sidian gripped his arms. He was firm and solid, his dark eyes steady on Raine. "Then let's collect everyone and put them someplace safe. Someplace with only one entrance, which we can guard."

Raine flinched away from his mate's stare. Looking at Sidian in that moment felt blasphemous. He couldn't do it. Not while surrounded by hideous death and fire and proof—irrefutable proof—that dragons were the dishonorable, disgraceful monsters Sidian had initially believed.

"Okay," he said, addressing his feet.

Sidian's hands gripped his shoulders harder, as if demanding something. Raine kept his head down. He couldn't look. He *couldn't*. Eventually, Sidian stepped away with a sigh.

Wylan opened the narrow servants' entrance and helped Lissy inside. Her body shook with shock and pain, but she was no longer sobbing. Raine trailed after them, hollow and listless. Upon entering the keep, he finally raised his eyes. For an instant, Raine couldn't breathe.

He was home. In Chambrin Keep's kitchen. Scents of dried herbs and cinnamon chased away the oily aftertaste of dragon fire. Raine's eyes grew misty as he stared at the kitchen tables, heaped with autumn produce and day-old bread. His mind catapulted a decade into the past, when he had helped Wylan and Tavish, the head cook, make fruit preserves and pies. Wylan had snuck him the best berries to snack on whenever the cook's back was turned.

Tavish had let Raine gift their best pie to his father, which happened to be blackberry. His father had praised it effusively, then ate the whole thing. Years afterward, Raine discovered that his father hated blackberries; that he had feigned enjoyment at every bite, refusing to dim the dazzling pride in his son's smile.

A hand slipped into his and squeezed, drawing Raine out of the memory. He felt Sidian's stare like a weight on his cheek but pretended not to notice. Looking at Sidian was akin to skewering himself over and over while peeling off his own skin. It *hurt*.

"You need medical attention," Nyx said, addressing Lissy. He spoke to her like a child, his words measured and gentle. "I've had training. I served as a medic my first year in the guild. Is it alright if I treat you?"

Her arms hovered near her chest, crossed like a bat's so as not to touch anything. The burns looked worse now. Her hands were red and misshapen, the flesh of her palms filled with pus. Blisters bulged along her forearms in a bed of mottled, wet-looking skin.

Raine had never experienced pain from fire. And since he was a dragon, he never would. But his father had told him burns were one of the worst things a man could feel. That if the injury was severe enough, a man would rather die than suffer it.

Lissy's sweetly rounded features were gouged with agony. Her forehead was sheeny, as if she had a fever. Slowly, she nodded, her mouth white and trembling.

"There are healing supplies in a storeroom nearby," Wylan said. "It's stocked with tinctures and salves I made personally. You're welcome to anything you need."

Nyx guided Lissy toward a chair by the woodstove. He waited until she was seated to look at Wylan. "Show me."

They trailed after Wylan, who shuffled down a corridor at a pace Raine hadn't thought the old man capable of. The keep was dead silent, and they passed no one on their way to the storeroom.

"It was a great commotion when the dragons arrived. I heard the screams first, then saw everything through my bedchamber window," Wylan was saying. "I flung open my door and found Moranda there, along with several of the staff. With General Olan and most of the keep gone, we didn't know what to do. None of us are battle-trained."

Raine snorted. That was putting it lightly. The only staff within the keep's confines this late at night were domestic workers. Cooks and maids and a few footmen. They wouldn't know which end of a sword to point, had they confronted the dragons. And since none of them served the guild, they only had access to steel. No amount of prowess could have compensated for such useless weapons.

"Where is the rest of the staff?" Raine asked. "Did they venture outside with you?"

He couldn't bring himself to care overmuch for Moranda's fate, but she was technically innocent. None of the domestic staff had been involved with the Cavern. His father had always kept that business separate from the keep, housing the curtain guards and dragon handlers on other parts of the grounds.

"No, no. We were seeking a secure place to hide when Lenka said her sister, Lissy, was working late in the garden. I went to retrieve Lissy while Moranda led the others to safety. They were heading towards the chapel when we parted."

Wylan paused to open a heavy oak door on their right. The room was square and plain, its walls lined with shelves. There were many glass jars, labeled with Wylan's meticulous handwriting. Nyx wasted no time gathering the supplies he needed, taking several jars and a steel box of bandages and medical tools.

"I'll take care of Lissy," Nyx said. The jars clinked as he adjusted his burden. "Find the other servants and get them someplace secure."

Raine hesitated, but Sidian said, "Once the girl is treated, you do the same."

Nyx nodded, already turning to rush back to the kitchen.

Raine and Sidian followed Wylan, who went the opposite direction. Three turns later, they reached the chapel foyer, which was really just a broader section of corridor outside the sanctuary.

The chapel's double doors were more decorous than the keep's main entrance, inlaid with gilded filigree depicting the Divine Father's palace. Opening the chapel doors would similarly part the miniature palace doors.

Raine pushed one of the chapel's iron-levered handles, but it was locked.

He knocked, calling out, "Hello, is anyone in there?"

There was a clatter coupled with several frightened squeals. Raine poised his fist to knock again when the door swung open. Something hard thwacked the side of his head before he could react. Throwing his arms up, he dodged the next swing and squinted through pain.

Moranda stood in the doorway. She wielded a broom like a pole axe, her hair a disheveled curtain over her heaving shoulders. Raine didn't know what made his eyes water more, being brained with a broom or the sight of Moranda in her nightdress. Her unbound breasts strained against cotton too sheer for modesty. Shuddering, he averted his eyes and prepared to block her next swing.

"You." She bared her teeth like a dog. "You cursed fucking ghoul. This is all your doing, isn't it, blanch?"

Raine tensed, acutely aware of Sidian's presence. Moranda's pejoratives had lost their ability to wound, or so he thought. But having his mate overhear the old slurs somehow made them new again. He felt her words like a knife. They sliced him open, spilling shame.

"I'll explain later," he said, wary but urgent. "Right now, we need to get everyone to safety."

Moranda spat, a frothy wad that narrowly missed his toes. "I will keep myself and my girls safe. I need no help from an aberration like you. You're the reason we're in this mess. I know it. Every breath you draw is an offense to the Divine Father, and this is his punishment. The keep will be destroyed for housing you, for permitting your taint."

Raine burned with humiliation. It was like fate wanted Sidian to see every ugly side of him at once, and Raine couldn't take anymore. He opened his mouth, convinced he was about to bid Moranda farewell like she so flagrantly wanted. Only, his conscience overtook his tongue. What came out was, "Look, Moranda. I know you don't like me. And, honestly? You're not my favorite person, either. But the keep is under attack as we speak, and everyone here is in danger. So will you please come with me, just for an hour or two? We need to get you somewhere safe—"

"I'm not going anywhere with you. Go ahead. Try and make me. I've been waiting for a chance to end you since the day Arastus brought you here. You were small and defenseless, an infant. A few minutes in the washhouse was all I needed to drown you." Raine's flesh crawled at her smile as much as her words. "But there was never an opportunity. Arastus watched over you worse than a mother hen. I should have never given up. I should have found a way to scrub your existence from this world like the blight you are. I wish Arastus was alive, if only to see the look on his face when he realized I was right."

She swung again. Raine reacted too late, his body numbed by her venom. Screwing his eyes shut, he braced himself. The broom handle whistled softly through the air. His eyes flew open at the sound of wood striking flesh inches from his cheek.

The side of a hard, unyielding warrior pressed against his. Sidian snatched the broom from Moranda's grip as easily as if she were a child with a stick, then threw it to the floor. The lines of his sinew stood out starkly beneath his Guardian uniform, his entire frame primed with violence.

"Strike him again, with either words or weapons, and I will end you." Sidian's voice was satin smoke. Calm and collected. Raine shivered, recognizing the lethal intent behind it. His mate meant every word.

Moranda looked Sidian up and down, openly taking his measure. A sneer wrapped around her face, as if she found him wanting. Sidian didn't react beyond the faintest uptick of his chin. His stance was disarmingly loose at first glance. Moranda had no clue he was a predator ready to pounce. Raine read her death in the callous twist of her lips, which parted to spew more hate.

"I don't know who you think you are—"

A shattering crash ripped through the chapel, cutting off Moranda's fateful diatribe. Beyond the double doors, three hulking dragons smashed through the chapel's glass-domed ceiling. They plummeted in a waterfall wave of glittering shards and crashed into the central rows of prayer benches, scattering cushions and wood splinters.

The maids within screeched and fled through the doorway, bowling Moranda over like a herd of panicking wildebeests. They huddled behind Raine as the dragons inside the chapel rose and shook themselves off. It was two against one. A green squaring off against a purple and red.

As one, the three dragons stood on their hind legs and walked a circle. Talons crunched glass and broken furniture as they waited for an opening to attack each other.

"Get out of here," Sidian hissed.

For a wild instant, Raine thought Sidian was addressing the dragons inside the chapel, but then his mate darted an irritated glance at the maids pooled behind them.

They didn't leave. Instead, they clung to Raine's back like a pile of timid kittens. Their panting breaths echoed around him, and Raine felt his own annoyance spike. Sidian was right. Now wasn't the time to have a dozen defenseless domestics underfoot. One wrong move, and he would end up elbowing some chit in the face. There was no room to fight.

Wylan walked into view, hurrying to Moranda's side. She was still prone on the floor, but her head lifted at his approach. Poor Wylan seemed as frail as a withered vine next to her stout girth, but he knelt to help her stand. The wrinkles on his forehead turned puce with strain, his knees wavering.

It was the last thing Raine wanted to do, but he found himself crossing the narrow foyer to aid Wylan before he collapsed. As Raine reached for Moranda's waist, she jerked upright, knocking into Wylan. The steward fell against the wall as she rounded on Raine.

"Do. Not. Touch. Me."

"Are you okay?" he asked Wylan, ignoring the mad woman before him.

Wylan righted himself and smiled, albeit faintly. "Right as rain," he said, an old joke between them that squeezed Raine's heart.

"Glad to hear it. Will you take the staff someplace safe to hide?" Raine asked. He glanced meaningfully toward the circling dragons, then back to the steward. "Preferably somewhere without a giant glass ceiling," he added.

Moranda turned to follow Raine's gaze and froze, peering straight into the chapel. The purple and red dragons faced them. Their focus was on the green dragoness, still caught in a stare-off. They might not have ever registered their human audience if Moranda hadn't chosen that moment to demonstrate the precise extent of her lung capacity.

She shrieked, long and loud and piercing. Moranda might have shattered the chapel's domed glass if the dragons hadn't already smashed it to pieces.

Raine had no idea who the three dragons in the chapel were. But in the split second that the red and purple dragons clocked them, their reptilian features sharpening with malicious intent, he knew who those two weren't.

"Run," he yelled. At the same time, the dragons roared, drowning him out. "Run," he repeated, stepping sideways for Wylan and Moranda to pass more quickly.

Moranda raced down the corridor, barreling through the clustered maids with the brute force of a bull. A few of the maids stumbled, but their companions caught them before they fell. Without a backward glance, they fled after their mistress, their nightdresses lifting high over their calves as they pumped through their terror.

Wylan was the only one who seemed torn. He watched the women flee, then eyed Raine and the chapel. He looked ten times his age, frail and vulnerable.

"Wylan, go," Raine barked, needing to squash the debate in the older man's eyes. "I'm relying on you to keep them safe."

As Wylan hastened away, the red and purple dragons dropped to all fours and charged at Raine. The green dragoness spat a snarl of flames and threw herself into their path. The red male careened into the green female. They tussled across the chapel in a mountain of flashing scales and teeth.

Sidian drew his sword and leapt between Raine and the purple dragoness as she reached the chapel's exit unimpeded, her jaws snapping. Sidian slashed a wide arc. Scales split and blood ran down the purple female's chest. She drew back with an enraged screech.

A resounding crash came from the chapel. Then, the red male dragon appeared beside the purple female, puffing gray smoke from his nostrils as he beheld Sidian. The breath sawed out of Raine at their proximity to his mate. They were too close. A single stream of dragon fire would blister Sidian's bones to charcoal.

Sidian blocked the chapel doorframe like a protective shield. His stance was open and ready, his longsword poised for a thrust as he faced them. There was no fear in his posture; only nerve and grit and boldness. Every taut line of his body said, *try me, if you dare*.

The red dragon's maw parted on a crushing roar that blew Raine's braid back. Sidian swung his sword. The red male pivoted and lashed his tail, smacking the center of Sidian's stomach. Sidian clutched his midriff with a choked groan, then raised his sword and slashed.

The two dragons jerked backward, evading the blade. Another puff of smoke poured from the red male's nostrils. This time, the smoke was thicker and darker. A precursor, Raine realized with a sickening jolt.

Raine lunged into Sidian's side, throwing them both to the stone floor. They landed rough, Sidian's sword nearly taking out Raine's eye as they flailed.

A trunk of fire blasted through the chapel doorway in their wake. Not a warning flare or a quick breath meant to foil a foe. No, it was a long, hot wave designed to incinerate Sidian where he stood. If Raine hadn't spotted that black smoke ... If he had reacted just a second later ...

A shiver frosted his spine. Then, the world turned red. Blood red. The same vibrant hue as his target. The red dragon stepped out of the chapel, his chin poised higher than a king's. Raine wrenched Sidian's sword from his hand, the movement too fast and unexpected for Sidian to resist.

Raine could have been wielding the bone of his own relative.

He didn't care.

He could have been wielding it to strike down one of his own parents.

He didn't care.

Through a crimson haze of red-on-red, he drew back his arm and struck. His shoulder jarred as bone met bone. The sword glanced off the red male's ribcage instead of cutting into the soft, vulnerable viscera beneath. A darting numbness zinged up Raine's wrist. The sword slipped and fell from his slackened fingers as the red dragon thrashed, flames spraying wide.

Violet eyes locked on Raine, and the purple dragoness charged as a huge green shape flew from the chapel like a cannonball. The green dragoness knocked into the red male. Together, they tumbled into the purple female.

Flames shot in all directions. Roars boomed and crashed against the corridor walls. The three dragons fought like feral cats—a flurry of fangs and claws too tangled to determine who had the advantage.

Until the red and purple dragons pinned the green female. Their milky talons, as long as daggers, dug into the green female's neck and shoulders. Her wings fluttered uselessly, pinched against the floor.

Raine's heart was in his throat as he watched, his body clenched with the urge to intervene. He snatched Sidian's fallen sword and forced himself to wait. There would only be one chance to get this right. Only one chance to sever the heads of the vile dragons pinning one of his friends.

He inched closer, getting a better read on their colors. The pinned female's scales were the tender green of sweet peas and baby asparagus. *Eva.*

The purple female growled, low and menacing. Her fangs sparkled against the flickering sconces as her mouth neared Eva's throat. Eva thrashed and spat fire, engulfing the purple female's head in orange flames.

Breathing fire on a fellow dragon must have been a gross insult of some sort, because the purple dragoness puffed up with greater malevolence. A cruel, cunning gleam entered her eyes as she raised a paw, fanning her talons into a serrated line meant to cut deep.

Eva bucked wildly. The red male's arms jerked and trembled as he fought to hold her down. The purple dragoness stared unwaveringly at Eva. She waited for an opening with the patience of a canny lioness, her thickly muscled arm poised to deliver a killing blow.

There was no time to wait. Raine had to act. The two dragons were so focused on Eva, they wouldn't notice him until it was too late. He would sneak up behind them and, with one smooth swing of Sidian's longsword, he would send both of their heads rolling.

Raine rushed forward, his plan already unfolding in his mind's eye.

Sidian's gray coat pulled taut against his chest as someone grabbed him from behind, yanking him to a halt midstride. He turned, scowling his urgent frustration. Instead of heeding Raine's wordless demand to *let go*, Sidian snatched back his sword.

"Of the two of us, I'm the one trained to slay dragons."

Sidian stepped around him as if the matter was settled. Raine fisted the cloth between Sidian's shoulder blades, halting his mate the same way he'd halted Raine.

"Of the two of us, I'm the one who is fireproof," he gritted, tugging Sidian backwards.

Sidian tried to jerk free, but Raine held fast with one hand, the other going for Sidian's sword. Sidian turned and swiped his leg. Raine buckled as his feet flew from under him. He clenched his fingers hard into Sidian's Guardian uniform and dragged his mate down, too. They landed in a heap. Eva's life-or-death plight was all but forgotten as they grappled for the sword.

Another crash reverberated from the chapel, followed by a barrage of roars. They froze, each with one hand on Sidian's hilt. As one, they turned and looked toward the commotion.

Less than ten feet away, six—no, seven dragons engaged in an all-out battle. A sky blue dragoness—Evin, he was sure of it—tore into the red male pinning Eva. The red dragon was forced to release Eva to defend himself against Evin's furiously swiping talons.

Two green dragons, Oka and Carrisyne, intercepted the purple dragoness as she went to aid her red companion. A darker blue dragon lunged defensively in front of the purple female and snapped his wings, sprawling Oka and Carrisyne down the corridor.

As the dragons continued to rage, flames licked the stone floor and ceiling. A fiery orange current shot in Raine and Sidian's direction, falling inches shy of their flesh. Raine's cheeks and neck heated against the fire-lashed air as trepidation iced his innards.

Enough was enough. The dragons were too close and too dangerous for Sidian. Raine had to get his mate to safety.

He released Sidian's hilt, yielding his hold on the sword. If things got any worse, his mate would need it more.

They climbed to their feet and surveyed the calamity. Walls shook. Stones cracked. The dragons clashed with the catastrophic violence of a maelstrom.

More flames snaked in their direction. Raine snagged Sidian's elbow and dragged him backwards. He hissed through his teeth as the fire curled right where Sidian's head had been.

It was like the whole damned world was determined to cook his mate right before his eyes.

"We need to get out of here." Raine tugged Sidian's arm meaningfully, directing him down the corridor. Sidian wrenched his arm away.

Raine drew up short and turned to find his mate's mouth pinched in displeasure.

"I'm not hiding with the housekeepers."

Over Sidian's shoulder, four more dragons dove through the chapel ceiling and flew into the small foyer to join the fray. It was absolute madness.

Raine shoved Sidian against the wall, sheltering him before he was burnt or crushed in the chaos. Sharp, twisting limbs struck his back and sides as the dragons fought, but Raine barely registered the pain. All his concentration was spent on shielding his mate.

"Okay." Sidian rested a palm over Raine's thudding heart. "You're right. We need to get out of here. We're closer to the chapel."

Raine winced at the truth of it. They would have to navigate a teeming mass of fire and muscle to reach any kind of safety. He already had to press ever deeper into Sidian to avoid being absorbed into the fracas.

After a minute, they had their opening. The dragons were concentrated on the other side of the foyer. Raine dropped his arms and trailed Sidian to the chapel. They hugged the wall as they moved, dodging fire blasts and wing thrusts as the fighting spread in their direction once more.

As they reached the double doors, a purple dragon barreled at Raine. Head-over-tail, the dragon somersaulted across the floor like a scaly boulder. The wide, horrified eyes of Eva met his, and he knew she hadn't meant to fling her opponent at him. That knowledge wouldn't make the impact hurt any less. Raine grit his teeth, bracing himself.

A hand dug bruisingly at Raine's chest. He heard the fabric of Sidian's coat rip as the world turned upside-down. The hand clutching Raine whipped him like a stone. He soared through the chapel's doorframe, away from the chaotic fray. He caught a glimpse of the chapel's ruined dome, a fleeting impression of jagged glass and the cold light of distant stars. The floor flew up to catch him, meeting his back with chastising force.

"*Oof.*" The breath whooshed out of him. He blinked, looking up at Sidian. His mate's black hair fell over his eyes, shading them as he stared down at Raine. It took several laboring gasps before Raine managed to speak. "Did you have to throw me so hard?"

"You're welcome," Sidian said, sounding smugly satisfied as he offered Raine a hand.

Overhead, dragons careened through the shattered dome in a swift, glittering line. Raine grasped Sidian's palm and wrenched his mate to the floor as the dragons swooped by.

"Seriously?" Raine scowled at the dragons, who continued whizzing through the chapel. They were fighting midair like a bunch of pissed-off, overgrown eagles. "Is there a sign on the roof inviting everyone to the chapel melee?"

Sidian gestured with his sword. "From high in the air, that broken dome probably sticks out like an island at sea."

Wonderful. The chapel was filled with colliding dragons. Their violence was savage, with no regard for anything around them. "We need to figure out a way to stop this before they bring the entire keep down. I won't lose any more innocents to this senseless fucking slaughter. *I can't.*"

Sidian tensed. His crouched posture went from wary bystander to alert hunter.

"You won't," he said simply.

Before Raine could ask what the hell that meant, Sidian sprinted across the chapel. He was a blur of black in the twilit chapel, a flitting shadow in the ruins of a once grand sanctuary.

Raine grew hot and cold by turns as he tracked Sidian's progress, gripped by the worst fear he'd ever experienced as, one by one, the embattled dragons noticed him.

Betony's storm was ruled by a dark agenda: vengeance. No matter how extensively Evin and Naiah's thunders engaged them, fellow dragons weren't the objects of their animus. Humans were.

At the sight of Sidian, of a human after many long moments fighting fellow dragons, the parents' bloodlust was thickly palpable. It permeated the air, swirling seamlessly into the miasma of acrid char and smoke that wafted on the night breeze—carrying the stench of burnt flesh and bone and outbuildings through the shattered dome above.

One dragon dropped out of the skirmish and came after Sidian. Then another. And another. Until Sidian looked like the leader of a small, charging dragon army.

Or the target of one.

Each heartbeat struck Raine's chest like a hammer blow. His gut was a bottomless void of fear that consumed him as he frantically measured the distance between Sidian and his closest pursuer, a grass-green dragoness.

The dragoness coughed an arc of flames at Sidian's back. The bright orange fire sank away unfed, Sidian just out of reach as he raced toward ...

That was Aly. Raine knew her vivid scarlet hue from any other red. She and a blue dragon—Zane, if he had to guess—were backed against a wall on the opposite side of the chapel. Aly spewed flames defiantly into the face of the palest purple dragoness Raine had ever seen.

Betony. The storm mother. She slammed her tail against the floor, spraying wood splinters like water. Her roar was as powerful as ten dragons combined. It ripped through the chapel on a shockwave of crushing sound and spinning dust. Something inside

Raine buckled against it. He fell to his knees, as if his legs had been axed. Around him, the rest of the dragons dropped, too.

Including Sidian's pursuers. A rush of dizzying gratitude swept through Raine, so powerful it would have knocked him over if he hadn't already fallen. The only two left standing in the wake of the storm mother's roar were Betony ... and Sidian, who continued sprinting with the swift silent grace the guild was known for. The storm mother's back was to the chapel, or she might have taken heed of the incoming danger.

She roared again, emphasizing her outrage as she loomed over Aly and Zane, who were pinned to the floor by the same invisible force as the rest of the dragons. Her fangs snapped shut, cutting off the terrible sound as a milk-white longsword caressed her neck.

"You possess a resonant roar. Good to know," Sidian said, his voice more gelid than a glacier. "Call off their attack, right now, or die."

CHAPTER TWENTY

It took longer than usual for Raine's bathwater to boil. Then again, maybe that was just him. His shoulders hunched as he stared, waiting for the pinprick bubbles lining the bottom of the iron basin to rise.

The crackling fire beneath his tub set his teeth on edge. He couldn't stop recalling the carnage and chaos that fire had so recently wrought. It had been dragon fire, not these flint-struck flames. And it had consumed flesh and bone, not seasoned logs and kindling. The difference registered in Raine's mind, but not in his raw, twitching sinew.

Sidian's eyes dug into his back like cattle prods. Raine pretended not to notice. He couldn't bear to look at Sidian. He felt as foul and slimy as a putrid wound. What must Sidian think of him now?

"Are you sure you don't want to go help put out the fires?" Raine asked without turning. "Someone's got to keep Betony in line."

After Betony had transformed into her human form, standing stark naked in the keep's chapel with Sidian's blade at her throat, she'd issued a ceasefire. In moments, the chapel had filled with the nude human figures of her storm, everyone having followed her example by shifting.

Perhaps Raine should have stuck around to sort out the confusion or help find clothes they could wear. But his whole body had trembled as he stared at the dragons. *Murderers.* That's all they were to him. Callous and craven killers. He hadn't had it in him to assist them with anything, and fled before he did something he might regret.

"Are you trying to get rid of me?" Sidian asked instead of answering.

"No." It was a feeble lie that only made him more ashamed. Of course, he wanted Sidian to leave.

Your kind are rabid and spineless. Those were Sidian's words, once upon a time. And look how fucking right he'd been. His mate deserved so much better than to be in Raine's lowly presence.

Several bubbles broke the bathwater's steamy surface. *Finally.*

Raine tore off Sidian's coat. Despite his turmoil, he purred as he submerged himself in the precious basin. His washtub held so much more than boiling water. It was comfort. Solace. Home.

Sidian sighed from his seat at the vanity. "You look like a parsnip in a stew."

"A delicious parsnip," Raine declared, closing his eyes as the boiling water buffeted him gently, very much like a vegetable in a stew.

Sidian hummed thoughtfully. "A delicious parsnip," he agreed in a voice slightly huskier than normal. And much, much closer.

Raine's eyes opened, and he jolted. Sidian was no longer at the vanity. He hovered near the edge of the washtub, staring intently at him. Heart stammering, Raine tore his gaze away.

"Raine."

Raine fiddled with a washcloth, working a round cake of vanilla soap into a lather against it. He did not look up.

"Raine. Look at me."

The authority in Sidian's voice was absolute. Raine gave Sidian the barest glance possible, his gaze going no higher than his mate's neck. Sidian made a harsh sound in the back of his throat, dragging Raine's gaze the rest of the way. He met eyes slitted with anger, set in a severe countenance.

"Why are you avoiding me?"

Raine couldn't hold his stare. His chin tucked to his chest as he worked his vanilla soap into the washcloth with renewed vigor, as if enrapt with his task. "I'm not."

"Have I done something to offend you?" The question was posed with heartbreakingly careful neutrality, as if Sidian was concerned about his answer and trying to hide it.

It obliterated something inside of Raine's chest. He thought it might be his heart.

He shifted his shoulders, facing his mate directly for the first time since the fighting ceased. "Are you kidding me?" he asked, straightening himself with his palms against the tub bottom. "Did you not just see what happened?"

Raine's face crumpled like wet tissue. He turned his head, offering Sidian his profile as he continued. "I don't know how you can stomach the sight of me. I understand if you can't and you're just too good a friend to show it. There are numerous guestrooms. I will have Trista prepare one for you—"

"Stop."

Sidian's quiet, husky command was more powerful than a shout. Raine bit his tongue. His racing pulse drummed the silence, drowning out the burbling water and crackling flames. The silence stretched until he knew, with painful clarity, that Sidian waited on him to meet his gaze.

Raine felt raw and exposed, as if his skin had been stripped, revealing every ugly thing that had once been concealed by his beautifully deceptive packaging. He forced himself to face Sidian, his back rigid, muscles taut as stone.

"You once said you did not hold all of humanity responsible for the crimes of a few." Sidian's statement was not a question, but he paused as if waiting for a reply.

Raine recalled the day he'd flung those words at Sidian. It was after Tayo had attacked him in the woods; Sidian, blinded by his hatred of dragons, couldn't reconcile Raine's innocence. Particularly when Raine's innocence had meant Sidian's journeyman and fellow Guardian was the villain.

Raine issued a shallow nod, which must have satisfied Sidian because he continued.

"I am no longer the man I was when I took you into custody. The man who accused dragons of lacking honor. And I no longer hold all of your kind responsible for the crimes of a few."

"I'm responsible for everything they did," Raine burst. His mind screamed, *shut up, shut up*, but his mouth kept moving, as if possessed by the urge to paint himself in the grimmest light possible. "I was in charge, remember? You said it yourself. A great leader would have been able to control their unit, and *I didn't.*"

"I was fucking with you. We all were," Sidian countered. "You weren't in charge of them. Betony was. You were meant to guide us here and find a discreet path to the war dragons. That's it. End of story."

Raine shook his head, shoulders slumping. "Maybe if I had embraced my role as leader, that slaughter could have been avoided." He swallowed, his mouth dry and burning. "It's just as Lukor said. They might have listened had I bothered giving them orders, but all I did was avoid them. I made Betony address them in my stead. No, Sidian." He slashed his arm through the air when his mate tried to speak. "This is reality. It sucks and I fucking hate it, but I can't hide from it. And I don't want you to, either. You have to know this is my fault. I'll be damned forever before I let you believe lies about me, even pretty ones."

Sidian's dusky mouth bracketed with anger. "Fine. I concede that things might have gone differently if you had tried speaking to them. That is no guarantee things would have gone better. I think we've all realized by now that lives were going to be lost coming here, no matter what. And what I saw tonight was you risking your life to defend the innocent. If you think I will revile you for your display of valor and integrity, think again."

Sidian marched to the vanity and snatched the chair before returning to the tub's edge. He straddled it backwards and crossed his arms over the wooden backing as he faced Raine. Their gazes were level over the tub rim.

Sidian glared at the boiling water, then at Raine. "Had you deigned to bathe in water that wouldn't kill me, I could have joined you."

Raine's stomach swooped. The image of Sidian joining him threatened to overtake his senses. His favorite person and his favorite activity wrapped together? It felt closer to a blissful fantasy than anything that could happen in real life.

Sidian's disappointed scowl diminished Raine's fevering blood. He took in the smudges of ash and dirt on Sidian's skin, the greasy sheen of his hair. There hadn't been time or warm enough weather to bathe on their way to the Hellhole. Nyx and Sidian had performed quick shaves at water crossings while Raine and Naiah's thunder shoved damp rags beneath their clothes, cleansing their skin as best they could whilst fully dressed—a pitiful substitute for real baths.

Too many days had passed since they'd soaked themselves in volcanic hot springs, and Sidian didn't have to be as fastidious as a dragon to crave soap and warm water.

"I'm sorry," Raine said, feeling like an inconsiderate lout. He moved to the other side of the tub and grabbed the ash pail from the floor before offering it to Sidian by its wire handle. "Here."

Sidian accepted the ash bucket graciously and knelt below the tub. Several shovels of ash put the flames to bed. With the fire out, the water would cool, but it would take forever for it to reach a temperature safe for Sidian. Raine frowned, considering.

Aha. There was over a foot of space between the water and the tub's edge. He could mix the cooler water from the spigot with the scalding water of his bath. Raine operated the pump, swiftly working the lever until the water rose an inch from the rim.

Sidian dipped a finger.

"Still too hot," Raine surmised, watching his mate's skin redden where it had been submerged.

"It'll cool down soon enough." Sidian settled in the chair, draping his arms over its back.

Raine reapplied soap to his washcloth since he'd dropped it in the water. The bathing room was quieter than ever without the noise from the fire. He tried not to think too hard about his mate watching him as he bathed. It was old hat, by now. Or should have been.

But this time was different. This time, Sidian knew they were mates. He had touched Raine. Kissed him. Found pleasure with him.

Raine's blood quickened with the direction of his thoughts. His cock began to harden.

Raine squeezed his thighs together, horrified. What kind of perversion did he suffer from, that he could think of sex now, with the dying screams of the keep's guards still reverberating off the stone walls? His blood heated as the water cooled, and Raine wracked his brain for a distraction.

"So, what story do you think Naiah will tell tonight?"

"I don't think she's doing a story tonight."

Raine grimaced. Sidian was probably right. Naiah had regaled them with tales of dragon history each night on their journey from Moontop to the Hellhole. She seemed to really enjoy it. Raine knew he enjoyed listening. But after what they'd just endured ... The mood wasn't exactly set for stories.

"*You* could always tell me a story," Raine suggested hopefully. The more he learned about dragons, the more he wanted to know.

Their history was fascinating, focusing on individuals and communities. He'd never realized how impersonal human history was. It was so bland, so meaningless in a way that dragon lore never was.

"I had other plans." Sidian's voice was a smoky promise.

Oh, no. He'd nearly forgotten Sidian's intentions of consummating their bond. Raine's mind was unchanged. They could not mate. He didn't care if it meant a slow, painful death of heartsickness. Sidian wanted a wife. A human wife. And children. Sidian was not going to throw away his future to save Raine's life. Not if Raine had any say in it.

Sidian shifted on the chair, his stare smoldering. Unease trickled down Raine's spine even as lust ignited in his lower belly.

Fucking hell. He would rend his beating heart from his own chest and present it to Sidian if the man asked. How was he going to find the strength to deny his mate anything, let alone something that Raine himself yearned for with his entire being?

"I think we should stick to a story," he said weakly.

Sidian's rich brown eyes were decadent with heat. He blinked, long and slow. "Very well," he murmured. "You can have a bath-time story."

Raine rolled his eyes at his mate's feigned obtuseness even as his belly flipped. The man knew Raine meant for the story to be at bedtime. But Sidian already said he had *other plans*. Plans that made Raine hotter than any amount of boiling water.

It didn't matter. He would thwart Sidian one way or another. He had to.

He had to because he loved him.

"Blaming yourself for events beyond your control is a trait you and the Dreaming Mother share." Raine straightened in surprise. Sidian surveyed his reaction with a hint of smugness, aware he'd snared him like an oblivious turkey. "The Dreaming Mother doesn't always have dreams. Sometimes, she has nightmares."

Nightmares? Gooseflesh pebbled along Raine's skin though his bathwater was still on the verge of scalding.

"Her sweetest dream and her worst nightmare share one thing in common. Both found a way out of her world and into ours. Thus, dragons and ichneumons were created."

Raine tilted his head. "Ichneumons?"

Sidian nodded. His expression was absolutely serious. "They're a type of weasel, long-bodied with narrow snouts."

A laugh escaped Raine before he could help it. "It sounds like the dreams and nightmares got mixed up. Oh, come on," he said at Sidian's quelling glare. "If massive, fire-breathing dragons are her dreams, how can harmless little weasels be her nightmares?"

"Who said they were harmless?"

"Well, they can't be capable of greater destruction than dragons." Raine's lips twisted into a bitter smile. "As Betony's storm was kind enough to demonstrate."

Sidian's mouth pressed into a firm line. "What does the Dreaming Mother love above all else? Her dragons," he stated, not waiting for Raine to respond. "She cherishes all of you. So, what do you think her worst nightmare consisted of?"

"Apparently, it consisted of weasels," Raine said drily.

"Ichneumons are the mortal enemies of dragons." Sidian's tone was stiff and chiding. "In the womb of her nightmares, they were equipped to kill your species with brutal efficiency. Fortunately for dragons, it worked both ways. They, too, were equipped with the unique means to destroy the ichneumons."

Raine's ironic humor abated. The way Sidian spoke ... It was like something terrible and violent had occurred. A war of sorts. Dreams versus nightmares.

"Either species killed the other on sight. It was a bloodbath that lasted for decades," Sidian said, confirming Raine's thoughts. "And every time a dragon perished, the Dreaming Mother blamed herself. So great was her dismay, the earth crumbled and split. Rivers sank through the cracks and disappeared. Volcanoes spewed enough ash to choke the sun and sky, which resulted in a hundred-year winter. Her guilt was poisonous to herself and her loved ones," Sidian said meaningfully. He skewered Raine with a pointed look.

Raine's head fell back on a sigh. "I understand." He glimpsed Sidian's skeptical expression. "I won't wallow in blame," he added more earnestly. "After you reminded me of what happened with Tayo, it sunk in. No part of his cruelty or corruption was your fault. And the indiscriminate violence of Betony's storm is not mine."

A complex mixture of emotions spread and mingled like watercolors over Sidian's features, too fast and too blended for Raine to determine any one of them. In moments, his expression shuttered to impassivity.

"Tayo was a lesson," he said gruffly. "Like tonight. Our responsibility is to learn from them and not repeat our errors. The Dreaming Mother discovered this truth, as well. Once she made peace with her turmoil, the earth ceased breaking. The volcanoes swallowed their bilge and lava cooled to stone."

"What about the ichneumons? Dragons are still around, so I assume they found a way to destroy them."

"In a manner of speaking." Sidian trailed the water with a fingertip. The temperature must have been right because he reached for the black zipper at his throat and pulled it down. The Guardian jumpsuit peeled away as if he was shedding black snakeskin. Sidian stepped out of his crumpled hose like a god born from darkness.

A smattering of dark curls trailed down the carved V-shape above his pelvis. Raine's silver eyes followed those dark curls like a pigeon chasing breadcrumbs. Sidian's cock bobbed, flushed and heavy with arousal, at the base of his curls.

As Sidian set one foot over the side of the tub, Raine stood. Water sluiced down his frame, trailing the gentle ridges and hollows of his torso. His mouth went dry at Sidian's hawklike scrutiny. His mate seemed captivated by the water beading down Raine's abdominals and lower, where it dripped from his jutting erection.

Sidian's other leg followed, bringing him fully inside the tub. As he stalked closer, Raine edged away.

"I don't get it," he said hurriedly, desperate to stop his mate from the carnal intent simmering like flames in his eyes. "What happened?"

A flash of confusion told Raine his mate had forgotten all about the ichneumons. Sidian blinked, as if struggling back to his story. "The dragons and ichneumons were evenly matched for a time. The ichneumons were able to sneak and hide. They used ambush tactics to great effect. But it took a dozen ichneumons to take down a single dragon, and they suffered heavy casualties to accomplish it. Their ambushes occurred less and less frequently. Until there weren't enough ichneumons alive to organize another attack. The few survivors fled north, choosing to make their homes away from dragon territory."

As Sidian spoke, he inched forward. His steps were so smoothly perfect, the bathwater didn't murmur or swish in his wake. Raine watched, entranced and a little awed by his mate's graceful stalking.

Sidian gripped his wrists, jolting him from his stupor. Their cocks dragged together lazily as Sidian leaned forward, closing the distance between them.

Raine's lips parted without permission. He held his breath as Sidian neared, equally desperate and terrified to feel his mate's mouth on him. This perfect, gorgeous, supreme man whom he loved.

Whom he loved.

Fuck. What was he doing? As Sidian's warm breath caressed his lips, Raine broke away and retreated several steps. Water sloshed and sprayed with his movements. The edge of the tub's rim caught him mid-thigh, and he fell backwards.

"Oof." He landed solidly against the stone floor, slipping on a splash of soapy water. Sidian smirked down at him over the washtub, his proudly erect cock peering over the rim. Raine closed his eyes and groaned.

CHAPTER
TWENTY-ONE

Raine stood at the threshold of his bedchamber and stared, his posture slack with dismay. Water droplets leaked from his hair, trailing down his back and shoulders and legs. A towel, wrapped snugly around his waist, absorbed what it could. The rest of the water formed a shallow puddle at his feet. And still, he stared.

Well-muscled arms snaked around Raine's waist from behind and pulled him against a toned chest. Raine closed his eyes and savored Sidian's strength, inhaling his clean, soapy scent and that underlying sweetness that made his blood sing.

"Hey," Sidian murmured, a hint of a question in his tone. Raine knew the moment Sidian peered into the bedchamber around him. His frame stiffened to a statue.

Raine wasn't sure who had destroyed his room and belongings. It was a tossup between odious Olan and the various hunters who had lain in wait for Raine's return, hoping to catch him unawares.

His four-poster bed was stripped of its linens, the mattress gutted as if a coterie of groundhogs had made their burrow within. His armoire, carved of the same polished walnut as his bedframe, was smashed to splinters. The desk he'd used throughout his boyhood was upturned, legs broken. Everywhere, there were split pillows, goose down, broken glass, and scattered pages torn from his favorite books.

In short, the place was savaged.

Sidian tugged him backwards. "Come on," he said with aching tenderness, as if Raine was as delicate as a white violet petal.

He let his mate direct him to the other bedchamber—his father's. It was mercifully untouched. Raine wasn't sure he could have borne it if his father's things were also ruined.

In fact, the room had been left in such a manner, it served as a brutal reminder of Arastus Chambrin's untimely demise.

Everywhere, there were signs of a life interrupted. His father's spare boots rested in a corner. A steel sword balanced haphazardly against a desk littered with correspondence, most of it opened. An unfinished missive was set aside, as if his father had grown weary and decided to finish it later. The bed linens were rumpled from his father's abrupt midnight awakening, from when Raine had barged in, begging for assistance. Assistance which had gotten his father killed.

Raine slumped on the edge of the bed, half-expecting his father to enter the chamber any moment, though he knew it was impossible. Surrounded by his father's smell and personal belongings made his death feel both unreal and final. A sharp pain and a dull throb all at once.

The mattress dipped as Sidian sat beside him. Without a word, he reached both arms around Raine and pulled him into his chest. Raine clung to him, wrapping his arms around Sidian's bare, silken back, still steamy from their bath. Sidian hugged Raine to him so tightly, it was as if he was trying to fuse their bodies.

Raine closed his eyes and relaxed. Every fiber of muscle, every string of sinew, every line of bone turned into soft, malleable clay in Sidian's arms. He wished he was clay. Wished they both were, so that they could fuse together in truth. So they could be one body instead of two. Then this wonderous feeling could last forever, surely.

He absorbed Sidian's comforting strength like a flower in sunlight. It sutured his cracked and bleeding heart, soothing wounds he thought could never be healed.

Hours or minutes later, Raine straightened from their embrace. "What are we going to do?" he asked. Frustrated anger warred with despair as he considered the clusterfuck ahead. They had a castle full of murderous dragons and petrified humans to contend with, let alone the corpses and ruined structures outside. "Their actions can't just go unpunished, right?"

Sidian's arms fell away gently, his hands running down the lengths of Raine's arms in a parting caress that made him shiver. Raine remained motionless as Sidian stood and moved towards their rucksacks, which rested near the doorframe. The knot of his towel was loose, threatening to unravel as he walked.

Raine swallowed, tracing the powerful planes of his mate's back and the curve of his ass. He wasn't willing Sidian's towel to fall. *He wasn't.*

"There's no justice system in place for this situation," Sidian said calmly. He knelt and rifled through his pack, an unfair test of his towel knot's integrity as well as Raine's control over his rogue, roving eyeballs. "Those dragons answer to Betony's authority alone, and I don't foresee her exacting any sort of punishment."

Raine looked away, suffused with bitterness. "How could she, when she'd have to punish herself, as well?"

Betony could have used her "resonant roar" to stop her storm at any time. But no. She'd been as eager to murder the keep's human occupants as the rest of the parents. Instead of instilling order, she'd taken her pound of flesh along with them.

Sidian extracted two spare Guardian uniforms and tossed one to Raine. He caught it and let the slippery black fabric pool in his lap. For whatever reason, his mate insisted upon garbing him like a hunter.

Gazing at it, he saw a different Guardian uniform in his mind. The one his father had extended to him months ago, when Raine had come crawling through the chimney in search of aid with that doomed rescue mission. Clenching his fingers into the fabric, he ached at the memory. If he'd never asked his father to help free the Cavern dragons, Arastus Chambrin might still be alive.

Raine imagined going back in time and changing things. Imagined leaving twenty-one frail, filth-crusted dragons in their cages in exchange for more time with his father. And he suddenly knew he wouldn't change things, even if he could.

The Nine had already been onto his father. They'd been toying with him like some sort of game piece. Slowly stripping his authority. Leaving him in the dark. And once his father ran out of usefulness, they would have ordered his execution on a discreet slip of parchment, passed from a blood-soaked chieftain's hand to one of their Guardian units.

By freeing the Cavern, his father had died a little sooner. But he'd also lived to see his dream accomplished. It was a shattering realization, but it eased Raine in a way nothing else had, to know that his father wouldn't have changed anything, either.

At the sound of a zipper, Raine looked up. Sidian, now fully outfitted, pushed his damp hair back and surveyed him. "Your focus can't be vengeance, or you'll be just as bad as Betony's storm."

Struggling back to their earlier conversation, Raine blew out a breath. "Maybe I don't care about being bad."

At that, Sidian smiled. "You couldn't be bad if you tried. You are so pure, it should be nauseating."

"Bullshit." Raine sputtered. "I'm *bad*. In all sorts of ways, too," he added, scowling as Sidian's smile morphed into a smirk. "I cheat at wrestling," he said. "And card games, even when there are silvans involved. I steal and break rules and lie to get out of trouble. And I'm so vain, it's obnoxious. I think that nobody is better looking than me. Well, I think you are," he amended. "But only you. And I feel smug about it."

"Smug about me or smug about yourself?"

Sidian's face was deadpan, but his eyes glimmered in a way that made Raine suspect his mate was teasing him. He bristled, indignant that Sidian wasn't taking him seriously.

"Both," he snapped, throwing up his hands. "I'm smug about how good I look, and I'm even more smug over you. So, there. I'm not pure, at all," he finished hotly.

"I see." Sidian nodded, looking grave. "Thank you for clarifying. I'm confused about another matter, however." He stepped closer.

Prowled, really. His shoulders swayed as he walked, his gaze sharper than a knife. "How can you be smug about having me when you insist on not having me?"

Raine jerked his eyes away and stared at the floor. His pulse thrummed with the cadence of panicked wings. "You already know why I can't have you."

Did they have to talk about this again? Raine hated thinking about it, let alone discussing it. Being flayed alive had to hurt less than this miserable reality—having his mate so, so close ... and yet, so very far. A vast, insurmountable chasm would always separate them.

"Look at me." Raine's gut clenched at Sidian's low, commanding tone. When he raised his eyes, Sidian said, "Explain it to me again, because I still don't understand."

"You told me yourself," Raine said haltingly, determined to keep his voice steady and his eyes dry. "You don't like *men*. You plan to have a wife someday."

Surprise spread across Sidian's features, widening his eyes as his mouth opened. "I did say that," he murmured, almost to himself. Louder, he said, "In my defense, I had no way of knowing my wife would be male—"

"Excuse me?" Raine slapped a hand to his chest. A wave of outrage washed through his despair. "If we mated, I would not be your *wife*. I would be your husband."

"Same difference." Sidian shrugged. It was absolutely not the same difference, but before Raine could say so, Sidian continued. "It doesn't matter how you label it. Husband. Wife. Mate. None of that changes what we are to each other."

"And what's that?" Raine demanded.

"Everything," Sidian replied, as if it were obvious.

Raine's mind unraveled like a thousand snipped threads. In the span of a single heartbeat, he replayed Sidian's response half a dozen times and still didn't understand. His mate almost sounded like …

Raine couldn't bring himself to complete the thought. The impossibility of it made him *ache*.

"No." He shook his head, trying to clear it. "I'm not your choice, Sidian. You only want to mate with me to save my life. You aren't attracted to me, and that's *fine*," he stressed. "It's fine. You are who you are. You have every right to your preferences, but I won't be some … some lifelong regret or the world's saddest pity fuck."

Sidian's jaw worked silently, as if he couldn't decide what to say first. Abruptly, he turned and marched to his pack. He dug through it and extracted a rectangular object. Then approached Raine and extended it with an impatient jerk of his arm.

There, hovering inches from Raine's chest, was a stunning calfskin book. Intricate silver foils were stamped into the cover, which depicted an iridescent sea horse. Accepting the book, he tilted it this way and that. The seahorse sparkled like an ever-shifting moonbow, exactly like his hair.

"What is this?" Raine asked, already peeling back the cover. He fanned the book's lusciously thick pages. All of them were blank.

"A sketchbook," Sidian said. "I gave Nyx some silvans before he went to Pashun. I told him which shop to go to and what to purchase. Ask me why."

Raine looked up, his heart palpitating in his throat. "Why?"

"Because I love you."

Raine sucked in a breath. He couldn't have heard that right. He must have misunderstood. Sidian was trying to say he loved him as a friend. That *had* to be it. There was no other possibility.

His neck craned as Sidian stepped closer. "You asked me if I *liked* men. I don't. Now, ask me if I *like* women."

Raine trembled, his hands as shaky as an unsettled sea where they gripped the sketchbook. He already knew the answer to this question, so why was he so affected?

"Do you like women?" he asked once he was sure he could get the words out without his voice quavering like the rest of him.

"No," Sidian said, his voice hard. "I don't."

"But-But what about Lyka and—"

"I said it before, and I'll say it again," Sidian said, cutting him off. "I'm not the same man who took you into custody. I don't like men and I don't like women. I like *you*. I don't just like you. I love you. And you love me."

Raine's mouth fell open. "What?" He forced a laugh. It sounded like a moose dying and he stopped. "I never said that."

"You don't have to." Sidian narrowed at him. "The way you look at me ... It's the same way dreamers gaze at stars and sailors stare at the sea. As if I am everything you'll ever want or need. As if I'm the answer to your life's purpose."

A tear splashed on Raine's hand, where it covered the sketchbook. He blinked down at it in surprise, and another tear plopped. He hadn't realized he was crying.

He also hadn't realized quite how transparent he'd been. All this time, he had worked assiduously to spare Sidian from any love-laden confessions, but none of his restraint had mattered. Because, apparently, he'd been showing Sidian instead.

A familiar callused palm cupped his chin and pulled his misty gaze upward. "And since you still haven't realized," Sidian whispered, smoothing the moisture from his cheek with a thumb. "It's the same way that I look at you."

Raine's face crumpled. He dropped the sketchbook to shove Sidian's hand away, then buried his face in his palms. "I'm either dreaming or I'm dead." He moaned through his fingers. "Oh, fuck. Did I die during the attack on the keep?" He raised his head, aghast. "I did, didn't I? And you said my focus can't be vengeance. Are you kidding? They killed me. There'd better be some fucking vengeance."

As Raine stood, the uniform and sketchbook slid off his lap and onto the floor with a soft thud. He sucked in a breath, unprepared for how close it put him to Sidian. He could count each individual eyelash.

Without any warning, Sidian's hand fisted his hair and tugged him forward. He claimed Raine's mouth with brutal swiftness. Raine gasped in shock, and Sidian's satin tongue invaded, moving against his in long, sweeping strokes that caught his blood on fire.

Raine gripped Sidian's shoulders, stretching black lotus silk as his fingers dug for purchase. His body was too molten to stand unsupported. Without Sidian to cling to, he would have melted to the floor, as formless as lava.

Surprise had made him pliant, parting his lips sweetly for Sidian's plunder. But now, desire raged like a furnace, making him bold. He met Sidian's kiss stroke-for-stroke. Sharp, vicious need throbbed between his legs, where all his iron concentrated.

Again, without warning, Sidian tore away. His mouth was wet and swollen. Raven black hair fell into his pitch-dark eyes. His shoulders heaved as he sucked air.

"You're not dead, idiot. Right now, you have two choices. Get dressed so we can see to the aftermath of the attack, or lay back and prepare for me to consummate our bond from now until next week."

CHAPTER TWENTY-TWO

Raine heard the noisy hum of feasting dragons long before he and Sidian reached the great hall. They walked quickly, side-by-side with a matching stride that made his chest swell. They were acting like a pair, moving in sync as if they were two sides of the same silvan. Two halves of the same soul.

Sidian caught his stare from the corner of his eye and smirked. Raine's ears grew warm. His answering smile felt shy, but he couldn't help it. Hours from now, he was going to join bodies with Sidian. They were going to be lovers. It was as thrilling as it was mortifying.

And almost too incredible to be true. He might yet think he was dead or dreaming, but Sidian had cured him of that notion while he was getting dressed. Raine massaged the right globe of his bottom, where his mate had decided to *pinch* him. Sidian obviously didn't know his own strength, because it had seriously hurt.

It also worked. Raine was awake. He knew it. He knew that everything that just happened was real and true. It didn't make it feel any less like a dream, but at least he knew it wasn't. And if his faith started to slip, he could always prod the bruise forming on his ass cheek to remind himself.

The din grew impossibly loud, like stepping inside a beehive, as they entered the hall. The enormous oak dining table, designed to fit a squadron of soldiers, was full on one side. Betony's storm, draped with an eclectic assortment of linens to shield their nudity, ate from heaping platters of roasted pork and mutton. It was a feast fit for a holiday and could have only been prepared by the kitchen staff.

Raine's lips curled in a sneer. What kind of demented bastards demanded a hot meal from the very people they sought to slaughter? As their jaws worked and lips smacked, he wanted to bash their teeth in and watch them choke to death on bones and blood. He wanted retribution for the innocents they harmed. The people they murdered.

Fortunately for them, his fury was tempered by the radiant joy and love filtering through his bloodstream. Raine wanted many violent ends but found the control to abstain. Sidian's palm slid into his, and Raine's anger cooled further. His mate was right. If he lashed out at Betony's storm, it would only perpetuate an endless cycle of death and destruction.

Hatred couldn't be vanquished with more hate. They had to educate the parents. Foster empathy and respect. Build a bridge between species and find a way to coexist harmoniously.

Lenka appeared, an overburdened tray of sliced venison balanced on her palms. She wore a powder blue nightgown, her dark hair slick with sweat from the kitchen stoves. Raine squeezed Sidian's hand roughly, seeing red as she served the monsters who had attempted to kill her sister, Lissy.

Who had attempted to kill *Sidian*.

Scanning the table, Raine sought dragons with telltale wounds on their chests and ribs. He might not be able to sentence Betony's storm to death or incarceration, but one of these dragons had dared to breathe fire at his mate. Another tried to murder a cowering maid. Neither was going to slide.

Frustration thrashed in his chest as he surveyed the dragons. Blood stains marred each of their draped linens. Splotches large and small bloomed like red ink across their chests, sides and backs. Some were dark and dry. Others were bright, still bleeding.

No dragon was better off than any other. It was the perfect camouflage, the perpetrators indistinguishable by injuries alone.

Lenka approached the table with the cautious bearing of an abused stray. She flinched as a female dragon with emerald hair snatched the platter impatiently, without a word of thanks.

"We need more water," a red male snapped.

"And pork," a blue male added beside him, waving a T-bone mauled to its gristle. "Well, go get it," he barked when Lenka hesitated. He leaned over, addressing the red male beside him as he said, "Humans are so feeble-minded. Killing the rest of them would be an act of mercy."

Lenka backed away from the table until she was a few steps from an exit, then swiftly spun and darted through. For a moment, Raine was tempted to shove the blue dragon's greasy leftover bone through his eye socket.

No. He clenched his fists and forced his gaze away from the table. He needed to check on Lenka and the rest of the staff. They were his priority, not the cretins laying waste to the keep's winter larder. Raine skirted the hall, trying not to draw attention to himself as he made his way to the door Lenka disappeared through.

After a few steps, he realized Sidian was following him. "No," he said, turning to place a hand on his mate's shoulder. "You're probably famished. Stay. Eat." Raine pointed at the far end of the table, where Nyx sat with Tejayla on his right side and two empty chairs on his left. "You can sit by your brother."

"Where are you going?"

"The kitchens," he answered, more curtly than he intended.

"I will accompany you."

Raine took in Sidian's firm mouth and slanted brows. The stubborn tilt of his chin. Swallowing a sigh, Raine nodded.

Hot, humid air enveloped them as they entered the kitchens. Steamy plumes wafted aromatic garlic and thyme and scalded milk. Trista pulled trays of freshly baked bread from an oven while Ivarra keeled a vat of pudding, her cheeks flushed and damp from the heat. Wylan stood at an old, scarred table, where he was breaking down whole, roasted hens. He separated breasts and thighs, passing them to Lenka. She arranged a tray with the pieces, dressing them with gravy.

"What the fuck are you doing?"

Everyone halted. It was as if time itself froze. Ivarra's arm stilled over the large, steel pot she stirred. Trista's hand paused near the loaves she was spreading with butter. Wylan dangled a roasted thigh by its ankle joint mid-air. Lenka was a statue beside him.

Wylan recovered first, wiping his greasy hands on a worn towel as he faced Raine. "Young Master, forgive me. We're working as quickly as we can to serve your companions."

Rage surged, threatening to burst the veins throbbing in Raine's temples. "Why? I didn't ask you to do that. I wouldn't. Those dragons" —he gestured vaguely in the direction of the great hall— "almost killed Lissy. The Divine Father knows who all is dead. It's nearly midnight. The kitchen should be closed." He paused, panting heavily as he took them in. Trista and Ivarra, chambermaids. Wylan, a steward. Lenka, a laundress. "Where are all the kitchen staff? Where's Tavish? And Melly? Ellowyn? Rance?"

"In Rokeshin, Young Master," Wylan said. "With General Olan and the brigade."

Raine kneaded his forehead where his pulse pounded his skull. "Okay. Fine. What about Moranda and her crew? Where are they?"

Wylan twisted a hand towel, eyes darting. "Well, uh. The thing is ... Nyx can tell you."

"O-kay," Raine said slowly. There was so much going on, he wasn't even going to touch that. "Listen. Not all the dragons in the dining hall are bad. Some of them are dear friends and the best people I know. But I would never, *ever* expect you to serve them. The only thing you should be worried about is grieving. Tallying the dead and preparing them for the Divine Palace above."

Trista set down her spoon and butter boat. Tears glistened in her honey-brown eyes. "We weren't sure what to do. When we saw the d-dragons, they looked human, but we knew right away they weren't. A dragon lady—Evin—told us we were safe. She wanted to know of a good place for everyone to await you. We were so afraid, especially because some of the dragons kept making comments. It sounded like they meant to finish us off. It was Wylan's idea to have us serve food to occupy them until you reappeared."

Wylan nodded, his wrinkled face resembling an earnest raisin. "Many of them looked upon us with such violence, I feared they would resume their assault. Feeding them has kept them occupied, and now you are here to direct matters as you wish." He bowed deeply.

Raine clenched his teeth but didn't correct Wylan's deferential display. Terror and grief were stark in the staff's eyes. These humans craved order and direction. After the hell he'd brought to their doorstep, the least he could do was be the strength they needed.

"Finish cooking the food underway, then close the kitchens," he announced.

They scurried like mice, working their stations with renewed purpose. Wylan lifted a meat cleaver, its square blade streaked with grease and bits of herbs, and resumed carving the hens. His arthritic hands were slow and unskilled. Raine imagined Oka watching and almost cracked a smile. The green dragon wouldn't last ten seconds before pushing Wylan aside and taking over.

"I don't understand," Raine said. Lenka grabbed the now-full platter of poultry and left for the dining hall. Wylan continued transferring breasts and thighs to another serving platter, which had rested beneath the other. "Where are the war dragons?"

"The war dragons were relocated a sennight ago." Wylan set his knife down to face him once more. "It was a matter of great discretion. Only General Olan and the dragon handlers know their whereabouts."

It was such a strange answer, Raine could only blink. The war dragons had never left Chambrin Keep. Not *ever*. It didn't make sense. Had the Nine anticipated that the parents would attack the keep and decided it was too risky to have the war dragons present?

But then, that didn't explain why the soldiers were also away.

"What business does Olan have in Rokeshin, that he needed the entire brigade and kitchen staff to accompany him?"

"General Olan was already in Rokeshin. He is away from the keep much of the time, in meetings with the Nine. The soldiers and the majority of the staff left only recently. To attend the succession." At Raine's nonplussed look, Wylan added, "Chieftain Brandor of Rokeshin has passed."

Ah. Well, that explained the droves of traffic on the roads. Thousands of Valdenians flocked to a chieftain's resident city whenever they died, to pay their last respects.

Sidian's fingers dug into Raine's bicep. He leaned in and whispered urgently, "This is our chance."

The warm current of Sidian's breath teased his ear, and he shivered. What was Sidian talking about? Raine opened his mouth to voice that very question, then promptly shut it. If his mate had to speak in hushed tones, presumably he couldn't elaborate without privacy.

Addressing Wylan, Raine said, "Once the kitchens are closed, please gather the remaining staff to help collect and identify the dead outside. We'll place them in the Roost, for now. The lower level is fine. We'll arrange a pyre in the morning."

The steward hesitated. "Young Master, what of the dead we can't recognize?"

There are bound to be plenty of those, Raine thought grimly. "If there are doubts, we can set those bodies aside in a separate pile."

He made for the garden exit, Sidian on his heels.

"Where are you going?" Trista called, her voice high and thin.

"To get started," Raine answered without turning.

The scents of smoke and char greeted them on a rush of cold wind. Fire blazed along the bathhouse roof in the distance, flames lashing the black sky like hellish whips. The bleachers in the training yard were nearly consumed. Reams of foul smoke billowed from all directions, indicators of the many fires he couldn't see from the garden's narrow vantage.

It had evidently been too much to expect Betony's storm to come snuff out their fiery ejections. No, they'd rather sit at his father's table and gorge themselves. A lavish feast for a massacre well done.

The heels of his father's spare boots clipped against the flagstone path as Raine walked forward aimlessly. He didn't know where to begin. Deceased guards peppered Chambrin's grounds like smoky charcoal slabs. Even using a process of elimination, they might not be able to identify each individual corpse. Fire was a terrible, defacing death. Most of the dead were bound to be charred beyond recognition.

A hand grabbed his shoulder, halting him. Raine allowed himself to be turned. Sidian's eyes shone like dark stars as he drew Raine to him, their noses almost touching.

"The Nine will be in Rokeshin." Sidian spoke tensely, dropping each word like a weight. "All of them."

"The succession ceremony," Raine said, nodding. "To think, we damn near ended up in Rokeshin. It would have been a disaster. Well" —he grimaced— "an even worse disaster."

If such a thing were possible. Though, Raine had to concede it was. Going to Rokeshin would have sealed their death warrants. Not only would all nine chieftains be in Rokeshin to attend the succession, but so, too, would the bulk of the guild and Valdenia's military. Not to mention half of the country.

Raine had never lived through a succession, but previous ones were occasionally talked about. Until the succession was complete, stores would remain closed. Business would cease. Valdenia would hold its breath like a great dragon, and not come alive again until it exhaled, expelling flames onto Chieftain Brandor's pyre and sending his spirit to the Divine Father's palace.

"You aren't getting it," Sidian said, shaking him slightly by the shoulders. "We should have gone to Rokeshin. We need to go *now*."

"Are you insane? All nine Chieftains are there. It'll be swarming with Guardians and soldiers. We need to find out where Olan stashed the war dragons and try to reach them while the chieftains are distracted."

Sidian rested his forehead against Raine's.

"Aren't you sick of running?" Sidian's fingertips skimmed Raine's shoulders and neck. Pleasure sparked along his skin, raising gooseflesh as Sidian's hands buried into the base of his damp braid. "The Nine are gathered. That makes them vulnerable. To attack," he stressed, his breath warm on Raine's mouth.

"Attack?" Raine echoed dumbly. It was difficult to concentrate with his mate so close. Sidian smelled like one of his favorite soaps, a blend of cedar and clary sage that was sweet and bright yet warmly relaxing. Raine wanted to melt over him like a pat of butter.

Sidian groaned and stepped away, withdrawing his hands from Raine's hair. "Maybe you'll think more clearly if I give you some space." His dry tone didn't mask his breathlessness any more than his Guardian hose masked …

Oh. Raine arched a brow as he beheld Sidian in all his turgid glory.

Following Raine's gaze, Sidian glanced down at himself and snorted. "Unlike you, I remain capable of higher thought processes during arousal."

"My thoughts are coming along just fine, thank you," Raine said in a deliberately prim tone, as if he wasn't inwardly panting for it as bad as Sidian. Worse, even. "Are you actually suggesting we go to Rokeshin and assassinate all nine leaders of our country? That is *treason*. A crime I was seriously offended to be accused of in my wanted posters, by the way. And even if I was willing to do something that crazy, we would never get near them. They'll be surrounded by the entire guild and a veritable army."

"What will you do after we retrieve the war dragons?" Sidian gesticulated wildly as he spoke. "Disappear into a volcano? Flee north like the ichneumons? Keep living in fear and secrecy as the guild picks you off one by one?"

"I haven't thought that far ahead." Raine rubbed the back of his neck, looking away. "Reaching this point feels impossible already. I can't—" He stopped, then carefully amended his statement. "Before an hour ago, I wasn't able to see a future for myself," he admitted softly.

Sidian snatched the dark, silken material on his chest, wrenching Raine to him with an audible growl. "Well, you fucking have one," he said menacingly, then shoved him away. "So, start thinking like someone who is going to be around for the next thousand years. You retrieve the war dragons, then what? The Nine will never stop hunting you. They created a secret society dedicated to eradicating your entire species. Watchtowers litter the country, manned twenty-four-seven so no dragon can fly undetected. They dispatch hundreds of trained warriors bearing weapons crafted from the bones of your ancestors to kill you."

Raine's mouth worked silently but no sound came. He didn't know what to say. The plight of dragons was hopeless when looked at directly. He preferred to glimpse their situation peripherally, in small doses. That way, things didn't seem so insurmountable. That way, he could keep going.

Sidian's features twisted with scorn. "You're a fucking dragon. It's time to stop acting like prey. We need to eliminate the threat at the source. The guild is only an instrument. The Nine are the hands that wield it."

Everything Sidian said made sense. Terrible, damning sense.

It was like Raine had been zoomed into a painting, focused on a single detail. Sidian's words yanked back his head and forced him to take in the convoluted canvas in its entirety. The matter was plain, their only solution evident.

"You're right." Raine sighed. "That was always the next step. I just didn't want to see it. But Sidian, attacking them in Rokeshin is impossible. It'll be an exact replica of Gargantha's invasion, with us outnumbered thousands to one. There'd be no contest."

"You're right," Sidian said easily. Raine straightened hopefully, then slumped as Sidian continued. "But we don't have to fight the guild or army. Our targets are the Nine. We treat it like a mission. An assassination. Get in, do the job, get out."

"You're not hearing me. Sidian, *please listen*. It's a suicide mission. We'll kill the Nine, probably. If we're lucky. But there's no way we're making it out of Rokeshin alive afterward. Not with that many hunters on us. Why don't we plan it for after the succession? That way, there's no rush. We can be careful. Stalk them in their home cities and hit them at their most vulnerable."

"Interesting. Tell me, then. When are the Nine at their most vulnerable?" Sidian touched a finger to the side of his chin and regarded Raine silently.

Raine rubbed his palms against his sides, hesitating. For some reason, Sidian reminded him of a spider. His question, an invitation to join him on his web.

"I don't know. When they're asleep in their beds? Darning their socks? Taking a shit?"

Nearly any answer was better than *hanging out in the military capital of Valdenia*. At least, Raine thought so. But Sidian shook his head. His arms crossed over his chest, stance widening. He looked like a strict captain about to school his undisciplined unit.

"The Nine are paranoid. They have traps and extreme security measures in place to protect them in their home cities. They are *never* unguarded. The rule of thumb is, if you see one chieftain, at least four Guardian units are lurking unseen. That's their minimum guard."

"It's because they failed to capture all the dragons," Raine said, his stomach sinking. "They know the free dragons can strike at any moment, so they protect themselves."

Sidian nodded. "It explains why they employ the guild to hunt you all so obsessively."

"Not because dragons are evil," Raine murmured. "But because they're afraid."

"They should be afraid." Sidian's visage darkened. "They should be terrified, considering how guilty they are."

Raine thought of Eddic, Tyrus, and Vanwert. Of Pare and Brandor and Morseth. He didn't need guilt to feed his fear. It blossomed all on its own, a snarling topiary of constricting vines and jagged thorns.

"Are you sure it's not better to wait?" He was being a coward, but he couldn't help it. The Nine were so foul, so off-putting, they made him want to flee the country. Hell, flee the planet, if possible. Was there a way for dragons to get back inside the Dreaming Mother's dreams?

"If we wait to attack the Nine one at a time, they'll be forewarned and go to ground. They'll erect so many defenses, it'll be impossible to reach them with our limited numbers. But if we take them out all at once, before they can prepare or hide, we can win. Their agenda will die with them."

"That just means we must attack them at the same *time*, not the same *place*. After the succession, we can split up and send smaller groups of dragons to all nine cities. If we set a date and time, then attack in unison, the chieftains won't be forewarned or have a chance to hide."

"In that scenario, if just one chieftain gets away or defeats us, it'll all be for nothing. I've seen some of their defenses. It's better to take them out while they're gathered in a strange city, where they lack the advantages of their homes."

Raine's temples started throbbing again. He didn't like this. Thus far, he'd undergone two rescue missions, and both ended in absolute disaster. The first had cost Raine his father. The second, his home. Over a dozen fires continued feeding around them. In the morning, almost every building sans the keep and Roost would be little more than hollow, blackened ruins.

Sidian wasn't suggesting a rescue, though, was he? As a matter of fact, it was the precise opposite of a rescue mission. He wanted Raine and the dragons to embark on a murder mission.

The difference wasn't between saving lives and taking them, Raine realized with a start. It was about passivity versus action.

They hadn't been rescuing dragons. They'd been stealing them. As if *they* were the criminals. And worse, they'd done so while enabling the Nine to continue their dragon slaughtering campaign unchallenged.

Inaction was only justifiable to a degree, and the fire was blazing now. Too hot to be denied.

Rokeshin or no Rokeshin, it was time to face the enemy and remind the Nine of who they were dealing with. Not prey. Not criminals. Not cowards.

Dragons.

"Think about it this way," Sidian continued, unaware of Raine's racing thoughts. "Rokeshin is so stacked with soldiers and

Guardians, us going there is the last thing the Nine will expect. Which means they will never be more off-guard than now. That's why this is our chance—"

"Okay," Raine said, cutting him off. "I agree with you. We need to go to Rokeshin. I didn't want to believe you because I was afraid. I still am, to be honest." Raine swallowed, clenching his fists. "But I'm more afraid of what will happen if we don't go."

Sidian's features grew impossibly soft before tightening. "You have no reason to fear," he said, deadly serious. "I'll slaughter anyone or anything that tries to harm you."

A flippant retort danced on Raine's tongue, but it melted away like spun sugar at the raw emotion emanating from Sidian. For the first time, he recognized the dark intensity lining Sidian's expression as love.

"Likewise," he whispered.

CHAPTER TWENTY-THREE

Locating charred corpses in the dead of night proved difficult. Burnt bodies were lost to shadows and rubble and overgrown grasses, transforming his and Sidian's task into a grisly scavenger hunt.

That's exactly what Raine felt like, too. A scavenger, seeking the cooked carrion of the keep's guards.

Perhaps it was wrong of him, but Raine was relieved that all they found were curtain guards. Betony's storm hadn't massacred a bunch of defenseless domestics, as he'd feared. These men might not have deserved this fate, but none of them were exactly innocent, either.

Together, he and Sidian transferred the guards' ruined bodies to the Roost. Without ever discussing it, they alternated who got the head or feet, working in grim silence.

Many of the bodies were dry, dragon fire having blazed every last drop of moisture from their remains. Those corpses were as light as children, spilling ash over Raine's hands and arms.

It was worse when the bodies were moist. Their black flesh was a brittle overlay that split with the slightest pressure, revealing raw pinkish-red insides no eyes were meant to see. The first time he grabbed onto a wet one, the body slipped from his fingers, leaving slick black peels like burnt potato skins on his palms.

"I need another bath," he muttered through his teeth as they deposited another heavy, wet corpse into the vacant Roost.

They were supposed to be separating the bodies into two piles. Those that were identifiable and those that required ... investigating. But it had turned into a matter of wet versus dry. The dry, withered corpses of ash and bone automatically went into the mystery pile, and the wet ones went into the other. Their flesh, while ruined, was still mostly present and might lead to successful identifications.

Sidian wiped his brow with his forearm. Weak starlight filtered through the Roost's dual entryways, illuminating the gray smudge across his forehead as his arm dropped. "I'm exhausted. You're exhausted. The staff are exhausted. It's getting harder and harder to find bodies. We should turn in and resume in the morning."

Leave the dead to litter the grounds like trash? It didn't sit right with Raine. Who cared how tired and hungry he was, when these men would give anything to possess such earthly complaints once more?

He opened his mouth to tell Sidian he couldn't stop yet, but his gaze caught on his mate's slumped shoulders. Sidian's eyes were cast in shadow, but Raine could picture the purplish bruises underneath them.

The dead guards took precedence over Raine's earthly needs, but nothing came before his mate. They would have to resume on the morrow.

"Young Master." Raine jumped in surprise as Wylan's silhouette appeared in the ground-facing entryway. "The kitchen is closed, and we're here to help."

Weariness bent Wylan's spine like a sickle. The crooked backs of the pajama-clad staff behind him weren't much better. Towards the back of the group, someone released a three-syllable yawn. It set off a chain reaction that ended with Raine's own jaw cracking wide.

"Don't worry about it," he said. "The rest can wait 'til morning. Find your beds, all of you."

Raine wanted to say more. *Thank you for everything* and *I'm sorry*. He wanted to offer them enough silvans to retire rich and fat. He wanted to give them plots of land with farms and forests. And he really wanted to present them with the heads of certain dragons on golden platters.

But, like Sidian said, they were exhausted. None of that would erase their pain, and he didn't want to keep them from their well-deserved rest a moment longer.

"What about the dishes, Young Master? The meal is ongoing, but there will be much work to do once your companions are through supping."

"They're still eating? How long have we been out here?"

It felt like hours, but that was wrong. The sky was as black as it had been when they began.

"An hour," Wylan answered. He peered at the corpse piles, his voice noticeably thinner as he added, "You've been very efficient."

Yes, well. The unpleasantness of their task had lent him and Sidian a certain measure of swiftness. They must have gathered forty corpses in as many minutes before their progress slowed.

"Leave my *companions* to me," Raine said firmly. "Tomorrow promises to be a hard day for everyone. Go to bed, please. I need you fresh for the morning."

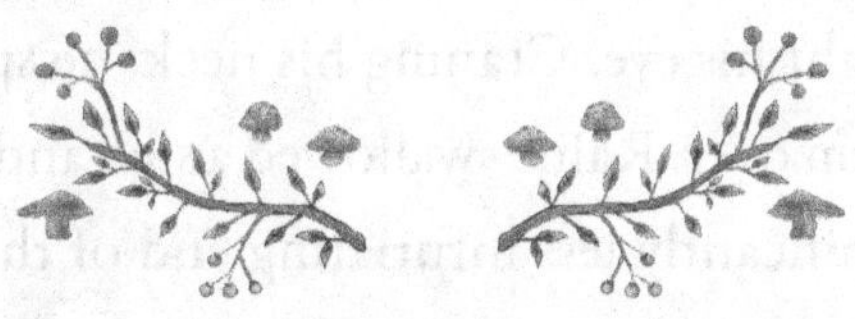

The feast dwindled, all but finished. Gone were the towering platters of roasted pork and pheasant. Most of the trays were empty, their surfaces streaked with grease. Here and there, Betony's storm nibbled at leftovers as they conversed with the sleepy, contented air of the well-sated.

They were sated, alright. Sated on rich food and violent slaughter.

It was sheer luck that their victims had been guards who served the Nine and not droves of innocents. Betony's storm hadn't cared either way. Raine thought of Lissy, of her ruined arms and agonized screams.

Resentment welled in him like foul, black blood. He wasn't in the mood for this shit. He altered course, intending to go straight to his bedchamber. The oblivion of sleep called to him the same way he imagined the bottom of a bottle beckoned drunkards.

Sidian grasped his forearm, preventing his escape. "No. You can retire after you've eaten."

Raine didn't bother asking how Sidian knew exactly what he'd been planning. The man was eerily keen sometimes. "I'm not hungry," he lied.

Just then, Raine's stomach groaned. It was an audible, beastly growl, as though he housed a starving wolf beneath his belly. A coolly arched brow was Sidian's only response. He did not let go of Raine's arm.

Motion caught his eye. Craning his neck, he spied Nyx, who was waving them over. Raine swallowed a sigh and let Sidian lead him to the significantly less infuriating end of the dining table. The tightness in his chest eased, a knot he hadn't realized was there, as he met the sweetly kind smiles of Naiah and Evin.

While Betony's preternatural storm mother powers aggravated and subdued, the two den mothers bolstered him, body and spirit. He returned their smiles, feeling both warmed and energized, like he'd just rolled out of a hot hearth after a nap. Further down the table, Nyx patted the empty chairs beside him.

There was more food on this end of the table. Raine snagged the lip of a tray and dragged an untouched, clay-baked trout in front of the empty chair next to Nyx, then took the seat beside it.

Sidian sat before the trout, knowing it was his without asking. Raine retrieved trenchers of roasted vegetables and buttered bread, positioning them where both he and Sidian could reach.

Lenka appeared at his shoulder and placed two heaping flagons of ale before them. Raine started to thank Lenka automatically, then froze and glared at her. "What are you doing?"

"Bringing you a drink." She put her hands on her hips, her bloodshot gaze direct. "I'm not going to serve those monsters and leave you thirsty. Not when you're the one I should have waited on."

"I've got it from here," he said, raising a palm. "The best way for you to serve me is to get some rest."

"I'm not tired." Lenka wet her bottom lip and leaned forward, lowering her voice. "Unless you'd like to retire with me?"

Raine's brows furrowed, both at her odd phrasing and her audacity. It was nice that she cared about his sleep, but the chit was overstepping her position. A laundress wasn't going to dictate his bedtime like a nurse to a toddler.

"There are matters I must see to before I can retire."

Sidian turned in his chair and regarded Raine with glacial sharpness. Raine gulped reflexively, wondering what he'd done to earn his mate's reproach.

Lenka leaned closer, invading his personal space. Her bosom nearly brushed his chest. "That's okay. I know where your bedchamber is. I will make sure the blankets are good and warm for when you join me."

Raine gaped as Lenka's meaning clicked. Sidian's glare continued to gouge icicles into his flesh, promising painful retribution for not rejecting Lenka's advances immediately. Raine's tongue knotted painfully as his desire to set Lenka straight warred with his need to reassure his mate.

Lenka took his silence as approval, her gaze bright with heated anticipation. "Don't keep me waiting—"

Thwack.

Lenka cried out and cupped her head. Raine's neck snapped to Moranda as Lenka shrank away. The head housekeeper's teeth were bared, and a vein throbbed in her neck. In her hands, she wielded a mop like a club.

As much as Raine despised Moranda, he had to give credit where credit was due. The woman was no slouch and clearly knew her way around the keep's cleaning cupboards. It really was too bad Moranda couldn't turn that mop onto her own crusty soul and give it a good scrubbing.

"Wanton bitch," she spat, shaking the mop at Lenka. "I warned you, didn't I? I told you to stay away from that fucking blanch. I won't have any of my girls part their legs for that, that *thing*. Leave. Right now, get out. You're not welcome here, and when I'm finished spreading the word, you won't find a job within a hundred miles of my castle."

Tears filled Lenka's eyes as she looked from Raine to Moranda and back again. Moranda shouted a war cry and swung the mop again. Raine caught the handle and yanked, aiming to disarm her in the same manner Sidian had earlier.

Only this time, Moranda was ready for it. She held firm and yanked the mop back. Raine didn't have to deliberate his next move. He simply released the mop handle and grinned as she toppled backward. Her legs splayed like scissors as she fell on her back. The dingy gray mophead landed on her head and fanned over her mouth.

"How the hell did she get out of the closet?" Nyx wondered aloud.

"I released her," Lenka said in a small voice while Moranda righted herself.

Nyx sighed, leaning back in his chair. "I wish you hadn't. I told Moranda she couldn't come out until she decided to be a decent person."

"Helda and Cosette were stuck in there, too. They were yelling for help through the door. I couldn't just leave them," Lenka said apologetically.

The way Lenka avoided looking anywhere near Moranda reminded Raine of a child petrified of a malignant specter. As if Moranda couldn't hurt her so long as she didn't look. Too bad Raine knew from experience it didn't work that way. It was always better to keep a wary eye on those who had it out for him. That way, when they inevitably came swinging, he could be ready.

The mop handle stung his palm as Raine caught it again. This time, Moranda had aimed for him, right at the bridge of his nose. Still clutching the mop, his brows climbed his forehead as Lenka's words penetrated.

"You locked her staff inside a closet with her?" he asked Nyx, convinced he had somehow misunderstood. Moranda tugged at the mop with all her strength, grunting as her color heightened. Raine held tight with ease, inciting a slew of sputtering curses.

"Yup," Nyx said, sounding almost cheerful. "They seemed like nice girls. I hoped their decency would rub off on her."

Raine gawked at Nyx, askance. Locking Moranda up was akin to a public service. He had no protests there. But her *staff*?

"Um, no offense, Nyx" —Raine raised his voice so he could be heard over Moranda's garrulous insults— "but you sound like a total maniac."

"Somebody's egg was scrambled before they hatched," Oka said from the chair opposite Nyx. He whisked the air around his ears, demonstrating scrambled brains specifically.

"Mother worried the air on Moontop was too thin," Carissyne announced, a few chairs down and across from Raine. "She said it might damage a human's brain if they breathed it for too long."

Her popinjay green eyes darted meaningfully at Nyx. Raine felt more than saw Sidian's nod.

"I didn't want to say anything, in case it was a delicate subject, but I'm afraid my brother's mind is all but gone," Sidian said gravely. "We're lucky he's still able to eat and relieve himself independently, I think."

Moranda roared in frustrated anger, drowning Nyx's objections. She released the mop and swept them with a vulgar hand gesture. Envy pricked Raine as he noticed Lenka slinking away in the background. *She'd* been Moranda's original target, but here he was, stuck with the fallout.

His gaze snapped back to Moranda as she spat, "You think it's funny to lock me up and ignore me? Laugh while you can, because the joke's on you." She pointed at Raine, her dark eyes shining with malice. "I hope you enjoyed your meal, you pestilent wight, because it'll be your last."

An eerie smile crept over her mouth like a string of mealworms. It wasn't enough to suppress Raine's appetite, though it was a near thing. He wanted to correct her by saying that he hadn't yet enjoyed anything thanks to her damned interruption, and could she please go away so he could finally fucking eat?

"What are you talking about?" Sidian demanded.

His low, smoky voice puckered Raine's flesh, and he shivered. Moranda shivered, too, though likely not for the same reason. Her features paled at whatever she beheld in Sidian's stare, but as she glanced back at Raine, her mouth twisted in a sneer.

"The first thing I did after Lenka released me was visit the mews," Moranda unveiled with relish. "A carrier pigeon is delivering a message to General Olan as we speak. He said you might show up here. And now, he'll return to eliminate you once and for all. I still can't decide what to do with your rank carcass afterward. Even feeding you to Drooger's pigs seems too noble a disposal."

"I warned you of the consequences, should you strike my mate with either words or weapons." Sidian's even tone and placid expression should have made him sound less threatening, not more. He pushed out his chair and stood. His movements were as measured and smooth as a coiling serpent as he approached Moranda. "Yet you have done both."

She stood her ground, scoffing dismissively. "You're a Guardian of Vale, and I'm a loyal countrywoman. If anything, you should be turning your sword against that thing behind you. Blanches are bad luck. An omen of death." Sidian paused before her. She seemed to take his stillness as encouragement, becoming more animated. "Look around you. Chambrin Keep is in ruins. The guards are all dead. And it is all the fault of that cursed blanch."

In a blink, Sidian's longsword was drawn and poised.

Raine's conscience bucked violently. Things had gone far enough. "Sidian, don't."

But Sidian was already swinging, his sword sparkling like a billion white jewels as it slashed toward Moranda's throat. Raine tensed, his viscera a black funnel of sickly anticipation. Moranda gawped at the downward arcing blade, disbelief stark on her countenance. It was the last expression she would ever make, and Raine was probably going to hell because all he could think was, *I am not cleaning up her head after this.*

The dragon bone sword halted mid-swing and hovered.

As Moranda's expression shifted into triumph, Raine snapped out of his daze.

Sidian had heard him and seemed willing to listen. But Sidian wasn't yet convinced to let Moranda live. His sword quivered, eager to resume its lethal arc.

Very gently, as if cajoling a tiger, Raine said, "We cannot kill her, Sidian. We don't have the authority to sentence her or anyone else here for their trespasses, remember? If we do, it makes us just as bad as them."

The sword wavered but didn't lower. Sidian didn't look away from Moranda's throat. The triumph gradually seeped from her expression, replaced by dawning horror. There was no mistaking Sidian for anything other than deathly serious.

"You have to set a good example for me," Raine sang thinly, running out of ideas on how to call Sidian off. He'd already used his best argument. "I look to you for the right thing to do, you know."

"Screw that," Aly yelled, approaching them from the great hall's eastern entrance. A wrinkled sheet was wrapped around her like a sheath dress. Zane trailed her in a matching sheet he'd punched head and arm holes through, wearing it like an ungainly tunic.

"Where the hell have you been?" Raine asked, only now realizing they'd been absent all this time.

"I had to pee and got lost. This place is a freaking maze." Aly took the vacant seat across from Raine, and Zane settled in beside her. "I didn't hear everything that awful woman said, but I heard enough. Slice her head off," she ordered Sidian.

"No. *Do not slice off her head*. Moranda," Raine barked, commanding her attention. Even inches from death and pale with fear, her features still etched with loathing as they lit upon him. "Consider yourself banished from Chambrin Keep. Indefinitely. Pack your things and leave the premises at once."

"Or what?" she snarled. Her eyes darted toward Sidian's sword, betraying her nervousness.

"I'll kill you," Sidian whispered, dropping his arm.

CHAPTER
TWENTY-FOUR

For the love of the Divine, please let there be no more disruptions. Raine's ravening stomach gnawed at his spine, and he wouldn't be held accountable for his actions if he didn't eat in the next five minutes. Pulling both of the flagons of ale Lenka had brought to his side of the table, he placed a crystal ewer of plain drinking water before Sidian's plate, long since familiar with his mate's preferences.

Sidian arrived shortly thereafter, having taken it upon himself to escort Moranda off the property. There was a relaxed, satisfied edge to his features that made Raine wonder if Moranda had actually made it off the mesa, or if her body had somehow joined the smoldering corpses in the Roost. He decided he didn't want to know.

Instead of tucking into his trout, Sidian pulled a tray towards Raine, one loaded with sweetmeats and soft cheese. "Normally, I would make you have dinner before dessert," he drawled. "Today can be an exception. Eat."

Raine plucked a pumpkin tart with a pecan crust from the tray and swallowed it in one bite. Sweet and savory notes burst across his taste buds. He moaned aloud, then rapidly downed two more.

Aly stared at his tray dubiously. "We couldn't tell what those things were, so nobody ate them."

"They're terrible," Raine mumbled through his mouthful. "You'd hate them. They're made of squash. It's very mushy and bland."

He poured a small pitcher of heavy cream over another tart before cramming it into his mouth.

"I can't believe you eat that stuff." Oka's face scrunched with disgust. "It was bad enough dining on cooked meat rubbed with *plants*."

Oka shuddered, as if his meat had been covered in feces instead of rosemary and garlic. Raine suppressed a laugh, not wanting to choke on his tart. It was splendid, flavored with maple syrup and cinnamon.

Aly elbowed Oka in his ribs. "You just don't want to admit it was the best food you've ever eaten." She leaned forward conspiratorially, her eyes glittering like garnets. "Oka ate all the beef. I mean, *all of it*. He's half-cow right now. I can't figure out where he put it."

"Oi," Oka protested, and they fell into a familiar pattern of playful bickering. Raine absorbed it like sunshine after a monsoon, grinning as Nyx and Jaska ganged up on Aly.

He felt Sidian's stare and turned to find fawn eyes fixed on him. His mate reached out a hand and swiped the corner of his mouth with a finger, revealing a white droplet of runaway cream. Sidian's lips closed around his finger, sucking the cream off. Raine averted his gaze, his heart hammering riotously.

"What's the matter?" Aly smirked, looking fiendish. "Does watching Sidian lick cream off his fingers remind you of something else?"

Her smile was so obnoxiously sly and knowing that Raine returned it with one of his own. "So," he said, addressing Zane. "Has Aly shown you her prized possession?" Aly's eyes narrowed. "It's thick and long and black—"

"I will end you," Aly said sweetly, twin spots of color staining her cheeks.

Zane glanced at her with such naked curiosity, Raine knew he was going to bring this conversation up later, when he and Aly were in private. He grinned as Aly's palms flattened on the table, elbows bent to launch herself at him. It had been ages since they tussled, and he was ready.

An imperious voice cut through the hall. "Where are our children?"

Raine stiffened but did not look down the table to see who had spoken.

"They aren't here. We can see that much," a male piped in. "I saw you speaking with the humans. What have they said? Where are they?"

In truth, Raine was surprised the dragons had waited this long to inquire. He was out of charity with them, however, and didn't care to answer. Instead, he ate another tart, this one stuffed with apples and walnuts. The crust crumbled like sand on his tongue, and he moaned appreciatively, not missing the sharp inhale Sidian took at the sound.

Many chairs scraped against stone as Betony's storm stood from the table. Raine was still chewing stewed apples and crust when they surrounded his end of the table, thin faces lined with impatience. Betony moved behind Aly's chair to stare at him directly.

"My storm is grateful for your aid as well as this replenishing repast. That being said, it is time for answers. Our children are gone. It's something I should have anticipated." She curled her fist and glanced at her storm. "The humans knew we would come. They feared our wrath. Our strength. They hid our children, knowing we would rescue them." Stare refocusing on Raine, she said, "We pressed the humans for our children's whereabouts after our battle, but they insisted upon ignorance. What have you heard? Did they tell you where they are?"

Raine swallowed. His once delicious tart went down like ash, souring his stomach. "Battle," he repeated, wide-eyed in outrage. "Lady, what you call a battle, I call a butchery. You and your storm slaughtered over a hundred men. And not one of you stopped to question their identities or ponder the possibility of their innocence." His voice held more bite than the air above the distant white-capped mountains.

Betony drew back as if slapped but recovered quickly. Her silvery-purple eyes flashed with steel. "There are no innocents here. Every human in this wretched place played a part in our interment below ground. While we were rotting away in cages, wallowing in filth like swine, these humans trod on us above, carefree in the sun."

"If guilt is a matter of knowledge and proximity, then I am more culpable than anyone." Raine met her gaze evenly. "And the precious offspring you salivate after like dogs chasing a bone? Are equally blameworthy, by your reasoning." He sneered at the denial etched across her face. "You're a fucking hypocrite and a disgrace to dragons. If you so much as look at one of these humans the wrong way, I will meet you on the field of honor. Do you understand me?"

Betony's breaths came fast and shallow. He could tell she was unused to being addressed in such a manner. Storm mother or no, Raine didn't care. She wasn't in charge here. Wasn't in charge of him or Chambrin Keep.

Lorrivare stretched his arm around her, but she shoved him off roughly. "We will not touch the remaining humans," she said with a chilly disdain that Raine appreciated. If Betony didn't like him, he knew he was doing something right. "We will not even overstay our welcome. Tell us where our children are, and we will leave without delay."

Raine barely refrained from snapping that they were never welcomed in the first place. "Thanks to your storm" —his voice dripped venom— "there are only civilians here. And none of them know your children's whereabouts."

"Then who does?"

"Only the general of the keep knows where the war dragons were taken. And he is presently in Rokeshin, attending the succession."

"What succession?" Lukor demanded from his seat several spaces from Zane's left.

Raine's lips firmed as he eyed the quarrelsome dragon. Not so quarrelsome anymore, he amended, eyeing the wintery blue head of hair resting at Lukor's shoulder. Naiah caught his look and smiled kindly at him.

With a long-suffering sigh, Raine explained all that Wylan had shared.

"It's probably why the Guardians fled the forest surrounding the Hellhole so abruptly," Raine added near the end. "Almost the entire guild will be in attendance."

"And you wanted us to go to the safehouse in Rokeshin," Aly said without a shred of tact. She leaned forward and pointed at Lukor, in case the dragon in question forgot his complicity.

Raine shot a vindicated look at Sidian, as if to say, *See? I'm not the only one who thinks Rokeshin is the most dangerous city in the country right now.*

Sidian rolled his eyes, but it was Betony who said, "Then to Rokeshin we go."

Aly twisted like a ferret in her seat to stare up at the storm mother hovering behind her. "Are you daft? They'll kill you."

"My life is meaningless without my children," Betony said frostily. "When you become a mother, you will understand why nothing stops me."

"Actually ..." Raine's sigh was long and drawn. "We've decided to go to Rokeshin, as well."

"What?" Aly cried, gobsmacked.

Betony inclined her head rigidly at Raine. "So long as you do not slow us down or interfere, you may accompany us," she said, as if granting him permission.

Her sanctimonious attitude grated like pumice stones. *Like I'm going anywhere with you and your demented dragons.* He didn't say so aloud, though. Mostly because he'd already stuffed another tart into his mouth.

One of the parents approached Betony, a slender blue female. A large bloodstain soaked one side of her sheet. Betony was quietly attentive as the female whispered in her ear. She looked down at her storm, her features creased with worry. It was a new expression for Betony. Or, at least, it was an expression Raine hadn't yet seen from her.

"My storm requires rest before we leave," Betony said haltingly, now eyeing Raine. "I hope your low opinion of us won't prevent you from offering a small area where we can sleep and heal."

Raine's gaze flicked down the length of the table. Betony's storm was noticeably wearier than before, as if they could scarcely hold themselves upright. Pale except where they were bloody. Railthin from two centuries of starvation and confinement, they didn't look like monsters who violently captured a castle. They looked like refugees. They looked like they'd lost.

It doesn't matter how they look. It matters what they did.

A refusal formed on his tongue, one as brutally swift and merciless as Betony's storm had proven themselves to be.

One of the parents caught his eye. A green male. While they were all thin, he was thinner than most. As gaunt as if he'd been rescued from the Cavern days ago instead of weeks. His eyes were red-rimmed and sunken. His cheeks were craters that showed just how hollow a skull truly was. He could probably still fit through the bars of his old cage, if he had to.

His old cage, which waited a mile beneath their feet. Open, empty, and crusted with filth and despair.

Raine pressed his lips together and faced Betony. He could hardly believe what he was about to say.

"You can stay in the Roost," he said at last. "The tower outside. It's where your children lived until recently. There's straw and fleece to bed down in the loft."

"Thank you," Betony said, the words stilted and unnatural.

Raine hoped they entered the Roost through the ground level and tripped over the corpses piled there. He hoped they got smeared with ash and decay. He hoped they had nightmares, tonight and forever after.

His smile was a baring of teeth. "You're welcome."

Evin and Naiah's thunders were quiet as Betony's storm shuffled from the hall. Several of the dragons weren't able to walk unaided. Others, like the blue female that had approached Betony, had fatal-looking splotches of blood across their sheets.

The hall door closed behind them, and Raine shook his head. "What makes them think they can take on the Guardians and soldiers in Rokeshin when they can barely walk?"

He had meant it as a rhetorical question, but Nyx answered. "They're rough now, sure. But after a few hours in their dragon forms, they'll be fit for anything."

Huh? "What, are you saying they'll be healed or something?" To his surprise, Nyx nodded. Raine frowned. "I thought dragons only healed twice as fast as humans."

"Normally, yes. But as a storm mother ages, her powers increase. If Betony has come into her resonant roar, it means she can also generate a healing resonance," Nyx explained. "She can only produce it in her dragon form, and dragons can only absorb it in theirs.

But if I'm right, so long as her storm sleeps in their dragon forms, they'll be fully healed by dawn."

Oh. "That's ... pretty cool, honestly."

"Alright, cut the crap." Aly swiped her dishes aside and pressed her palms on the table to lever herself over Raine. "When the hell did you decide to go to Rokeshin? Better yet, *why* are you going to Rokeshin?"

He opened his mouth to say, *Ask Sidian,* but he was stalled by a voice both sorrowful and kind.

"Raine, I know I said it was important for all of us to stick together." Evin hesitated. Then, her features hardened like iron. "But if you're going to Rokeshin because of what I said earlier, about staying with Betony's storm to maintain unity, please know that I no longer ask that of you. The events of this evening were an atrocity I never imagined possible. I'm so sorry, Raine. Every time we look to you for aid, you pay for it with pain."

Raine's throat knotted, his grief rising to the surface as if summoned by Evin's reference to its source. Beneath the table, Sidian laced their fingers and squeezed.

"Our plans have nothing to do with Betony's storm or finding the war dragons," Sidian assured her. "We seek to eradicate the Nine, once and for all."

Nyx straightened as understanding lit his features. "The succession. It's genius."

"I thought the succession was why we should avoid Rokeshin." Lukor's purple brows puckered mutinously. "Now you're saying it's a reason to go. Anyone want to start making sense?"

"The Guardians make a peaceful life impossible for all of you," Sidian said. "But they don't choose to hunt dragons. That directive comes from a higher authority."

"The Nine," Evin whispered. The dragons nearest went quiet and still.

"Yes." Sidian nodded. "Our numbers are no match against the Guardians of Vale, but if we narrow our targets down to their leadership, we stand a decent chance. Now is the best time to act. The Nine only assemble when one of them dies. It could be decades until the next succession."

"We can take them out all at once," Nyx said approvingly.

"But that's insane," Aly burst. "Hello, am I the only one here who remembers that every city in Valdenia has mandatory inspections at their gates? We can't even get inside the city."

"Actually, we can," Sidian said.

Raine snorted. Of course, Sidian had already thought of a way around the gatekeepers.

"If you're referring to those wigs I bought, forget about it." Nyx gestured around the table. "When Naiah's thunder shifted to fly here, they left their bags and belongings behind."

"We don't need the wigs," Sidian said. "I know of a secret entrance into the city. A way that is unguarded."

"Bullshit." Lukor glared down the table. "There is no secret way into Rokeshin. We've been sneaking in and out of that city for two centuries. If there was an entrance other than the main gate, we would have found it."

"That's the funny thing about secret entrances," Sidian drawled, unphased by the three hundred pounds of seething muscle challenging him. "They're designed to remain undetected."

Tendons corded against Lukor's skin. Raine tensed, prepared to throw himself in front of Sidian if Lukor attacked. Naiah rested a palm against Lukor's forearm and whispered something in his ear.

The purple dragon didn't relax an inch, but somehow the energy shifted. Attack no longer felt imminent. *Well, not physical attack*, Raine mentally amended, as Lukor's lip curled back to expose his upper teeth.

"You must think yourself clever, human. But I've been alive longer than you can imagine. I know how mankind operates. How cowardice makes you deceitful. This is a setup." Lukor nodded as if to agree with himself. Taken in by his own conspiracy, he said, "You want us in Rokeshin. You want us where the hunters are."

"Enough," Raine snapped. Bloodthirst beat at him like a thousand furious wings, demanding he eliminate this threat to his mate. But his disdain for Betony's storm—at their mindless, animalistic bloodshed—was sharp and present. Raine refused to be anything like them, and he resisted his darker impulses until reason prevailed. "Lukor, I get where you're coming from. I do. But respectfully, shut the fuck up. Keep your mouth off my mate and keep your shitty conjecture to yourself."

The dragon's features twisted into a baleful sneer. "When your mate's secret entrance turns out to be a prison cell, I'll have all the evidence I need. But by then, it'll be too late."

Raine's knee-jerk comeback was cruel and ugly, but before he could hurl it, his gaze caught on the small, pale hand stroking Lukor's arm. Naiah's snow wolf eyes gazed at him the way his father might have—as if she understood all that he felt and believed him capable of acting noble despite it. He didn't have to turn his head to know Evin wore a similar expression.

Fucking den mothers.

"Lukor," he said, keeping his tone carefully neutral. "If you will recall, you also believed my father was the enemy. You were wrong then, and you're wrong now."

Raine wasn't sure, but he thought Lukor flinched at that. His response, when it came, was simply a curt, "We'll see," that made Raine suspect he wasn't the only one on the receiving end of a Den Mother Doom Stare.

"So, to be clear, we're going with the secret entrance method?" Oka asked.

As one, they looked to Sidian, who nodded. "It's a secure tunnel that will allow us to enter Rokeshin unseen." His dark eyes darted to Lukor. When the purple male looked away, Sidian continued. "We can't plan the assassination until we're inside."

"We have to study their layout and security patterns," Nyx said in agreement.

"Exactly," Sidian said. "The Nine will gather outdoors when they light Brandor's pyre, but I hope to eliminate them before then. If we delay until the burning day and something goes wrong, we won't get another shot."

The dragons hung on Sidian's words, their eyes fierce with purpose. All except Evin. Her sky-blue gaze was banked with unease.

"My first instinct is to decline this mission," she said slowly. "It's too dangerous. If we fail, the consequences will be catastrophic. It'll be the end of us."

"But if we succeed ..." Savere let his sentence dangle. Raine didn't have to be a mind reader to know they were all finishing it privately, each in their own way.

If we succeed ... If we succeed ... If we succeed ...

"We already live like we're dead," Oka said, folding his arms. "So, we really don't have anything to lose."

"No," Evin murmured, sad and thoughtful. "I don't suppose we do."

CHAPTER
TWENTY-FIVE

An insistent knock rippled through Raine's consciousness. He tried to lift his head, but it was too much effort. His body felt like a leaden anchor lodged deep within sand and mud. Sidian jerked awake beside him, dipping the mattress as he got up.

Another series of knocks was interrupted as Sidian flung the door open. "What?"

"Are you two sleeping?" Nyx sounded both disbelieving and entirely too awake.

"Is there a reason we wouldn't be at ... six in the morning?" Sidian hissed.

Six in the morning? Raine groaned and buried his face into a pillow. No wonder he felt like a mangled steak.

He and Sidian had stumbled into bed well after midnight, both utterly wrung out. Sidian hadn't even tried to consummate their bond. He'd simply smoothed Raine's hair back and held him close, his eyelids drooping shut as he whispered, "Get some sleep."

"Everyone else is up," Nyx said, his voice coming closer. A hand shook Raine's shoulder. "Come on, kid. We've got places to go and chieftains to assassinate."

Raine rolled onto his back with a huff and blinked blearily at Nyx. "It's still dark outside. Come back after sunrise."

Sidian walked around the bed and fell back onto the mattress. "What he said."

Raine's stomach flipped as Sidian's arms banded his chest and pulled them together. His mate was sleep-warm and pliant, molding his frame against Raine's with the sinuous flexibility of an octopus. It spoke volumes of Raine's weariness that all of him remained equally soft and pliant while folded in Sidian's snug embrace.

"Look at you two," Nyx gushed, ignoring his dismissal. "You know, we've been so busy, that I haven't had a chance to congratulate you guys properly. I mean, this is so surreal. My little stinkbug and my little scamp are mates. What were the odds?"

Raine attempted to smother his laugh, but it was no use. Sidian felt his muscles shake and pinched his side. Raine yelped. "Ouch, hey. I'm sorry, okay? But stinkbug?" He didn't bother trying to stifle his next bout of laughter. "It gets me every time."

Sidian's soft snort sent a puff of hot breath against Raine's crown. "You have no room to talk, princess."

"No." Raine moaned. "It's bad enough Aly calls me that. Knock it off."

"Oh, princess," a sly voice called from the outer chamber. "Is Sidian nailing your gorgeous ass or is it safe to come in?"

It was official. The Dreaming Mother definitely conspired against him. Raine would not be convinced otherwise, not ever.

Sidian muttered something that sounded suspiciously like, "I wish."

Raine flushed, his gaze darting to Nyx. Fortunately, Sidian's brother's attention was fixed on the doorway.

"I'm in here, too," Nyx said. "We're all perfectly decent, I promise."

Aly smirked unrepentantly as she tripped through the door, Zane and Oka trailing her. Aly and Oka must have snatched their packs with their talons after they transformed last night, because they wore their usual muted garb. Zane, meanwhile, was outfitted in the maroon button-down and linen trousers favored by the keep's footmen.

"She compliments your appearance frequently," Zane said, his cerulean eyes narrowing.

"Oh, come off it." Aly threw a hand on her waist. She pointed the other at Raine as he dragged himself upright on the mattress. "Have you ever seen a prettier dragon? His hair glitters like a creamy rainbow." Aly's compliment was underscored by a note of envy.

Zane picked up on it, as well. His glare melted into a wry smile. "There is at least one prettier dragon. At least, if you ask me." His stare was hot and earnest on Aly. Her cheeks bloomed a pale rose.

She truly was beautiful. Unfortunately, Raine knew precisely how beautiful since she'd thrust her naked bosom in his face within hours of making his acquaintance. That information was probably best kept between him and Aly, however.

"And you're the handsomest," she whispered without a trace of deception, leaning forward to steal a kiss.

"Seriously? I am a man," Raine grumbled, not caring about their special moment. "I'm the handsomest. Not the prettiest."

He *hmphed*, jerking his chin toward Sidian, who sat upright beside him. His mate's gaze was incendiary as it moved over Raine's face and chest. "I'm with Aly on this one."

Nyx held his hands up, as if to say, *Don't ask me.*

Oka leaned against the doorframe, his grin more wicked than the Nine.

"Shut up," Raine grunted, before Oka could embarrass him further.

"I was merely going to say Betony's storm is about to leave," Oka said with mock affront.

Nyx nodded, his expression sobering. "That's actually what I came here to tell you. Since the guild has assembled in Rokeshin, Betony decided there's no reason her storm can't fly there."

Raine frowned. "The sky watchers—"

"Have been called to the succession," Aly finished. She shared a *what the fuck* look with him, then shrugged. "I guess the entire guild is in Rokeshin, not just most of them."

"Impossible," Sidian said, frowning as he climbed out of bed. "The guild has strict protocols in the event of a succession. Only seventy percent of active units may attend, and the turnout is usually less due to ongoing missions and scheduling conflicts."

"We heard it from Wylan, who heard it from some guy named Olan—he runs this castle now? Or did, until we took it." Aly batted her hand, unconcerned about the technicalities. "Anyways, Olan was already in Rokeshin, but he sent a letter here, releasing every man and woman from duty so they could attend the succession."

Sidian's brows flattened with skepticism. "The men and women stationed at this keep are attending the succession. So, what? That doesn't mean all five thousand members of the Guardians of Vale are reporting to Rokeshin."

"Aly has the right of it. Olan's missive states the entire guild is to attend," Nyx said. "It's penned on Eddic's personal stationery and sealed with his signet. Allegedly, the guild's policy has changed. The Nine believe that, since every chieftain operates as a commander-in-chief of the guild, each Guardian's final respects should be obligatory."

Raine ignored his protesting muscles as he staggered out of bed. He was glad he'd gone to sleep fully outfitted in a Guardian jumpsuit, seeing how his father's bedchamber currently served as a meeting parlor.

"That's why that watchtower was abandoned. The one we saw on our way here," Raine mused, searching around for his father's boots.

They weren't under the bed or by the door. He turned to check near his father's desk and stopped. Sidian held a pair of boots out by their calf guards. As far as demonstrations of his mate anticipating and meeting his needs went, it was an unremarkable gesture, but Raine's belly fluttered as if his mate had presented him with gold or jewels instead. He accepted the boots, hoping his smile wasn't as dopey as it felt.

"Yup," Oka said. "According to that missive, all the watchtowers should be unmanned. We can fly nearly the whole way to Rokeshin, then find a good patch of countryside to land and shift before blending in as humans on the road."

"That's a bad idea in broad daylight, even without sky watchers," Sidian said, voicing Raine's misgivings. "If the entire guild is headed to Rokeshin, that's thousands of witnesses to their flight."

"Again, that's why I'm here." Nyx rolled his eyes as if Sidian should already know. "Flying to Rokeshin under the cover of night will be easy with the guild distracted. But leaving now is a death sentence. The Guardians are concentrated in Rokeshin. They'll see Betony's storm when they land, if not sooner. Those dragons will be captured or killed if someone doesn't talk Betony down."

The way Nyx was looking at Raine put his back up in alarm. "What, you think I can convince Betony to wait?" Raine asked, incredulous. There was no reasoning with the storm mother's brand of crazy.

"Evin is speaking with Betony right now," Nyx said. "And it's not going well. She's managing to stall them, but that's it. They're going to fly off any minute."

"I tried backing Mother—Evin—up." Oka straightened from the doorframe and stepped into the bedchamber. "We all did, but she ordered us to silence."

"Naiah did the same to her thunder," Zane added.

And dragon hierarchy being what it was, the thunders had been forced to obey their respective den mothers. The dots began connecting rapidly in Raine's mind.

Evin wasn't having any luck swaying Betony, and the other dragons couldn't even try. Which left *him* as the only dragon free to help Evin convince Betony to hold off until nightfall.

But just because he could attempt to talk reason into Betony didn't mean he cared to. Because of her and her storm, his gut was a constricting knot of rage and blame. Of guilt and shame. A knot that grew tighter and more convoluted whenever he was forced to *think* about Betony's storm, let alone *see* them. Let alone *interact* with them.

"If Betony wants to leave now, who am I to try and stop her?" Raine dropped his father's boots to the floor and began wiggling his feet inside, speaking all the while. "And anyway, I don't want to go to Rokeshin with them. Let them go on their own. If they get captured, they'll deserve it for being so stupid."

Boots secure, he glanced up to find Nyx's hardened gaze fixed on him. Raine gulped, instantly transported to a time when that look meant he was in for a whipping.

"I've dedicated the last decade of my life to freeing those dragons." Nyx's words were edged with censure. "Me and Arastus." Raine flinched, and Nyx's gaze softened. "I understand what you're feeling, Raine. You're hurt and angry, and you have every right to be. But so do they."

"They don't have every right to destroy my home and slaughter any humans they fancy."

"No, they don't," Nyx said quietly. "What they did last night was wrong. But letting them get captured or killed by the guild is wrong, too. They're in a bad place right now. In here." He pointed at his head. "And here." He pointed at his heart. "So even though we can't control their actions, we have to steer them as best we can. We have to try to protect them from themselves, because their damage isn't their fault. If they're out of their minds, with fear or anger, it's because we made them that way. It's not fair to expect them to act normally or rationally after two centuries of captivity and abuse. I know it's hard, but they needed us in the Cavern, and they need us now, too."

Raine's jaw ticked as he resisted the empathy stirring in his gut. "Yeah, well, Zane was also trapped in the Cavern. You don't see him acting like a bloodthirsty maniac."

Raine's blood felt riddled with broken glass just thinking about their callous disregard for human life. The way they'd destroyed his home.

He'd sympathized with Betony's storm enough to offer them the Roost. It was more than they deserved.

"My case is different," Zane said. "The humans couldn't take my eggs away, since I didn't have a mate." He hesitated, then appeared to make a decision. "The others ... You can't possibly imagine the suffering they endured. Even though I witnessed it firsthand, I don't think I can come close to knowing how they felt." Zane looked at Aly. "Not only did their eggs get taken, but they couldn't protect their mates. Couldn't provide for them. They had to watch them starve and fade, unable to do anything about it."

Zane glanced at Sidian before refocusing on Raine. His voice was heavy with meaning as he asked, "What if it had been your mate down there? How would you feel after two centuries of watching humans beat and starve your mate? I don't have the same mindless impulse for revenge that the others do, but I think I would." He looked at Aly. "I think I'd be the worst of them."

Raine imagined Sidian among those recovered from the Cavern. His fawn eyes dull, his ribs hollow. Frail and filthy and tormented. Raine's spine became a shaft of ice. The cold splintered and spread through him, so gelid it burned.

He jumped, startled when a pair of solid arms squeezed around him, drawing him into a crushing embrace. The black lotus silk covering Sidian's shoulder was soft against Raine's cheek as his mate cradled his head, pulling him closer.

"You're shaking," Sidian whispered against his ear, smoothing a hand down his braid. "It's okay. I'm okay."

Raine nodded against him. For minutes or hours, he soaked in his mate's warm strength. Let it thaw the icy terror that had encased him. He heard Nyx speaking with Zane and Aly, with Oka occasionally chiming in. But their voices were muffled to Raine. His senses were trained on Sidian with primal urgency, a part of him still convinced his mate was in danger.

The entrance door to the sitting room cracked open loudly. Raine straightened, body tense and primed for anything as he stood in front of Sidian.

He relaxed as Tejayla skidded inside the bedchamber. Carissyne and Sarasana followed on her heels. The pair yelped, unable to halt their momentum as they tumbled into Tejaya. The three went down like toy blocks. Amari and Amara appeared at the threshold. Their identical purple crowns shook back-and-forth as they eyed the pile of flailing limbs near the bed.

"You've got to stop them," a voice cried from behind the twins. Eva shoved her way inside the room, her pea-green hair as wild as her expression. "Betony's storm is about to fly off. My mom and Naiah are trying to reason with them, but they're not listening."

Nyx cursed and bolted from the room. His pace was frantic, as if his swift arrival was the difference between life and death.

It may very well be, Raine thought gravely.

Zane's probing had led to a revelation, of sorts. Raine now understood why the dragons were so angry, at least. He'd destroy anyone who hurt Sidian. He'd burn down entire worlds for his mate. But he also liked to think he'd ensure he was burning down the *right* worlds and the *right* people.

But those dragons' freedom was what his father had lived and died for. And Raine couldn't let his father's death—his dream, his life's purpose—be in vain.

Clutching that thought close, he chased after Nyx.

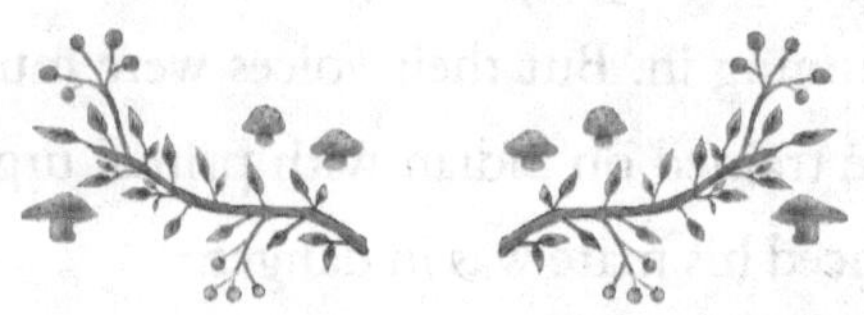

The grounds stank of char and fire. Nearly every outbuilding was a blackened husk. Chambrin Keep looked like a ghost town. A ruin.

The sky rapidly paled with the encroaching dawn. Already, it was a middling shade of blue with a mere suggestion of stars, their brilliance washed out with the onset of a new day.

Raine nearly forgot his purpose for rushing out here as he spotted Wylan and Ivarra staggering across the training yard. They struggled toward the Roost, balancing a long, shadowy lump between them. Raine's chest constricted at their limping pace. The urge to interpose and overtake their burden dug into him like spurs.

"In a minute," Sidian said, following his gaze. "You can only do one thing at a time. Naiah and Evin need you now."

Nyx stood with the den mothers. Together, the three faced Betony's storm. Who were *naked*. Raine swallowed a groan. He really, *really* didn't want to see Betony naked. Or any of them, for that matter.

At least Evin and Naiah were dressed. As well as their thunders, who stood and watched the proceedings from the sidelines. Chambrin's few remaining servants must have distributed garments to Naiah's thunder. Clothing wasn't cheap. Most of the staff made their own. It was an act of incredible generosity, and Raine made a mental note to compensate them for it.

"Peril is irrelevant to us," Betony was saying to Evin as Raine and Sidian reached them. Her storm fidgeted, some muttering mutinously as they waited for Betony's signal to fly. "The only thing we care about is reaching our children as quickly as possible, no matter what."

"No matter what?" Raine asked, staring fixedly over the top of Betony's silvery purple hair.

Evading eye contact was impolite, but Raine didn't care. He'd already endured enough trauma. If his pupils dipped any lower, Betony's exposed breasts would show in his peripheral vision. He suppressed a shudder.

"No matter what," Betony echoed. Her pugnacious tone dared Raine to challenge her.

So, naturally, he did. "I believe waiting until tonight to disembark falls within the scope of *no matter what*."

Although he wasn't looking at her face, there was a vague impression of a denial forming. Before she could issue it, Raine continued.

"There's a difference between reaching Rokeshin as quickly as possible and reaching your children as quickly as possible. What do you want? To reach the city posthaste and be thrown into cages? Or to arrive a little later than you'd prefer and have an actual chance of finding your children? Because that's the decision you're making right now."

There was a long, fraught pause. Gusts of wind howled in the spaces between them. He wished he could see Betony's face and get a hint of her thoughts.

"Grandmother, I beg you to consider Raine's words," Evin said into the stretched silence. One slender hand gripped Raine's shoulder, but her attention was on Betony. "There is a safehouse in Rokeshin, as I said. You are more than welcome to stay with us. If we are cautious and work together, we can find your children and defeat the Nine. Together."

Betony made a rude noise in the back of her throat. "You've had two centuries to make headway against the humans. Your progress has been underwhelming, to say the least. So, forgive me if I choose to do things my way."

"Are you saying you won't help us?" Evin's nails were trim but sharp, biting through the black cloth of Raine's jumpsuit with enough force to break skin.

"I'm saying we have different ideas of what constitutes *help*." Betony's gaze darted at the brightening sky. Her lips pursed. "If we agree to stay in your safehouse, you will not interfere with my storm's objectives."

"But-But we have the same objectives," Evin sputtered.

Raine had never heard her sound so uncertain, so lost. It hardened his heart even more against Betony, if such a thing was possible.

"Do we?" Betony stepped closer.

Raine took a large step back. Too large for politeness, but seriously. There was a chance—a hideous, horrific chance—that

Betony was his *mother*. And that meant her naked bosom was coming nowhere near him, thank you.

Evin held her stance, shoulders squaring as she faced Betony. They were nearly nose-to-nose, Evin's summer blue gaze clashing against Betony's frosted lilac.

"Yes," Evin said firmly. If Betony had intended to intimidate Evin, it backfired. Evin rose to Betony's silent challenge, a column of unyielding steel. "We both want the same things. We're on the same team."

"Not from where I'm standing." With pointed exaggeration, Betony peered at her storm, then at the dragons crowded near Evin and Naiah. As she spoke, her voice seeped with accusation and disgust. "Do you know what I think? You've spent so long living among humans, you've started to identify with them. You sympathize with them. Protect them."

"You make it sound like that's a bad thing," Evin said softly. "Like I'm somehow a traitor for it."

"Aren't you?" Betony's head tilted sideways.

A pang of dread snaked through Raine's entrails at the familiar gesture. His father had always likened Raine to a curious pup when he did it. His eyes dropped involuntarily to Betony's face.

Betony looked like a pitiless hawk.

"Grandmother, please." Naiah stepped forward. "Not all humans are the enemy. Even if you don't believe so, allowing such opinions to divide us will only weaken us. We must remain united in our cause to defeat the Nine if we wish to succeed."

"We never agreed to that cause," a green male called. It was the stick-thin male from last night, the one who'd roused Raine's pity.

"That's right," the red female beside him said. "We are going to the human city to find our children. Nothing more."

Other dragons uttered similar sentiments, limbs jostling with unrest. Betony's stare didn't quell them this time. After a moment, Raine realized it was because she wasn't trying to. The storm mother was content to watch and listen as her storm riled themselves into a disorderly mob.

Naiah and Evin exchanged a look. They seemed at a loss, neither willing to undermine Betony's authority by curbing her storm's mounting protests.

Zane marched forward, passing the den mothers as well as Betony to address the agitated parents. He waited until he had their attention to speak. "I understand how you feel. In many ways, I agree with you. But Evin and her thunder freed us from the Cavern at great risk. We should be open to returning the favor, particularly when it pertains to vanquishing our mutual enemies."

Bitter laughter leaked from a hyacinth-purple female. "You're a spark-struck fool, Zane. Don't you think it's funny Evin's thunder waited two hundred years to rescue us? And what a coincidence. It turns out they *need* us for something. They dismissed our torment until our capture was inconvenient for them. Until they required our help to solve their own problems."

"The timing isn't favorable," Zane agreed. "But given our predicament, I don't think anyone could have come for us soon enough. Help was always destined to arrive too late. The instant the earth closed over us, it was too late."

Several heads bowed. In thought or shame or memory, Raine couldn't say.

"I don't ever want to be caged again." Zane's voice roughened with emotion. "I don't ever want to go a single day without seeing the sky. I never want to hear the anguished cries of parents separated from their young. The Nine are our ultimate oppressors. They are the ones who would see us back there. We all have a stake in this fight. It's our lives or theirs. I can't speak for the rest of you, but as for me? I'm with Evin and Naiah. This has to end, once and for all."

There was a long pause.

"Fine," the green male declared. "We can help them with the Nine *after* we retrieve our children."

"Retrieving your children will be no hardship once the Nine are dealt with," Sidian said coldly. "It was through their orders alone that you were caged, and your children taken. And they'll continue to hunt, kill, and use all of you. Unless we stop them."

Nyx moved closer to the dragons, standing at Zane's side as he said, "Our window of opportunity is narrow if we hope to eliminate the Nine. When one dies, another takes their place. To remove the constant threat to your lives, we need to get rid of the Nine in one fell swoop. While they are gathered for the succession."

"We will rescue our children first," a dark blue male toward the back of the throng insisted. "The human general can only hide them from us for so long. We will go to Rokeshin and extract the truth from his craven lips before we kill him."

Somewhere in the middle, a green crown nodded. "Once our children are at our sides, we will sever the heads of the Nine too quickly for them to multiply."

Raine's demure gaze evaporated under a hot wave of irritation. "Spoken exactly like dragons who've been locked in a cage for two hundred years." His glare flitted from one defiant face to the next. "Do you honestly think you can swoop into a city packed with thousands of trained dragon slayers and survive the encounter?"

For the first time, he watched doubt and uncertainty play across some of their features. He continued pressing.

"The human general you seek is Olan Chambrin. My understanding is that he is with the Nine. Which means he will be surrounded by Guardians. How do you expect to interrogate him when you can't even reach him?"

"If the Nine are so well-guarded, how do *you* intend to reach *them*?" the red female in the front row asked.

It was a good question, one he didn't have an answer to. His mouth opened and closed as he fumbled for a response.

"By not flying there in broad daylight, for a start," Sidian drawled. "Tell me. Do you know the face of the man you seek?" He waited a beat. Nobody spoke. "There are thousands upon thousands of humans in Rokeshin. If you arrive in full view of the city, it will incite mass hysteria. General Olan will slip away in the chaos even if you could recognize him. Which you *can't*. Your mission requires observation and planning. Secrecy and caution are paramount."

The red female near the front went to speak again, and Betony held up her palm. Her storm straightened as one and eyed her attentively.

"I acknowledge your point," Betony told Sidian. "But we are beyond caution. Caution kept us locked below ground for two centuries. Caution killed ninety percent of the dragons who weren't captured with us. When we strike, we will be swift and bold."

Sidian's gaze narrowed. "There's a difference between boldness and folly."

Betony narrowed right back. "That is why I'm agreeing to wait." A gasp tore from Evin. "We will fly to Rokeshin with you and yours after this day's sun has set," Betony said, now addressing the den mother. "I make no promises beyond that."

CHAPTER TWENTY-SIX

The morning was brisk, the sun too newly risen to have mellowed the air. Pale fog curled from Raine's lips as he walked the keep's familiar footpaths. His gaze swept over the charred ruins of his home, assessing the destruction so he could organize the most efficient way to clear it.

The Roost and the keep were formidable, with thick stone walls and slate rooftops, and it showed. Neither had suffered much damage from Betony's storm. In fact, the Roost was untouched entirely, and the chapel was the only part of the keep that required attention.

Everything else was in shambles.

Where sheds and storehouses once stood, there was only burnt grass and rubble. The bathhouses and workshops were gutted and frail. The barracks were nothing more than hollow stone, their wooden infrastructure consumed to ash.

Almost everything else was in shambles, he corrected as he approached the dovecote. Situated between what used to be an apple crib and a woodshed, the squat stone building was unharmed.

Raine cracked the door and peered inside. A conical roof opened above, spilling light and fresh air through the space. Feathery wings fluttered as homing pigeons shifted in their nesting boxes. Some cooed. Others grunted at his intrusion.

"We have time," Sidian said over his shoulder.

Raine closed the door and turned. His heart skipped a beat as their eyes met. For a second, he forgot what he was going to say. He was lost in every detail of his mate. That rigid jawline. Those graceful brows. The raw power woven into his sinewy frame. And always, *always,* the liquid velvet depths of his eyes.

"Time for what?" Raine managed, only a touch breathless.

The skin around those perfect fawn eyes crinkled in a knowing way, as if Sidian understood the effortless impact he had on Raine.

"Time before any Guardians or soldiers show up." Sidian ticked his chin at the dovecote.

Raine hadn't forgotten that Moranda sent an alarm to Rokeshin. Thanks to her, torrents of hunters were likely enroute to the keep. The Nine weren't in the habit of sparing resources when it came to capturing or killing dragons.

"It will take them at least two days to get here," Sidian assured him. "We'll be in Rokeshin before they're even halfway here."

"I know," Raine said.

By sending word to Olan, Moranda had hoped to see Raine defeated or worse. Too bad for Moranda, he wasn't going to remain at the keep long enough to greet whatever forces were underway. Her call for arms wouldn't so much as inconvenience him.

In fact, "Moranda did us a favor, didn't she?" Excitement quickened his veins. "The more forces the Nine send here, the less we'll have to contend with in Rokeshin."

"Figured that out, have you?" Sidian's lips twitched, then he sobered. "We're fortunate Betony agreed to wait. Her storm would have flown right over any reinforcements headed here, instantly redirecting them back to Rokeshin."

"Why didn't you mention that when you were talking to her earlier?" Raine's blood chilled at how disastrous that would have been. "She damn near decided to leave."

"Look around." Sidian directed his gaze at the many ruined outbuildings. "Betony's storm is high on victory. It's hard for them to perceive any humans as threatening after annihilating so many with ease."

"This wasn't a victory." Raine heard the edge in his tone but couldn't help it. "For victory, there must be a battle. No part of this was a battle. They slaughtered those guards. They didn't even check to make sure they weren't civilians."

Sidian nodded slowly, his expression considering. "Did you know dragons don't have designated warriors or soldiers?"

Raine blinked, then shrugged. "No. What does it matter? Betony's storm clearly imagine themselves as such, even without a label."

"In dragon society, there are no warriors because they are *all* warriors," Sidian explained. "Dragons believe the responsibility to protect and defend falls upon everyone. It never would have occurred to them to ensure this keep wasn't full of civilians because they don't understand that concept."

"So, I'm wrong and it was a victory, after all?" Raine sneered. "Awesome. I guess they can pat themselves on the back for a battle well fought."

"No," Sidian said, frustration bleeding into his voice. "That's not what I'm saying. You asked me why I didn't explain Moranda's missive to Betony, or the reinforcements it will have summoned here. It's because, to her and her storm, this was an enormous and easy victory. Right now, the guild's strength and numbers are immaterial to them. They feel invincible."

Boots scraped against rubble, announcing Jaska's approach from the north. Oka and Savere trailed the midnight green dragon, their progress hindered by the wreckage.

Jaska's sharp features were intent as he reached them. "We want to help. Where do we start?"

Raine hoisted another fragment of the bathhouse's crumbled walls and tossed it onto a growing pile of previously mortared limestone. His shoulders ached but he kept moving. He only had one day to assist the staff with this dismal mess before he left for Rokeshin.

He was going to make it count.

On the bright side, the frosty air no longer bothered him. Nonstop exertion saw to that.

He had stripped the olive-green jacket he pilfered from his father's closet hours ago. Sweat leaked from his hairline. He paused to wipe his brow, smearing grit and dust across his skin. His braid felt damp and heavy.

Lifting another misshapen segment of wall, Raine resisted the urge to glance at the tower piercing the sky behind him. Wherein Betony's storm brooded over their missing hatchlings and did fuck-all to help with anything. Never mind that they were the ones who caused all this destruction.

Whatever. It was better this way. The keep's staff was fragile and frightened. They didn't need the added stress of dodging the dragons who had killed all the guards and razed their home mere hours ago.

Besides, Evin and Naiah's thunders were absolute stars. The amount of work they had accomplished, together with Raine and the Wade brothers, was staggering.

One hundred and eighteen corpses had been collected and identified. Some cadavers had been trickier to place than others, resulting in the world's most macabre guessing game, since only half the guards had remained at the keep. The rest were attending the succession.

Sidian, Nyx, and Oka were currently building a pyre large enough for all the dead. Its size was ghastly, stretching from one end of the training yard to the other.

Meanwhile, Raine and the rest of Evin and Naiah's thunders worked at clearing away the ruined outbuildings. It was the most grueling, painstaking work imaginable. Raine yearned for a giant broom to appear out of nowhere and sweep the rubble straight off the mesa.

He squinted at the sky, but alas. No divinely wielded cleaning instruments descended. If he wanted the bathhouse taken care of, he'd have to see to it himself.

Go figure.

Only three of the bathhouse's five walls were standing. Criss-crossing beams had once formed a striking cedar starburst overhead, centered directly over the bathing pools.

The bathhouse's trusses were star-shaped no longer. Most of the beams had fallen when the walls crumbled.

Most, but not all. Two massive beams still clung to their brackets overhead. It was going to be a pain in the ass getting them down.

Raine had been deliberately stacking all the loose bricks and stones beneath the area where the joists met the rafters. Now, all he had to do was scale the rubble and take the beams down. After which, demolishing the rest of the bathhouse would be safe and straightforward.

Raine slowly climbed the leaning cairn of rocks and wall fragments. It was broad at the base but narrowed quickly. Stones shifted and wobbled, threatening his purchase. Somehow, he made it to the top without the whole thing collapsing. His gut tightened at what he found.

The lower beam was snugly secure and uncompromised. It would take effort to pry it loose, but no matter.

The issue was the beam sagging above it. The bolt securing the upper beam was half a shake away from breaking loose. And if the upper beam broke free, it would fall into the lower beam and knock it loose. Then, both beams would descend and crush Raine's skull before burying him inside the rocks he was perched upon.

To prevent that deadly sequence, all he had to do was free the incredibly secure lower beam without jostling the upper beam. If it moved even a fraction, he was in for a world of pain.

He took a deep breath and held it while he worked at the lower joist. It had already broken off where it met the opposite wall, so he pulled with all his strength, encouraging it to release on this side so he could drop it to the ground.

At first, the bolt was so rigid that it was like trying to rend an atmos tree from the earth. But Raine was stubborn. Many carefully controlled breaths later, the beam finally began to flex with his efforts as it loosened.

Encouraged, Raine gripped the cedar joist and yanked harder than ever. Gritting his teeth, he held his breath and strained.

The bolt dislodged with a sudden jarring crack that reverberated through his bones. His arms faltered as the entire weight of the lower beam sagged against his hold. The rockpile beneath him began to crumble, unbalanced by the additional weight. Worse, above him, the upper beam dipped sharply as its bolt released from the wall.

Raine's stomach dropped faster than the unbalanced stones beneath him as he realized what was about to happen. He had only seconds. Frantic, he cradled the loose beam in one arm and used the other to push against the beam slipping down overhead.

The rockpile shifted, toppling faster. His body sank with the jumbling stones, until his fingers could no longer support the beam above him. As his hand fell away, Raine squeezed his eyes shut and prepared for crushing pain.

A wall of wind knocked into him. He released the beam he was clutching, and it was immediately swallowed by tumbling stones. Raine rode the rockwave as best he could, hopping along the larger fragments to keep himself from being similarly buried. The rocks stopped falling almost as soon as he reached the ground.

An abrupt clatter boomed behind him. Raine whirled. He half-expected to find the bathhouse's remaining walls collapsing upon him. Instead, a huge wine-red dragon landed in the center of the rubble. The falling beam that might have killed Raine rolled harmlessly where the dragon tossed it.

A thousand knuckles cracked, and Lorrivare stood before him. Raine threw a gritty palm over his eyes.

The male snorted. "You're oddly bashful for a dragon, aren't you?"

Raine lowered his hand but kept his gaze skyward. "I don't have to be bashful to not want to see you naked. There is a coat on a rack to your left—"

"I'm already decent," Lorrivare drawled.

Raine looked over and relaxed. The male was outfitted in the wrinkled sheet he'd worn the previous evening. The last time Raine had seen Betony's storm, they'd been nude in anticipation of flight. They must have donned their sheets after their trip was delayed.

None of them had left the Roost since, let alone sought Raine out. He frowned. "Do you need something?"

Lorrivare's eyes narrowed, looking more like blood than wine. "I came to offer my assistance with your task when I discovered you amid an accident. I transformed in time to catch the joist before it crushed you. You're welcome," he said pointedly.

Raine scoffed. "You've been lazing around in the Roost all day. Why start being useful now?" It was a rhetorical question, and Raine didn't pause for an answer. "Just go back to the tower and sit with Betony and her other bloodthirsty brutes while the rest of us clean up your mess. We'll come get you when it's time to leave."

Lorrivare gave him an odd look. "My mate and her storm are not in the tower." He stepped around the remaining walls of the bathhouse and glanced outward.

Irritation lashed at Raine as he hastened to Lorrivare's side. If Betony's storm was out there creating problems for the staff, he was going to …

His inner tirade cut off.

Thin, somber dragons dressed in rust-stained sheets were everywhere. A blue male and purple female were helping Eva and Evin clear away the remnants of a workshop. Two green females helped Lukor with another. The barracks—or what was left of them—were being steadily stripped to their foundations by Naiah, several members of her thunder, and three more strangers in bloodied sheets.

He sucked in a breath as he found Betony. The storm mother seemed too proud—and selfish—to help anyone, let alone humans. But there she was, walking between Sidian and Oka, the three of them carrying armfuls of splintered wood fragments. They set their burdens at Nyx's feet. Nyx grabbed from the pile and carefully slotted the wood into the pyre, while the trio flitted from site to site, collecting anything and everything that was wooden.

It was a shock seeing Betony in action, but Sidian swiftly stole Raine's attention. His raven black hair gleamed in the sun, appearing darkly exotic amid all the heads of vibrant green and red and blue.

Like Raine, Sidian had stripped his coat in his exertion. Muscles flexed and rippled beneath his jumpsuit as he worked. Raine was captivated by that rugged strength.

Too captivated.

Earlier, when Sidian was splitting logs for the pyre, Raine had been so enthralled that he walked nose-first into the bailey's stone walls no less than a dozen times. To spare himself from a flattened nose and further humiliation, Raine had traded jobs with Oka, who had been dismantling the ruined bathhouse.

"Betony regrets last night," Lorrivare said quietly. Raine's skeleton jerked. He had forgotten about the dragon beside him. "We all do."

"Since when?" Raine asked, bitterness bubbling to the surface.

"Since the moment our heads cleared." Lorrivare's sigh was troubled. "When the humans upon the battlements saw our approach, they brandished weapons of our bone from their sheaths. I was overcome with rage. We all were," he said mildly. "And we let that anger rule us."

Something close to empathy wormed through Raine's chest. He ignored it. "Right now, there's an innocent maid inside the keep with her skin melted to the elbows. She's suffering so profusely, she probably wishes she was dead. If your lot had their way last night, she would be."

Lorrivare faced him fully and nodded. "You're right. Our anger was misplaced. We destroyed your home and harmed an innocent because of it. For that, I am truly sorry."

Try as he might, Raine could find no trace of artifice or deception. Lorrivare reeked of sincerity.

Sidian's words from earlier returned to him. Betony's storm had attacked the keep without any concept of civilians. Of innocents other than children.

Well, they were fully apprised now.

"Your apology is accepted," Raine said gruffly. "But you won't be able to plead ignorance the next time you feel overcome."

"The next time we draw fire, it will be against those deserving of it," Lorrivare said, an assurance. "Until every human involved in persecuting us is dead."

"I thought all you cared about was getting your children back. Now, you are swearing vengeance on the entire guild?" Raine shook his head, frustration welling. "One of the reasons we are targeting the Nine directly is to stop this violent cycle with the fewest casualties possible. What is any of it going to mean, if the second the humans lay down their arms, you force them to pick them back up?"

Lorrivare held his stare, but not for long. He looked away, scanning the horizon. "You make a decent point. Our children *are* our priority. And war is not what is best for them."

That hadn't been Raine's point, but it was true and, more importantly, it supported an end of human-dragon conflict. "We will vanquish the Nine," Raine vowed. "They might not be the original Nine who incarcerated you and weaponized your children, but they are the ones responsible for perpetuating that agenda. The rest of the humans have just been pawns, like yourselves."

"Just like us? I didn't realize any humans were placed in cages, too." Raine's lips twitched at Lorrivare's droll tone. Possibly, the male wasn't trying to be funny. And really, it wasn't. "We will help with this," Lorrivare said, reverting to their original subject. He indicated the destruction around them. "As much as we are able. And later, I will speak with Betony about the merits of ... peace."

CHAPTER TWENTY-SEVEN

Raine eyed Carissyne's approach warily from where he leaned against the keep. She'd worked herself to the bone clearing away the barracks with Naiah and others. Smears of ash lined her arms and neck. Her skirt was torn and covered with dust. She should have been exhausted, but those popinjay green eyes glinted with mischief.

Raine's fight-or-flight response system began threading his sinew with tension at the vulpine curve of her smile.

"Are you ready?" Carissyne asked, bouncing on her soles.

"For what, a nap?"

"No. For your next lesson." Her hand curled over his right bicep, and she tugged. "On accessing your dragon form, remember?"

The fine hairs along Raine's nape prickled. *Not this again.*

"No, thank you," he said, careful to keep the panic from his tone. Carissyne was a predator. If she sensed his fear, it was over with.

"Really? We're flying to Rokeshin soon. Don't you want to use your own wings to get there?"

Of course, he wanted to use his own wings to get there. But there was no chance in hell he was going to consume the still-beating heart of a mountain lion or any other animal to accomplish it. He shuddered, his tongue folding back on itself to evade the imagined taste.

"I've decided against any more lessons. My change will come when it comes." He shrugged, hoping an insouciant air would encourage her to drop it.

Instead, Carissyne pursed her lips, looking mulish. "I think you should reconsider. Our fire is at its strongest the first few days we use it. You'll be an entire army unto yourself. Sounds like something that might come in handy, don't you think?"

Before Raine could determine how much of Carissyne's argument was fabricated, the better to lure him, he heard the sound of gravel crunching. His pulse fluttered as he glimpsed Sidian's approach. Aly and Zane walked beside him.

Once the pyre had been finished, Sidian had joined the couple in clearing out the glass and wreckage within the chapel.

Raine had objected to Sidian's involvement in that particular task. Glass couldn't cut dragons, but Sidian was human. There were other, less dangerous jobs he could perform.

When Raine said as much, Sidian had given him a flat look and said, "I know how to kill a dragon seventy-two different ways, with my bare hands. I think I can handle a broken window."

The trio had disappeared inside the keep to tackle the chapel less than an hour ago, and now they were here. It seemed too brief for their job to be done. Had they been forced to stop because of an accident? No sooner than the thought struck him, Raine snatched Sidian's hands. He tried turning them over so he could inspect his mate's palms and fingers for injury.

Sidian extracted his hands and rolled his eyes.

"I'm fine." He held up his palms for good measure, showing smooth tanned skin devoid of any cuts or blood. "See?"

Relief rolled through Raine, but he schooled his expression. "You were lucky," he said with excessive seriousness.

Sidian coughed a surprised laugh. "You're ridiculous."

His dark eyes dazzled Raine, glowing with warmth and affectionate humor. Raine's lower stomach swooped and fluttered like a net of magpies. Sidian's features morphed into a hungry look, and Raine's mouth went dry.

"Sidian, tell Raine he needs to learn how to shift into his dragon form," Carissyne demanded.

Sidian's lips twitched as he surveyed him. Raine glared, silently promising pain if his mate sided with her.

"I can think of a few occasions where your wings would have saved us a lot of trouble," Sidian mused. Raine's mouth fell open, but his mate wasn't through betraying him. Devious mirth creased his eyes as he added, "You should take Carissyne's lessons whenever she offers them."

Aly's red mouth formed a circle of surprised delight. She eyed Carissyne appraisingly. "That's such a good idea. I wish I'd thought of it." To Raine, she said, "It can take decades to learn how to shift. The sooner you start, the better."

"Decades?" Carissyne drew back, then her face cleared with understanding. "Evin is your den mother, isn't she?" Aly had barely begun to nod when Carissyne continued. "She is such a stickler, I bet she never shared any of the shortcuts."

Before Aly could ask, Raine stepped between them. "No." He slashed his arm through the air for emphasis. "Don't listen to her. They aren't shortcuts. They're cruel and unusual torture methods."

If possible, Aly looked even more intrigued. She pushed Raine to the side, like a piece of furniture in her path. Her garnet eyes latched onto Carissyne. "Tell me more. No, tell me everything."

This was why Raine had once thought Naiah's thunder ate male dragons. Because females of all species were deranged. His best friend included.

He clapped his palms together loudly. "Well, you two go ahead and bond over animal cruelty and sadism. But don't expect me to stick around and be your willing victim."

Carissyne and Aly scarcely registered his retreat. They were already bent together, conversing with ecstatic glee. Zane eyed Raine pitifully, as if he yearned to accompany him away from the plotting females. But devotion to his mate won out. Zane remained fixed like a resigned stanchion at Aly's side.

Raine's steps slowed as the bailey wall came into view, but only so he could throw an elbow into the ribs of the man walking beside him. "I can't believe you encouraged that insanity. You're supposed to be on my side."

Sidian massaged his ribs as if in pain. An obnoxious smirk belied the performance. "What? I spoke the truth. If you had your wings, we could have flown up and down Moontop to search for Nyx instead of nearly perishing from hypothermia. That's just one example out of many."

Raine shook his head. "If you think wings are that important, then *you* go learn to fly. I'm almost positive the identity of Carissyne's pupil doesn't matter to her. Any victim will do."

"Except I'm not the dragon here. You are."

"Just flap your arms really fast. I'm sure it'll be fine," Raine deadpanned.

He had no warning. One minute, he was crossing the flat, scorched lawn near the bailey. Then, sheer agony puckered his abdomen and sides. He screeched and attempted to escape the onslaught.

Sidian's merciless fingers kept their purchase, wriggling beneath his ribs. Tears streamed down Raine's face as he howled with tormented laughter.

"Stop," he gasped. "Please, no more."

He continued to beg, though he was soon insensate to the words pouring out of him. His knees buckled, and he tried rolling away.

Sidian seemed to anticipate Raine's every squirming evasion. His evil, wretched fingers didn't falter. Raine's back pressed against the cold ground as Sidian pinned him, straddling his hips. All the while, Sidian's hands took Raine apart. Skimming up and down his sides and across his quivering stomach.

Raine twisted and bucked. His lungs felt raw. His sides ached. "Please, Sidian. Oh, please."

Above him, Sidian stilled. Raine's panting breaths were loud in the silence. He became excruciatingly aware of the palms against his sides. They felt hot and firm against his skin.

Sidian's grip tightened. "Say that again."

Huh? Raine blinked dazedly up at Sidian. His eyes were so dark, Raine couldn't distinguish his irises from his pupils. Sparks danced through his belly. His heart thumped like a fist. "Say what?"

Sidian moved his hips. A shallow, deliberate thrust that grinded his ass against Raine's cock. Raine's lips parted on a strangled moan. He was hard. Rock hard, his cock large and leaden against his belly. And he hadn't even realized it.

"My name," Sidian said, his voice rough with demand. "Say my name while you beg me."

Raine choked on his tongue. Desire flooded him, a disorienting wave of heat and need that constricted his lungs.

This wasn't a good idea. They had the barest shred of privacy, splayed in the shadows of the keep's inner curtain. On the other side of the gray stone wall, mere paces away, a pyre scattered with dead guards awaited a torch.

"Later," he gasped. Sidian didn't like that. Eyes darkening, he rolled his hips again. A sinuous motion that should have been outlawed. Raine's cock wept against his tights. "You're going to make me come." Sidian moved again. Raine shoved his fist into his mouth to muffle a sob. "Please don't make me light the pyre with a wet spot on my jumpsuit."

Cursing sharply, Sidian leapt off of Raine and stood. He pulled Raine to his feet, then blew out a shuddering exhale. "Apologies. I'm always accosting you without meaning to. If you can believe it, I expected our situations to be reversed." A self-deprecating smile traced Sidian's lips. "This has been humbling, to say the least."

"Do you mean you expected *me* to always be accosting *you*?" Raine asked, aghast. How could his mate think something like that of him?

It wasn't that Sidian wasn't accostible. He was very accostible. *Too accostible*. But until last night, Raine had believed his affections were one-sided. Sidian had to know that Raine would never, *ever* push himself onto his mate under such circumstances.

Sidian smirked. "I did. In fact, I counted on it." He leaned against the bailey wall and crossed his arms, as smug as a cat with a canary in its belly.

It probably had to do with how flabbergasted Raine looked. His eyes were open so wide, his eyeballs would roll right out like marbles if he wasn't careful. "But I swore I wouldn't mate with you. I told you I wouldn't let you sacrifice your future."

"I recall." Sidian snorted. "I knew how much you wanted me and figured you couldn't resist for long. I intended to tease and tempt you until you couldn't take it anymore and jumped me."

"It would have never worked," Raine said, only now realizing how true it was. He had agonized over his weakness for no reason. Never would he have yielded to a consummation that doubled as cage bars to his mate. But, "When did you start wanting to mate with me? Not just to save my life, but because …"

"Because I love you? Because I want you?" Sidian's eyes glinted with devilry. "Because all I can think about is sinking my cock into your pert, pretty ass? Bending you over and having you beneath me?"

Heat rose beneath Raine's face. His head probably resembled a snow-capped strawberry. "All of that, I suppose."

"It took longer than it should have." Sidian shoved his hands into his coat pockets. His features sobered. "When we met, I was closed off from the world. Insulated by anger and bitterness."

Raine recalled his mate's brooding ice. How he seethed with enmity. A husky voice that cut deep. Velvet eyes that craved Raine's demise.

"My bedmates were always impersonal. Women who could have been anyone. Then you came along ..." Sidian shook his head at a memory. A wry smile traced his lips. "I didn't understand what I was feeling. I thought I cared for you like a little brother. Someone to guide and protect—"

Sidian broke off the instant he glimpsed Raine's features. It started with a snicker, something of a half-chuckle. But it quickly grew, until Sidian was clutching his sides and guffawing at the sky.

Raine was not amused. Cold horror snaked through him like a dozen fanged eels.

A little brother. A LITTLE BROTHER.

"Stop," Sidian choked, leaking laughter. "Making that face. Seriously, stop. I can't continue until you do."

"I don't know if I want you to continue," Raine managed. His mouth felt frozen, locked in an appalled grimace.

"If it helps, I don't think of you as a little brother anymore."

"When," Raine said rigidly, "did you cease regarding me as a sibling?"

"Earlier than you surmise," Sidian drawled, hints of mirth still teasing his mouth. "I've been hounding you for sex this entire week. Do you really think—"

"I don't know what to think," Raine burst. "Please, tell me when you started feeling something *not brotherly* for me."

"I would have to say, it was probably sometime during our journey to Moontop," Sidian said musingly. A wicked smirk crept over his face. "About the time you started dry-humping me in your sleep."

Raine's mouth fell open. His blush grew scalding.

"You were a very hot armful," Sidian continued, low and smoky. "I wasn't used to sleeping against anyone. I didn't expect to revel in it. But I did. I basked in your heat. The silken feel of you. Your warm, sweet scent. Your size and strength only made everything better."

Raine drew in a breath. Then another. He thought he might be wheezing. "You-You've wanted me that long?" His mate's lips curled into a sly affirmation. "But, then, why didn't you say any-thing?"

"I luxuriated in your besotted gaze for weeks," Sidian said gently, making Raine sputter. "You always make your feelings known, even when you seek to hide them. Knowing how intensely you felt for me made it that much harder to control myself. But you are the purest thing in my life, and I refused to take advantage of your infatuation like some lecherous cad."

Raine's mouth pinched. "I'm a grown man. Dragon. *Whatever*. You wouldn't have been taking advantage of me."

"Yes, I would have." Sidian's tone was blunt. Matter-of-fact.

"Fine." Raine shook his head but decided to let it go. "Why didn't you tell me how you felt once you knew we were mates? You were fine with consummating the bond to save my life, but you didn't breathe a word about wanting me." *Of loving me.*

Sidian arched a brow. "I assure you, I did. My ardor was quite evident."

Raine fidgeted, feeling foolish. With hindsight, Sidian's ardor *had* been evident. Not clinically executed flirtations meant to lure

Raine into consummation. But real, genuine desire. "It's just that, you were so focused on preserving my life. Of the consequences if we didn't mate."

"Imagine that. Me, not wanting you to die."

Raine scowled. "You know what I mean."

"I do." Sidian frowned, considering. "You said I deserved to choose. I *thought* you were referencing the predetermined nature of our bond. Not some presumed lack of reciprocation on my part."

Raine's mouth opened and closed, but no sound emerged. He was speechless. Fuck, had he truly been so abstruse? In hindsight, he was forced to admit that, yes. Yes, he had been.

Sidian's gaze went distant as it scanned the horizon. "When you finally shared your little misapprehension—that you believed only a woman could make me happy? Everything became clear. I realized you had no idea what I felt for you."

Fawn eyes pinned Raine abruptly, arresting him. "I corrected my oversight immediately." An ironic gleam entered Sidian's stare. "Which is more than I can say for you."

Raine blinked. "Come again?"

"Like myself, you never gave voice to your sentiments." Shrugging casually, Sidian added, "You still haven't, if we're being technical."

As his mate's meaning penetrated, shame nearly brought Raine to his knees.

"I love you," Raine burst, frantic to rectify his mistake.

Part of him was still afraid that the strength of his attachment would disturb Sidian. But he'd be damned if he stood here and kept a single scrap of it to himself. By allowing fear to bind his tongue, he had failed his mate. That stopped now.

"I love you so much," he continued, more raw and open than if he'd been turned inside out. "It's more than love. I'm obsessed with you. You own me, Sidian. Body and soul. You have since the day I hatched, wearing my human form because my soul yearned for us to match the day we met. Your face is the wallpaper that wraps my mind. I'm consumed with thoughts of you—"

"You think I'm unaware of how you feel?" Sidian's dark stare throbbed, holding him captive. "Even if you weren't so fucking demonstrative, shouting your love with every glance and gesture, I would still know your heart." He snorted at Raine's expression. "You're a dragon and I'm your mate. I will always be perfect in your eyes."

Abandoning his position against the curtain, Sidian marched right up to Raine. Firm fingers gripped Raine's chin. His stomach fluttered.

"You covet me. Crave me. Adore me. With a passion unrivaled by anything in this world. It fucking petrifies me—the influence I hold over you. And I've got news for you."

Sidian's other hand reached around Raine and gripped the base of his braid, tugging him closer. Their breaths mingled.

"It works both ways. I'm putty in your pretty fingers. You tempt me by breathing. I can't stop touching you, even though it makes my need a thousand times worse. You're so fucking responsive, and you don't even realize it. Your eyes follow my every move. Your body faces me whenever I'm in the same room, regardless of who you're speaking with."

Sidian's hand slid from Raine's chin to his neck in a satin caress, making him shiver.

"It's instinctive. Subconscious. And every time I touch you, you fucking melt."

Sidian's fingers clenched around Raine's throat. It hurt *good*. He whimpered. Sidian groaned, gripping him even tighter before drawing back.

"Come on." His gaze flickered to the sky. "It's almost sunset."

Dragons lined the curtain wall along one side of the pyre. Hands clasped, heads bowed, features solemn—Betony's storm was displaying admirable tact considering the pyre was laden with their enemies.

Perhaps Raine should have told them that their presence wasn't expected. Even humans didn't hold honorable services for the foes they had vanquished.

But they were already here, interspersed with Evin and Naiah's thunders. Raine left them be.

On the other side of the pyre stood the keep's staff. In direct contrast to the dragons, they were lively. They smiled and laughed, clustering close together for warmth as the sun sank.

True to Valdenian form, there were no tears. Self-control was paramount at a funeral pyre. Humans believed that whatever emotions they projected would be the last impression the dead received of this realm. It was the responsibility of the living to fill their final flesh-bound moments with joy.

Raine took a steadying breath. The air still tasted like smoke and char. Scents that should have come after a pyre was lit, not before.

A flare of orange flame caught his eye. Raine's gut clenched reflexively. For a hideous moment, he thought one of the dragons had transformed and was breathing fire.

His stomach relaxed as he spied the head of black hair glinting off the flame. It was Sidian. In his right hand was a lit torch.

Raine could have kicked himself. He had completely forgotten the single most important element necessary for his role. Prayers were all well and good, but it was fire that the dead required to rise.

Sidian's fawn eyes were more liquid than usual in the flickering light. They curved with his smile, which somehow both teased and bolstered Raine. Their fingers brushed as Sidian passed him the torch. Sparks shot up Raine's spine at the contact.

Together, they faced the pyre and assemblage. It was almost funny how miserable the dragons looked next to the beaming humans. Their confusion was palpable. Dragons didn't channel grief into a celebration of the life that was lived. Instead, Requiems formed iron weights in their chests until their lamenting roars shook earth and sky.

There would be time to explain the differences between human and dragon customs later. For now, Raine simply appreciated their efforts.

And now, it was his turn to make an effort. To muster some final words for the dead before he sent them off.

He'd never been close to the curtain guards. His father had always kept them at a distance. Raine hadn't discovered why until Lukor informed him that the weapons they kept arduously concealed were the milk-white of dragon bone.

These men ... They had been Raine's foes, too.

Throughout his afternoon of dull labor, Raine had ruminated on his reactions whenever Guardians died around him. And he realized that he'd been projecting his love for his father and Sidian onto his enemies. His thoughts were always an insistent thrum of the hunters' innate goodness, even though he had no proof of their characters.

The men before him died defending Raine's home, and for that he was grateful. But the lines had been drawn for over two centuries. Raine would still strive to preserve as many lives as he could until the Nine were vanquished, but he would no longer mourn the loss of men and women that served their cause.

When he spoke, his voice was steady. He kept his words brief but honest. "These men were dedicated and loyal. They lived well and died bravely. May their spirits rise straight and swift."

"Their palace rest is well earned," the staff chimed.

Twilight descended in a rush, unveiling the stars as Raine cast the torch onto the pyre.

CHAPTER TWENTY-EIGHT

Raine's arms wrapped around Sidian's waist from behind, holding tight as Oka careened through the dark sky. This high off the ground, the air was thin and bitterly cold. His braid whipped along the night wind like an angry asp. He kept expecting his next foggy exhale to turn into snow. Snuggling closer into the small of Sidian's back, he savored his mate's contoured strength and heat.

Sidian was the only one who knew where the secret passage into Rokeshin was, so he sat in front of Raine, straddling Oka's wing joints. The position placed him as close to Oka's dragon ears as possible, so he could issue directions to the green dragon as needed. The rest of the dragons followed behind them in an arrowhead formation.

Thus far, Olan's missive regarding the guild's policy change proved eerily accurate. Every watchtower they passed was unmanned, as if all the sky watchers had vanished on the breath of a desperate dandelion wish. Logically, it was a good thing since the Guardians' absence enabled their brazen flight. But each vacant platform only heightened Raine's unease.

The very thing making their journey to Rokeshin so easy was also going to make their next objective immensely difficult.

Unless, of course, half the guild was on their way to Chambrin Keep.

Clenching his thighs around Oka's body for added purchase, Raine leaned over to scrutinize the shadowy ground below. He'd been intermittently scouring the earth throughout their flight in hopes of spying whatever reinforcements the Nine had sent in response to Moranda's alert.

But no matter how carefully Raine inspected the passing forests and fields, he couldn't detect so much as a hint of a hunter army. They must have made camp beneath one of the wooded canopies along the route. Raine abandoned his search with a huff.

At least the Guardians' concealment worked both ways. Raine couldn't see them, and they probably couldn't see the huge group of dragons arrowing through the night sky right over their heads. The hunters had no idea they were rushing further and further away from the dragons they pursued.

Raine's ass and ears were both numb by the time he detected the faint glow of an enlivened city in the distance. Rokeshin's many lamps created a soft, pulsating dome against the blackness. It diluted the stars but helped illuminate the ground.

He sucked in a breath as he surveyed the snaking road far below. A teeming mass of people stretched for miles. From his aerial perch, they resembled a huge colony of ants crowding an endless strip of honey. Packed shoulder-to-shoulder, they pressed forward in a painstaking progression toward Rokeshin.

There was no mistaking them for the reinforcements sent to Chambrin Keep. They were going the wrong way, for starters. And even this high up, Raine could detect the motley array of both guild-issued and civilian coats and travel gear.

Thank the Divine Sidian knows a secret way into the city. If they had to wait in that interminable line to gain entry to Rokeshin, Raine would have turned around and left. Assassinations be damned.

He snorted as he recalled Lukor's suspicion that Sidian was taking them somewhere nefarious. Sidian could be escorting them to a hovel of inbred cannibals, and Raine would find a way to establish healthy boundaries with them before going to bed. Anything was better than that hellish line.

Sidian said something to Oka, but the wind ate his words before Raine could interpret them. Oka's body tilted as he veered right. Without looking back, Raine knew the dragons behind them had also veered right. Dragons in flight were as fluid as starlings. They moved in sync like a hive mind. It was stunning to see, and Raine looked forward to his dragon transformation if only so he could understand how it worked.

His stomach fluttered as Oka swooped lower. They had flown far enough away from the road that no one was around to witness their descent. They passed another vacant watchtower before dense woods yielded to grassland. The gently rolling hills, black in the night, resembled a tempestuous seascape.

Sidian gave more directions to Oka. They flew lower still, then landed on the crest of one of the many small hills. Soft thuds sounded the arrival of the others. Raine and Sidian dismounted and turned away from the dragons so they could shift and garb themselves.

Fortunately, with so many of Chambrin Keep's residents out-of-town for the succession, the dragons had been able to borrow clothes and shoes without issue. Backpacks were a different story. Betony's storm had been forced to use their bloodied sheets like sacks to carry their articles.

Wind howled through the fields, flattening calf-high grasses in great gusts. Raine shuddered, huddling in on himself. His hood suddenly rose and covered his head. Raine looked sideways at Sidian and found his mate glaring at him in the near darkness.

"Take better care of yourself."

Raine frowned. "You don't even have a hood." His eyes widened. "By the Divine, Sidian. I'm so sorry. Here." He fumbled with his coat buttons.

"Stop." A hand closed over his, halting him. "I'm not trading coats. The hood isn't just for warmth. You need to be able to hide your hair."

"I'll put on my wig." Raine tried to resume unfastening his coat. Sidian's grip tightened, keeping his hands still. "Damn it, Sidian. Stop being such an ass. I'm trying to take care of you."

Sidian's glare softened, as if Raine hadn't just snapped at him. "I know the cold bothers you more than it does me, no matter how you try to hide it." He closed the gap between them, sandwiching their hands. His breath was a shock of heat against Raine's frozen ear. "You can take care of me in other ways."

Raine's blood had been as sluggish as slush, half-frozen like the rest of him. Right up until Sidian said *that*. His veins imploded with quicksilver heat. It spiraled through him with dizzying speed.

Sidian's lips brushed against his ear. A slow, deliberate caress. Raine gasped as his cock turned to stone.

"Hey, guys," Nyx chirped, plopping his pack onto the grass next to theirs. Sidian growled softly against Raine's ear before pulling away. "Aww, Raine. You look so adorable bundled up. Remember that time I took you sledding?"

Raine almost didn't hear Nyx. He was too busy reeling from the exquisite sensations caused by Sidian's low growl. "Um, what? Oh, sledding. Yeah."

"Are you okay?" Nyx's palm covered his forehead. "You don't have a fever. I think we should get you out of this cold."

Even in the dim starlight, Raine caught the wicked glimmer in Sidian's eyes. "His senses do seem addled."

"Are we talking about Raine?" Aly asked, bounding over. Her grin was blinding as she adjusted her pack.

"Zane, actually," Raine said, lifting his chin. "We're still confused about why he's so taken with you."

"Nice deflection," Aly simpered. "But considering that addled is your default state, I'm certain Sidian was referring to you."

Raine opened his mouth, but at that moment, Evin reached them.

"Hatchlings." It was her den mother tone, somehow both gentle and strict. She eyed Raine and Aly a little longer, ensuring their compliance, then looked to Sidian. "We are ready when you are."

"Where is it that you are going?" Betony demanded, edging her way through the throng of her storm—all of whom were now human-shaped and dressed. "We agreed to arrive here discreetly. Nothing more has been discussed."

"I know of a secret passage into Rokeshin," Sidian said. "My understanding is that Evin has a safehouse within the city."

"Yes. It belonged to Velissa's thunder until the hunters found them." A shadow crossed Evin's face. She blinked it away, her gaze earnest as it found Betony. "Please join us there. I know our purposes differ, but that's no reason for us to separate."

"How is it safe for us, if others were found?" Betony asked.

Good question. Raine looked to Evin with the rest of their company, curious.

"They were overtaken by hunters while visiting the site of the massacre. It was a foolish thing to do. Many of us warned them to stop the habit, but Velissa's thunder was a mournful one. Each of them had lost a mate there. I think ... I think they knew what would happen."

Sorrow creased Betony's eyes. "Velissa was always so sentimental." She huffed a sigh. "Very well. We will rest at your safehouse, but do not forget—our purposes here are different. Tomorrow, my storm will commence our search for the human, Olan."

"Thank you, Grandmother. I promise we won't interfere with your mission."

Betony's chin lifted. "See that you don't."

Less than an hour later, they were crossing another blunt, grassy hill when Rokeshin's imposing stone walls came into view. But that wasn't what drew Raine's attention.

Nestled directly against the city barrier was a grand estate. Two steeply sloped rooftops framed a much broader, longer rectangle. Judging from its windows, the manor house was four stories high. It was an ostentatious dwelling, serving no purpose beyond hearth and home for an obscenely wealthy family.

Raine surveyed the estate in bewilderment. He didn't think people were permitted to build so close to city fortifications. Even more unusual than its location was the solid, eight-foot-tall palisade hemming the property. The fence was so wide, it stretched out of view on either side.

"What's this place?" Nyx asked, peering down alongside them.

"Roke Manor. It's the ancestral seat of the Roke tribe's founders," Sidian said. "It's also where the Roke stables are located."

Even Raine, who had lived his whole life removed from horseflesh, knew of the Roke stables. Their powerful, stocky war horses were coveted by every army in the world. Once, they had been the vale's richest export—before Valdenia had formed and sealed itself from trade.

Raine traced the pointed pikes of the palisade with new eyes. It was built higher than necessary to keep prized horseflesh from wandering off. He readily gathered the fence's alternate purpose—to keep thieves out.

"We aren't going there, are we?" Raine asked. His eyes widened as he looked from the manor to his mate.

"We are," Sidian confirmed. He arched a brow at Raine, his gaze sharply intent. "Problem?"

Raine bit his lip as he considered his mate. "No. It's just, that place looks hard to sneak into. Is there another way to the secret passage? One where we don't have to break into a giant, fenced-off estate?"

"There isn't," Sidian said. He smiled mysteriously, then added, "I've been here before. We won't have any issues."

Raine regarded the night-veiled estate uncertainly. He couldn't make out many details in the darkness, but it seemed too grand not to have guards or some sort of security. Raine looked back at his mate and caught a flash of something he couldn't identify before Sidian's expression shuttered.

"Okay," Raine said reluctantly, wondering what Sidian was trying to hide. Was he upset at Raine's lack of faith in his plan?

Raine's heart winced at the thought. Sidian deserved a mate with utmost confidence in him. Raine resolved to keep his objections to himself. It didn't matter that the estate was gated and possibly guarded. Sidian had probably already accounted for those obstacles.

If any of the other dragons had reservations about approaching the manor house, they didn't voice them. Not even Lukor. Raine kept glancing over his shoulder, expecting someone—anyone—to show curiosity or concern. When they didn't, Raine felt even worse for doubting Sidian. He was Sidian's mate, and he was demonstrating less trust in him than *Betony*.

His thoughts swerved as he saw Jaska shift his backpack with a pained grimace. Was Jaska injured? Concern pricked him, and he fell back into step with the dark green dragon to ask, "What's wrong?"

Jaska flicked a sideways glance at him before staring forward. "Just some wing strain."

"Is there anything that will help it? Bandages or ointment? I can go find out if Nyx brought any medical supplies." Raine began to turn, intending to scan the crowd and locate Nyx.

Jaska grabbed his shoulder to keep him straight. "Don't worry about it. The same thing happened on my flight to Chambrin Keep. I slept in my dragon form last night, and Betony's healing resonance cured everything. She'll do the same tonight, when we next rest."

"Yeah, but who knows when that will be?" Raine frowned. "You're hurting now."

"Even if Nyx has something to help, he won't have enough for all of us." He snorted at Raine's expression. "I'm not the only dragon whose wings have weakened with disuse. Every dragon here is strained."

Raine turned around. This time, Jaska didn't stop him. He surveyed the dragons, noticing their stooped backs and glazed expressions for the first time. They kept stumbling, barely managing to stay upright.

No wonder none of the dragons had reacted to where Sidian was taking them. They looked too knackered to speak.

"Like I said, we'll be fine after a night of Betony's healing resonance," Jaska said quietly.

"We're nearly there," Raine said, trying to ease some of the pained resignation pinching Jaska's features.

Jaska shook his head tiredly. "We're nearly to the passageway, perhaps. We still have to walk through Rokeshin to reach the safehouse."

"You might be able to rest at the manor tonight," Sidian remarked without turning.

The base of Raine's spine tingled with alarm. He'd thought the plan was to sneak by the estate unseen, not *sleep* there. "How is Roke Manor a place we would be welcome? If the owners don't try to kill us, their guards or massive war horses will."

"I think you will find yourself very warmly welcomed," Sidian said in a dry tone as they reached the palisade. A worn, gravel path continued beyond a scrolled metal gate.

Sidian stepped aside and dug through one of the ornamental shrubs bracketing the entrance. After a bit of searching, he extracted a smooth, brown rock. It looked familiar. Raine learned why when, seconds later, an iron key spilled from the hollow stone and into Sidian's open palm.

Sidian unlocked the gate and held it open, stepping aside until everyone entered before relocking it.

Evin and Naiah separated from the throng, looking dead on their feet as they trudged over to them. Evin offered Sidian a tired smile. "I take it the passage is on this property?"

"It is," Sidian said, "but I will see if we can spend the night here, if you'd like to continue in the morning."

Naiah's toilworn gaze lifted with hope. "The people living here," she began, then paused to peer at the manor. "Are they safe?"

"Yes," Sidian answered succinctly before striding up the path to the front door.

"Wait," Raine called nervously. Gravel crunched beneath his boots as he hurried to catch up. "It's not that I don't trust you," he whispered urgently as they neared the manor's doubled entrance. "But who the hell lives here? Sidian, we're putting the lives of every free dragon on the line right now."

Sidian halted before twin cherrywood doors. Each possessed a stained-glass window featuring a silhouetted stallion. The horses mirrored each other, their muzzles meeting where the doors would open.

Sidian's dark eyes slanted to Raine. He radiated confidence. Too much confidence. The cocksure kind that invited a humbling disaster. Raine's stomach flipped as Sidian began hammering at the door like a tax collector.

"You can't knock like that," he whisper-yelled, pale with fear. "It's the middle of the night. You're going to piss them off."

"It's a big house," Sidian said blandly. "I'm making sure they hear me." He waited half a second, then pounded the door even harder. His hooded gaze was fixed on Raine, as if he couldn't be less bothered at who answered.

This was a bad idea. Sidian clearly believed whoever lived here would help them, but what if he was wrong?

The answer was so obvious, Raine didn't have to think about it. He steeled himself, suddenly and inexplicably calm.

If Sidian was wrong, Raine would protect his mate at all costs. It was that simple. He braced himself as the door flew open.

A short, dark-haired woman shrieked and launched herself at Raine. "Moonbeam!"

CHAPTER TWENTY-NINE

Raine flung out his arms and managed to catch the woman just as she smacked into his chest. Her delicate appearance belied a core of wiry strength. He gasped as she reached round his neck and squeezed, cutting off his air supply.

"I can't believe you're here," she gushed, squeezing harder before releasing him.

"I can't believe *you're* here," he said faintly, still recovering from whiplash.

Rosa—*Rosa*—was here. Behind her, the polished floor of an entrance hall gleamed beneath a crystal chandelier. The light spilled out of the manor, softly illuminating Rosa in a poppy red nightdress. Her dark hair was swept into a messy updo, and her left leg was encased in a lumpy white cast.

Raine shook his head slowly. Rosa's presence was too surreal. "What are you doing here?"

"I believe that's *my* question, Moonbeam." She drew herself up to her full height, which was underwhelming given that her crown reached as high as Raine's shoulder. "You're at my house, after all."

"Your house?" Raine's eyes widened, then immediately narrowed at Sidian. "Are you telling me that, all this time, you've been taking us to Rosa's house? Why the hell didn't you just say so?"

"I wanted to surprise you." Sidian shrugged, then refocused on Rosa *Roke*, apparently. "We require a place to rest. Can you sleep thirty-six?"

Rosa blinked twice, rather owlishly, then gazed beyond them for the first time. "Oh, wow. I see. Yes. Yes, I can manage that. Come in. Come in." She receded into the manor, gesturing for them to follow.

Raine made sure his stare promised payback as he caught Sidian's eye. "That wasn't funny. You should have told me."

"I was going to tell you when we first saw the manor." Sidian leaned forward, his voice a low, husky taunt. "But then I saw how nervous you were. Your eyes were so big and pleading. It was how you looked when I was reading my brother's book." His mouth brushed against Raine's ear. "It's how I imagine you'll look when I finally sink my cock in you."

Raine stuffed as much righteous indignation into his expression as possible with all his blood surging to his prick. Sidian had been making him nervous on purpose. He had enjoyed watching Raine sweat and squirm. Why did that set Raine's blood on fire?

"What's happening?" Nyx asked.

A flush ignited Raine's cheeks, but Nyx wasn't looking at him. He was too busy poking his head through Rosa's doorway like a curious cave bear.

"We can stay," Raine said, though his answer didn't seem to matter much to Nyx, because the man was already entering Rosa's ridiculously huge house.

"We should inform the others and get everyone inside," Sidian said.

A smirk lingered on Sidian's lips. It miffed Raine even as his belly tightened. He wanted to press his tongue into the seams of Sidian's mouth and see if he tasted as superior as he looked.

Prying his gaze away, before he did something embarrassing, Raine looked at the dragons assembled on Rosa's shadowy lawn. They hung back far from the manor house, prepared to flee. Their stooped, shivering postures made him think they wouldn't have been able to get very far, had Roke Manor indeed proven dangerous.

"Are there really enough bedrooms for everyone?" Raine asked, walking toward the space where Evin and Naiah huddled next to each other, their thunders behind them.

"Yes," Sidian affirmed. Their shoulders brushed as they walked. "Roke Manor existed before the city. Three centuries ago, Chieftain Roke lived here with his extended family. He designed it to house up to five generations, so no Roke would ever be without a home."

Raine grabbed Sidian's arm, halting him before they reached the dragons. Hard, coiled muscles met his fingers, and Raine's stomach swooped. Fuck, Sidian was strong.

Sidian gazed at him in question. Raine cleared his throat, hoping to mask his sudden breathlessness. "How is this place safe? If Roke Manor is home to multiple generations, doesn't that mean Rosa isn't the only one living here?"

Raine didn't doubt that they were safe with Rosa. But up to five generations of her family? If a single member of Rosa's family recognized Raine from his wanted poster—

Shit. An even worse thought struck him. "Rosa is a Guardian. What if some of her relatives are, too? They'll take one look at our group and report us. We won't survive the night."

"The Rokes are staunch supporters of the Guardians," Sidian said, his voice carefully neutral. "However, they are presently occupied with serving guild terms."

"Serving guild terms? But the entire guild is in Rokeshin," Raine hissed. "That puts them pretty damn close to home. What if someone drops by?"

Sidian shook his head. "They won't. The Rokes have diminished in number over the years. Only Rosa and her parents remain." Raine made to interrupt. Sidian quelled him with a look. "Her parents will not visit their country estate with their daughter in residence. They don't get along."

That Sidian knew so much about Rosa and her family reminded Raine of their history. Captain and journeywoman, yes. But also, ex-lovers. How often had Sidian come here? And why? Were his visits strictly guild business ... or erotic interludes between missions?

A tight, uncomfortable feeling formed in the pit of his stomach, as it always did whenever he imagined his mate with another. Raine swiftly buried the sensation before it spread. Humans weren't like dragons. Sidian was entitled to his past, regardless of what Raine's instincts thought.

Movement drew his gaze to the manor. Rosa exited her house, tightening a night robe as she approached. Her leg cast made her gait awkward, though her face showed no discomfort. Nyx grumbled, trailing closely behind her. Raine caught phrases like, "stubborn woman," and "shouldn't be walking."

Rosa didn't seem to hear him. She halted before the dragons, smiling in welcome. "If everyone would like to follow me, I will show you to your rooms."

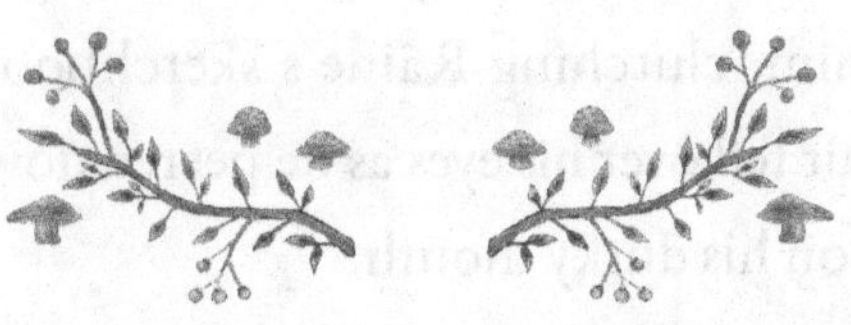

Someone shook Raine's shoulder. He groaned, swatting blindly as he buried his face into a pillow. "Not now, Father. Five more minutes."

He was so warm and comfy. Plush cushions cradled his frame like a divine embrace, upholstered in a material as sleek and smooth as water. Raine was content to spend the rest of his life right here, floating on this silken river of a bed.

A hand smoothed back his hair. His scalp tingled pleasantly, and he shifted his head encouragingly. The hand stroked across his crown more firmly, and he purred. *Paradise.*

Distant voices grew louder until they filled the room.

"Thank you, but I can manage it," a feminine voice was saying. There was an edge to her tone, as if she was repeating herself.

"You shouldn't be running around this much. Your leg requires rest," a male responded.

That's Nyx, he thought muzzily. *Talking to Rosa.*

"Who do you think you are, my doctor?" Rosa's voice dropped to a sultry whisper. "I know what my body can handle better than you do."

Even more voices entered the room, drowning out Nyx's reply in a sea of nonsensical chatter. Someone shook Raine's shoulder again. A soft mouth touched his ear. "Time to get up."

Raine shivered and jerked upright, blinking blearily. Sidian stood before him, clutching Raine's sketchbook in one hand. Raven black hair fell over his eyes as he peered down at Raine, the hint of a smile on his dusky mouth.

"Look who's awake," Aly cooed, popping up at Sidian's elbow. She looked as cheerful as a new daisy. "Your timing sucks. While you were taking your little princess nap, Betony stuck her foot inside a lit fireplace to warm her toes and almost burned the whole manor down."

"You should have seen it," Oka said, coming up beside Aly. His leafy eyes sparkled despite the tired bruises under them. "Her coat and clothes went up in flames, and she started flapping around like an angry gull."

"Lorrivare and Savere tackled her before she set too many things on fire." Aly's expression filled with glee. "They had to roll her up in a rug to smother the flames."

"Seriously?" Raine felt his lower lip protrude and knew he was pouting, but he didn't care. How could he have let himself miss that?

Well, alright. He knew how.

Too many dragons had needed to be settled into their guestrooms. Raine had grown bored of the proceedings, especially when it seemed like Rosa intended to situate everyone else before showing him or Sidian to a room. So, he'd wandered off and stumbled upon the most delightful parlor.

The wallpaper was enchanting, with thousands of life-sized hummingbirds flitting around wildflowers. Raine had obsessively studied the pattern, mesmerized by the unique sheen of the hummingbirds' feathers and the elaborate detail of the flowers.

His brain had imploded with designs and inspiration, and he'd perched before a dying hearth to sketch in his journal for the first time. He didn't remember falling asleep, but he must have.

"Seriously," Rosa echoed. She set a tray on a low table with a sigh. "Luckily, only one guestroom was ruined, and it's not like there aren't fifty more. Please, make yourselves comfortable. All this hovering makes me feel like a bad hostess."

Sidian sat next to Raine on the plush loveseat. A current of awareness sparked where their hips and thighs pressed together. He felt Sidian's gaze on him but didn't meet it. They were too close. Electricity zinged perilously through his bloodstream. He tugged a throw pillow onto his lap, positioning it directly over his groin. Just in case.

Aly and Oka joined Zane on a fern-patterned sofa. Nyx waited for Rosa to sit in a white velvet armchair, then reached down to prop her casted leg onto a matching ottoman. He even unfolded a sherpa blanket and spread it on her lap before taking a seat next to her.

Raine glanced between the pair, wondering what the hell was going on. Hadn't they just been arguing? And now, Nyx was acting like Rosa was as precious and fragile as a doll.

Rosa screwed the blanket up in her fists and shot Nyx a scathing glare, then looked over at Sidian and Raine. "I'm thrilled to see you guys, I swear." An edge in her tone belied the sentiment. "But can one of you please tell me why there are over thirty dragons and one obnoxiously suffocating control freak in my house?"

Nyx scoffed. "Call me whatever you want. It doesn't change the fact that someone needs to step in and make sure you're taking care of yourself."

Rosa barked a humorless laugh. "Based on what? You've known me for two hours."

"And in that time, you've done nothing but prove my point over and over."

As Nyx and Rosa continued to argue, Raine plucked at a loose thread on the embroidered pillow in his lap. Nyx and Rosa were strangers, yet he felt as if he were listening in on a deeply private conversation. He glanced around the room, trying not to pay attention to their exchange.

Aly and Oka were observing Nyx and Rosa with avid interest. Zane sat between them, staring at the ceiling. Aly held a pastry in her hand, some sort of scone. As she nibbled, her eyes never wavered from the quarreling pair.

"I bet you're one of those imbeciles who thinks every woman needs a man," Rosa spat hotly. "Let me tell you, *Nyx*. I don't need a man. Not for anything."

"Not for anything?" Nyx's inflection was weird. Low and exaggeratedly husky, almost like Sidian's.

"Not for anything," Rosa repeated, tossing her head. "There is nothing a man can do for me that I can't do for myself."

"Oh, I don't think that's true." Nyx leaned toward her, his voice satin soft. "I'm sure there are some things only a man can give you."

Sidian's hand slipped beneath the pillow to grasp Raine's thigh. Lightning struck through Raine, a white-hot streak that nearly scorched him to ash. He gasped, then took hold of Sidian's wrist to stop him from sliding his palm upward.

"Stop," Raine whispered. Sidian's fingers dug deeper into his thigh. Raine's cock throbbed in answer. "Your brother and Rosa are *right there*," he added desperately.

"Then let's go to our room," Sidian muttered, his voice rasping with frustrated desire.

"We can't just disappear," Raine said thinly. "Rosa deserves to know what's going on. And since you're the one who brought us here, you can tell her."

"Yes, Captain," Rosa chimed, startling Raine. He shifted away from Sidian, feeling awkward for more reasons than he could explain. "If I'm going to be housing illegal guests, I think I deserve to know what's going on. *And are those the missing breeding dragons in my guestrooms?*"

"They are," Sidian said smoothly.

Rosa sat straighter in her chair, utterly intent. "Tell me everything."

Sidian did, beginning with the events at Silvan Dredge. Raine listened raptly as his mate revealed details that were new, even to him.

It was policy for a captain to report to a guild master upon completing a mission. Sidian had cited that exact policy as an excuse to leave Eddic's side while Raine had been strapped down in the interrogation room. Sidian had, in fact, reported to a master—relaying Rosa's whereabouts as well as the trouble they had encountered with Tayo and Garreth's unit.

But after arranging Rosa's rescue, Sidian had secretly raided the guild's stored explosives. He placed small bombs strategically throughout the prison, ensuring they would go off at varying intervals, maximizing the destruction and chaos that had enabled their escape.

Nyx took over the narrative, covering the time after they arrived at Moontop as well as the true version of Gargantha's invasion. To Raine's surprise, Rosa listened to him without a hint of her previous hostility. There was an absorbed look on her face, as if she was memorizing Nyx's every expression. Occasionally, she interjected to say things like, "I knew the Nine were suspicious," and, "That's so awful."

By the end, she looked grim. "Going after the Nine during the succession isn't feasible. You can't walk down a single street in Rokeshin without running into Guardians." She pursed her lips and seemed to deliberate before saying, "I think you should take the dragons and leave Valdenia. Escape to the Northerlands."

"We're not going anywhere," Oka said. He climbed to his feet, nearly upsetting the tray of scones with his knee. "This is the land we were dreamed into. We belong here."

"Fleeing north is the only way you'll survive," Rosa argued.

"No, it isn't. It's a great way to kill us, though." Oka loomed over her, eyes flashing.

"Back off," Nyx said firmly. "She's human. She doesn't know what she's suggesting, and either way, it's not a reason for you to threaten her." To Rosa, he said, "No dragon will ever agree to leave Valdenia. They believe that they were dreamed into this world by a slumbering dragon deity, the Dreaming Mother. According to dragon lore, Valdenia is the land featured in her dreams.

Leaving this land means leaving her dreams. And if they leave her dreams—"

"We vanish," Aly said.

"Or die," Oka said, nodding.

"Or pop her dream bubble, thereby waking her up. Causing all of Valdenia and everyone in it to collapse into a void of nothingness," Zane said in a drowsy monotone, still facing the ceiling.

"Or that." Nyx massaged his forehead. "Suffice to say, there are multiple theories—the consensus being, dragons can't leave Valdenia."

"Oh." Rosa sighed. "I understand. Or at least, I think I do. But you still shouldn't have come here."

"It's a good thing we did," Nyx said, frowning at her. "You should be on complete bed rest. Someone should be cooking your meals and delivering them to your bedside. Helping you dress. Changing your sheets. Doing the wash ..."

As Nyx ticked off the various tasks Rosa required assistance with, her face turned an alarming shade of puce. Her expression was one Raine had seen several times. On Lukor, whenever he was gearing up to commit murder.

Before Rosa could spring out of her chair and ensure Sidian's older brother was actually dead and not just faking it, Raine cleared his throat. Loudly.

It worked better than he expected. Instantly, Raine found himself the center of attention. As he searched for something intelligent to say, Raine's gaze met Sidian's. His stare was dark and filled with heat.

But then I saw how nervous you were. Your eyes were so big and pleading.

Raine shivered at the memory, more grateful than ever for the pillow in his lap.

"So, um." He tugged at his coat collar and struggled to form a single, coherent thought. "How did you know Rosa would be home?"

Sidian's cool response was at odds with the fire burning in his eyes. "When an injury renders a guildmember incapable of fulfilling their duties, they are sent home to convalesce. Rosa's leg was broken when we left her. It was an educated guess she would be here recuperating."

"When I was a journeyman, I broke my ankle and got sent home for the summer," Nyx exclaimed. His face lit up with memory. "Mom kept baking me pies and pastries. It's her way of fussing," he added as an aside to Rosa, who no longer looked eager to throttle him.

A corner of Sidian's lip ticked fondly. "I remember. We both gained twenty pounds because you insisted on sharing with me."

"Thank the Divine Father I did, or I would have gained forty pounds."

Aly observed her half-eaten scone curiously. "Pies and pastries make you gain weight?"

"Please don't talk about weight gain right now," Rosa groaned, trying and failing to touch her foot where it was propped on the ottoman. Her leg was wrapped too thickly to bend, and she huffed. "I'm so sick of this cast. After being bedridden for weeks, I thought the worst was over. *Nope.* Now this damn thing itches all the time. I feel like I have leg lice."

"Here." Nyx bent forward and scratched her foot. She moaned, arching into it. Nyx whispered something too low for Raine to hear. Rosa's face reddened, although this time, it wasn't from anger. She looked at Nyx as if trying to peer through his clothes. The sultry curve of her smile indicated she liked what she saw.

"Maybe later, if you stop annoying me," she purred.

Raine really, seriously did not want to know what that was about.

Oka cracked a yawn as he shifted his weight. "Sorry, guys. I'm sure there's plenty more to talk about, but there's a huge bathtub calling my name. My wings are killing me after hauling Raine's heavy ass all the way here."

"I am not that heavy," Raine squawked. "You were carrying me *and* Sidian." Oka massaged a spot on his back, and Raine recalled Jaska's words from earlier. The dragons had all gotten wing strain from their flight to Rokeshin, and Oka was the only one who had carried two fully grown males on his back. "Shit, Oka. I'm sorry. Jaska said your wing strain will heal after a night of Betony's healing resonance."

"Relax. I was screwing with you." Oka grinned and rolled his shoulders. "And yeah, Jaska is right. It's honestly hard to decide what I want first. A bath or a few hours of rapid healing."

"Do the rapid healing," Raine said quickly. "That way I can use the bath."

His filth was horrendous after cleaning up burnt buildings and corpses all day. His hair, skin, and clothes were smeared with ash and residue. Not to mention he stank like smoke and sweat.

A bath was bliss on a normal day. Right now, it would be the equivalent of entering the Divine Father's palace.

"Why would Oka have to wait for you to take a bath?" Rosa asked, sounding confused. "There's a private toilet and bath attached to every guestroom. Just use your own."

"What?" Raine gaped. He'd been wasting his time in this—admittedly gorgeous—parlor when he could have been steeping himself in hot, soapy water?

Sidian smirked. "You'd have known that if you hadn't wandered off while the rooms were assigned."

"You." Rosa jutted a finger at Raine, emanating triumph. "Mister 'I'm An Innocent Dragon Baby,' my ass. Care to tell me why you and the captain are sharing a room?"

"Well, uh ..." Flames engulfed his face as Rosa leered at him. Why the hell had Sidian asked for them to room together? Even if they were going to end up in the same bed, Sidian could have let Rosa assign them separate rooms.

Sidian's smug smile bordered on obscene. "Because he's mine."

CHAPTER THIRTY

aine awoke to an empty bed and a dull ache in his chest. He slid his palm over the vacant, rumpled space next to him. It was cold.

He sat up slowly and surveyed the guestroom. Last night, it had been too dark to make out the details. But now, sunlight beamed through the windows, reflecting off elaborate cherrywood furniture polished to a jeweled shine.

The four-poster bedframe was carved so that each bedpost depicted a rearing stallion. There was a matching armoire, breakfast table, and coat stand. Whoever crafted the set was as meticulous as Savere. The horses were so lifelike, Raine half-expected them to break free from the bedposts and canter off.

As he slid off the bed, his toes sank into plush carpet. He sighed at how lovely it felt. Perhaps he would install carpet at Chambrin Keep. Cold stone floors were miserable, especially in the winter. He shelved the thought as he dressed, opting for a loose lawn shirt and tights since Sidian wasn't around to force a jumpsuit onto him.

He shoved his boots on at the last second before he was out the door.

Wandering down several long, identical hallways—each lined with equestrian tapestries and expensive-looking sculptures—Raine found the broad, spiral staircase that led to the main floor. He navigated past the hummingbird parlor as well as several salons and studies.

Where the hell is everyone? It was possible they were still sleeping. But he knew Sidian was awake, at least.

"Hello?" he called out, hoping someone was around to hear him.

"We're in here," a feminine voice chimed back. Raine thought it might be Amari's.

Following the sound down a nearby corridor, he discovered several familiar faces situated around an oval-shaped dining table.

Savere nodded in welcome before resuming his current woodcarving—a tiny, exquisitely detailed hummingbird. Raine couldn't contain his grin. How often were he and Savere inspired by the same observations without realizing it?

"No. Absolutely not," Rosa was saying as she half-walked, half-hobbled into the dining room. A platter of steaming dishes tilted dangerously as her balance faltered.

Sarsana, who was trailing her, snatched the platter before the bowls toppled. "I'm only trying to help you."

"And I appreciate it," Rosa snapped, then grimaced. "I'm sorry. It's that asshole Nyx's fault. He won't let me do anything. It's driving me insane."

"Why?" Sarsana asked, looking mystified rather than offended. "Had I known that breaking a leg would make Nyx wait on me like my own personal servant, I'd have done it years ago."

Rosa shook her head. "You say that now, but the reality is different. I feel more smothered than a gravy steak."

Raine slid into the chair beside Jaska, who was so intent on setting a ruby into a ring that he didn't look up.

Amari smiled at him from across the table, already serving herself from the tray Rosa had brought.

"Does anyone know where Sidian is?" he asked, reaching for a plate. The tray held scrambled eggs, sausage, and oatmeal. His stomach grumbled as he took double portions of everything.

"Yes. He went into Rokeshin with Nyx a couple hours ago," Rosa said, sitting between Sarsana and Amari.

Raine jerked, accidentally spilling a forkful of eggs. "What? They went *where*?"

"They wanted to know if it would be safe for dragons to walk the streets. I haven't spent enough time in the city to know the answer, so they decided to go themselves. They'll be fine," Rosa assured him. "*They* don't have sparkly hair and eyes like jewels. It's important to know if concealing your hair will make any of you stand out or seem suspicious."

The ache in Raine's chest intensified. Somehow, knowing how far away Sidian was made the distance more painful.

After a dragon sparks, a courtship tie forms. Essentially, you cannot leave my side until our bond is consummated.

Sidian had told him that. At the time, it explained so much. But now, Raine understood something he hadn't grasped then. He might not be physically capable of leaving Sidian's side, but the same wasn't true for his mate. Unfettered by instincts that ran soul-deep in Raine, Sidian could go wherever he wanted.

And apparently, he wanted to go into a city teeming with their enemies. Without Raine by his side to protect him if things went south.

Raine scooped his eggs and crammed a mouthful without tasting anything. His chest twinged.

"You finally finished it," Savere said. Raine looked up at the dragon's uncharacteristically marveling tone. "May I?"

Jaska deposited the golden ring he'd been working on into Savere's waiting palm. Savere turned it over beneath the bright overhead lamps. Everyone sighed or gasped as the ring's rubies sparkled with the brilliance of countless fiery stars.

"Hang on," Raine said. "I always thought you worked on loads of different jewelry pieces. Do you mean you've been working on the same ring all this time?"

"Yes and no." Jaska smiled quietly at the ring. "I began crafting it eighty years ago. I made dozens of other pieces during that time, but this was the only ring."

"How did you get it to be so sparkly?" Sarsana breathed, sounding as hypnotized as a moth to real fire.

"Centuries of dedicated craftsmanship," Savere said, answering for Jaska. He passed the ring back to the midnight green dragon. "Much like its recipient, it has no equal."

"You craft jewelry like a human," Betony said, her voice coated with contempt. She stood at the end of the table, sneering as she eyed the ring. Jaska's fingers curled around it, hiding it from view. "That practice is unnatural for a dragon. Have some respect. If not for yourself, then for your superiors."

The room lapsed to brittle silence. Raine opened his mouth to rip Betony a new one, but Jaska silenced him with a look as sharp as a Guardian's knife.

"My apologies, Grandmother." Jaska pocketed his ring, along with his tools and a few loose gemstones that sat near his plate.

Betony's nod was so sanctimonious, it must have insulted every higher authority in existence. "It isn't entirely your fault. Your den mother should have curbed that nasty habit long ago. As well as yours," she added, pointedly eyeing Savere's hummingbird carving. "Wood is for nests and fires. What you do is a waste of time and resources."

Raine gnashed his teeth, quietly fuming. He wanted nothing more than to tell Betony where she could shove her unwelcome opinions, but that would only upset Jaska and Savere further. They really adhered to the 'storm mothers are supreme' philosophy.

He'd never been more glad to be raised human.

"With all due respect, Grandmother, I find Evin to be a superlative den mother," Savere said tonelessly. "My flaws are my own and should not reflect on her leadership."

Betony might have had something venomous to spew at that, but her attention had already shifted to Raine. She stared at his plate with almost comedic abhorrence. "Do you always consume the fare of rats and bovines for breakfast? You are a dragon, or so you claim. Where is your meat?"

Raine glanced down at his oatmeal, which was sprinkled with cinnamon and dried cherries, then back up at Betony. He'd already finished his eggs and sausage, but instead of saying as much, he widened his eyes and blinked innocently.

"Oh, I don't eat meat." He gave a theatrical shudder. "Just the sight of it makes me ill. I mostly live off vegetables and fruit. This oatmeal is such a treat. Thank you, Rosa." He beamed at her.

Before Rosa could do more than blink, Betony had a total meltdown. "You. Don't. Eat. Meat." Her silvered lilac eyes were glassy with horror. "You are no dragon. I knew it," she spat. "I knew you weren't one of the children. You've made no effort to connect with my storm, and it's because you already know that none of us are your parents. You're an imposter. A spy. A pretender trying to strip our freedom."

Raine shook his head, astonished. He had lied about not eating meat to nettle Betony. It was supposed to be mild payback for her verbally shitting all over his friends. And now, he was a spy posing as a dragon in order to recapture them?

"Wow," he breathed. "That's some ironclad logic you're working with there. But I'm curious. How is it that I survived getting fire breathed all over me?"

"Humans are capable of great trickery," Betony said fiercely. "You may fool the others, but you do not fool me. You've been trying to control our movements since you arrived. I command my storm. Not you, or Evin, or the thousands of insignificant humans you claim to be a threat."

"Betony," Lorrivare said, cautiously approaching his mate from behind. His wine-red gaze swept the table, lingering on Raine. "What's going on?"

"We are leaving." Betony's pale hair swayed like a cape as she spun to face her mate. "That silver-eyed imposter seeks to waste our time. He wants our children to suffer, and us along with them. It took me longer to catch on than it should have. I can only blame myself for putting so much trust in Evin's judgment. I should have known better. Every member of her thunder makes it clear that her perception has been compromised for decades. Alert the others. We fly within the hour."

She clipped from the room without waiting for a response.

Raine's knuckles whitened around his spoon. Slowly, rigidly, he resumed eating. If there was an infinitesimally small part of him that stung at Betony's words, at her absolute rejection of him as both dragon and potential offspring, he didn't acknowledge it.

Lorrivare sagged like a great weight had befallen him. He opened his mouth, but decided against whatever he'd been about to say. His jaw snapped shut as he disappeared after Betony.

Jaska stood upon Lorrivare's exit and moved toward the opposite hallway.

"Where are you going?" Amari called.

"To get Mother and Naiah," he said without slowing. "They are the only ones Grandmother listens to. Perhaps they can reason with her."

"The horses," Rosa exclaimed, leaping from her chair. Her cast thumped heavily against the ivory-tiled floor as she hastened away.

There was a brief pause where everyone looked as nonplussed as Raine felt. Then, Sarsana and Amari pushed back their chairs and hurried after Rosa.

Raine looked at Savere, the only other person left in the dining room. "What was all that about?"

Savere sighed. "I have no idea, but we should probably follow them."

"Rosa," Raine cried, spotting her distant figure near a row of open barns.

Raine and Savere kicked into a jog until they reached her.

"You shouldn't be out here." She looked around anxiously. "I've only gotten two stables put away. The studs are still grazing."

"So, that's what you meant by *the horses*." Raine felt like a proper numbskull. "You're putting them away."

"Yes, and I need to find the studs before those other dragons come out here. I don't want them to get hurt."

Raine and Savere fell into step beside Rosa as she headed toward open field. The ground swelled gently beneath them, gradually enough that he didn't feel the climb but steep enough to conceal the pastures ahead.

"It's probably fine," Raine assured her. He massaged his arms against the chill, wishing he'd grabbed his coat. "Horses are afraid of dragons, remember? They'll stay far away if Betony's storm comes out here."

"No, you don't get it," Rosa said. "Roke horses are *war horses*. They don't run from a threat. They pursue it."

Uh oh. Raine was starting to see where Rosa was going with this. Savere, too, because he asked, "Where are Sarsana and Amari?"

Rosa stopped abruptly. "Why are you asking me that? They were with you in the dining room when I left to come out here."

Two high-pitched screams sounded beyond the hillcrest. Raine and Savere's gazes met in mute horror. As one, they bolted up the hill.

Then skidded to a halt, their boot heels scarring the sod. Six Roke war horses—if those prehistoric behemoths could be called horses—thundered towards them. They were the size of ox-wagons and looked like they ate Garganthan moose for breakfast.

Sunlight glinted off their glossy coats. Black, brown, red, tan, cream, and a dappled blue. All pounding the earth with breakneck fury as they chased Amari and Sarsana. The dragonesses were fast, but the Roke war horses were faster. They flew across the grass like wingless dragons, the dappled blue in the lead.

"Fly," Savere shouted.

The females kept running as if they hadn't heard him. The war horses were swiftly gaining. Raine cupped his hands to amplify his words and yelled, "For the love of the Divine Father, they're going to trample you. *Fly*."

"This is my only dress," Amari panted. "And coat. And shoes."

"Same," Sarsana gasped.

She wasn't as fast as Amari. The dappled blue stallion's shadow fell over her. She sped up, energized by a fresh wave of urgency. It wasn't enough. The dappled blue edged closer, its shadow grazing the back of her sparkling red hair.

"That's great," Raine called, "because being run over by six huge horses will leave your clothes *more* intact."

Amari and Sarsana exploded into their dragon forms, shredding their garments in an eyeblink. Beating their wings in short, rapid bursts, they rose into the air. The dappled blue stallion brayed and snapped its teeth at Sarsana's wingtip as she lifted out of range.

"Keep low," Savere yelled frantically. "Don't fly higher than the city wall."

They adjusted their trajectory at the last second, staying low. Their hind talons skimmed the grass as their wings guided them towards the manor.

Rosa stumbled as she reached the hilltop. She braced herself with one hand on Raine's shoulder and the other on Savere's. "I really hate this stupid cast—" She broke off. All the color drained from her face, leaving her complexion strangely gray. "Run. *Run.*" She spun around and began hobble-jogging down the hill.

Raine stared at the incoming herd of Roke war horses, momentarily captivated by the deathly fury gleaming in their dark eyes. It reminded him of how Sidian had looked when they first met, his velvet brown gaze seething with hatred.

His heart fluttered with absurd nostalgia, as if Sidian's intent to kill him had been the equivalent of a romantic picnic.

"Come on." Savere seized his arm and yanked.

Raine snapped out of his daze and sprinted after Savere. The ground trembled beneath him as hot breath ghosted over his nape. He reached Rosa, who wasn't halfway down the hill, and scooped her up midstride.

"Those are the Roke horses?" he asked, crushing Rosa to his chest with an arm under her knees and another across her back. He pumped his calves for all he was worth, resisting the fatalistic dread that battered his psyche like riled hornets. "Who the ever-loving-fuck rides those things?"

"Anyone who can get their hands on one," Rosa said proudly. "No other horses in the world are like ours. The Roke stables are what drew the first foreign merchants here. Without them, we wouldn't have silk or potatoes or turkeys."

"I'll be sure to recall and appreciate every potato I've ever eaten while they're stomping me into a flesh puddle," Raine panted.

Rosa's fingers dug into his chest where she gripped him. "Run faster."

"I'm trying."

Savere was a few paces ahead. And since Raine was carrying a whole-ass woman and still keeping up with him? He figured he was doing pretty damned good.

Rokeshin's towering border wall loomed beyond the stables. They were racing towards a dead end. Raine didn't know what to do. Veer left and continue sprinting across the rolling lawn? Or veer right and try to make it back inside the manor house? He didn't have the breath necessary to ask.

Two figures in black, guild-issued cloaks appeared at the edge of a stable. At once, Raine realized that his heart no longer ached as though an invisible string was stretched taut to breaking.

Sidian and Nyx threw back their hoods and froze, taking in the scene.

"The whistle," Rosa screamed. "It's hanging by the stalls. Blow it twice, as loud as you can. Hurry."

Nyx threw himself into the stable while Sidian drew his sword.

Rosa went as wooden as a board in Raine's arms, then screeched, "No. You will not hurt any of my horses, captain or not."

Sidian didn't seem to hear her. His gaze was fixed beyond Raine's shoulder. He charged forward, his sword poised for a long, diagonal blow.

Time slowed. Each beat of Raine's heart lasted a century as his mate's demise played out in his mind.

Sidian would cut down the dappled blue stallion and miraculously leap over its tumbling body. And as his boots hit the grass and he raised his sword for another strike, the five other Roke horses would be on him. His body would be dragged beneath their sharp, frenzied hooves. He wouldn't even have time to scream.

Sorry, Sidian. Raine signaled Savere before twisting a sharp right, knowing the horses would follow them. Their dragon scent had the studs wild with the need to crush the predators invading their territory. The maneuver wouldn't earn him any points with Sidian, but he didn't care. If he had to choose between an irate mate and a dead one ... There was no choice.

Raine focused all his attention on running. To slow or stumble meant death, even for him. Hooves couldn't pierce his flesh, it was true. But if Tayo's rock-pelting games had taught Raine anything, it was that blunt force didn't have to break skin to wound him. In that way, his organs and sinew were as vulnerable as any human's.

Another wave of hot breath gusted his nape, and Raine braced for pain.

A whistle blew twice, bright and piercing. The hoofbeats thundering dangerously close began to slow, then ceased.

"You can stop," Rosa said, wriggling in his arms until he halted. "It's safe for now, but I need to put the studs away while they're docile."

Raine set Rosa down and hung back with Savere while she and the Wade brothers corralled the war horses. The dappled blue was the most willful. It tossed its head and stomped at Rosa's cajoling. Before it disappeared into the stable, it gave Raine a vindictive look filled with too much intelligence for any horse. Raine shuddered against the chill morning air.

"That spotted horse wants me dead," he whispered.

Savere rolled his eyes. "They all want you dead, or did you think the rest of the herd was coming to our rescue?"

"Are you alright?" Sidian asked, reaching them. His eyes raked Raine intently from head to toe, searching for injuries.

"We're fine," Raine said. "Nyx's timing was excellent."

"Good," Sidian said curtly. "Now, do you mind telling me why you were just on the brink of a violent death? I was gone for *two hours*."

Raine was suddenly reminded of how he'd awoken that morning. Without Sidian, yes. But also in a bed, his hair brushed and braided, and wearing snug sleep shorts.

The last thing he remembered from the night before was lingering in his bath, too leaden to move a muscle. He must have fallen asleep, which meant Sidian had retrieved his unconscious figure from the tub and prepared him for bed, all without Raine waking.

Heat climbed his neck as he imagined Sidian toweling his skin dry and putting undergarments on him.

Sidian watched him silently, exuding frustrated anger. Perversely, his mate's agitation sent a spike of sharp arousal through Raine. His body thrilled at Sidian's intensity, as if it was a prelude to mating.

Raine tried to quell his burgeoning erection by focusing on the reason behind Sidian's upset. And that reminded him that he had an upset of his own.

"I can't believe you left me behind," he said in a rush. "I have a wig, damn it. It would have been safe enough to take me along.

What if you'd been found out? What if you were killed or imprisoned or whatever?"

"I was never in danger. I blend in. You don't. Not even with a wig. Your features are too fine. People gaze at you overlong." Raine blinked. Once. Twice. Three times. Was Sidian saying he was *too beautiful* to blend in with a crowd? A silly smile threatened, but he suppressed it at his mate's dark glare. "I left you here to preserve your safety."

"If you had taken me with you, I wouldn't have nearly gotten trampled," Raine couldn't resist pointing out.

Sidian's response was low, smoky, and ominous. "Believe me, I'm aware. You won't be leaving my sight for the foreseeable future."

CHAPTER THIRTY-ONE

Rosa and Nyx arrived with their elbows linked. Her face was pink with pleasure, dark eyes shining as she gazed at Nyx. They shared a private smile and looked seconds away from kissing or worse.

Hadn't Rosa complained earlier that Nyx was a smothering asshole? Neither Sidian nor Savere appeared confused, and Raine knew he was missing something.

Savere cleared his throat. "What did you discover in Rokeshin?"

Nyx looked up. His smile was sheepish as he surveyed them. "It's better than we anticipated. The entire city is packed for the succession. There are Guardians everywhere, but their primary focus is crowd control. They aren't peeking under hoods or cowls. Or giving any undue attention to individual citizens."

"I have a plan in mind, to get at the Nine," Sidian said. Unlike Nyx, he appeared grim. At his next words, Raine understood why. "For it to work, we need the assistance of every dragon here. Including Betony's storm."

Raine winced, wondering how he was going to tell Sidian that what he perceived as a formidable task was actually an impossible one. And all because Raine had pretended to dislike meat. It would have been ridiculous if their situation wasn't so dire.

The sound of distant yelling came from the direction of the manor house. Raine's stomach plummeted as Sidian, Nyx, and Savere started running toward the manor. It looked as though he wouldn't have to tell Sidian anything. The unfolding spectacle would do it for him.

Raine followed at a more sedate pace, matching Rosa's speed. He couldn't trick himself into thinking it was out of chivalry. Not with the anxiety pooling in his gut. It grew larger the closer they came to the manor.

As they crested the hill nearest the house, Betony's voice rang out, sharp and vicious. "—a disgrace. Your thunders act more human than dragon, and I will not subject my storm to this perversity any longer." She caught sight of Raine and sneered before facing Evin and Naiah. "If you want to play 'human' and be led by that pretentious spy, be my guest. I haven't lost my way. I haven't forgotten what I am. What *we* are."

"You don't have to remain with us if that is your choice." Evin's voice was quiet. Raine strained to hear her as he crossed the lawn. "But there's no need to endanger your storm by flying into the city. Permit me to guide you to the safehouse. Use it freely, as we discussed."

Up close, Raine could see the harsh tension lining Sidian's eyes and mouth. There was a bleakness to his expression, as if he was watching his plan shatter before his eyes. Sidian must have decided Betony's aid was beyond their reach because when he addressed her, he dedicated his focus to damage control as opposed to re-cruitment.

"I know how tempting a direct attack on Rokeshin must be. But remember, you're going to have to locate your target first. Otherwise, you run the risk of accidentally killing General Olan before you identify him, let alone question him."

Betony's storm huddled near the manor house, watching Sidian. They were all clothed and shod, much to Raine's relief. Lorrivare must have neglected to tell them they were leaving on wings instead of feet.

Betony's lips pinched as she considered Sidian. "As always, your reasoning is sound," she said grudgingly. Her features hardened. "You should know that the one who claims to be your mate is a liar and an imposter." Raine sucked in a breath. "Raine Chambrin pretends to be a dragon as well as one of my storm's offspring. He is neither. His father was both human and our captor. Raine Chambrin intends to betray us and continue his father's legacy."

Sidian looked absolutely flummoxed. Which was fair. Without the breakfast scene from earlier for context, Betony sounded nut-tier than a pecan tart.

Raine girded himself and stepped forward. Betony's gaze swiveled to him, reptilian in its emptiness.

"I lied, okay?" he said. Triumph twisted her features, and Raine scowled. "Not about being a dragon or Sidian's mate," he snapped. "I lied about hating meat. It isn't true. I eat meat all the time. Why, I'm practically carnivorous. I enjoy roasted pheasant and beef stew and bacon. And" — acid coated Raine's tongue, but he forced himself to say — "I'm sorry for my dishonesty. I didn't realize how much it would affect you."

Betony closed the space between them, her steps measured and purposeful. Once she faced him directly, she smiled. It raised the hairs on the back of his neck.

"I don't care what you eat," she said, her tone a saccharine knife. "I don't care what you say or what you do. None of that changes who you are and who you aren't."

"Well, that's ... true," Raine said slowly. "And nothing you say changes who I am, either. To be clear, is this an official disowning thing?"

There was a peculiar pang in his chest, but he ignored it. If Betony had gotten one thing right, it was that Arastus Chambrin was his father. He didn't need birth parents.

"We can't disown a child who was never ours," Betony said with a contemptuous smile.

Raine wanted to scratch the hideous expression off her face. He wanted to tell her that they couldn't disown him because he disowned them *first*. They were nothing to him. *Nothing*.

But Betony had already turned, dismissing him to address her storm. "We will accept Evin's offer to use her safehouse. Sidian is correct. We've allowed love and concern for our children to overwhelm our reason. We must find the human who knows our children's whereabouts before an attack can be made."

A warm, callused palm grabbed Raine's hand. Sidian's velvet eyes were upon him, glittering a thousand questions.

Raine's throat knotted. He suddenly recalled being very young and bruising his knee on a fall. He'd waved off Wylan's hovering concern and strode confidently away. But the instant his eyes met his father's in the corridor outside their rooms, he had burst into tears like a pricked waterskin.

Raine looked away from the abundant love in his mate's gaze. He had to, before it revealed the truth of his pain. Not to Sidian, but to himself.

"I don't think that's necessary," Lorrivare was saying, his tone gentle but insistent.

"I disagree," Betony said flatly.

Predictably, Lorrivare zipped it. *What the storm mother says, goes.*

"We will utilize the safehouse and hold off our attack on one condition," Betony said, now facing Evin and Naiah. "The imposter is not welcome there. I don't even want him to know where it is located. Otherwise, the deal is off, and we fly right now."

Evin's sky-blue brows furrowed. "Grandmother, I know you think Raine is some sort of spy, but—"

"Fine," Raine interjected. Both Evin and Naiah began to protest. He cut them off. "I don't need to visit the safehouse. It makes no difference to me, so there's no reason to argue."

Betony wasn't going to concede. She was convinced Raine was an enemy, so it made perfect sense that she didn't want her storm's location known to him. He would have lauded her for finally displaying some shred of prudence if she didn't have the truth so ass-backward.

"I'm not leaving Raine behind," Sidian said in the soft, husky voice he used whenever he expected to be obeyed without question.

Betony picked up on that thread of steely command. Instead of challenging Sidian, she nodded. "So long as he is kept away from the safehouse, I have no objection to him accompanying you."

The secret passage into Rokeshin turned out to be an underground tunnel. Nestled in the weeds behind the center stable was a round, cast iron lid. None of the dragons were eager to be belowground, but the city wall rose only twenty feet away from the opening. Their passage would be brief.

"It's like being back in Moontop," Tejayla said, thick with distaste once everyone was inside and underway.

Ahead in the darkness, the Wade brothers guided Betony and her storm through the passageway. Evin and Naiah's thunders followed behind Betony's storm, unsubtly buffering Raine from the parents. He was too grateful to call them out on it.

Not everyone held a light to see by, causing them to walk in clusters. At the very back of the throng, Raine balanced a silver candle holder. Tejayla and Carissyne pressed into his sides, walking slightly behind him so that, in Tejayla's words, they could *sacrifice Raine and make a run for it* if any hunters or tunnel-dwelling monsters showed.

The dirt floor was mostly level, but the odd dip threatened to trip them, making their progress slow. Small offshoots occasionally opened in the tunnel walls, but Sidian kept them moving straight.

They walked much further than Raine anticipated, given the city wall's proximity to the tunnel entrance. They had to be passing underneath roadways and buildings by now.

"Where do you think this leads?" Tejayla asked, just as Raine was really beginning to wonder.

"The city," Carissyne deadpanned.

"Yeah, I know that." Tejayla huffed. "But where in the city? What if we pop out in the middle of a street?"

"Sidian would not have suggested this route if it opened someplace unsafe," Naiah said lightly, a few paces ahead of them in the darkness.

She was right.

Fifteen minutes later, they climbed out of the passage and into the empty cellar of a townhouse. It was musty and damp with a dirt floor and creaky wooden steps that sagged dangerously beneath Raine's weight.

Everyone congregated upstairs, in a sitting room that was never meant to entertain thirty-plus guests. Dusty sheets draped the furniture, and the air was nearly as stale as the cellar. Raine didn't ask whose house they were in, assuming it was one of the wealthy Rokes' inner-city residences. Fortunately, a vacant one.

Dragons murmured to their neighbors as everyone shuffled to make room. The dragons gradually quieted as Sidian spoke, projecting his voice to address the group from a spot where Raine couldn't see him.

"We're in the heart of Rokeshin. It's a militant city, set up as Valdenia's first line of defense in the event of invasion. The buildings here are solid stone. Every roof is topped with battlements. Wings and fire aren't sufficient to penetrate such fortifications. Keep that in mind, should you feel the urge to attack. The Rokeshin Citadel is two blocks away from where we are now. The man you seek, Olan Chambrin, is within the citadel."

The room exploded with animated chatter as Betony's storm all talked at once.

"Quiet," Betony barked. Her storm's obedience was so instantaneous that, for several rapid heartbeats, Raine thought his ears had failed him. To Sidian, she said, "All this time, you have known where our target is?"

"An educated guess," Sidian said coolly. "The citadel is impregnable, so don't think you can force your way in to reach him. My advice is for you to stake out the castle gate and watch for anyone in a red military jacket with gold shoulder patches. Few men will be wearing that uniform. General Olan is one of them."

Aly squirmed her way through the crowd and smiled at Raine. Sidian and Betony kept talking, their voices projected so all could hear.

Aly cupped a hand to his ear and whispered, "Is it true that Betony's storm disowned you?" He nodded. "What shabby little shits," she hissed. "They're lucky I wasn't there. Evin and Naiah made all of us wait inside, and now I know why. I'm glad we're dumping them at the safehouse. *Good riddance.*" Her voice softened as she asked, "Are you okay?"

"Yes," Raine whispered. It felt like only half a lie.

Around them, everyone began pulling their hoods up and tucking their ears through the loops hidden inside—a crucial modification Raine was relieved Jaska had thought to do.

Sidian appeared before him, a black cloak fastened up to his neck.

"Evin and Lukor are going to take Betony's storm to the safehouse. Nyx is going with them so that he can act as the speaker if any Guardians stop them. It's unlikely but not impossible. Naiah's thunder is accompanying them, as well, so each of them is able to locate the safehouse in the event of an emergency."

"What about the rest of us?" Aly asked.

"We'll follow them until we reach the citadel's barbican. That's where we'll stop and wait."

Aly scoffed. "So that Raine doesn't know where the safehouse is? Because he's secretly an evil, lying human who might try to kill them in their sleep? If he did, they'd deserve it. They're morons."

Sidian's lips twitched. "Regardless of their aversion, we wouldn't have accompanied them. The citadel doesn't only host General Olan. It's also where the Nine stay. And the city square outside the barbican is a prime location to analyze the citadel's security and assess infiltration options."

Evin called out, "Everyone, stay close and keep your hoods secure."

As the door opened, a line of vivid sunshine bisected the room. The outside air filtered in, crisp and lovely. Raine breathed deep, relishing its freshness after trekking the stuffy tunnel passageway. Around him, the room emptied rapidly. He felt like a rock in the shallows, standing motionless while everyone poured around him to exit.

Soon, only Jaska, Savere, Oka, and Zane remained in the townhouse with them. Sidian reached out and tugged Raine's hood up. Their eyes met and lingered.

"We ready?" Oka asked, clapping Raine's shoulder.

Sidian nodded. "Stay close. The streets are chaotic with all the festivities."

"Festivities?" Aly exclaimed. "I thought everyone loved the dead guy."

"Chieftain Brandor was both beloved and highly venerated," Sidian said as they made for the exit. "Our country grieves him greatly. But unlike dragons, humans don't express their sadness immediately. First, they celebrate the life of the deceased."

"Seriously?" Aly sounded aghast. "Yeah, humans are definitely not like dragons. Grief wrecks us."

Sidian paused at the threshold, his hood downcast. "I know," he said, his voice as soft as goose down.

Raine swallowed against the knot in his throat, but before he could find words to reassure his mate, the world exploded with light and noise.

The townhouse opened onto a white-bricked road that was packed with so many people, he thought they might be a mob. His gut lurched with instinctive panic. Then, he noticed their easy body language and casual, meandering footsteps. No one was paying them any attention. The pressure in his veins alleviated.

"This way," Sidian said, turning left onto the street.

Raine fisted the back of his mate's cloak, so that he wouldn't lose him as they moved.

Sidian hadn't exaggerated when he said Rokeshin was a militant city. It looked more like a fortress maze than anything. There was no space between houses. They lined the streets in solid walls of square, gray stone. Battlements ran the lengths of the conjoined rooftops.

As they progressed, the crowds never thinned. People either wore rough, serviceable clothing or armor of mixed leather and steel. The atmosphere was zealous with celebration. Drinks flowed freely. Everyone seemed to have a cup of mead in one hand and food in the other.

"May Brandor's spirit rise straight and swift," a man with a ruddy complexion crowed, raising a cup at the side of the street.

Everyone cheered and saluted the sky with sloshing cups before swigging their drinks.

"Who needs a refill?" a man shouted.

Raine's stomach went hard with fear, his steps frozen on the brick path as he saw the Guardians. There were six of them. Two units. Black jumpsuits peeked out from their guild-issued jackets. They all carried boxy trays that were secured to their torsos with leather straps. Upon the trays were pitchers of gorgeous amber mead and stacks of paper cups.

Raine's grip on Sidian's cloak stretched taut, spurring him back into motion. He hurried after Sidian, eyes still on the proceedings. People held up their cups, and the Guardians topped them off. The hunters were friendly and encouraging, urging everyone around them to partake in the refreshments.

"Since when do Guardians act like servers in a pub?" Raine asked aloud, unable to contain his incredulity.

If Sidian had an answer, he withheld it as a Guardian appeared before their group. The golden cuff around his bicep proclaimed him a captain.

"I see your hands are empty." The captain plucked a pitcher of mead from the tray secured to his waist and started pouring cups. "Take a drink," he said, offering the first cup to Raine, who stood nearest to the tray.

"Oh, um. I don't have any silvans on me," Raine said apologetically.

The captain scrutinized him, peering beneath his hood closely. Raine resisted the urge to tug at it, relieved that he'd worn his wig. His white hair was so bright, Sidian had worried about its detection even with a hood, so he'd made Raine slap the wig on as an extra precaution.

"You lot must be new to the succession," the captain said. Easing back, he gestured to his tray and said, "Refreshments and housing are being provided to all by the Nine. If you need a place to stay, there are large tents erected in select districts. You'll find concession stands posted on every street. You have but to wait in line and give your order to be served."

Raine looked around and noticed details that had eluded him previously. The glassy eyes and flushed faces of a people bolstered with unlimited spirits. Men and women laughed too loud and too long at every little thing. Strangers leaned on each other, tripping and stumbling to stay upright.

In the middle of the road, a handful of youths tried to assemble in a drunken pyramid, collapsing clumsily before they could stack three rows of their companions.

The captain pushed the tray toward him meaningfully. "Drink." It wasn't a request.

Their sobriety already set them apart from ninety percent of the revelers. Raine didn't want to draw more attention to their group by refusing. He took a cup and smiled his thanks before downing it.

The captain grinned approvingly, showing a shiny, silver-capped tooth. "All of you, come now. I insist."

The drink was delicious. Woodsy and smooth with a crisp finish, like biting an apple. Raine reached for another and gave Savere an encouraging smile. The dragon accepted a cup with poor grace but didn't protest, thank the Divine. The others followed suit until everyone held a paper cup except Sidian.

When the captain pressed him, Sidian said, "I don't drink."

The captain's brows knitted. He jerked his chin and said, "Lower your hood, sir."

It was the first instance of a Guardian requesting such an act. Raine froze at the order. Luckily, Sidian did not. He moved with easy confidence, giving away nothing as he pulled his hood down.

"Captain Wade," the man exclaimed with surprised pleasure. "Of course, you don't have to drink. Your service honors Chieftain Brandor more than any toast."

"Thank you," Sidian said simply, features schooled in a bland mask of aloofness.

The Guardian eyed the rest of them with renewed interest, as if they might all be heroes of the guild beneath their hoods. A frisson of foreboding prickled Raine's spine. They couldn't afford anyone looking at them too closely. He thrust his cup in the air, nearly catching the captain's nose with the rim.

"May Brandor's spirit rise straight and swift," Raine called loudly. All around them, his toast was echoed as over a hundred people drank at once. The dragons behind him took the hint and drained their cups with feigned enthusiasm.

"That was delicious," Jaska remarked, staring at his empty cup as if it performed a magic trick.

The captain grinned. "We know a thing or two about good spirits. Only the best for this momentous occasion, eh?"

Even Savere snatched another cup before the captain ambled away.

"Forget Brandor," Oka said as he plucked a third drink from a passing journeywoman. "May the spirit in this cup rise straight and swift to my mouth."

"It will rise straight and swift to your head if you are not more circumspect," Sidian said warningly.

"I know you don't like to drink," Raine said. "But you should try this stuff. It's fantastic."

Sidian's dusky mouth tightened as he eyed the cup in Raine's hand. Catching Raine's gaze, the irritation eased from his expression. "My father liked drink overmuch," he murmured, his voice so quiet that Raine wouldn't have heard him without his enhanced senses. "He wrecked his ship and nearly died because of it."

Raine's breath caught, and he grasped Sidian's hand. "You weren't onboard, were you?"

It was a foolish fear. Even if Sidian had been onboard, he had clearly survived. He was walking right beside Raine, hale and whole. But the thought of his mate in such peril, even years past, threatened to send him spiraling.

"No." Sidian kept hold of Raine's hand as they progressed. "The weather was poor, and the sea too agitated for safe sailing, so I was made to stay home. My father should have stayed, too. But he was drunk and stubborn. He said we couldn't afford to miss a full day's fishing."

Bitterness seeped into Sidian's tone. "Money was so tight, yet we never lacked for rum. He drank more than usual that day, waiting for the weather to turn. He was on his second bottle when he stumbled out the door. By that point, it had been years since I last saw him walk straight. We received news of his shipwreck the next day."

Sidian's grip tightened around Raine's fingers so fiercely, he might have thought his mate was trying to hurt him if he didn't see the bleak, inward stare Sidian wore. It made Raine's heart ache so painfully, the brutal grip on his hand was forgotten.

"My mother was inconsolable with anguish, and I swore to never touch alcohol, not for any reason. Not after the unnecessary pain and hardship it wrought upon our family."

"Your father is alive, though. Right?" Raine asked tentatively. He had vague recollections of Nyx referencing a father, but what if the shipwreck had occurred since then?

"Yes. He washed ashore days after we'd given him up for dead. To his credit, he realized his drinking had nearly destroyed my mother as well as himself. He hasn't touched spirits since." Quieter than a whisper, Sidian added, "I think my solidarity lends him strength."

Raine squeezed Sidian's hand, suffused with too much tenderness to bear. In the pressure between their palms and fingers, he swore a silent and irrevocable vow to never be the cause of his mate's suffering. He only ever wanted to ease Sidian's heart and add light where there might otherwise be darkness.

CHAPTER THIRTY-TWO

Their progress through Rokeshin was inevitably slowed by the masses. A twenty-minute walk became an hour's affair. The effect was further compounded as they reached the next street over and were forced to a standstill.

The street was no longer simply crowded. It was a crush of bodies packed so tightly, a rat couldn't squeak through.

"What's going on?" Jaska asked.

Raine stood on his tiptoes to see what the holdup was. He was taller than most, but there were a lot of people, and it was difficult to make sense of the chaos.

Hoping for a better vantage, he began jumping up and down. Each bounce of his heels revealed more details. The crowd seemed intent upon tables lining the side of the road. Two men and a woman, all Guardians, were positioned behind it. Their hands were busy as people came up to them, but he couldn't see what they were doing.

Sidian glanced at him and snorted. "It's a concession stand. We're caught in the line."

"Can we go around it?" Aly asked.

"No way." Oka's face tilted up as he sniffed the air. "Do you smell that? Whatever it is, I want some."

"We aren't here to eat," Savere admonished, sounding every inch the stern older brother.

The throng crawled forward a few steps. People had their empty cups at the ready as they discussed the merits of the cherry duck dumplings versus the pork skewers.

"Everyone else is waiting in line," Sidian murmured, glancing back to address their group. "Ignoring the concessions will make us stand out. Not in a good way."

Savere's mouth tightened as Oka smirked at him, exuding insolent victory. The rest of the dragons simply nodded, angling their feet to follow the line.

Warm spices perfumed the air. Thyme and sage and something sweet.

When they reached the stand, everyone except Sidian held out cups for a refill. There were trays of steamy pink meat on sticks, shiny crescent dumplings, cream-filled pastries, and roasted nuts in cones. One Guardian oversaw drinks and the other two, the food.

Oka piled his arms with two of everything, his grin so wide it reached his ears. Raine's sweet tooth won out, and he took several pastries and a cone of nuts, which he discovered were glazed in salted honey. He moaned around a mouthful, inspiring Aly to snatch two servings for herself. Sidian graciously accepted a drink at the insistence of a Guardian. He handed it off to Raine once they were far enough away from the table.

Raine munched happily as they continued. Now that they were beyond the concession stand, the foot traffic flowed like a river, directing them toward the citadel looming ahead.

In minutes, they reached the city square. It was huge—a flat, open space spanning the length of several city blocks. An area designed to hold an entire army of mobilized soldiers.

The crowds were thickest here. Guardians, soldiers, and civilians mingled with merriment. Spirits flowed. Food was everywhere. Musicians played rousing sets with fiddles and bladder pipes. People danced and toasted and danced and ate.

Their group was starkly somber by comparison. Silently, they stared up, up, *up* at the citadel. Built on high ground, it towered above its curtain. A monstrosity of gray stone and too many spires, like an obelisk's hand clutching a fistful of pikes.

A hundred paces from the city square, at least a thousand Guardians were stationed along the defensive curtain, maybe more. Watchful and unmoving, they crowded on top of the citadel's battlements like a wolf spider's innumerable young.

Raine stared at them, stunned. He hadn't truly comprehended the full might of the guild. Until now.

"Um, Sidian." Raine swallowed, his voice as weak as his knees. "That's a lot of Guardians," he pointed out lamely.

He couldn't see Sidian's expression through the side of his hood, but when he spoke, his tone was grim. "I know. I saw them earlier." Sidian's gaze swept the battlements slowly, as if tallying the Guardians. "I don't think the Nine sent any reinforcements to Chambrin."

The news hit Raine like a fist of solid dread. He gasped. "But—But why wouldn't they?"

They'd been counting on Moranda's letter to summon reinforcements to Chambrin Keep, leaving less opposition for them to face in Rokeshin. If what Sidian said was true, that meant the entire guild was here. Present and on high alert. How the fuck were they going to get anywhere near the Nine?

"The Nine have always been exceptionally paranoid," Sidian said. His voice was cold and calm, like a sea in dead winter. "They must have realized their vulnerability, the target they present. My guess is that they are putting their personal protection above recapturing the breeders, if only for the duration of the succession."

"What are we going to do now?" Aly asked, pressing around Raine to look over at Sidian.

"What we came here to do." Sidian stared at the citadel, motionless and intent. "The circumstances aren't ideal, but our mission remains the same."

Sidian fell silent as a trio of young women appeared beside them. They chattered excitedly, pointing at the skyline above the citadel. Like everyone else in the city, they were deep in their cups, their movements exaggerated and clumsy.

"It's almost time," one girl said giddily. Her dark hair was a mass of sweaty tangles. She was flushed and overheated, an abundance of alcohol keeping her warm without a coat on.

"Are you sure we didn't miss it?" one of her companions asked. She wasn't wearing a coat, either, but her dress was long-sleeved and thick with fleece.

"I'm sure," the third girl answered. "They practice at the eleventh—"

Before she finished speaking, a bell tolled from behind them, mounted high in the belfry of the austere sanctuary that trimmed the square. Each strike of the clapper reverberated in a ponderous boom that drowned all other sound.

Once ... Twice ...

It continued, booming eleven times in total.

The first girl squealed. "We're just in time."

Confused, Raine looked to Sidian for an explanation and froze. A hard, troubled frown carved ridges around Sidian's eyes and mouth, but it was the stricken look in his eyes—like a man trapped in a sinking ship—that raised gooseflesh down Raine's neck and arms.

He tracked Sidian's gaze, his chest already pounding with reciprocal fear. What he found robbed him of breath. His entire body went numb, encased in ice.

Beyond the citadel's curtain, winged silhouettes were sailing into the air. Their distance made them appear as small as tree lizards. They moved in harmony, like a rainbow ribbon that danced and spun at the whims of an invisible hand.

Or, a not-so-invisible hand. Because mounted to each of the war dragons' backs was a rider. They were too far away for Raine to identify, but he knew with preternatural certainty that they were the dragon handlers; Bulloch, Thatcher, and the rest of the men charged with the daily care and training of the war dragons.

Rage buried Raine like an avalanche as he surveyed them. Each handler gathered reins in one fist and brandished a whip in the other, snapping sharp leather thongs against the dragons' sides as if they were nothing more than simple-minded beasts to subdue and control.

"I'll kill them," Jaska breathed. He crushed the paper cup in his fist. Mead spilled over his hand and dripped to the ground. The cup followed as he dropped it and took a sudden step forward.

Zane splayed a palm over Jaska's chest, halting him. "I understand how you feel, but now is not the time."

Sidian looked back at them and nodded. His hood veiled his eyes, but his jaw ticked as he spoke through his teeth. "Zane's right. We can't react."

"Neither can we stand by and do nothing," Savere said, his tone coated with malice as he watched the riders usher the war dragons through a series of complex aerial maneuvers. Their commands were punctuated with harsh shouts and cracking whips.

"If you interfere, you will doom us all," Sidian warned.

One of the war dragons diverted from the group and flew an exuberant circle around a turret. Her scales gleamed like lavender glass as she twirled, fragmenting the sunlight in a thousand brilliant rays.

Aching fondness broke through the dull horror binding Raine. It was Yip. The youngest of the war dragons and his most constant playmate. She was a radiant gem brought to life, mischievous and bold against the pale blue sky.

Her portly rider slammed the handle of his whip against her skull. Not once or twice, but repeatedly. He beat her viciously, his bulk heaving with each blow. Blood roared in Raine's ears, his veins pulsing with impotent fury.

A guttural growl rasped the air. Deeper and more bloodthirsty than his worst nightmares. Raine wrenched his gaze away from Yip and turned.

Oka, Zane, and Jaska each fisted a section of Savere's coat as they pinned him in place. And Savere—ever stoic and un-flappable *Savere*—was observing Yip's handler with a snarl, his leafy green stare as empty and merciless as a black-footed leopard. And Raine knew, as sure as the sunrise, that the man riding Yip was already dead. He just didn't know it yet.

Gradually, Savere relaxed. His eyes still gleamed a promise of death, but he was no longer about to burst out of his clothes and fly for Yip's rider. The others realized the same because they released their hold on him and stepped back.

When Raine looked towards the citadel, Yip had rejoined the other war dragons' formation. Her rider's whip now rest-ed against her flank, poised to crack rather than bludgeon. It didn't really make anything better.

"I need a drink," Jaska announced, then broke away to locate one of the Guardians toting trays of mead.

"Same," Aly and Oka said in unison, darting after Jaska before the crowd swallowed him. With an audible sigh, Zane followed dutifully after his mate.

Around the city square, spectators *oohed* and *aahed*. Voices rich with pride—and slurred with spirits—they exalted the war dragons' strength and the Nine's sagacity. Valdenia was both powerful and protected. The greatest country in the world.

"So," Raine said, dragging out the syllable as they continued watching the war dragons fly choreographed circles around the citadel. "This might change some things."

"Not as much as I feared," Sidian murmured. He jerked his head, wordlessly indicating the iron-gridded portcullis centered in the barbican. "At the twelfth bell, that gate will open to admit mourners into the citadel."

Raine's eyes widened. "They're allowing visitation?"

It was normal for the living to visit the dead one last time before the pyre. But with thousands of mourners piling into Rokeshin every day since Brandor's passing, how on earth could the Nine keep such a thing organized?

"Thus far, they have," Sidian said. "Tomorrow is the final day. The last of Brandor's mourners will be admitted by the sixteenth hour, and his pyre will be lit at sundown."

Raine whistled through his teeth. That wasn't much time to come up with a plan. Brandor's passing must have occurred earlier than he thought. He had assumed they would have multiple days to observe and prepare. He had assumed woefully wrong.

"You intend for us to pose as mourners to infiltrate the castle," Savere said quietly.

Sidian nodded. "It will be more risky without Betony's support, but there are too many Guardians concentrated outside to sneak through any other way. I'll go by myself today and analyze the security within the citadel. We can fine-tune a plan for tomorrow based on my observations."

"What happened to not letting me out of your sight?" Raine's voice squeaked in outrage. He cleared his throat. "You aren't going alone," he added darkly. Glaring a silent threat, he dared his mate to argue.

Sidian arched a brow, unfazed.

Raine's scowl deepened. "I mean it."

Sidian's lips quirked in amusement. As if he was a panther who'd just been confronted by a kitten. "We don't know if they check underneath hoods before allowing Brandor's visitors inside the chapel."

"My wig—"

"Does nothing to disguise your eyes," Sidian said smoothly. Stepping closer, he tucked a finger beneath Raine's chin and lined their stares. "I need to verify that the visitation isn't a trap before you step foot in the citadel. The Nine's security may be lax elsewhere to lull us into a false sense of security."

"I believe we have a more immediate concern," Savere said, drawing their gazes. "The second Betony's storm sees their children, nothing and no one is going to stop them from attacking. I doubt Brandor's visiting hours will be extended to accommodate a full-scale dragon assault. They're going to ruin your plan before you can implement it."

Jaska and the others silently rejoined them as Savere finished speaking. Aly used Raine's shoulder to steady herself in a way that told him precisely how many tiny paper cups she'd enjoyed.

Sidian's mouth pressed into a thin, hard line. That troubled look was back in his eyes. "I advised Betony to stake out the citadel."

Alarm twisted Raine's stomach. "We need to keep them away from here."

"Don't look now," Aly slurred. "But I think you're probably definitely too late."

All around them, jocularity bled into shock and stillness. Thousands of arms lifted, pointing at the sky. Raine followed their stares and gaped in open-mouthed horror. His face blanched white as every drop of blood drained to his feet.

Twenty winged silhouettes cut through the air like glittering blades. Flying straight for the citadel.

CHAPTER THIRTY-THREE

The war dragons didn't hesitate. As if they'd been primed for this exact scenario, their lazy ribbon-like formation shifted into a seething death cyclone. Betony's storm didn't make it beyond the citadel's outer curtain before they were surrounded.

The war dragons encircled their parents in a seamless corkscrew formation. Betony's storm was either too delusional or too stupid to flee. They flew in a compacted triangle, making themselves an easy target for their spiraling children.

Every time the war dragons lapped Betony's storm, they narrowed their corkscrew. Raine felt like he was watching a gigantic rainbow serpent constrict a lame calf. Some of the parents emitted high-pitched barks and whines. The war dragons ignored them. They were lethally focused—conditioned to take down any threat to their humans.

A silvery lavender dragoness broke free from the storm's triangular cluster. *Betony.* She flew for the closest war dragon, a mammoth-sized red male. *Mayhem*. Betony chirped something at him. It sounded sharp and desperate. A plea and a demand wrapped in one.

Raine's gut clenched as she came within striking distance. Mayhem was one of the more brutal war dragons.

There was a flash of glittering white teeth, then a yelp as Mayhem's maw snapped around her throat. In a blink, he was plummeting toward the ground, wings tucked into his sides. Betony flailed helplessly, struggling and failing to escape his hold on her neck.

A wine-red dragon belted an anxious roar and started after them. Lorrivare didn't make it ten feet before Violet, a purple female, clamped her fangs down on the base of his tail. Raine cringed. He didn't have a tail, but he found himself massaging a phantom pain on his backside as Lorrivare ripped the sky on a fiery scream.

The war dragons reacted as if they'd received a signal. Suddenly, each of them pivoted and latched onto the nearest invading dragon.

One by one, the war dragons drove their parents into the ground beyond the citadel's curtain. Raine couldn't see past the barrier, but he counted each impact as microquakes rocked the pavestones beneath his feet.

Dust clouds rose beyond the wall. Vicious snarls and cracking blows followed. Along the battlements, Guardians aimed crossbows loaded with milk-white arrows at the inner courtyard.

All too soon, the sounds of conflict ceased. The Guardians eased back their weapons and proceeded to watch what Raine could only guess was Betony's storm's official recapture.

"Do you ever think—*hiccup*—that you should have lied when Betony asked where that—*hiccup*—Olan guy is?" Aly asked.

"Only every other minute or so," Raine said drily.

Contrary to his sardonic tone, tangles of barbed wire coiled around his chest, shredding him. Guilt and misery seeped from the wounds in place of blood.

It didn't matter how ignorant and offensive Betony's storm was. It didn't matter that they had disowned him.

This wasn't about them. It was about a son honoring his father.

And right now, Raine was seriously fucking failing.

Oka looped a heavy arm around the shoulder not claimed by Aly. "On the bright side, now we don't have to worry about twenty loose cannons going off at the wrong time and wrecking everything."

"Are you daft?" Jaska hissed. "That *just* happened."

"I disagree," Sidian said quietly. As one, they turned to him, but he was observing the citadel. "If the Nine were on guard, waiting for a strike, it is possible that Betony's storm did us a favor."

"They will think the danger is done. The threat contained," Zane murmured appreciatively.

Trumpets blared, blasting a tinny tantara that quieted the city square. Raine hadn't noticed how noisy and chaotic the crowd had gotten. Only the sudden absence of crying and screaming made him realize it had been occurring at all.

In the distance, bodies emerged on a railed balcony centered high above the citadel's entrance. The trumpeters ceased as a robed man stood at its center. There was a cylindrical object in his hand, which Raine identified as a blowhorn when the man raised it to his mouth to address the city square.

"Greetings to you all," Chieftain Eddic's voice called out. "You have my sincerest apologies for the startling scene you've just witnessed. We strive to keep our dragons' reflexes sharp, and I'm afraid we got a little carried away in their training exercises today. There is no cause for alarm. I have asked General Olan and the officers involved to please save any future mock battles for outside the city walls."

Eddic paused as someone spoke in his ear. Nodding, he continued to address the crowd. "Visiting hours will stay the same. Those of you who have not wished Chieftain Brandor farewell have until the morrow to do so." Eddic raised a fist in the air and called, "May Brandor's spirit rise straight and swift."

Raine's skeleton hummed as thousands of voices chanted back, "His palace rest is well earned."

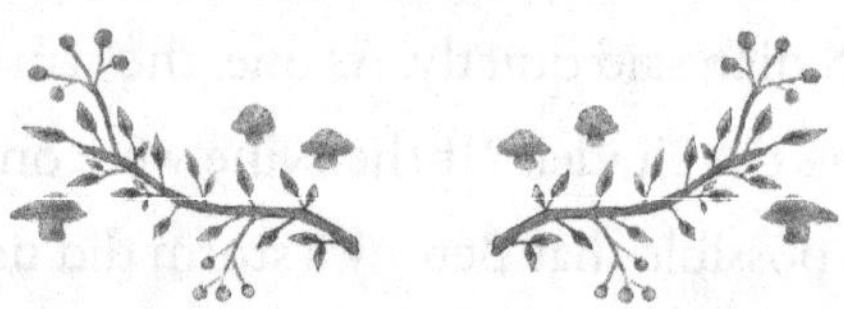

"It's going to be alright. Sidian's got this," Aly said bracingly from her perch on a white velvet armchair.

Raine scarcely registered her words. He was too busy slogging through mires of trepidation and fear as he paced the hummingbird parlor.

After Betony's storm was recaptured, Nyx's group—or, rather, what was left of them—had arrived in the city square. The Wade brothers then ushered Raine and the remaining dragons back to

Rosa's manor and promptly dumped them here, so they could scamper right back to the citadel.

Not going to leave my side for the foreseeable future, my ass. Raine wanted to scream. He understood his mate's logic. Sidian had to ensure dragons could get into the vigil undetected. But oh it rankled. And terrified. He felt so fucking helpless.

There was a dull ache in his chest from Sidian's absence, but he scarcely registered it. His pain was nothing, *nothing*, when his mate was in potential danger.

"The captain will return," Rosa said. "To this day, no recruit has outdone his score in reconnaissance training. He knows what he's doing. So, just sit down and relax."

Raine continued to pace. He was infected with nervous energy. His muscles itched for a fight. Not play wrestling, but a real fight.

It was too bad Lukor was preoccupied. If any dragon here would be willing to give Raine a down-and-dirty (and distracting) brawl, it was him. But spurred by the indomitable, no-nonsense Betony, Lukor's group had blitzed through Rokeshin's festivities without partaking in a single bit of mead or dumplings. It was now well past lunchtime, and Lukor was in the dining room, demolishing trays of cold meats and cheese with the other snack-deprived dragons.

"Look. I'm trying to be nice," Rosa huffed. "But if you keep pacing like that, you're going to ruin an authentic Strowan rug that was gifted to my family before this manor even existed."

Raine halted, staring down at the rug in question. It was the creamy blue of a blended sky. Gold glimmered in loose, swirling lines that offered the impression of wind or sun, or both.

"It's not like we don't have dozens of fancy rugs, mind you." A thread of self-consciousness entered Rosa's tone. "But my mother is exceptionally fond of that one. This is her favorite sitting room, and I don't want to deal with the headache if you scuff the pattern."

"Sorry," Raine murmured. He frowned thoughtfully at the mention of her mother, recalling Sidian's assurances that Rosa's family wouldn't visit with their daughter in residence. "Why don't you get on with your parents?"

Silence greeted his inquiry.

Raine looked up and found Rosa's lush mouth pressed into a tight line. "Shit, I'm sorry. It's none of my business. I didn't mean to—"

"No. It's fine." Rosa smiled thinly. "And we do get on. For the most part. But my mother caught an illness that left her barren after she had me. Leaving this sweet womb" —Rosa slapped her lower belly to demonstrate— "as the only one capable of producing the next generation of Rokes."

"What's so wrong with that?" Aly asked, cocking her head.

"Nothing at all." Rosa's smile turned wry. "Except that I insisted on pursuing a career instead of settling down and shelling out babies."

Aly's eyes bloomed wide. "Do you not want babies, then?"

"Perhaps someday." A peculiar gleam entered Rosa's eyes. "If I ever find a man I want to have them with."

"Interesting," Aly mused. "Are you sure you haven't found one yet? Because there's a man hereabouts that seems pretty keen to acquaint himself with your womb."

Twin spots of pink splashed Rosa's cheeks as she barked a laugh. "He wishes. That man is a pest."

"I don't know." Aly touched a finger to her cheek, but too much mirth played about her mouth for the gesture to appear contemplative. "I've never looked at a pest the way you look at Nyx."

"*Nyx?*" Raine asked over Rosa's squawking protest. He had known there was something off about their interactions, but what Aly suggested was, well. It put things in a different light, that was certain.

Aly shook her head at him. "You're so dense. Thank the Dreaming Mother you have Sidian, or I'd be worried for your survival at this rate."

"Well, pardon me for not realizing that barbs and threats are some sort of mating ritual," Raine grumbled, rubbing absently at his chest. Right at an invisible seam that felt ready to split from being pulled taut too long.

"Wait a minute." Aly's eyes narrowed suspiciously. "Don't tell me you're still in your courtship." Raine hastily dropped his hand, but it was too late. A hot, guilty flush was already climbing his neck. Aly's lips formed a stunned red circle. "*How?*"

The heat spread, engulfing Raine's ears as Rosa and Zane's gazes fixed on him, too. "Well, um. What do you mean, how? It's pretty self-explanatory." Raine shrugged awkwardly and willed her to drop it.

"Duh. You guys haven't had sex yet," Aly said bluntly. "I know *that*. But, why? What are you waiting for?"

"Is it because Sidian is human?" Zane asked carefully. "Has he—That is, does he reciprocate your feelings?"

"Are you blind, Blue Boy?" Rosa snorted. "The captain looks at Moonbeam like he wants to eat him. Alive and squirming," she added with a wink.

"I know that, too," Aly said impatiently. She glared at Raine, her features wreathed with adamance. "So, what gives?"

Raine chewed his lip as his gaze flitted from one probing stare to the next. Aly and Rosa sat in the matching white armchairs, Rosa with an ottoman tucked under her leg cast. And Zane was on the fern-patterned sofa, his previously indolent posture now attentive as he eyed Raine with frank intrigue.

"It's ... complicated."

"Don't care," Aly said shortly. "I take back everything I said about Sidian being good for your survival. It's obvious you're *both* too dense to live. Do you know how dangerous it is to leave your bond unconsummated? If Sidian dies before you mate—"

"I know the consequences," Raine growled. He dug his nails into his palms, feeling more beast than man. "I cannot endure any speculations about Sidian's death. Not right now, *please*."

Aly winced. "Sorry. That was my bad. I promise you, Sidian is going to be fine. Did you see the line forming for Brandor's visitation? It was insane. And every human in it looked just like Sidian and Nyx. They blend right in."

"They didn't look a thing like Sidian," Raine protested. "And he won't blend in. He's too tall and too handsome. Too well-known by the guild. People *recognize* him."

"Yeah, and the guild obviously hasn't been apprised of his new loyalties. When that one hunter recognized him, he was thrilled to run into *Captain Wade*." Aly simpered his name with an eye roll.

"It's true," Rosa assured him. "I haven't heard a whisper of the captain defecting. And since he's my immediate superior, I'd be informed before most."

"Isn't that strange, considering he blew up half of the guild's headquarters?" Zane asked, cerulean brows furrowing.

"Humans are strange, so who knows? And anyways, we're not talking about that right now," Aly said stiffly. She pointed an accusing finger at Raine. "We're talking about why you haven't sealed the deal with your mate. Well?"

Aly was like a winter-starved wolf stalking a lamb. She wasn't going to rest until she got her kill.

Raine blew out a sigh. "We had a minor misunderstanding. But we've worked it all out. Everything's good now."

"Wait a minute," Rosa said slowly. "Does that mean what I think it means?"

"If you think it means we had a minor misunderstanding, but we've worked it all out, then yes," Raine deadpanned.

Rosa grinned. "Is my little Moonbeam going to experience lovemaking for the first time tonight?"

"You're so lucky," Aly gasped. "You get an actual bedroom. My first time with Zane was at the Hellhole. In the meat cellar," she added, as if Raine had asked. "It became the unofficial hook-up spot for mated pairs. Poor Oka nearly lost his mind when he found out."

Raine's nose scrunched. "I don't think I needed to know that. Ever."

Judging by the way Zane closed a palm over his face and groaned, he agreed.

"Act prissy all you want, princess." Aly sniffed. "But if the only way you could have Sidian was inside a communal sex-slash-meat cellar, your ass would be banging in there, too."

Rosa clamored out of her chair and began thumping for the parlor's exit.

"Where are you going?" Raine asked.

She threw a saucy grin over her shoulder without slowing. "Jaska's room is next to yours. I'm going to move him further down the hall, so you and the captain will have more privacy."

"Wait." Raine started after her, his tone strangled with panic. "You're not going to tell him *why*, are you?"

He collided with a dark figure and almost fell. Strong arms steadied him. "Tell who what?"

Raine blinked into curious fawn eyes and flushed. "Oh, um. You're back," he cheered weakly. "H-How was the vigil?"

Sidian's amused smirk told him just how pathetic his prevarication was.

A high-pitched squeal sounded from down the hall. Rosa's voice rang out. "Put me down, you overbearing oaf. I said I can *walk*."

"Informative," Sidian murmured, his gaze never wavering from Raine's. "Come on. Everyone's meeting in the dining room."

CHAPTER THIRTY-FOUR

The wallpaper in Raine's ensuite was deepwater blue. Fat, round lily pads floated throughout, teeming with freshwater flora and fauna. Raine twisted inside the tub, bathwater murmuring as he traced the wall's pattern, marking the differences between the frogs and dragonflies as he bathed.

But no matter how diligently Raine fixated on the frogs, his mind invariably wandered to the massive king-sized bed in the next room.

He was gripped by a nameless dread. The fear that he would disappoint his mate. Their consummation loomed over him like a loose stalactite, the threat of doom mounting every second.

Raine cupped his face and groaned. This wasn't going to work. All he wanted was to please Sidian, but he didn't know how. There'd been rows and rows of erotic books at Love Play, and he cursed his previous indifference towards sex. Had he bothered to flip through a few volumes, he might be more prepared.

How did men even make love? He had a vague notion, but it seemed so ... *indecent*. It couldn't possibly be that, but Raine rather thought it *was* that.

The bathroom door opened, sucking out all the warm, humid air that built up. Sidian leaned against the doorframe, mouth twitching. "I should have known this is where I'd find you."

"Sorry," Raine blurted, feeling chastened despite his mate's wry tone. He hadn't meant to make Sidian search for him.

Raine had remained in the dining room long enough to absorb the basics of their plan for tomorrow. But between Aly's incessant innuendos and Rosa's obnoxious, waggling eyebrows, he had grown more and more flustered. Until he couldn't take it anymore and sought the respite of a bath.

"Did you need me for something? Has the plan changed? I should have stayed longer. I'm sorry—"

"The plan hasn't changed." Sidian stepped into the room and approached the tub.

Each quiet tap of Sidian's boots against the blue tile floor made Raine's stomach flutter. Tall and broad and handsome—his mate looked like the Divine Father's model of a heroic warrior. Raine tried very hard not to peer between Sidian's legs, but it was a lost cause. Garbed in body-hugging black silk, his mate's groin was as snugly outlined as the rest of him. And just as impressive.

Raine's pulse tripped, arousal flooding him. He swiftly wadded his washcloth and tucked it over his lap, right as his mate reached the edge of the tub.

A teasing gleam entered Sidian's eyes. "What are you thinking about that has you so pink?"

"Nothing." He cursed inwardly as his cheeks warmed. "It's the water. It's really hot."

Sidian's mouth curved knowingly as he dragged his gaze from Raine to the water. "Hm. I can see that," he drawled.

Raine winced, flush deepening as he realized his error. Not a single curl of steam wafted from the water's surface. It was glaringly tepid.

"Your bathwater isn't even dirty," Sidian added, almost accusing.

"That's the point." Raine lifted his chin. "I'm through with being a grimy outlaw. From now on, I am staying clean if it kills me."

Sidian smirked, slow and secretive. "Don't count on it. I have plans for this evening that will make you filthy."

Raine's breath hitched. That husky voice, rasping those words, melted his brain out of his ears.

Belatedly, he parsed their meaning.

"What do you mean? Is sex *dirty*?" Raine drew back, scandalized, accidentally splashing water onto the floor.

"Don't worry. I'll clean you afterward." Sidian's fawn eyes danced wickedly. He bent down, leaning forward. Warm, soft lips caressed Raine's ear as he whispered, "Then dirty you up all over again. And again."

Raine shivered, goose bumps prickling. He gasped and dropped his washcloth as Sidian nipped his ear.

"Enjoy your bath," Sidian murmured, straightening. His eyes trailed hungrily down Raine's body before he turned and left, shutting the door softly behind him.

Fuck.

Raine slumped against the tub. Heart thundering, he eyed the closed door as if it was a coiled rattlesnake. Anxiety shredded his innards to ribbons.

Last night, Raine had fallen asleep in the bath by accident. Perhaps he could pull off the same trick tonight? That would give him a chance to raid the marketplace for a naughty bookstore tomorrow. Was there such a thing as a *How to Please Your Mate* guide? Or step-by-step instructions on how two men made love? Or something, anything, that would spare him from a humiliatingly awful performance and Sidian's inevitable disappointment?

It doesn't matter if there is, he thought morosely. Even fake sleep was impossible in his current state. Electricity enveloped his bones, emitting a low-level hum that buzzed through his skin. His body was too alert, primed for something more ancient and physical than battle.

Raine's stomach pitted to a whole new level of trepidation as he realized ...

Tonight was going to be a first for him *and* Sidian.

His mate had only ever been with women. Would Sidian's hands trace the firm, masculine lines of Raine's body and find him wanting? Was he going to reach for soft breasts and rounded hips, and realize he didn't want to consummate their bond, after all?

*I don't like men, and I don't like women. I like **you**.*

Raine squeezed his eyes shut and wrapped those words around him like a cocoon, willing them to permeate as he finished his bath.

His mate wanted him. Not to save his life, but because he loved and desired him.

Raine's confidence grew as he sat before the vanity, brushing his hair until it was dry and gleamed like a lush curtain of opal moonlight. He massaged the strands with vanilla oil before weaving his hair into a long, thick braid.

As he oiled the rest of his body, he noticed the light slanting through the porthole window. It was the gilded roseate of advancing twilight. Raine had lost track of time. It was later than he'd thought.

Nerves zinged through him, threatening to steal his composure.

There's still time, he reminded himself. Not much, but some.

Raine drew a fortifying breath. Then another. Throwing on a white cotton robe, he squared his shoulders and reminded himself that he was fit and gorgeous—if not particularly experienced or female.

It was a comforting thought, but he knew something that would bolster him more than any pep talk.

Intending to raid Rosa's liquor cabinet and sneak some liquid courage before Sidian came to bed, Raine opened the door.

And froze.

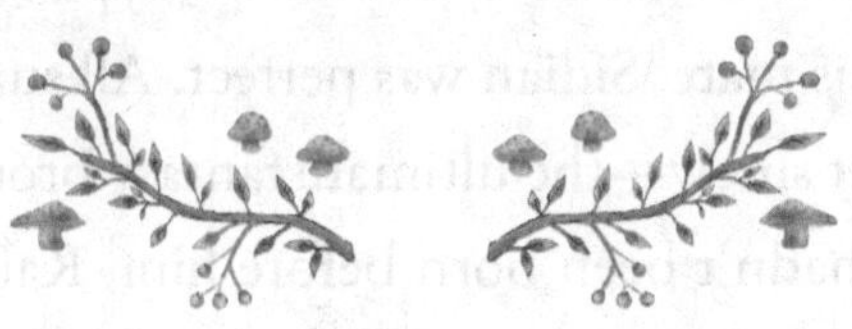

Sidian rested with his back against the headboard, the bed neatly made beneath him. He wore a pair of snug black underwear and nothing else.

Hands tucked behind his head, he looked indolent and intense. Like a panther sunning in a tree. His dark eyes moved lazily over Raine, as if he were a fat deer grazing below the canopy.

Raine gulped and almost choked on his spit. His throat was tight and dry. It took several swallows to moisten it. "Y-You're back early. Is there something we need to talk about?"

They were going to talk about Raine's heart condition if it didn't slow down soon. His pulse thundered so fiercely, he dimly accepted the possibility of his chest exploding.

"Strip."

Heat spiraled through Raine's center at the smoky command. Sidian's delivery was cool and composed, and hinted at consequences should Raine resist.

His hands shook as he reached for the belt of his robe. It was tied in a simple knot, but Raine fumbled with it, as if all his fingers had turned into thumbs. The tie finally loosened, and he shoved the robe off, hoping his mate couldn't tell how flustered he was.

Looking up, he was seared by the heat in Sidian's stare.

"Come here."

Raine walked to the bed as if in a trance, hypnotized by the raw sensuality of his mate. Sidian was perfect. All sun-bronzed skin and sharply cut sinew—the ultimate fantasy brought to flesh.

If his mate hadn't been born before him, Raine would have thought he'd somehow dreamt him into being.

Raine's greedy gaze roved from the defined planes of Sidian's chest down to his narrow hips. Where a tight band of muscle arrowed into black silk.

Sidian's engorged cock strained beneath the fabric.

Raine stumbled at the size of it. He caught himself and halted two steps from the bed, unable to trust his legs.

The world tilted as he was abruptly yanked and flipped onto his back. Raine blinked up at Sidian, realizing he was now on the mattress. His head rested on the same downy pillows that had cradled his mate's back only seconds before.

Sidian's dusky mouth was hard, his eyes liquid velvet as he surveyed Raine like a meal.

Tejayla was wrong. At least about Raine. He was a rabbit, after all. Helpless prey, well and truly caught. Sidian devoured him with his gaze, bracing his arms against the headboard to line their profiles.

"H-Hello," Raine stammered. "Are you ... Are we ..."

Divine Father, kill him now.

"Tell me," Sidian murmured, ignoring his inane blather. "Have you ever touched yourself?"

Raine's heart slammed into his ribcage. "W-Why are you asking me that?"

Sidian's eyes formed dark slits. The muscles in his biceps flexed overhead. "I won't repeat myself."

His mate's voice was a promise of sex and pain—two things Raine wouldn't have put in the same sentence, but his cock throbbed as if it understood something his mind did not.

"I, uh..." Raine's eyes dropped like two bashful stones. He stared at his mate's chest as a full-bodied blush painted him pinker than the sunset. "No," he managed in a strangled whisper.

"Raine, look at me."

His mate's voice was a rasping lick of smoke and fire. Powerless to disobey, Raine slowly raised his head and lost himself in a fathomless fawn gaze.

"You're going to stroke yourself until you come. And I'm going to watch."

Raine's silver eyes went wide. Arousal and embarrassment surged through him, tightening his stomach. "But-But I don't know what to do."

His reaction coaxed a smile from his mate. "You'll figure it out."

Sidian released the headboard and moved down the bed. Settling between Raine's thighs, he clasped a hot palm on each of his knees. His stare was unwavering. A silent, unyielding demand without a hint of doubt. Because Sidian knew Raine could deny him nothing.

Raine's stomach squirmed with mortification as he eyed his cock. It jutted towards the ceiling, tip glistening with moisture. Raine felt each thump of his heart in his palm as he reached down. His abdomen twitched and fluttered as his muscles shifted.

His fingers wrapped the base of his length. Sidian licked his lips. His eyes were blacker than midnight. Ravenous.

Raine sucked in a breath and concentrated on his cock. He couldn't watch Sidian watch him. Not without losing his nerve.

He gave himself a soft, timid stroke. And gasped. More moisture seeped from the tip, coating his palm. He should have found it repellent, but he didn't. Not when it offered such wonderful slickness on his next pull.

Fuck. He glanced back at Sidian and his hand went still.

Sidian's features were tense, jaw clenched. His sinew thrummed with the effort of his restraint. And all that pent up frustration was for Raine.

What was going to happen when his mate snapped?

"Keep going," Sidian rasped, guttural. Feral. A beast.

Raine's cock wept and he moaned, squeezing harder on his next stoke. Hot sparks danced at the base of his spine. Sidian's fingers clenched around his knees. Raine felt himself swell as the heat deepened and spread. His whole body constricted, shivering with the force of an invisible current.

His palm slicked upward once more. Sidian's fingers clenched harder, digging cruelly as if he was trying to shatter Raine's kneecaps.

A sudden violent wave crashed through Raine. His muscles seized and spasmed as he came, his arousal warm and wet where it splashed across his stomach.

Raine shuddered as his palm skimmed the tip of his cock. It was achingly sensitive, and he jerked his hand away.

"Very good," Sidian murmured, drawing Raine's gaze. His mate's expression was hooded, almost satisfied except for the stark hunger in his eyes.

Raine's cheeks glowed at the mess he'd made. His hand was wet, and he didn't know what to do with it or the cum all over his belly. He recalled the one other time they'd done anything like this. Sidian had wiped their spend on a discarded jumpsuit.

"Should I go get something to clean this up with?" he asked, then frowned. "Wait. What about you? You didn't get to—" His blush deepened as he searched for a way to phrase it.

"Do you think I'm done with you?" Sidian smirked, running his palms up and down Raine's thighs.

"I don't know," Raine confessed, acutely aware of how ignorant he was. "You wanted me to ... finish, and I did, but you haven't."

"I had you finish because you were bursting with it. You need to last longer than fifteen seconds for me to take you." Sidian's caresses grew firmer, massaging the backs of Raine's thighs where they met the curve of his ass. "That, and I've fucked my hand while imaging you like this a dozen times over."

"What?" Raine squeaked. "When?"

"You're a very heavy sleeper." Sidian's lips twitched at his expression. "In all my fantasizing, I failed to factor in how tormenting it would be to look and not touch. I hope that brief little taste of self-exploration has satisfied you, because from here on out, your pleasure is mine."

Raine was still trying to wrap his head around the idea of his mate *masturbating beside him* when Sidian scooped the cum from his stomach.

"I have to open you before we go any further. It will be easier if you turn over."

Raine's mouth fell open as he stared. Sidian was holding his spend. In his *hand*. "What are you talking about? And why do you have *that*? It's dirty. Let me get a towel."

"Turn over," Sidian repeated, inserting enough steel into the words that Raine knew it wasn't a request.

Raine hesitated, realizing that position would place his bottom right where his mate's hand waited. He eyed Sidian uncertainly, but his mate was a fortress, his countenance shuttered. Raine moved cautiously, the white linen sheets cool and smooth against his knees as he shifted so his back faced his mate.

He gasped as Sidian reached around his midsection and hiked him up, singlehandedly maneuvering him so that his rear end was higher. The position spread his cheeks apart. Cool air caressed his most intimate flesh. Mortified and exposed, Raine cinched his legs and started to sit up.

"No." The voice of a demon addressed him, low and throaty. "Lean forward all the way and spread yourself."

Raine's stomach flipped at the odd command. Distantly, he registered that he was panting. Short, shallow breaths that moistened the pillow he was clinging to.

"Good," Sidian purred. That one small sound hardened Raine's spent cock to stone.

Sidian swept Raine's braid to the side, exposing his spine. "Stay still."

Raine's stomach clenched with excitement. He had no clue what his mate intended. His heart pounded as his cock wept, every inch of his flesh sensitized with renewed lust.

A warm, rough palm stroked his spine and slid downward. Prickles of pleasure fanned over Raine's back, and he sighed, relaxing deeper into the mattress.

When Sidian reached Raine's bottom, he traced the globes with a gentle, almost reverent touch. Raine's haunches trembled, his cock throbbing as each caress inched Sidian's hand closer to his center. He stiffened when he felt Sidian brush his opening.

"Fuck," Sidian whispered huskily. "You're so fucking pretty. Like a tight little flower bud, all quivering and eager for me to open you."

Raine's cock swelled painfully as his belly clenched with shame. His mate's words dripped with desire, but he was talking about Raine's hole. A part of him he'd never imagined another would see, let alone admire. His ears burned as he imagined how exposed he was.

Something probed at his entrance, soothing the rim. Raine felt a slippery wetness as the pressure grew stronger. It was Sidian's *finger*. Raine tried to flinch away. Sidian's iron grip held his hip in place. "Stay. Still."

He barely recognized Sidian's voice. Hoarse and darkly authoritative, it was choked with need. Raine stilled.

Sidian worked him open slowly. His movements were meticulous and controlled, and Raine gradually relaxed.

Suddenly, his mate pressed inside him to the knuckle. Raine gasped. It felt strange. And unbearably intimate.

Sidian's finger disappeared, and Raine was surprised at how bereft it made him. The mattress dipped as his mate reached for something on the nightstand. Raine twisted to see, but Sidian pinned him with one hand between his shoulder blades, reminding him without words to keep still.

Raine hugged the pillow and waited. In moments, the warm scent of cinnamon reached his nose. Sidian's finger returned to his entrance, sliding inside him tenderly and with slightly more ease than before.

The cinnamon smell grew stronger as another finger joined the first. Raine hissed, his body squeezing uncomfortably tight around the intrusion.

"Shh." Sidian stroked his back in time with his fingers. "You're doing so good. Try to relax. Let me in."

Raine moaned, arching subtly into his mate's hand. Something was happening. The idea of Sidian's fingers went from embarrassing to erotic. It felt nice. Sensual. His mate was worshiping his hole with his hand, and it made Raine's prick ache. His body was seeking something, behaving as though he could find release this way. It was mindless instinct, and he gave over to it. Rocking his hips, he took Sidian's fingers deeper.

Sidian growled, and a third finger entered on his next stroke. There was a flicker of pain as Raine's body adjusted. His breaths grew ragged. He felt so full. Exquisitely full. He rocked harder against his mate's hand.

"Not yet." Sidian pinned his lower back. "You're still too tight. I need more oil."

The smell of cinnamon mixed with the vanilla wafting from Raine's skin. He savored the delicious aroma as his mate pushed slick wetness inside his hole. Oil dribbled down Raine's thighs and warmed his sack as Sidian worked his fingers deeper, until Raine felt open and drenched.

His body jolted as Sidian touched something inside him. Something molten. His nerves went white-hot with more pleasure than he could endure.

Sidian cursed sharply, his warm breath fanning the base of Raine's spine. Raine would have been embarrassed to realize how close his mate's face was to his opening, but his mind was too fractured from that electric shock of ecstasy.

"Turn around," Sidian said, his command rough with desire. Raine's limbs shook as he turned over and faced Sidian. His stomach glistened with the copious smears of his excitement.

Sidian's pupils were blown wide, turning his eyes into voids. He reached down, tearing the thin cloth of his underwear with an impatient jerk. Then he grabbed Raine by his shoulders and guided him backward.

Raine's eyes widened as his head hit the pillow. "Is this—I mean, are we—"

Sidian claimed his mouth in a bruising kiss. Raine moaned, all thoughts evaporating as Sidian laved his tongue, sucking it into his own mouth. His mate's cock was harder than Raine thought possible, an iron bar prodding his abdomen.

Their kiss ended slowly, by degrees. With a sweet, parting suck on the tip of Raine's tongue, his mate drew back and regarded him.

"It is. We are." Sidian's gaze was firebright, his features etched with desire. With the need to possess and ravage.

Raine's heart punched his chest as Sidian positioned himself. His cock was as big and bronze as the rest of him. Beautifully shaped, but with an unnerving girth. Translucent slickness seeped from its flared head.

The blunt press against Raine's hole felt like the span of ten fingers. It *hurt*. Raine's breath faltered as Sidian pressed deeper. Only the tip of his leaking cock was lodged inside Raine's hole, and it was too much.

He flinched, and Sidian went perfectly still. His hands came up to smooth Raine's brow. His soft mouth followed, pressing warm, gentle kisses over Raine's forehead.

Raine's lashes fluttered shut as those downy kisses trailed over his eyes, then found his mouth. They kissed, long and slow. Raine lost himself in his mate's mouth. The smooth glide of his tongue and the delicate bite of teeth on his lips.

"So sweet," Sidian murmured into his ear. He nibbled at the lobe, and Raine shivered. "You're taking my cock so good. You were made for it. Made for me."

Sidian's hips moved, driving his cock deeper. It stung, and Raine clenched. Sidian hissed, then wrapped his arms around Raine and gathered him to his chest.

"Easy," Sidian whispered, turning his words into a caress as his mouth brushed Raine's ear. "You've got to relax. Open that pretty hole for me. Let me make you feel good."

Inch by agonizing inch, Sidian worked his way in. Raine felt full to bursting, but Sidian kept giving him more. All the while, he played with Raine's ear. Murmuring words heavy with praise and soaked with desire.

"You're so fucking sweet. So perfect and tight on my cock. Easy, now. Easy. Relax. That's it. You're taking me so good."

Those steady vibrations against Raine's ear were like a hot stroke against his cock. He whimpered and writhed, desperate for friction against his arousal. His movements shifted his hips, until he was fucking himself with shallow, clumsy thrusts against Sidian's cock.

"Stay still for me. Don't squeeze—*Fuck*." Suddenly, Raine's braid was snatched in a vicious fist. His neck arched painfully, eyes watering from the stinging pressure at his scalp. "So fucking greedy. You want my cock so badly? I'll give it to you."

Sidian rocked forward, seating himself fully in a single thrust. Raine dragged in a gasp, annihilated. The size and rigidity of Sidian's cock stretched him beyond anything he could have prepared for.

His mate cursed, low and rough, then slammed their mouths together. It was a direct contrast to Sidian's previous kisses. As brutal and unforgiving as the hand fisting Raine's hair and the cock penetrating him deep.

Sidian tore away to glare at him. His mouth was swollen and panting from their kiss. "I'm going to fuck your little sweet spot until you scream."

He released Raine's braid and grabbed his hips. His dark eyes were merciless and unwavering as he drove into Raine, sinking deeper than before. Raine sucked in a breath and fisted the sheets, overwhelmed. It was too much. He wasn't made for Sidian, after all. There was no way he could handle this. His hole was too small. Sidian was too big.

His mate adjusted his angle and, "*Oh*."

White-hot, nerve-melting pleasure obliterated Raine. He held onto Sidian, his mouth slack on a silent scream as his mate pounded into him. Each thrust was more devastating than the last as Sidian's cock rammed against that mysterious place inside him.

The onslaught of ecstasy was too much for Raine's body to contain. It flooded the space around them in a blinding light.

Impossibly, Raine's pleasure heightened. It was like he was both filling and being filled. He sensed a hot, silken hole strangling his cock. At the same time, Sidian's cock smashed into that electric bundle of nerves, shattering Raine in pure bliss.

He came, feeling the hot gush of Sidian's spend as if it were his own. As if he was coming across his stomach and inside his own squeezing tight hole.

Raine didn't know how long he laid there, eyes screwed shut as he experienced the most profoundly intense sensations of his life. When the last tremors faded, he opened his eyes to find Sidian staring down at him. His mouth was open, his eyes heavy and glazed as he watched Raine, rapt and adoring. Raine blinked at him, dazed with euphoria. And love. So much love, it ached.

Sidian pressed his mouth against Raine's forehead as he carefully withdrew.

"You," Sidian rasped against his cheek. "Are exquisite." He pressed a gentle, chaste kiss against Raine's lips.

Raine's answering smile was soft and shy. "So, it was good? You weren't disappointed about ... anything?"

Sidian's gaze turned incredulous, then narrowed. "After such a brief sample, I'm reluctant to answer. We'll have to go again to make sure."

Arousal, sharp and sweet, sang through Raine's veins in tandem with the heat in Sidian's eyes. His mate stood from the bed and held out a hand. His cock was half-hard and continued to lengthen as he waited for Raine.

"Where are we going?" Raine asked, letting his mate pull him from the bed.

He flushed as wetness seeped from his hole, coating his thighs.

Sidian's dark eyes raked over him with a devious smile. "To take a bath. I promised to clean you up before making you messy again."

CHAPTER THIRTY-FIVE

Raine woke to Sidian trailing feather soft kisses down his stomach. A large, callused palm squeezed his cock. He sucked in a breath.

"S-Sidian." He moaned, threading his fingers through his mate's black, silken crown. He was already hard and throbbing, his hips unconsciously thrusting for more.

Sidian's kisses grew hotter as he nibbled and licked his way south. He reached the space between Raine's thighs and swallowed his cock without warning. Raine's spine arched as he cried out. Sidian's hands were like vise grips on his hips, pinning him down as he worshipped Raine's cock with his tongue.

Raine whimpered and moaned as his mate laved at the head before sucking him down. His balls drew up tight as his belly clenched. "I'm going to—"

He broke off as the world fractured. Sidian's mouth turned gentle, delicately working Raine's cock through his spasms.

Open-mouthed and panting, Raine's mind was vacant as aftershocks of ecstasy rippled from his center. He didn't realize his mate had moved from between his legs until Sidian's mouth was claiming his. Sidian swallowed Raine's gasp and deepened their kiss. Raine's belly quivered as he tasted his pleasure on his mate's tongue.

Raine became aware of the iron shaft prodding his abdomen. He moaned into their kiss, fire quickening through his veins in response to his mate's need. Sidian growled against Raine's mouth and wedged a hand between them.

Without breaking their kiss, his mate worked himself with short, rough strokes. Sidian's arm jerked once, twice. Then he groaned, low and hoarse. His teeth sank sharply into Raine's full bottom lip as he spilled himself over Raine's stomach.

Raine's jaw dropped on a sharp exhale as an orgasm blasted through him. It was as if Sidian had been pumping Raine's cock instead of his own. His toes curled, hard as stones, and he shuddered through wave after wave of pleasure.

"I don't think I'll ever get used to that," Sidian rasped as their tremors faded.

"Used to what?" Raine asked, licking absently at his abused lip.

Sidian lined their stares, his gaze blissful and smug. "Feeling your pleasure through our bond."

"Wait." Raine's eyes widened. "You feel my what, now?"

"I feel your pleasure. And you feel mine." Sidian's brows rose at Raine's shock. "Don't tell me you haven't noticed. The bond formed on our first joining."

"I do feel you. Here." Raine's eyes dropped shyly as he pressed a marveling palm against his chest, directly over the spot where he felt impossibly bright and full. As if a universe of stars had coalesced beneath his skin.

Sidian's palm covered his hand and squeezed. "This is where your half of our bond resides. The other half is in me."

"Oh." Raine flushed, overcome. Their bond felt so natural, so *right*. As indelible as his breath and blood. How had he ever survived without it?

"The bond creates a bridge. Through it, we can transfer emotions and ... sensations." Sidian's mouth curled into a sultry smile, his own thoughts on the bond seeming less than pure.

Sidian leaned forward and skimmed his teeth against the shell of Raine's ear. Raine gasped, lashes fluttering.

"Mm." Sidian sucked his ear lobe, then nipped it gently. "You really like this."

Raine's breaths grew shallow as Sidian's mouth dropped to his neck and bit. They both groaned.

"But there's something you like even more than me playing with your ears. Even more than feeling me come." Sidian drew back and smirked. "Any guesses?"

Raine received an impression of heat and humor that wasn't his own. *It was Sidian's.* His mate was intensely aroused. And Raine was sensing it through their bond.

Sidian grabbed Raine's thighs and yanked him lower, nestling Raine's bottom against his cock.

"Well?" Sidian drawled. Their bond blistered as his thumb teased Raine's entrance.

Raine shook his head, incapable of speech. He just came, *twice*, and his cock was already a leaden weight against his belly. He writhed against his mate's hand, wordlessly begging for more. Sidian's eyes were dark as he swiped their combined essence from Raine's lower belly and pushed it into his hole.

Raine winced at the stinging stretch. He was tender after a long night of lovemaking. And now he knew why his cock kept hardening despite his exhaustion. It had to be the bond. Sidian was insatiable, and he was infecting Raine with his lust through it.

"Oh." He gasped, his spine almost snapping as his body arched with white-hot pleasure.

"Fuck, that's it." Sidian's features contorted, wrecked with Raine's rapture as he stroked his sweet spot again. "You fucking love this. Can you take more?"

Raine was already nodding. He whimpered as Sidian withdrew his fingers. His mate swiftly replaced them with something larger. Raine hissed at the intrusion. His body was reaching its limit, but he didn't care. He needed more.

"So greedy." Sidian kissed Raine tenderly even as his blunt cock mercilessly stretched his tender hole. "So sweet and hot and needy. You can't get enough of my cock."

Sidian rolled his hips in a long sinuous thrust, grinding his cock against Raine's sweet spot. Raine's mouth fell open as Sidian gasped. His mate's expression grew feral as he fucked Raine hard and deep.

Raine gave himself over to unearthly euphoria as his mate pounded into him, and then he felt Sidian's pleasure, too. His hole, soft and swollen from overuse, gripped Sidian's cock with searing heat.

"Sidian," he gasped, their dual pleasure too much to endure. His body shuddered, sparks flashing as the power of two orgasms crashed through him.

His mate's orgasm was longer than his own. Lush spasms that made Raine moan, hips undulating as Sidian filled him with cum and ecstasy.

They kissed, lazy and languid, as their blood cooled. Sidian sucked on Raine's bottom lip, then jerked back. There was something in his eyes, shock or awe, as he massaged his thumb over the sore spot on Raine's lip.

Raine gave him a questioning look, and Sidian's expression smoothed.

"I was too rough." He kissed Raine's bottom lip with infinite care, then untangled their limbs. "Come on." His gaze darted to their window, where the morning light shone high and bright. "We have a mission to complete."

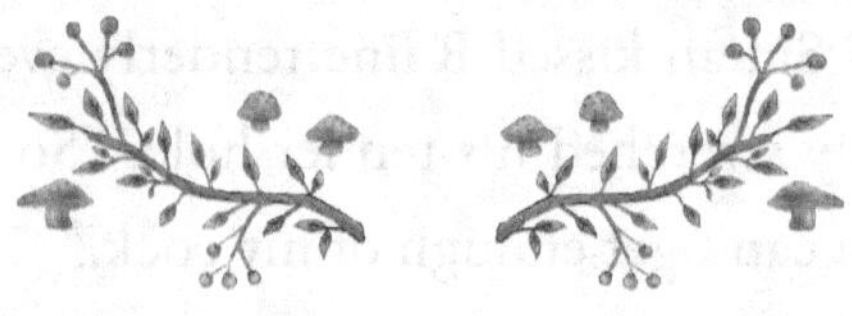

Raine hugged an elegantly wrapped bouquet of ivory roses to his chest and scanned Rokeshin's market district a third time, more urgently than the previous two.

Again, he failed to detect the tall, solid frame of Sidian. Even with a large, shapeless cloak concealing Sidian's face and form, Raine could have picked him out from the throng of last-minute shoppers.

Sidian wasn't here.

Raine might have been able to find his mate by playing a game of hot-and-cold with the ever-present string in his chest, chasing the pressure as it alleviated.

But the courtship tie that had tethered him to Sidian was gone. They had consummated their bond, replacing it with something infinitely more precious and wonderful. It glittered inside Raine's core, more radiant than the sun. And did absolute fuck-all in helping him locate his mate.

A hand clasped his shoulder. He startled, then turned with a hopeful smile. It slipped from his face as he encountered the wrong Wade brother.

"Oh, good. You've got your token," Nyx said, dipping his chin at Raine's bouquet. "Everyone else is ready. We have to get moving if you want to make it to the vigil before it closes."

"I can't find Sidian. Is he with the others?"

Raine knew the answer before Nyx started shaking his head. Sidian wouldn't have left his side. Not for anything.

Everyone had split up when they arrived in Rokeshin. The dragonesses went to the city square with Nyx while Sidian led the male dragons to the marketplace. They had to procure offerings to leave at Brandor's vigil. It wasn't required, but the custom was widely observed, and their group would have stood out without them.

Sidian had been a fixed companion at Raine's side as they explored the shops. But after the florist had wrapped and handed Raine his bouquet, he turned to discover his mate was gone. Vanished without a word.

"I don't know what happened." Raine thumbed a thorny rose stem, a well of foreboding burgeoning in his gut. "One minute he was there, and the next, he disappeared."

Nyx scanned the thoroughfare with a frown. "I don't see him. Come on. It's getting late. We don't have time to search the whole marketplace."

"What about Sidian?" Raine asked as Nyx ushered him away.

"My brother can take care of himself. We only have one chance to do this properly. He won't thank us for throwing it away by waiting on him."

Raine pursed his lips but had to acknowledge the truth of Nyx's statement. Their assassination plot was Sidian's grand scheme. His mate's fury would be absolute if Raine abandoned it now.

"He's probably waiting for us in the city square," Nyx added, angling them through the crowds. "Everyone else is already assembled near the sanctuary. I came to find you two since you were the only ones who had yet to show. I must have passed Sidian without realizing it."

That made sense. If Sidian hadn't been able to locate Raine in the market crowds, he'd have gone to the place where he was sure Raine would find him.

Raine perked up, doubling his stride. A sweet ache in his buttocks accompanied every step. A lingering discomfort that served as a delicious reminder of the previous evening. And that morning. He smiled to himself, eager to see the man who put it there. And possibly whack him upside the head with a dozen roses for worrying him like this.

The crowds grew crushing as they entered the city square. So many people were packed together, Raine marveled that the earth held their weight. Near the center of the square, he glimpsed a raised nine-point star—the symbol of Valdenia. Clean, dry lumber was piled artfully around it.

Brandor's pyre.

The vigil was ongoing, Brandor's remains not yet upon it. But everyone wanted a prime seat at the pyre. Mourners congregated in droves around the stacked wood, flooding the square like a squall tide.

Raine couldn't spot the dragonesses in the crush, but he knew they were in the thick of the crowd, maintaining their claim upon a strategic patch of flagstones. If Raine's group failed their task within the citadel and the Nine made it outside, it was up to the dragonesses to finish the job—a backup plan that was also courtesy of Sidian. His mate wanted nothing left to chance.

Which made it that much more concerning that Sidian had allowed them to be separated in the marketplace. As Raine spied a familiar cluster of hooded figures, his stomach sank to his feet. He knew at a glance that Sidian wasn't among them.

"It's about time," Lukor groused, crumpling an empty paper cup. In his other hand, he gripped a wax-coated condolence card decorated with peace lilies. "If one more hunter forces this swill onto me, I'm going to cram it down their throat."

"What are you calling swill? This stuff is incredible." Oka cast an easy grin and quipped, "May Brandor's spirit rise straight and swift," then downed a paper cup that appeared to have several empty cups stacked beneath it.

"Where's Sidian?" Savere asked, taking note of their absent companion.

"I'm not sure," Raine said. He glowered a silent threat when Lukor's amethyst eyes darkened. "We got separated at the florist."

"It changes nothing," Nyx said firmly. "The timeframe is too narrow as it is. We must act now, with or without him." His mouth tightened as he looked at Raine. "Do you want me to come with you?"

Their initial plan had been for Sidian to accompany Raine's group on the inside while Nyx remained with the dragonesses near the pyre.

Raine shook his head. "No. We'll be fine on our own. Besides, the females need a human spokesperson in case any Guardians approach."

Evin appeared at Nyx's shoulder, her serene features stamped with resolve. "Our group is as close to the pyre as we can get. You should join the vigil queue soon, before they stop admitting mourners."

Raine squinted against a slice of setting sun to survey the queue. It was hellishly long, but nowhere near the length it had been the previous day.

Sidian had planned their attendance to be near the end, limiting the amount of time they would have to hide inside Brandor's viewing room. Arriving late also ensured the piles of various tokens and offerings would be at their highest, providing them the most coverage for concealment.

"Let's go," Oka urged, half-jogging to secure a spot. A bottle of spiced wine sloshed with his movements, his offering to Brandor.

Lukor, Jaska, Savere, and Zane filed behind Oka. They stepped forward with the throng as more mourners were admitted through the arched stone barbican.

A small smile played at the corners of Evin's pink lips as Oka danced restlessly, his arm a frantic pendulum beckoning Raine over. "Better hurry before he becomes too unruly, and the hunters eject him from the queue."

Raine clutched his bouquet, thorns digging ineffectively into his palms, and gazed at the den mother who had once lost everything. Yet not an ounce of bitterness marred her heart. She was unfailingly kind, with a faith in others that both humbled and inspired.

It didn't matter that Betony's storm had spurned Raine. He already had a family.

"I accept your offer," he said, backing away. "It's an honor to join your thunder."

Evin's blue eyes lit with surprised delight before the crowd blocked her and Nyx from view. Raine shuffled to Savere's side and winced at the dappled stallion plush clutched in the green dragon's hand, his token to Brandor.

Savere caught his eye and smirked. "Don't worry. I bought you one, too."

"That better be a joke," Raine said, shivering at the toy's eerie resemblance to the stud in Rosa's stable.

The line crawled forward, and Raine scanned the city square endlessly for his mate. The only thing preventing his full-blown panic was the starbright bond inside his soul. It glittered and swirled a steady reassurance. Wherever Sidian was, Raine knew he was unharmed. Safe.

With only minutes left to be admitted into the vigil, they stepped forward to be received by the stern-faced Guardian serving as gatekeeper.

"How many?"

"Six," Jaska answered confidently, fingering the simple topaz brooch he'd brought for a token. "I realize the vigil is almost past, but better late than never. Brandor was a great man, gone too soon."

"That he was. Proceed." The hunter waved them on, already looking toward the group behind them.

There were over two hundred Guardians lining the stairs alone. Two on each step, they sandwiched Brandor's visitors as the line progressed.

Twilight was nearly upon them, and Raine worried the chieftains would halt the vigil and disperse the remaining queue. But as the sun's final rays gilded the horizon, the line began to move more quickly, as if the visitors were being hurried along.

Raine's wandering gaze snagged upon a crimson-clad figure on the battlements, which were now much closer after ascending so many stairs. The man was of average height and animated, gesticulating broadly as he smoked a pipe. Raine knew the weak bend of that spine, that feeble chin no amount of facial hair could hide.

Raine's body locked in a rigid beam as the man turned to survey the queue below. Raine couldn't be sure, but he thought the man's head jerked to study him. The line pressed forward, and Raine lowered his head, moving up to the vacated stair ahead. They were minutes from the ancient, doubled doors of the citadel, where the line disappeared into flickering torchlight.

Raine's stomach felt tight, as if caught between the jowls of two competing hounds. His instincts bellowed as he arched his neck, scanning the battlements to confirm who he'd seen.

But all he saw were black-clad hunters. Olan was gone.

The citadel loomed like a prehistoric beast, its doors open like a gaping mouth. Raine had the inexorable feeling of being eaten as he stepped off the long, tongue-like stairs and into a den of nightmares.

The line continued down a winding hallway and up spiraling stairs. Everywhere, there were Guardians. The shadows of the castle lived and breathed, fingering milk-white weapons as they passed. Raine stared at the floor, at patterned rugs made filthy with the grit and grime of thousands of visitors.

"Are you alright?" Oka murmured beside him.

Raine stared at Jaska's boots, copying his steps mechanically. Right, left, right left.

"I might have been recognized," he whispered softly. The walls didn't just have ears in this castle. They had hard eyes and silken black hose.

A sharp inhale assured Raine he'd been heard. "Someone from Chambrin Keep?" Oka whispered back, just as softly. Raine gave a slight nod. Oka's countenance hardened. "We'll take it as it comes."

A hand squeezed Raine's shoulder, and he looked back. Savere and Zane eyed him curiously, and Raine grimaced. There were too many Guardians for him to relay the possibility of their discovery.

"Be alert," he said instead, loading his words with significance. The dragons frowned, but then the line moved, spilling them into the viewing room.

Brandor's body was situated inside an open casket that sat upon a raised dais. He wore the dour, high-necked robes of a chieftain, his arms folded over his torso. His eyes were shut, and he seemed at peace.

The hairs along Raine's arms prickled as a sheet of foreboding frosted his spine. The sensation didn't alleviate until he was beyond the casket.

"Hey, watch it," a woman snapped from behind him. People grumbled, and many boots scraped stone as if they were pushed aside suddenly.

Raine turned to see Lukor backing away from the casket, his face more waxen than Brandor's as it blanched with horror. The purple dragon ignored the mourners, practically trampling them in his blind retreat.

Savere hooked an arm through Lukor's elbow and yanked him forward with a grunt. Lukor resisted, upturning a runner as Savere dragged him past the casket.

"Get ahold of yourself," a middle-aged man said. "We're all grieving."

"Sorry," Raine called over his shoulder as they hastened from the dais.

Savere looked eager to drill Lukor about his reaction, but the purple dragon jerked his head and hissed, "Not now. We need to find a place to hide."

The viewing chamber was overwhelmingly cramped, the number of mourners restricted only by the amount of floorspace. Guardians crowded near the entry points but remained absent from the actual chamber, lending as much room as possible for Brandor's visitors.

Gifts swelled in mounds from floor-to-ceiling. It may have once looked beautiful—the flowers and trinkets lovingly arranged around Brandor's remains.

But beauty had given way to grotesquerie, like a pretty maiden who caked on too much rouge. The small mountains looked less like towers of gifts and more like piles of trash.

Raine rounded the dais, following after Jaska.

The best hiding spot was instantly apparent. Depositing their tokens, they crept closer to a circle of potted trees and bushes.

One by one, they slipped inside the miniature copse. Raine made sure none of the mourners were looking before stepping between two tight-branched trees. They were several feet taller than him and packed with thumb-sized leaves, a perfect screen.

Inside the plant cover, Lukor tore off his hood and raked his hands against his scalp, skewing his topknot. A lock of purple hair fell behind his ear.

"It's a weasel," he muttered, pacing in a disoriented circle. "A fucking nightmare."

Savere placed a palm on each of Lukor's shoulders and steadied him. "What are you talking about?"

"That corpse," he hissed, gesticulating towards the potted ferns that concealed the dais. "It's an *ichneumon*."

Savere paled. "You're certain?"

"The feeling described by my late storm mother is unmistakable," Lukor said grimly. "I've never experienced such revulsion. The ichneumons have returned, and that corpse is one of them."

"Wait," Raine said, struggling to grasp everything. "That corpse is—*was*—a man. Not a weasel."

"We possess dual forms," Savere murmured, green eyes darting with rapid thought. "Perhaps they do, as well."

"Not possible," Zane protested. "Our humanity was a gift from the Divine Father. I doubt he and the Dreaming Mother conspired to grant that gift to her nightmares."

"Tell me you didn't sense it," Lukor hissed, pointing anew toward the casket. "Tell me you didn't feel the most powerful urge to tuck tail and run when you neared that corpse."

Zane opened his mouth, as if to do just that, then shut it with a grimace.

"What color are their eyes? The Nine?" Jaska asked abruptly.

Oka frowned. "What does that have to do with anything?"

"When we shift, our eyes remain the same in both forms," Jaska said, his words clipped with impatience. "That should go for the ichneumons, as well. Raine, you've been face-to-face with some of the Nine. Can you recall their eye colors?"

"They're yellow," Raine said, suppressing a shudder as he envisioned them. "But sort of brown, too. It's the same for all the Nine."

Oka looked ill. "Ichneumon eyes are yellow."

Jaska sighed. "Weren't you paying attention? Raine said their eyes are muddled. If the Nine were ichneumons, their eyes would be pure yellow. The hue of hornets. It has to be something else."

"No way. That they're yellow at all is too big of a coincidence." Oka edged away from the dais, as if Brandor's corpse was going to animate and attack any second.

"To kill a dragon, ichneumons burrow inside the dragon's body and destroy them from the inside." Zane's lips scarcely moved as he spoke, his cerulean gaze vacant with shock. "I once heard that, in their death throes, the dragon's eyes would bleed yellow."

The viewing room was over-warm, but Raine shivered. "The Nine weren't experiencing any death throes when I saw them. Their eyes held streaks of yellow, but they were healthy and un-suffering."

If insufferable, he mentally added.

"None of this makes sense," Jaska huffed. "Our ancestors should have pursued the ichneumons into Gargantha when they fled, superstitions be damned. We should have never stopped hunting them until they were all destroyed."

The weasels had fled north ... into Gargantha? Raine's lungs seized as his mind transported him to a cold night around a tall fire. When Idesta had claimed that King Normund went mad—*like a man possessed*.

"What if the ichneumons climbed inside bodies, not to kill, but to use?" Raine's pulse ticked faster as he considered it. "I think the ichneumons came back two centuries ago. The invasion—Gargantha's army didn't attack any of the human tribes. Instead, they marched straight for the Dragon Lands and ambushed the dragons. Why would they do that? Unless ..."

"Unless we are their mortal enemies," Savere said hollowly.

"The exact number of surviving ichneumons was never recorded." Zane was ashen, almost as sickly pale as he'd been in the Cavern. "But I'm willing to bet there were nine."

"Good," Lukor declared. There was no sign of the panicking dragon from earlier. Shoulders back and spine straight, he radiated calm, lethal purpose. "Today, we eliminate our enemies two-fold. The Nine die, and the weasels die with them."

The other dragons visibly collected themselves, responding to Lukor's conviction.

Jaska's knife-sharp features narrowed with intent. "When the Nine arrive, I'm going to raze them to ash where they stand."

"Not if I get them first," Lukor muttered. Shifting to his knees, Lukor peered between the two potted ferns. Raine angled his head and followed the purple dragon's gaze. Two mourners were laying floral bundles at Brandor's feet.

"What bothered you earlier?" Zane murmured, crouching beside Raine. "When we were in the hallway?"

"Someone who serves at Chambrin Keep recognized him," Oka said, dropping on Raine's other side.

"Maybe," Raine amended when Lukor twisted his head to stare. "I don't know for sure. He was on the battlements and saw me just before we entered the citadel."

Jaska closed his eyes and cursed.

"Let us hope he didn't," Lukor said evenly. He turned to survey the vigil, and Raine noted the lines of tension cording his neck and shoulders. The purple dragon was on edge and rightfully so.

They fell silent, tensely waiting for the vigil to end.

The stone floor was hard against Raine's knees. He shifted to get more comfortable and felt an accompanying twinge in his bottom. The pain was bittersweet, and he thought of Sidian. While he missed his mate fiercely, Raine was glad Sidian wasn't here. He didn't want his mate anywhere near the bilious weasels masquerading as men.

Though, in a way, his mate was here. Raine rested a reverent palm against his chest, where something alive and distinctly separate from himself pulsed in sync with his breath and blood. A small, irrevocable piece of his mate's soul.

Sidian's soul was fire and ice. Smoke and iron. Raine couldn't examine it too closely without his eyes misting in wonder. His mate had known hate, pain, and anger. He'd been fueled by fury for a decade. Yet his soul was all the more perfect for his darkness. Sidian was resilient and brave, with unbreakable honor and a love as boundless as the sea.

And he belonged to Raine. Now and forever, they belonged to each other.

One of the Guardians near the exit called out, "The succession ceremony will begin momentarily. Please make your final goodbyes and exit at this time."

The chamber grew loud as many people talked at once. They piled out of the exit, a doorway opposite the one they'd entered.

Lukor and Jaska shifted on their haunches, as if impatient to adopt their dragon forms. But to maintain the element of surprise, they had to wait until the Nine entered.

A door creaked open. Raine stiffened, his breath stilling as someone entered the room. They didn't come within view of their hiding place, pausing before they reached the dais.

"Now," Eddic's voice demanded.

Jangling metal clamored, sending frissons of alarm through Raine. Before he could react or identify the sound, a huge, black metal cage dropped over them. In a blink, the cage was surrounded by Guardians. They made quick work of bolting metal to stone, then flitted away, as if they had been lying in wait for that sole purpose.

Lukor shoved the ferns over roughly. Pottery shattered across the floor, spilling soil over Raine's boots. The unimpeded view revealed Eddic's gloating countenance. His yellowed eyes made Raine's flesh crawl with phantom maggots.

Next to him stood Olan, as odious as ever. An unpleasant smile stretched beneath his short, patchy mustache.

"Fancy seeing you here, snowballs. Or should I say *dragon*?" His coarse laughter turned to a cough. He doubled over, hacking like he'd taken water down his windpipe.

Eddic's thin-lipped smile tightened at Olan's prolonged cough-ing fit, a side effect of his smoking habit. "What a day of reunions this is, for you."

He rounded Brandor's casket, approaching the cage with his hands clasped idly behind his back. A calculated gesture to further demonstrate how powerless the dragons were. Raine bared his teeth but kept silent as Eddic continued.

"I trust you recall me well. And General Olan, of course. You must look upon him with great admiration, considering how eager you were to claim his identity." Eddic paused deliberately. His oily smile smeared over Raine's skin. "I do believe you'll find one more familiar face among us."

Raine clenched his fists, trembling with the need to reach through the bars and snap Eddic's wrinkled neck. He tensed to lunge. A sound halted him. The sharp, rhythmic taps of boots against stone. His gut bottomed out as his mind struggled to com-prehend what his body already knew.

A man stepped into view. He was clad in liquid black, with golden skin and tousled midnight hair. He had a wide mouth and chiseled jaw. The lines of his body beneath his Guardian uni-form were a masterpiece of musculature. The scabbard holding his longsword jutted over one broad shoulder.

Sidian's countenance was cold, eyes as hard as diamonds as they focused on Raine.

CHAPTER THIRTY-SIX

Raine drowned on air and despair as he stared. The bond inside of his chest grew sharp and painful. Like a shard of glass, it cut him with every breath. With every thought. With every beat of his heart, Raine's soul cracked and bled.

He knew, to the depths of his marrow, that Sidian's rejection would be the death of him. He could already feel a numbing coldness in his fingers and toes, his heart too hurt and sore to pump that far.

Eddic still imagined himself as center stage. He gestured to Sidian with a flourish, like a magician to their accomplice. "Captain Sidian Wade is one of our most elite operatives. I confess, I had reservations when I discovered his plans to aid your escape and accompany you abroad. Gaining your trust in order to reclaim the breeding dragons was too lengthy and farfetched a stratagem for my tastes. But we were getting nowhere fast with our interrogation, so I gave him the benefit of the doubt."

Eddic chuckled at Raine's brittle, shell-shocked expression. "Oh, yes. Captain Sidian has been a double agent this entire time.

Thanks to his exemplary efforts, there are no more wild dragons. Valdenia is finally secure from your blight and treachery."

Raine's knuckles whitened where his hands gripped the cage bars, the only thing holding him upright. Sidian looked as remote and cruel as a Northerlander god. Emotion shone only from his eyes. Hate. Contempt. A relief to be done with his charade of friendship and love.

Love. A prickling sting warned Raine of his pending tears. He turned away, and his knees buckled. Slumping to the floor, he squeezed his eyes shut, as tight as he could, but the tears still found their way through.

Inhuman laughter mocked him from behind. "We must ready Chieftain Brandor for the pyre," Eddic said. "Captain Wade, General Olan. Kindly aid your comrades in transporting your late ruler's remains to a preparation chamber. I will direct you."

There was noise, then. The sound of something heavy and wooden sliding against stone, then the strained grunts of men before they walked away.

"Raine," Oka said, crouching before him. He placed a hand on Raine's knee and shook it gently. "Hey." Raine raised his tear-stained face to Oka's leafy eyes. They were gentle with concern. "It's going to be alright."

It was not going to be alright. His mate *despised* him. Raine felt it in his core, a raw hatred that constricted his heart and lungs like deadly poison.

A harsh laugh lacerated the air. "I told you," Lukor breathed. "I fucking told you we couldn't trust him. He is a liar and a swine. A hunter who wields a blade of our bone. So help me, if my mate suffers from his treachery, I will craft a knife out of his own bones and gut him with it."

Lukor was as big as a bear and twice as mean. A sneer begging for violence marred his strong features.

Raine was all too willing to oblige. His limbs shook with murderous intent as he stood. Nobody was going to harm a single hair on Sidian's head.

"Shut the fuck up," he seethed. Broken pottery crunched as he narrowed the gap between them.

"Can't own up to your mistakes?" Lukor barked another humorless laugh. "How like a *human*," he spat. "You've done nothing but ruin our lives since the moment you showed up at our doorstep. Now we are trapped like rats, on the verge of extinction, and you put us here." A blunt finger prodded Raine's chest. "You and that dung-eyed traitor you thrust upon us. I will rend his heart from his chest if it's the last thing I do."

The dwindling thread of Raine's rationality snapped. He barreled into Lukor, taking them both to the floor.

Raine glimpsed a flash of teeth and wide eyes, set in a face reddening with fury, before his fist slammed into the center of Lukor's nose. Lukor caught Raine's fist on his next swing. His other hand wrapped around Raine's throat.

Raine pried against the chokehold, but Lukor's fingers only dug in deeper. The lack of air lent Raine a desperate strength, and his fist ripped out of Lukor's grip. Before Lukor could react, Raine punched the apple of his throat.

The fingers gripping Raine's neck fell away as Lukor collapsed. Clutching his throat with both hands, he turned onto his side and wheezed.

Raine stood above him, chest heaving. His instincts raked and clawed to finish the job. To destroy any threat against his mate.

Oka and Zane grabbed Raine's arms and dragged him away. Raine resisted, mindless with fury.

Savere moved in front of Raine, blocking his view of Lukor as he helped Oka and Zane restrain him. As one, they pressed Raine back against the cage bars.

As the purple dragon regained his breath, Raine's reason returned. He went slack, shaken by what he had almost done.

Jaska knelt on the floor and spoke softly to Lukor, who spat something crude as he sat upright. Jaska continued muttering as they stood, his own features sharp with anger. Lukor's jaw worked silently. Then, the baleful energy priming his body seemed to ease.

"I will not revoke my sentiments regarding your mate's treachery," he bit out grudgingly. "But I can understand how you were duped. It is not in us, to find fault in our mates."

The fractured pieces of Raine's mind puzzled enough to understand this was Lukor's version of an olive branch. But with fury no longer riding him, Raine could feel the cold numbness spreading to his arms and legs. And he knew Lukor's peace-making was immaterial.

Raine would be dead soon. No one had said so. They didn't need to.

A body not could survive without a heart, and Sidian was his.

Zane seized Raine's shoulders and drew them nose-to-nose. He looked deep into Raine's eyes, then cursed. "I think he might be heartsick."

Oka hissed and inspected Raine's features, as if searching for whatever had made Zane conclude his diagnosis. "That's not good. How long until ...?"

"I don't know." Zane probed Raine's unblinking eyes for several sluggish heartbeats. "Did you and Sidian consummate your bond?"

Raine struggled to speak, to respond. Part of him wanted to, but most of him was too numb. His mind was hideously blank, as if to protect him from shattering.

"Listen, Raine." Zane shook him. "If you haven't consummated your bond, it's possible the rejection process has begun. You must try to fight it."

"We have bigger problems than heartsickness," Lukor said. "The Nine will return any moment. All they have to do is skewer us through these bars with their bone spears and we're dead. We need to get out of this cage."

"There's no way out," Zane said, releasing Raine's shoulders with a defeated sigh. "I spent two centuries trapped in bars such as these. They will not yield."

Oka fingered the bars consideringly. "That's not true. They bent in the Cavern."

Zane shook his head. "Those bars were wideset, designed to hold our dragon forms. You only needed them to give an inch for us to fit through once we were human. Even that wouldn't have worked if we hadn't been starved to stick figures at the time."

The bars of their current cage were situated much more closely than the cages in the Cavern. Raine could follow their conversation, could understand their predicament. But everything felt

distant. Muted. Sidian's hatred had snowed him under, burying him.

"They still yielded," Lukor said stolidly. "Stand back."

Lukor's face screwed up, arms raised. He gave a little jump,
then gaped in slack-jawed stupefaction. A weak chuckle sputtered out of Raine. It sounded more like a death rattle than a
laugh, but Oka grinned broadly. "I agree with Raine. You look
ridiculous."

"You think this is funny?" Underlying Lukor's snarl was a
note of sheer panic. "I can't transform."

"No," Jaska breathed. He strode to the other side of the
cage and clenched his fists before him. His face scrunched as
if he was constipated. Raine's laugh that time was weaker, little
more than a wheeze. Jaska's midnight green eyes flew open
wide. "I can't transform, either."

A nasally laugh echoed through the chamber. Olan.

Something dark stirred in Raine's chest. It seemed only neg-
ative emotions moved him, now. Friendship and concern had
left him lifeless and bleak. But pulsating anger reinvigorated his
veins as his childhood bully walked over to them.

"Of course, you can't transform. Fools. Every single drink
and morsel to be had in this city has been laced with a special
venom. The toxin prevents you from swapping forms." He
smirked at them, close enough to the bars that dragon fire
would have left his doughy face a grinning skull. "Why do
you think so many Guardians are out there forcing people to
make toasts? You really are dumb animals." He laughed again.
"Didn't you wonder why there was practically no security? The
Nine wanted you to come here."

Jaska glared. "You think we're dumb? The foul creatures you serve have no care for man. They killed one of your own just to set a trap. I'm glad they intend to slay us. It's far better than what they might do to you, human."

Olan fingered his scraggly beard, as if it reaffirmed his manhood. "Brandor died of old age. He wasn't killed to lure you," he countered with a scowl. "But Eddic was wise enough to know how it would draw you here. And now, we have the war dragons, the breeders, and the leftovers. I hope you're ready to meet your maker."

More footsteps approached; Sidian, leading a group of hunters into the room like a parade of silhouettes. All of them carried wickedly sharp spears, their tips milk-white.

Raine's heart leapt at the sight of his mate. He traced every curve and contour of Sidian's face, like a greedy pirate pouring over treasure.

Perhaps Sidian did not hate him so much. Perhaps he had come to put Raine out of his misery.

But Sidian's eyes were chips of ice as they swept from Olan to the cage. Sidian looked as inclined to mercy toward Raine as a mongoose to a snake.

Olan's smile was all teeth, fuzzy and stained and as fetid as a sewer. "I bet you think they're here to kill you." He chortled at their blank confusion. "The Nine have something else in store for you, snowballs. Captain Wade has come to collect you for them."

A wordless terror filled Raine. He shrank back into the cage on a wave of pure instinct.

Olan howled with laughter, slapping his knee at Raine's display of fear. Raine didn't care. He retreated until his back hit something solid and alive. Arms banded around him, squeezing him against a firm chest.

Zane's voice was quietly urgent in his ear. "This is important. Did you or did you not consummate your bond?"

Raine drew short, shallow breaths as the hunters circled the cage.

"*Listen to me.* If your bond is complete, Sidian may be our only chance. He never drank any—"

Zane cut off as spears skewered the cage bars, intersecting the space like a deathly starburst. Sharp, glittering bone hovered near their throats and hearts, pinning the dragons in place.

Sidian drew the sword from his back and stepped forward.

The cage had a door. One they'd overlooked. It lined up with the black metal bars perfectly. Sidian inserted a key into the lock before meeting Raine's eyes. His gaze glinted a severe, silent warning, and then—

A tidal wave of love and reassurance crashed through Raine, nearly driving him to his knees. He gasped as his furiously pounding heart knitted the shattering pieces of his soul together, jarring them into place. And still, love—*Sidian's love*—swelled inside Raine's chest, so powerful and exquisite that he thought he might burst.

Sidian's mask slipped, flashing exasperation before schooling into icy hatred. At once, Raine understood.

His mate didn't hate him. *He was playing a part.*

And he was relying on Raine not to reveal his ruse.

"If any of you move an inch, the hunters will kill you," Sidian said coldly, dispassionately. As if it was nothing to him, a few dead dragons. He unlocked the door, then raised his sword defensively. "Raine Chambrin, you will accompany me."

A journeywoman retracted the spear aimed at Raine's chest with palpable reluctance. Fawn eyes narrowed at the arms encircling Raine's waist, and Zane slowly released him.

Raine navigated the cage with caution. His heart beat on hummingbird wings as he ducked under the crisscrossing spears that remained pointed at the other dragons.

"Stop there," Sidian ordered the moment Raine stepped through the cage door. The tip of his sword hovered at the base of Raine's throat as he closed and secured the cage. "Cuff him," Sidian demanded of no one in particular once the cage was locked.

A hunter stepped forward and bound Raine's wrists behind his back with familiar black metal manacles before moving away.

"Not so high and mighty now, are you, little lordling?" Olan sneered. He crowded Raine's face as he spoke, his breath hot and sour like fermented garlic. "You were never better than me. Your fair face, your strength and reflexes? None of it is human. You're just a pretty animal." Raine could see the fuzz coating his cousin's teeth as he bared them. "Livestock. And I, it seems, am your master now."

His palm reached out, as if to stroke Raine's cheek. Sidian's hand lashed like a viper, clamping around Olan's forearm before he could deliver the gross caress. "Our commanders expressed my need for haste."

Raine shivered at the husky timbre of his mate's voice. It was smoky and dangerous and entirely too similar to how he sounded in other, more intimate situations.

Olan's doughy features mottled with displeasure, but Sidian ignored him to address the other hunters. "Guard the cage until my return."

Sidian gripped Raine's bound wrists from behind and frog-marched him forward. After several paces, Sidian said, "You, as well."

"I am a general, *Captain*. I don't take orders from you."

"No, but you take orders from the Nine. They wish for their general to remain here. The dragons are cunning and have escaped too many times for us to take chances."

Olan snorted. "They aren't going anywhere on my watch," he said in a mollified tone. Raine didn't have to turn around to know Olan had puffed up like the world's ugliest peacock, inflated with delusions of his own importance.

Torches, spaced lavishly close, lit the path forward as they exited the viewing chamber. The corridor was empty, showing no sign of the hunters that had lined the hallway earlier. Raine guessed they were outside, awaiting Brandor's pyre now that the vigil was over.

Sidian's longsword remained balanced over Raine's shoulder, positioned to thwart any escape efforts. His other hand slid gently down Raine's spine before retightening around his wrists.

"What the fuck is going on?" Raine hissed. He tried to turn, but Sidian blocked his motion.

"Face forward and keep walking. We don't know who's watching," Sidian murmured close to his ear.

Raine moved forward haltingly, playing the part of reluctant captive. It wasn't difficult.

Sidian continued in a quiet rush. "Tyrus recognized me at the florist, while you were purchasing a bouquet. I approached him immediately, before he could notice you. When he revealed this scheme and requested my aid, I had no choice but to accompany him. It was that, or profess myself an enemy."

"Eddic said you planned on double-crossing me this entire time."

Sidian swore softly. "That was a long time ago."

"It was a few weeks ago," Raine cried out. He forgot to mind his volume and winced. "Sorry," he added, speaking softly once more.

Sidian squeezed his hands. "Turn left here," he muttered.

They entered another corridor. Raine moved slower still as his mate continued. "If you recall, that was before I got my brother back, when I thought all dragons were conscienceless beasts. Except you. Raine, back then, I thought you were an incongruity. That your morals and character were a side-effect of being raised human."

"If you thought I was an exception, why did you intend to betray me?"

"I only intended to recover the breeders," Sidian confessed, a note of apology in his voice. "I gave your map to my controller and explained in detail where I discovered you. It's my fault the Hellhole was compromised. My original plan was to help capture the other dragons while ensuring you slipped away somehow."

Raine's head spun at the implications. Lukor had been right not to trust his mate. The thought punched a hole through his stomach. "Fuck, Sidian. How long were you planning that?"

"Not long," Sidian said firmly. "Before we reached Moontop, I had already decided against it. I never brought it up because I didn't want to disappoint you."

The tension in Raine's shoulders eased. "I thought—" His throat pinched shut.

"I'm sorry," Sidian said hoarsely. "You wear your thoughts on your face, so I pushed hate and anger through our bond. I had to make you think it was real so you wouldn't give me away." A shuddering exhale tickled Raine's ear. "But I felt your anguish. It fucking gutted me, and I had to stop."

"I, uh, appreciate that," Raine said faintly, recalling his recent heartbreak all too easily. "What happens now? Do you have a plan?"

Sidian's tone flooded with dark promise. "I'm going to cut their fucking heads off."

Raine's blood petrified to stone. "Sidian, no. You *can't*."

"Watch me." Sidian tugged Raine's manacles, halting him, then gestured to an unmarked door. "This is us."

Shit. Sidian didn't know about the Nine. Panicking, Raine stepped between Sidian and the door before his mate could turn the handle.

Sidian frowned his impatience, plainly eager to send the Nine to whatever hellish afterlife awaited them.

Raine shook his head, eyes wide, and tried to indicate his need to talk. Preferably somewhere away from the door, since he couldn't risk the ichneumons overhearing.

A boot scraped stone on the other side of the door. Someone was approaching. Raine was out of time.

In a rush, he whispered, "The Nine cannot be felled by a blade. They are—"

The door opened.

CHAPTER THIRTY-SEVEN

An unfamiliar chieftain stood in the chamber doorway. Beneath his high-necked robe, a round gut protruded. His jowls were heavy and hung like a fleshy waddle over his too-snug collar.

The hairs covering Raine's arms stood on end. He locked his legs against the urge to bolt.

"Captain Wade, at last." The chieftain grinned like an affable host. "Please, come in." He made an expansive gesture, the yellow of his eyes almost indistinguishable in the dimly lit hall.

Sidian's blade was unwavering near Raine's throat as he forced him to enter.

Brandor was stretched out on a table. His skin was loose and waxy beneath a bright chandelier. On the opposite side of the table stood the other chieftains.

They regarded Raine as if he were a rabid wolf that might sink his fangs into them at any moment. Raine bared his teeth and they blanched.

The chamber held no other furnishings beyond another table. The sight of it seized Raine's blood. He recognized the table all too well, from his brief stint inside Obanth's prison. Leather straps dangled beneath its surface. Their metallic clasps glinted a morbid greeting.

Eddic pointed at the slab table. "Restrain the beast."

The sword near Raine's neck bobbed, as if Sidian had startled at the command. His mate recovered swiftly, lowering his blade as he unchained Raine's wrists.

A needle pricked between Raine's shoulder blades.

Not a needle. Sidian's sword. "Get on the table."

Raine drew an unsteady breath and hoped his mate couldn't feel how frightened he was. His legs wobbled, and he fell against the edge of the table. The surface was smooth and cold beneath his palms.

Sidian's face was a mask of hatred, his eyes gleaming like rocks slick with winter ice. "Lie back with your arms outspread."

Raine did so, his limbs trembling hard enough to shake the table. The grimace that twisted Sidian's features might translate as loathing to the ichneumons carefully observing them, but Raine caught a flash of the guilt and torment crushing his mate.

Bitter resolve drowned Raine's fear. If this was his end, so be it. But he didn't have to cause Sidian more distress by cowering like a dog.

Closing his eyes, Raine drew the slow, meditative breaths that had gotten him through so many trials. If he made it out of here alive, he owed Savere a fruit basket the size of Moontop for teaching him how to use his own breath to endure.

Tyrus strutted to the table once Sidian finished fastening the stays. He tugged Raine's wig off, and his braid draped over the side of the table. "Well, aren't you as pretty as a newly minted silvan."

Raine forced himself to meet the man's weasel-infested gaze. "And you're uglier than Brandor's decaying nutsack."

Someone chortled. "The dragon has teeth."

Tyrus reddened, his gray hair falling thickly into his eyes as he knelt over Raine's face. "Why should Nvek get it? I've wanted this one since the exams. Let him take one of the other dragons. We've plenty to spare."

"We've been over this, friend," Eddic said impatiently. "It is Nvek's time to transition, and he gets his pick as you will have yours. Captain Wade, please line the dragon's table with Brandor's, if you will."

Sidian went to the head of the table and grasped handles Raine hadn't noticed. Wheels rumbled across stone as Sidian dutifully moved him.

"I realize this must all seem strange to you, Captain Wade," Eddic said as Raine's table aligned with Brandor's. "It's time we let you in on our secret. You see, a holy power was bestowed upon us chieftains from the Divine Father himself. He has chosen us to safeguard Valdenia through the ages, and Raine Chambrin will play a crucial role in our destiny. I will explain it all to you later, before Brandor's successor is revealed. In the meantime, you may return to the viewing chamber and ensure the other dragons remain secured."

Raine's eyes went round despite the lamps half-blinding him. He wasn't here to be tortured or killed. It was far, far worse.

Brandor had been a mortal man, but the thing inside of him, *Nvek*, was not. And now that his fleshy puppet had succumbed to old age, the ichneumon required a new body. Raine's body.

The chieftains were intent upon Raine, and none of them noticed when Sidian didn't leave. His mate blended seamlessly in the background, a forgotten shadow.

Raine closed his eyes, thinking fast. Zane's bizarre parting words came back to him. If Raine's bond was consummated, Sidian was their only chance. But what did that *mean*?

Frustration clawed him, and he resisted the urge to bang the back of his head against the table. Raine was sharp enough to know he was missing an important detail, but his mind was too dull to sever it free. He didn't understand Zane's message, but his bond with Sidian had been realized, several times over as his sore ass could attest.

"Nvek chose well," Morseth said. His eyes were coldly appraising, as if surveying a finely crafted belt or new pair of shoes.

"We still don't know if it will work." Pare chewed his thumb, keeping his gaze averted. "To use a dragon ... It violates our nature."

"They are powerful and long-lasting," Eddic said sharply. "If Nvek succeeds, we might all wish to transition to their superior forms."

Beyond Vanwert's shoulder, Sidian raised his sword. *Fuck*. He was preparing to cut the chieftains down.

Sidian likely thought it would be a simple slaughter. The Nine were no warriors, preferring to command legions of men and dragons rather than risk their own hides.

Unless Raine missed his guess, the Nine were unarmed, as well. A clutch of hapless chickens waiting to be culled. Or so Sidian believed.

He had to stop Sidian before his mate made a fatal error, damning them both. But how could he when he was strapped to a fucking table? If he shouted a warning at Sidian, the chieftains would hear him, too.

Wait. Raine didn't have to tell Sidian anything.

He had a rapt audience of ichneumons trained on him. And whatever he said to them, his mate would overhear, as well.

"Fucking weasel," he spat, glaring hard at Eddic.

His heart hammered so powerfully against his chest, he wondered if it was visible through his coat. From the corner of his eye, he watched Sidian's blade lower a fraction of an inch. But it was still poised to slice through the back of Vanwert's unsuspecting neck.

"You're full of shit. You have no special power. You're nothing more than a nightmare." He offered Eddic his most aggravating smile. "It must really suck to have your own creator despise you. What do you think? That if you possess a dragon, the Dreaming Mother will start loving you?"

Sidian's sword lowered entirely, its point digging into the stone floor. His expression was concealed by the shadows, but Raine felt a tiny pulse of shock inside himself, like an echo. Relief surged through him, stronger than a riptide. *Sidian understood.*

"Too bad for you, possessing a dragon is impossible. If your friend tries to take me over, the fire in my blood will boil his mind and consume his spirit to nothingness," Raine continued blithely. Whether this was true or not, he had no idea. But he would spout as many lies as it took to keep Nvek from invading his body. "You should have remained in Gargantha with your tails tucked between your legs."

Pare and several others shrank back at Raine's diatribe, as if he had genuine fire in his blood and might spray it like venom at any moment.

Eddic's features contorted with fury, and he struck Raine across the face. The table rocked with the force of the blow.

Raine's face smarted, but no blood was drawn. Only dragon bone could accomplish that.

His breath expelled on a ragged gasp.

Eddic's urine-stained eyes slanted with a satisfied smile. He began to speak, but Raine wasn't listening. He was wrapped in memory as lush and decadent as boiled chocolate. Of teeth and a tongue, hot on his mouth. Of a passionate kiss that had left him breathless and bleeding. When Sidian had nipped his lower lip that morning, biting it like a delicious sweetmeat.

Zane's cryptic statement was now clear and obvious. Raine laughed, long and loud. He sounded demented, as if Eddic's punch had addled his wits.

Eddic struck him again, much harder. Raine's head snapped sideways, his ear hot and stinging.

"Enough of this," Eddic jeered. "Nvek has waited long enough in that human's reeking rot."

There was a riot in Raine's chest, like someone set off a brick of firecrackers. He panted, the feeling alien and terrifying in its intensity. If his hands were free, he would be clutching his sides. The pain was unbearable.

"I don't know, Vrrak." Morseth's brows pinched as he studied Raine. "The dragon doesn't look right."

The room began to spin. Raine closed his eyes and groaned. Sweat beaded across his skin, trickling down his ears and neck. A shudder wracked him, and he thought he might puke.

The ichneumons drew closer, barking at each other like squirrels as they argued. Raine looked ill. Wrong. Many of them already had reservations about using a dragon for a host. But to use a sick dragon, which appeared on the brink of death?

"I told you it was too much venom," the round chieftain said. "You made us drip our fangs dry every day for a moon cycle. If this fool was deep in his cups before coming here, he may be lost to its toxicity."

"Nvek will not thank us for transferring him to an ill dragon," Pare said anxiously. "We should call back Captain Wade and use him instead."

"No," Eddic snapped. "Nvek requested this form. We honor his choice."

Pare stumbled backwards and caught himself on Brandor's table. His sallow eyes bulged as he pointed wordlessly. The sound of a thousand branches snapping deafened the room, echoing the cacophony inside Raine's chest. Eddic and the others turned and discovered, too late, that Sidian had never left.

A massive figure emerged, blacker than the blank slate of the universe before stars ever burned. Raine's breath left in a whoosh as he stared.

Sidian was stunning. The lethal grace of his human form paled in comparison to the untamed malice that seethed as he uncoiled. Powerful muscles rippled beneath scales of polished jet. His teeth and talons possessed the cruel sharpness of a newborn predator, more cutting than untried razorblades.

The ichneumons scurried away, the acrid stench of their terror suffocating in the small, windowless chamber. Sidian blocked the only exit, and they piled behind Raine, fighting and shoving each other as they jockeyed for the best cover beneath the tables.

Sidian stalked nearer, and a pitiful cry rang out. Pare pleaded through broken sobs. "Please, please. I was against using the dragon. This wasn't my idea."

Heat blasted from Sidian's mouth. Flame followed. A huge, billowing breath that smacked Raine like a sledgehammer. The fire did not singe any part of him, but its forceful impact up-ended the gurney he was fixed to.

He landed rough, amid the fiery, flailing limbs of the Nine. A storm of elbows and knees battered him with bruising force. The ichneumons' agonized screams pierced his ears.

In seconds, the straps keeping Raine immobile burned away. He sprang from the fire, his coat smoldering to ash against his skin as he threw himself against the far wall.

Sidian's pitch-black scales were gilded by his own blazing breath, painting him with a reddish orange corona. He looked like the sun in full eclipse. Light and dark. Fire and shadow.

Sidian's large, black snout closed, biting off the flames. No noise came from the Nine as their charcoaled corpses smoked up the chamber. Raine squinted through the haze and navigated toward the dark shroud that was Sidian's dragon form.

"Come on," Raine said, half-strangled on smoke.

Sidian followed him through the doorway, his body nearly too broad to fit. Raine peered down the hallway and didn't see any hunters. *Good*.

"Change into your human form before anyone comes," Raine said quickly. "You can pretend the Nine sent you to retrieve the other dragons. All you need to do is get them out of the cage before the hunters find out the truth, and we're home free."

There was a pause. Sidian's eyes, a beautiful liquid brown that popped against his black scales, shut tight. Raine had the impression his mate was concentrating very hard. But when Sidian re-opened his eyes, Raine knew. The dire nature of their emergency had compelled Sidian's shift, somehow. And now, his mate had no clue how to reverse it.

Which wouldn't be an issue if they weren't in a castle crawling with elite dragon assassins.

"It's okay," he said with a calmness he didn't feel. "We've gotten through the worst. We'll figure this out."

A long, narrow-faced weasel hurled out of the chamber and down the hallway. Fleeing like a rat from a burning barn, the ichneumon flitted out of sight before Raine could do more than gape dumbly. Sidian reacted sooner than Raine, snaking back into the chamber. Raine heard his mate's flaming breath, like a concentrated windstorm.

Several minutes passed before Sidian emerged, his tail lashing agitatedly like a black whip. His wings fluttered at their joints, then flattened against his back and sides. Raine didn't have to speak dragon to understand the source of his mate's fury.

They'd both been lax, presuming victory instead of overturning the corpses to ensure no ichneumons had managed to survive.

Raine scraped his brain for a clever plan, then promptly gave up when he saw that he was naked. Sidian had torched away every scrap of clothing he'd worn, leaving Raine bare and covered in a sooty film.

"Damn it, Sidian." He felt around the center of his back and brought his braid around, inspecting it. His hair was dark and dull with ashy residue. He released it with a huff. "I'm so sick and tired of being grimier than a street urchin. I might as well become a beggar and live in a trash can, at this point. Why not? I always look the part."

He stomped his foot. The effect was ruined as his exposed penis jostled with the motion. Sidian's enormous dragon eyes stared at him, unblinking.

Raine shoved a greasy finger into his mate's chest. "I have no idea what your expression means, so I'm just going to translate it how I want. And right now, I would appreciate some contrition. Your apology is accepted."

Sidian snorted, blowing flames over Raine's body. If Raine had been human, he would be grossly disfigured or dead.

"Seriously?" Raine wiped at the soot on his face, but suspected he only succeeded in smearing it further. "Fine. I'm naked and you're a dragon. Now, all we have to do is get back to the viewing room and free the others before anyone stops us. Easy peasy."

They hurried through the halls but encountered no one until they burst inside the viewing chamber. Raine sucked in a breath, recoiling at the multiple rows of Guardians facing them. As one, the hunters brandished swords and spears of bone. There were three dozen at a glance.

Without hesitation, Sidian unleashed a stream of fire. It blew far and wide, engulfing the first row of hunters before they could dodge the infernal blast.

As charred bodies littered the floor, the unscorched Guardians fell back on each other in a chaotic frenzy. Raine darted forward and snatched a dagger, dropped from one of the Guardians who'd been killed on impact.

Rising up, he plunged the knife into the nearest retreating back. The man's scream stopped as Raine twisted the knife, angling it with the ruthless accuracy trained into him by his father.

Raine found himself and his knife without purpose as Sidian charged from behind, sweeping the Guardians with another devastating arc of fire. His range was insane, as if he possessed the firepower of fifty dragons.

In less than a minute, all the hunters were dead.

Around them, the mountains of gifts began to burn, having been caught in the crossfire. Raine's eyes stung as he hastened through the burning stacks, intent upon releasing his friends from the cage. Rounding the dais, his bare feet slid against the floor as he came to a halt. Sidian thudded into him from behind, but corrected himself before knocking them over.

Olan grinned, facing them from the far side of the cage. A white, sickle-shaped blade reached into the cage and curved against Lukor's throat. The threat of the blade kept the purple dragon's back pinned against the bars. Lukor's face was hard, his gaze ordering Raine to do what was necessary.

And what was necessary was strikingly clear. Because Olan's eyes were yellow.

CHAPTER THIRTY-EIGHT

"Whoa, whoa, whoa." Raine clamped his hands around Sidian's snout, cutting off his embers before he got Lukor killed.

A plume of gray smoke puffed into Raine's face, and he released Sidian once he was sure his mate understood. Lukor was an asshole, but he was part of Evin's thunder. *Raine's* thunder. And Raine would not allow him to die. It was not a fair trade, the life of any dragon for one of the ichneumons.

Olan laughed, his knife hand shaking carelessly. Raine zeroed in on the hairline of red trickling at Lukor's neck. "It seems we're at an impasse," Olan gloated. His eyes lowered, taking in Raine's nudity.

"Not one you're likely to win," Raine snapped, wishing very hard that he wasn't naked.

He noticed the other dragons, then. Jaska, Savere, Oka, and Zane. They were crouched near the floor, backs and shoulders tense, all eyes on Lukor and the bone sickle at his throat.

"Oh, really," Olan drawled. "That's quite humorous. Multiple thousands of soldiers and Guardians dwell within these walls. Do you truly believe one dragon can defeat all of them?"

Raine couldn't be certain, but if he had to guess, they were dealing with the profane nightmare that had inhabited Eddic. He was cruel, cunning, and—Raine suspected—the mastermind behind the Nine's schemes.

It was past time these weasels recalled their place in the food chain. They got off on subjugating predators, on killing and controlling dragons and humans alike. They seemed to have forgotten that they were the bottom dwellers here. The prey. Their reign of terror was always destined to be temporary—living on borrowed time in more ways than one. Borrowing the short lives of mortal men. Borrowing a few fleeting centuries of power before their nightmare ended.

"Maybe." Raine affected a casual shrug. "Have you seen Sidian's fire? It's outrageous. He can incinerate every Guardian and soldier before they make it through the doors."

The deadly sickle at Lukor's throat wavered with a fresh bout of the ichneumon's laughter. "Oh, no. You see, I was having a bit of sport with you. I knew better than to send for humans. Any minute now, my war dragons will blast through those doors. One signal from me, their esteemed master, and they'll tear you both apart."

Raine's heart skipped a beat. Roasting a barrage of human Guardians and soldiers like chestnuts would be nothing with Sidian's fire. Hell, they'd have been able to barricade the doors with the skeletons while they rested between rounds.

But if the war dragons came and wanted them dead, Raine and Sidian would die. There was no alternate ending to that grisly scenario.

Raine had assisted with their training firsthand; working alongside his father to hone the war dragons into supreme weapons. Until all of them were brutally lethal with claws and teeth and tails. They were fully capable of vanquishing any army, let alone two measly dragons, and one not even able to shift.

Raine pictured them, the hulking harbingers of his death. Fang, the biggest, with scales like glossed cherries. Yip, the youngest and most playful. Fern, the eldest, with the sweetest temperament. Blaze, the pacifist who loved knocking Raine on his ass but loathed true violence.

Slowly, Raine's eyes widened, lips parting.

Olan's features warped into a sallow smirk. "I see you comprehend your predicament at last, Raine Chambrin. Enjoy these final moments, for even if you kill me, it will not spare you from your own slaughter."

The ichneumon mistook his expression as acceptance of his fate. Raine was not about to correct the weasel's assumption, since it worked in their favor.

Putting his back to the ichneumon, he stared intently into velvet brown eyes. "We need to leave. Now." He injected as much urgency into those syllables as he could.

Sidian's head reared back as he bared his fangs. Raine cupped his snout with both hands, holding firm until Sidian's gaze refocused on him.

Trust me, he mouthed, softening his eyes imploringly. Aloud he said, "It's better to flee and fight another day than to perish for naught. Please, Sidian. We must go. Now."

Sidian's maw was set mulishly but he made for the nearest exit, trailing after Raine.

Olan's mocking laughter rang out behind them. "My war dragons are nearly here. You only hasten your demise."

Raine shut the door firmly behind them, muffling the ichneumon's grating mirth. When he turned, Sidian blew a stream of smoke into his face. Raine dispelled it with his hand and glared at the frustrated behemoth of black scales and shimmering fangs before him.

"Think about it, Sidian. The ichneumon sent for the war dragons."

As if his words had summoned them, the torch lit corridor began to rumble. The dragons were coming in hot, rocking the citadel like a stampede. Sidian shoved Raine behind him and faced outward, his frame tensed for battle.

"No, Sidian," Raine hissed, climbing over hard, scaly haunches to put himself before his mate. "You don't get it. He sent for the *war dragons*."

Before Raine could explain further, a solid wave of dragons rounded a distant corner, hurtling like jeweled comets straight for them. Sidian's tail whipped out and dragged Raine backward, trying to shield him. As shadowed scales and snapping teeth approached, Raine grappled with his obdurate mate.

"Let me go. You don't understand."

The meteor shower was upon them with Yip at the forefront. Her big, lilac head jerked with surprise, talons gouging stone as she dragged herself to a sudden halt.

The other dragons tumbled against her back. Several disgruntled roars shook the corridor as they righted themselves, shoving around Yip to see what the hold up was.

For a moment, they simply goggled at Raine. Then, with a wild, keening roar, Ruby's glittering body surged through the dragon jam and fell onto him.

A thick tail, darker than night, tightened around Raine's abdomen and yanked him away.

Ruby slammed into bare stone but recovered quickly. In less than an eyeblink, towering onyx scales lined with ruby red. Hair-raising snarls echoed through Raine's skull as they faced off.

"Damn it, Sidian. That's Ruby. She's my friend," Raine shouted, his voice lost in the guttural din of too many pissed off dragons in too small a space.

The tail wrapped around his midsection jerked, as if in shock. Sidian and the war dragons quieted.

Ruby barked a brief roar of inquiry, and Raine realized she thought Sidian was a threat to him just as much as Sidian thought the same of her.

"Put me down," Raine hissed, mindful of his volume now that the dragons weren't cancelling his words with their snarls. No doubt, Olan was salivating at the malefic cacophony that had sounded from the corridor.

Good. If the ichneumon discovered that the war dragons were among Raine's dearest friends, he would flee. Condemning dragons to centuries of restless uncertainty as they waited for history to repeat itself.

Sidian deposited him onto the floor, sliding Raine against his wonderfully scalding chest as he did so. In any other situation, Raine would have remained slumped against his mate, savoring that heat.

Instead, he moved forward and let Ruby snatch him in a greedy embrace. Her chest was warm, too, where her fire lived, though nowhere near as hot as Sidian's. Yip and Fang crowded around them, getting their hugs in, snuffling his hair with their warm muzzles.

Sidian roared, the sound an impatient demand.

Raine glanced over, and Sidian jabbed his tail meaningfully at the viewing chamber. At once, Raine understood. If they wanted Olan to believe that they were being viciously mauled, they required more noise.

Thinking fast, Raine gestured for Ruby and Fang. "I need you both to pretend-fight next to that door. Right over there, behind Sidian. Make it sound serious, and don't let anyone out."

They obeyed without question, gracefully snaking around Sidian. As the noises of a fierce dragon-on-dragon battle flooded the corridor, Raine beckoned the remaining dragons close.

The ichneumon thought these dragons were tame pets, broken like horses. That the war dragons had recently attacked and subdued their own parents must have bolstered that impression beyond all doubt.

But Raine knew the truth. These dragons were obedient purely out of ignorance.

He didn't know what poison the Nine poured into the war dragons' ears to make them thrash their parents so soundly, but any number of clever lies would have done the trick.

Too bad for the weasels, those lies wouldn't work with Raine. The war dragons *knew* him.

"I need the rest of you to listen."

They clustered around Raine attentively, and he realized there were only twelve war dragons in the corridor. They must have split up. The other half were likely approaching the viewing chamber's other entrance, so they could surround their targets before attacking.

"You reported here to eliminate two rogue dragons, correct?"

The war dragons chuffed their agreement.

"What if I told you one of those dragons is me?"

The dragons jerked back in shock. Wings fluttered and tangled in the too-narrow corridor, bones knocking painfully.

Shock swiftly yielded to understanding. One after another, the war dragons barked and roared with astonished delight. Yip surged forward, almost knocking Raine over as she pranced around him. The others followed, smooshing him in a ring of warmth and scales. They nuzzled his sides and hair, expelling hot air on chirrups of glee.

It tickled like hell, and laughter bubbled out of Raine. He shoved at their heads, gasping insults as tears streamed down his cheeks.

But it was no use. They were relentless. A pile of fire-breathing boulders determined to smother him with ecstatic affection. Because Raine wasn't just their friend. He was family. And now, he was a dragon, too.

A plan took form in Raine's mind. One that hinged entirely on the war dragons' cooperation.

Raine squirmed out of their suffocating circle and sent a quick prayer to the Divine Father and Dreaming Mother. Because no matter how close he was with the war dragons, he had no clue how they were going to react when he asked them to betray the one human they had been taught to safeguard and obey since infancy—the general of Chambrin Keep.

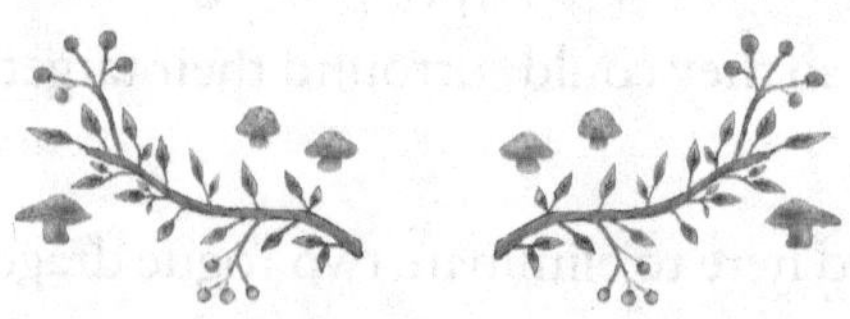

Raine laid on the floor next to Sidian and smiled his reassurance. This was going to work.

Sidian rolled his eyes, the gesture more fond than anything. His mate didn't quite care if Raine's plan worked. He intended to torch Olan to ashes whether or not the ichneumon stepped away from the cage to approach them.

Sidian hadn't said as much, but he didn't have to. His was the calm of a man who already knew the outcome.

Olan could run. Olan could hide.

But Olan wasn't doing either of those things. Instead, he was waiting.

And very soon, the war dragons were going to deliver exactly what he was waiting for: Raine and Sidian's corpses.

Fang got into position and looked to Raine for a signal. Raine gave him the ready, then shut his eyes. The world darkened beneath the shadowy veils of his eyelids as Fang smashed through the viewing room door. Polished oak cracked like cannon fire, trickling loose splinters over his face.

Raine remained limp and motionless as Ruby's serrated mouth dug carefully around his calf and pulled.

Aster took Sidian's ankle and followed. A willowy dragoness with scales like wisteria in bloom, Aster had the gentlest mouth. She liked to carry baby chicks and bunnies between her teeth, and Raine trusted her to handle Sidian with similar delicacy.

Tiny pebbles and debris scraped against Raine's bare flesh as Ruby moved him. It was like being dragged across a flat expanse of pumice stone. The grit couldn't abrade his skin, but it hurt just the same.

Raine ignored the pain and concentrated instead on taking slow, shallow breaths that couldn't be detected. There was no room for error. For his plan to work, Olan—now an ichneumon—had to believe Raine and Sidian were dead.

And the dead didn't breathe.

Raine's lungs protested their restricted intake, but he knew Sidian had it far worse. Dragon lungs were much larger than a human's. One wrong breath would expand Sidian's gleaming black sides and betray him instantly.

After a dozen paces, Ruby stopped and unclamped her teeth. Raine made a mental note to thank her later for depositing him in a manner that partially hid his chest and stomach, giving him more leeway to breathe.

A sudden shockwave of sound overwhelmed Raine. It was loud and crushing, and left almost no room for thought. The sound had more than one source, he realized as it went on. And then he knew.

They were Requiems. Desolate and heart-wrenching, they boomed from the cage and shook the chamber.

Raine's pulse quickened with excitement even as his gut shriveled with guilt. The other dragons' lament was a reassurance. Their ploy was working.

The Requiems ceased as abruptly as they began.

Olan was yelling.

"—mean it. If you don't cease your racket, right now, I'll spill his fucking throat first, and then finish off the rest of you!"

Silence fell. A throat cleared awkwardly. "Well done," Olan called, the praise unnatural and stiff. "Now, return to your stables." There was a long pause. "Go. You are dismissed."

The war dragons huffed and grumbled as they moved away. Raine kept his eyes shut, but he could tell from the sounds of their clicking talons that the war dragons were heading for the door opposite the one they'd entered through. He recalled the second flank of approaching dragons just as a shattering explosion erupted.

Raine's eyes flew open in time to watch the other war dragons pour inside the viewing chamber. Primed for a fight, they lashed out blindly.

Ruby, Fang, and the others struck back. The floor trembled as the dragons collided like storm fronts. Raine's features screwed back shut as a heavy green dragon rolled over him like a carriage wheel. He grunted, then turned on his side to survey the chaos.

A lone human shape caught his eye. *Olan.* He was skulking toward the far exit, away from the calamity. Raine scrambled to his feet. Now was their chance.

"Sidian," he shouted, then pointed.

In a flash of glossed ebon, Sidian was up and sprinting. Olan froze several paces from the exit, the portrait of petrified prey.

A booming roar rattled the walls, dislodging several stones from the ceiling. Raine turned toward the sound and cursed sharply.

Mayhem. Out of all the war dragons, Mayhem was the only one who had never meshed well with Raine. His scales were as red-hot as his temper, almost orange. When he took to the skies, he became a ribbon of pure, unadulterated flame.

Mayhem was the most ill-mannered and contentious of the war dragons, yes. But he was also the most fiercely protective. Panic hollowed Raine's entrails, replacing them with liquid terror as Mayhem bolted like a fireblast, intent upon the threat to General Olan's life.

Time slowed to a honeyed crawl. The brightly burning piece of Sidian's soul inside of Raine pulsed in time with his heartbeat.

The ichneumon must have realized he would not reach the door in time. Olan's frame curled in upon itself, braced for impact.

Flames fanned from Sidian's mouth as Mayhem lunged. Like a falcon intent upon the glimmer of fish underwater, Mayhem's talons extended, reaching for Sidian's unguarded back.

The most terrible pain wrapped around every seam of Raine, body and soul.

It was agony. Torment. Brighter than fire and darker than death. It exploded him into billions of shards, all too small to see.

Raine reassembled as the tips of Mayhem's curved talons touched Sidian's spine.

Sidian reared with shock. His fire-breath cut off as Mayhem's talons sank through flesh and scales.

Olan's head poked out of his arms like an anxious hedgehog. His frame slackened with relief as he saw Mayhem preparing to carve into Sidian.

Raine slammed into Mayhem before the red dragon could rake his claws down Sidian's back. He faintly registered the rainbow glint of alabaster scales as he pinned Mayhem to the floor and released a deep, menacing roar. Mayhem thrashed from side-to-side and tried to reverse their positions. It took all of Raine's strength to maintain his hold as Sidian lurched ahead.

Intent upon his target, Sidian loosed a wide fan of fiery death the instant he was within range. The entire viewing chamber washed a lurid orange, and Raine's gaze snapped to the fire. It was an impossible inferno, containing the heat and flames of a hundred dragons breathing as one.

If Olan screamed, it was drowned out by the hurricane *whoosh* of Sidian's fire.

The chamber rolled as Mayhem used Raine's distraction to reverse their positions. Raine looked up and saw his death in eyes that blazed like hot coals. He arched his back and tried to buck free. A red, taloned paw pinned his chest, drawing blood.

Sidian smacked into Mayhem like a missile, and the two went flying out of sight.

Raine leapt to his feet and ran to assist his mate. Then stumbled to a halt and stared.

Sidian was a whip of black fury, further aided by Clover and Blaze. As the three dragons subdued Mayhem, jewel-bright motion captured Raine's attention. He turned toward the cage.

Lukor and Zane stood side by side. Backs against the diamond-infused cage bars, they looked outward, observing Mayhem's takedown.

Oka, Savere, and Jaska, on the other hand …

Each of them had their arms stretched through the cage bars to cradle massive, scaly heads. Their faces were naked with emotion—tenderness and wonder and love—as they stroked the elegant lines of dragon necks and snouts.

A shit-eating grin split Raine's face as he drew closer, seeing who paired with who. Ruby and Jaska made sense. The midnight green dragon was obsessed with jewels, and she was more dazzling than her namesake. And by the Divine, hadn't Jaska been crafting a special ruby ring for eighty years? Raine had to doublecheck to be sure, but he would swear Ruby was eighty years of age exactly.

Oka and Violet were adorable. She was small, less than half Oka's size, with purple scales. Violet was shy but loved to laugh. *Oka will be good for her*, Raine thought, satisfied.

The shock that had him smothering a chuckle was Savere. Quiet, stoic Savere, whose gently reverent stare was fixed upon *Yip*. Yip, whose egg must have been steeped in pure mischief before she hatched. Savere's life was going to become very interesting, indeed.

Zane was the first to notice Raine's approach. His handsome features contorted with a grimace. "My mate is going to lose her shit when she sees you," he said gravely.

Raine's chest puffed with pride. While he had yet to observe his dragon form in a mirror, he'd glimpsed enough to imagine the picture he made. His scales put opals to shame. He couldn't wait for Sidian to see him all cleaned up and in the sunlight, where he would shine best.

"Quit preening and get us out of here," Lukor barked.

Raine ignored him to examine Olan's smoking corpse. The ichneumon had survived Sidian's fire once already, and Raine would be damned if there was a repeat. He reached the far wall and saw that Olan's flesh had burnt to bone, leaving only charred, hollow remains. Between a pair of human ribs was the sneering skeleton of a weasel. The epoch of nightmares was finally over.

The sound of rupturing stones deafened the chamber. Raine's tail caught painfully on the wall as he whirled, expecting to find a giant tunneling through the floor.

There was no giant, but the floor was wrecked where Ruby, Violet, and Yip had wrenched the bolted cage from the flagstones. Dust clouds unfurled through the air as they rushed to their mates.

A black dragon with velveteen eyes appeared next to Raine. Through their bond, Raine sensed Sidian's amusement as Yip pranced atop Savere, nearly flattening him in her excitement. And beneath that amusement was something profound and bright and more expansive than the universe.

It was love. And it was all for Raine.

Mercury eyes met fawn. The flames circulating inside Raine's dragon chest flared through his veins like magma as he sensed Sidian's desire. Hot enough to melt black diamond and so powerful, it consumed him. Sidian's stare went molten, and Raine wondered if Sidian was feeling his arousal, in turn.

Their heads bent. Raine had no clue how dragons kissed, the logistics of it. Mindless with need, he forgot to even consider it. Their mouths met in a scorching kiss.

Sidian devoured him. Sucking Raine's tongue into his mouth, he growled low and desperate. Raine moaned, a greedy, mewling sound that would embarrass him if he had any awareness of it.

Sidian tore away, breaking their kiss without warning. His dusky mouth was swollen and glistening. His golden chest heaved as he panted, muscles rippling with every breath.

Raine's eyes continued south, drinking in the gorgeous lines of Sidian's body. Sidian's *human* body. Raine glanced at himself and saw that they were both human once more. And naked. Their cocks were hard and straining between them.

Wicked mirth coursed through their bond, swift and wild and a little dark. Raine's expression narrowed with instinctive mistrust as his gaze found his mate's. Sidian's mouth curved into a smirk that made Raine's cock ache. The amusement spiked. Very deliberately, Sidian tilted his chin. Raine followed the angle, his neck prickling with dread.

Twenty-eight dragons stared at them, five of them with human faces and all of them rapt.

EPILOGUE: PART ONE

Raine tugged on the satin knot against his neck, inwardly cursing whichever sadist invented cravats. He had complained that morning when Sidian laid out his clothes, but his mate remained unmoved. As far as Sidian was concerned, if he had to wear a stifling doublet and tie, then so did Raine.

And Sidian had really been unable to avoid it, considering he was Nyx's best man.

A cool breeze cut across the gently rolling hills of Rosa's estate, carrying the sweet fragrance of primrose and hyacinth. Raine's hand fell away from his neck, his efforts of loosening the cravat futile. Sidian had fixed the knot with a deft expertise that left Raine feeling as trussed as a holiday roast.

With a sigh, he glanced around the expansive lawn, still a little jarred at how many people were in attendance for the reception. Over fifty rectangular tables were set up outside, all draped with cream linens and most of them occupied. The kitchen staff, equipped with extra hired hands for the grand occasion, cleared away empty plates and refilled wine goblets.

A band of sharply dressed minstrels warmed up their instruments on a pop-up stage. The bride and groom lingered over cake and fizzy spirits as they watched the minstrels prepare for an extended performance. The spring air sparkled with anticipation for the revelry ahead.

Someone smacked into Raine's side. He stumbled before catching himself. Aly leaned into him, giggling helplessly.

"Raine. *Raine.* You'll never guess." Aly chortled, her face flushed as crimson as her hair, which hung loose down her back.

Raine's own hair was in his customary braid, glinting like opal in the direct sun. Dragons no longer had to hide in Valdenia. They could even fly, the skies as open to them as the sea was to fish.

The guild had disbanded within weeks of the ichneumons' demise. There were still some anti-dragon grumblings from the more fanatic ex-Guardians, but their cause was doomed to failure. For every embittered human who still believed dragons were evil, there were a thousand more supporting dragon rights and freedom.

Raine smiled at his drunken friend, suspecting his own state wasn't altogether sober as he wobbled. They steadied each other with long practice and shared a grin.

"I'm half-sauced and can barely breathe thanks to the noose Sidian tied around my throat." He gestured to the cravat. "So, no. I will never guess. What is it?"

Aly snickered at his noose comment and thumbed the elegant knot choking him. "Sidian did a damn good job." Her red brows lifted appraisingly. "Honestly, you look like a sex kitten. I bet he did it on purpose because he thinks you're hot like this."

"Nobody is hot like this," Raine muttered glumly, inspiring another bout of snickers from Aly. Raine rolled his eyes. "I'm glad my asphyxiation amuses you. Now, what won't I guess?"

Aly's garnet eyes danced like she was about to share the juiciest gossip of the decade. She bent forward, and the low-cut bodice of her green silk gown threatened to spill her assets.

Raine caught himself before he reached out to tuck her bosom back in. It hadn't gone well the last time Sidian and Zane saw him do that. They hadn't seemed to care that breasts were as sexy as toadstools to Raine, or that his lust could only be inspired by a singular individual in all the universe, who was neither Aly nor female.

"Betony and Lorrivare found out that Mayhem is theirs." She tittered again, as if she hadn't just given him the most abysmal news possible.

The war dragons—or *children*, as their parents still termed them—were as put off by their overzealous, presumptuous parents as Raine. As such, they had mutually agreed to not reveal the order of their births. It was the only way the parents would know which dragons were theirs, after all.

But a fortnight ago, Betony and some of the other parents had initiated a plot to lure their children out of hiding. In the midst of Chambrin Keep's great hall hung a large tapestry. Listed on it was each mated pair of Betony's storm. Next to the couples' names were numbers. The numbers coincided with the order in which they'd produced offspring in the Cavern.

So now, Raine and the war dragons all knew who their parents were, while their parents remained impatiently ignorant.

Betony's storm waited like orb weaving spiders, counting on their children to become entangled in the net of their shattering revelation.

And it had been a shattering revelation, Raine thought grimly. His eyes searched for Mayhem. In a sea of jeweled hair, Mayhem stood out like a struck match. Like the other war dragons, he had learned to shift into his human form quickly. A feat chalked up to their lifelong military training, which made them uniquely disciplined and capable.

Mayhem was in the midst of a conversational cluster, an arm slung around Eva's waist. His mate.

It was hilarious when they'd all learned that Mayhem was Betony and Lorrivare's son. If the storm mother listed her least favorite dragons, Mayhem's name would be right under Raine's. Both of them bucked at her leadership, eschewing dragon customs and any efforts on her end to rule them.

First, Raine and Mayhem had bonded over their mutual rebellion. Then, roughly a fortnight ago, they'd bonded over their shared origins. Betony and Lorrivare had produced three eggs throughout their captivity. Mayhem, Fang, and Raine. Three males, two red and one white. All of them big and bold and stubborn. Raine had the impression Betony wished for docile hatchlings, creatures who would look to her for direction. *Pass.*

"How did they discover Mayhem is their son?" Raine hissed. His voice was pitched low, as if Betony or Lorrivare might overhear.

They wouldn't, as they were half a field away, along with the rest of the wedding guests. Raine and Aly loitered in the empty green between Rosa's manor house and the actual reception. After imbibing more than his fair share of roseberry wine, Raine had gone to relieve himself. Aly had caught him before he rejoined the festivities.

Aly pointed. Following her finger, Raine refocused on Mayhem's group. There was Mayhem. His mate, Eva. Eva's mother, Evin. And, *oh*.

Oh, shit.

Evin shoved her arm into Betony's chest, pushing her backwards. Raine regretted being out of hearing range as Evin lit into the high-handed storm mother. Lorrivare moved around the pair and seemed to be entreating Mayhem. Raine was too far away to read their expressions, but Mayhem's posture was insouciant. Almost smug.

"Mayhem told them," Aly said as they watched the scene unfold. "Betony tried pulling rank with Evin and me. She ordered us to relay any knowledge of parentage we possess or even suspect."

"Damn, that was stupid."

Evin had remained Betony's staunchest supporter, perhaps because she felt guilty for how the war dragons regarded her. As serene as a cloudless sky while also being kind and fair, Evin was a hit. The war dragons were drawn to her leadership style; a quiet, enduring authority that sought consideration and respect above all things.

Meanwhile, Betony exerted an overbearing dominance that only served to push the war dragons further away.

The storm mother didn't do well with the slight. She'd become more and more harsh in her dealings with Evin, fueled by spite that the war dragons preferred Evin to her.

Clarity bloomed like the sunny daffodils sprouted along the hedgerow. "Mayhem revealed his parentage to be a dick," Raine gasped. "Because he wants Betony to know Evin will be his den mother."

"Yup," Aly said on a nod. "Betony was saying once she identified her young, she was going to take them with her and *start a new dragon colony away from Evin and her degenerate thunder*." Aly's voice changed to mock Betony. "After that little announcement, she began pressuring me and Evin to reveal what we know. It was kind of funny, actually. She knows I can't stand her, and dangled the promise of her departure like a chicken on a string."

Raine snorted. "What does she think? That her fully grown offspring are going to follow her like lambs with a shepherd?"

"I don't think she sees you as real people," Aly confessed, a note of soberness creeping into her wine-soaked cheer. "Her time in the Cavern fucked with her head. With all of them. They spent so much time being seen as objects, they don't even realize how they're doing the exact same thing to their kids."

If Raine had a reply to that sapient insight, it wisped away like morning fog to high sun. Because Betony just fucking shredded her gown. Transforming into a long, silvery-lilac dragon, Betony attacked Evin, who exploded in a great ball of glittering blue and met her head-on.

"Well, I guess Mayhem is being true to his namesake," Raine said wryly as the two dragonesses took their fight to the sky. The females clashed like satellites in tangled orbits as they ducked and wove around each other.

"They better not singe a single tablecloth, or Sidian will have both their asses," Aly said.

Raine's eyes widened in alarm, and he scanned the reception for his mate. The guests resembled a flock of turkeys, their necks craned to watch the unfolding battle between Evin and Betony. Raine found his mate standing with Zane and a couple other dragons, his black hair standing out amid the jewel tones.

As his eyes locked onto his mate, Raine felt a tendril of cold rage unfurl in his chest. *Uh oh.*

Sidian. Was. Pissed. Nobody and nothing was allowed to fuck up his brother's big day. Raine watched Sidian's hand drop to the sword at his hip. A gorgeous blade forged of steel and black diamond, it was a gift from Nyx.

After the guild was disbanded, their dragon bone weapons were collected and interred in a mass grave. A monument was being built to mark the site—a bittersweet memorial for the dragons who had lost their lives when nightmares ruled. Nyx had presented the sword to Sidian the day after the bones were laid to rest.

Raine sent a wave of tenderness and calm down their bond. He knew from experience that it felt like being hugged from the inside out, as warm and soothing as a boiling bath. Boiling baths he and his mate now shared. The thought laced his wave of reassurance with a frisson of arousal.

Slowly, Sidian's hand fell away from the sheath.

His mate's head turned and found him unerringly, as if he'd known Raine's precise location this whole time. He probably had. Sidian was a wonderfully attentive mate. Passionate and possessive and never far away.

Sidian prowled toward Raine, his thighs bunching sinuously beneath his formal breeches. His jacket and waistcoat were tailored to accentuate his masculine shape; shoulders wide enough to lay on, a broad chest and narrow hips.

Sidian's dark eyes flashed as he reached them. "Why," he bit out, his husky voice uncharacteristically sharp, "are two dragons fighting at my brother's wedding reception?"

Raine's thoughts muddled as his blood surged south. His libido only registered his mate's intensity, and dismissed the reason behind it entirely. Sidian faltered at the unmistakable flare of lust. He rounded on Raine, exasperation plain in his features.

"I will take care of you later," he said with a hint of smoke. Lovely fawn eyes narrowed. "But right now, I want answers."

Aly poked Raine's side and smirked. "Is my sweet, little princess getting hot and bothered by his big, angry dragon?"

Raine's face heated, turning rosier than the wine he was half-drunk on. To Sidian, he said, "Betony tried using her storm mother status against Evin and Aly. To get them to tell her which dragons are kin to her and Lorrivare."

Sidian's dusky mouth tightened. "Knowing her, that's not a surprise."

"No," Raine agreed shortly. "But then Mayhem decided it would be funny to reveal himself as their son." Sidian's brows climbed his forehead. "Exactly. I guess Betony has this fantasy of stealing away with her beloved hatchlings and starting another storm from scratch, someplace far removed from us insolent assholes."

As one, the three of them surveyed the embattled figures above. Evin's long, azure tail shimmered as it lashed Betony's side. Pale purple wings beat frantically as Betony dodged another jab, then spat fire in Evin's face.

"If they singe so much as a single tablecloth ..." Sidian trailed off menacingly, then glared as Raine and Aly fell into each other, belting out laughter.

Zane appeared at Aly's side and tugged her gently away from Raine. She went readily and settled into the crook of her mate's arm. As her gaze met Raine's, they started giggling again.

To Sidian, Zane said, "We're going to give our best wishes to the happy couple while we can. Good luck with that." His eyes darted meaningfully toward the sky before they left.

Sidian's jawline was rigid, his stare accusatory.

Raine's giggles faded into a pout. "Don't look at me like that. I had no involvement with that mess."

"That *mess* is bleeding into every spare moment of our lives." Raine closed his eyes. *Not this again.* "You give them power over you by hiding your ancestry. I'm not asking you to welcome them into your life or even treat them as family. But you need to tell them. This situation is prolonged and worsened by your cowardice."

Raine flinched.

Sidian closed his eyes, his features etched with frustrated anger. Raine felt a tiny lick of apology inside his chest, and knew his mate was only being harsh out of love. And perhaps a little stress for the creamy white linens draping the tables.

"I'll tell them." Sidian's eyes flew open. "Next year, maybe," Raine added.

Sidian scowled. "Your father wished for you to know them."

"Low blow," Raine hissed.

His heart clenched at the mention of his father. He strove to honor his father's memory in as many ways as he could. Chambrin

Keep, once a militant stronghold, now served as a dragon sanctuary. Raine had even permitted Betony and her storm's residence because it's what his father would have wanted.

"You seize any excuse to put it off," Sidian said frostily. "Now there are dragons fighting at Nyx's wedding. Betony is not going to put her asinine notions to rest until she is forced to."

"I can't make the other dragons do anything—"

"They hold their tongues out of deference to you," Sidian shouted.

Raine jerked as if slapped. "*What?*"

No. Sidian had to be wrong. The parents were awful. Grasping and presumptive. They just *assumed* their children wanted parental figures. But even as Raine thought it, Sidian shook his head.

"Unlike you, they were not raised with the love of a father. Look at them." Sidian waved an arm at the distant reception. "Do you see war dragons on one side and their parents on the other, in some starkly drawn line in invisible sand? Because I see all of them mingling, exchanging pleasantries. There's Ruby and Jaska. Who do they stand near? Who is Ruby speaking with? What about Yip and Crash? Who is that with them?"

Raine swallowed roughly. The truth was devastatingly apparent, staring him straight in the face if he'd only cared to see it. Because they were with their parents, he saw. Nearly all of them, though their parents remained clueless.

"If they reveal themselves, a very brief process of elimination will subsequently unveil your parentage," Sidian murmured softly. "Mayhem was probably being an ass, but that was not his sole motivation for enlightening Betony and Lorrivare. He's trying to nudge things along."

Sidian's expression gentled, eyes heavy with understanding. The string of Raine's cravat tightened like a boa constrictor. He looked away from his mate's too-knowing gaze. "I need a drink."

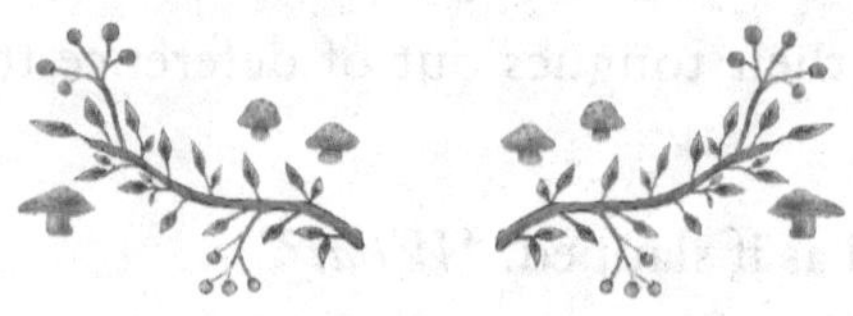

Sidian's stare was a brand between Raine's shoulder blades as he strode back to the party. Evin and Betony appeared to have reached a stalemate of sorts, each landing on opposite ends of Rosa's elegant lawn. The minstrels struck up a lively tune, a prelude to the first dance.

Raine snagged two bubbling glasses from a serving maid with mahogany curls beneath her uniform cap. Nyx and Rosa were engaged in a happy discussion with Lukor and Naiah, the latter's glow rivaling the bride's. Naiah and Lukor had randomly disappeared the previous month. When Raine had inquired about their absence, he learned more about dragon reproductive cycles than he ever wanted to know.

Naiah massaged her lower belly through her skirts, a secret smile on her lips. If Raine's edification had been sound, she would soon lay an egg and brood for a season. By summer's end, the first dragon to be hatched by its own flesh-and-blood parents in over two centuries would arrive.

Raine's eyes roved over the many clusters of guests. An unrecognizable emotion twinged in his gut as he saw Lorrivare—his biological father—in discussion with Fang and Mayhem. Eva was to the side, laughing at something Tejayla said.

Before he could think too deeply on it, Raine knocked back a flute of sparkling wine and placed it on an empty table. He kept the other glass tucked close to his chest as he joined his two brothers and their ... sire.

Mayhem noticed Raine first and smirked. Asshole. They were friendly enough these days, but Mayhem was Mayhem. He enjoyed being a pain.

Fang, Lorrivare's middle child—though Raine wasn't certain the wine-red dragon knew that yet—gave him a welcoming grin. "Tell me why one of the servers just told me, 'May the Sleeping Mother dream sweetly for you.'"

Raine blinked. "Really?"

Lorrivare nodded, his face a mask of cool politeness. "Another told me he hopes my spark comes swiftly." At Raine's confused expression, he added, "It is an old saying among dragons. Reserved for those who have yet to find their mates."

Fang grinned as Raine's puzzled frown deepened. "The humans don't always understand, but they have the spirit."

Raine tilted his head as he glanced reflexively at the nearest serving staff, a couple of young men carrying trays of roseberry wine and finger foods. "How do they know old dragon expressions?"

He thought it a fair question, considering he didn't know any old dragon expressions and doubted many of the war dragons did, either. But Mayhem shook his head at him in mock reprimand.

"Nyx considers you family, yet you don't make any time to read his book."

A blush warmed Raine's ears, and he sipped his wine, stalling out of guilt. "I've been busy," he said lamely.

The truth was, he liked when Sidian told him the stories. His mate's husky voice was smoke and satin, so decadent it was sinful. Sidian didn't read from Nyx's book, however. They were usually curled around each other in bed, lazily stroking hair or skin as they talked quietly about anything and everything. Once in a while, in those moments, Sidian would share a bit of dragon history from Nyx's book, *A Study of Dragons.*

It wasn't the most meticulous method for Raine to learn about his heritage, but Sidian's voice ruined him for reading the volume on his own. He made a mental note to have Sidian recount some of the other sections of Nyx's book since he clearly possessed huge gaps in his knowledge.

"It is my understanding that multiple thousands of copies of *A Study of Dragons* have been procured and consumed by humans," Lorrivare said stiffly. "And here you stand, a dragon blessed with prophetic hue and no passion or curiosity for your species. Your lack of interest is a disservice to the Dreaming Mother."

"I don't think the Dreaming Mother is offended that I haven't been to a book shop of late." This was why Raine couldn't tell Betony or Lorrivare what he was to them. They were so fucking eager to criticize everything he said or did.

Lorrivare looked at Raine like he was dog shit stuck to the heel of his boot. "My *son* Mayhem tells me you're the reason our children are so reluctant to come forward."

Raine flashed Mayhem a dark scowl. His eldest brother smiled angelically in return. Before Raine could say anything, Lorrivare stepped forward, inserting himself in Raine's personal space. The toes of their shoes almost touched.

"My mate cries herself to sleep every night," Lorrivare said, rough with anger and something else. Something fragile. "Devastated that she couldn't protect her eggs. And destroyed by the idea that our hatchlings hate her for it. Enough is enough. This sick game of yours ends now."

Beyond Lorrivare's shoulder, Fang stared at Raine, beseeching. He just wanted to know his parents, Raine saw. Know them as a son, and see if they could be a family.

Raine stepped away from Lorrivare, putting a respectable distance between them. It was Fang he looked at as he said, "I never meant to force anyone's silence. You and the others may declare yourselves with my blessing."

It was all he could manage. Raine might be a white dragon, but he was destined to be the black sheep of his parents' children. Betony and Lorrivare couldn't stand him, and the feeling was mutual. The gratitude that lit his brother's cherry red eyes wedged a shard of shame into his chest.

Without another word, Raine walked away.

EPILOGUE: PART TWO

Raine sat on the edge of his bed and toed off the shiny dress shoes that Sidian had made him wear. The bedchamber door flew open suddenly, the iron knob cracking against stone.

Sidian swept in like a tsunami and loomed over Raine, radiating the power and wrath of an earth-cleansing god.

"You," he seethed.

Raine clamped his legs shut and straightened, sternly informing his cock that Sidian's intense gaze was not a precursor to *that*. Sidian's eyes flared and Raine knew he detected his arousal through their bond.

"Me," he said weakly, hoping Sidian wasn't paying much attention to his body's reaction. They had been mated for half a year, and Raine still felt like a mindless, rutting animal around his worldly and controlled mate.

"Do you know how many rooms the Roke Manor possesses?" Before Raine could fathom this nonsensical question, Sidian gritted out, "*Eighty-seven*. I know because I checked every single one of them. Searching for *you*."

"Oh." Raine winced. He had left the reception immediately after speaking with Lorrivare, his thoughts a frustrated tangle of too many emotions to unravel.

Flying home at top speed, he had nearly fainted thanks to the Cravat from Hell that refused to untie or loosen. After redressing in the landing tent, Raine had chatted with Wylan about the various summer projects meant to make Chambrin Keep better suited to dragon occupancy. He had just returned to their quarters to bathe when Sidian burst in.

"Yes, *oh*." Sidian's handsome face twisted with outrage. "You couldn't spare a minute of your time to inform me of your departure?"

Raine looked at his stocking-clad feet, unable to meet his mate's accusing stare. "I'm sorry," he whispered, and meant it. "I wasn't thinking."

Silence stretched for an eternity. Then, a cool hand tucked under Raine's chin and lifted his head.

Sidian's features were as smooth and inscrutable as a river stone. Raine's pulse drummed in his ears as he gazed into his mate's velvet eyes. Sidian's thumb stroked his cheek.

"Don't do it again," he warned darkly.

Raine's mouth went dry at the promise of punishment in his mate's tone. He swallowed hard, clenching his knees more tightly together. "I won't," he rasped.

Sidian's thumb stroked Raine's full bottom lip. "What happened?"

Raine struggled to remember. His attention was fixed on the digit caressing his mouth, rubbing back and forth in the same tantalizing manner as Sidian's cock when his mate felt like teasing Raine, giving him a kiss of slick salt before pulling back.

"I was going to tell Lorrivare," he gasped. Sidian's thumb paused as his gaze narrowed. Raine rushed to add, "But then he acted like a total prick. He said I do the Dreaming Mother a disservice because I haven't read Nyx's book yet."

Thick lashes created brief, crescent shadows under Sidian's eyes as he blinked slowly. "Why haven't you?"

Raine shifted on the soft mattress and hoped Sidian didn't look down at his lap. Not that it mattered. Raine's lust burned hotter and brighter than a star down their bond. Even so, Raine wanted his mate to know he took him seriously and was capable of having a serious discussion without sex on his mind. Although that last part was debatable.

"Because I like hearing the stories from you."

Sidian snorted softly. His thumb resumed its slow, back-and-forth motion, like a pendulum against Raine's lips.

"I did the next best thing though," Raine said. "I was too irritated to declare myself, but I gave the other dragons my blessing. By this time tomorrow, Betony and Lorrivare will have figured it out themselves."

Surprise flashed in Sidian's eyes, there and gone as quickly as the glint of sun on scales. "Hm." His mate hummed noncommittally, the pressure of his thumb increasing.

Raine parted his lips like the greedy thing he was, and Sidian pushed his thumb into his mouth. Raine moaned, sucking the salt from his mate's skin. Sidian's lust ripped through him like a bomb, white-hot shrapnel imploding through his core.

"Take off your clothes." Sidian pulled out his thumb and trailed his hand down to Raine's cravat, which still somehow looked immaculate. "Except this. Leave this on."

Raine couldn't remove it if he wanted to, but he didn't say so. There wasn't enough air in his lungs for speech. He stood on unsteady legs. His hands were as clumsy as untried dragon paws as he fumbled with the buttons on his waistcoat.

Sidian went to shut their chamber door, then dimmed the oil lamps, bathing their room in a soft glow. While Sidian was busy, Raine redoubled his efforts to shed his clothing, not wanting his mate to witness the majority of his awkwardness.

As Sidian approached him once more, Raine was naked. His cock was peaked to full erectness. Wetness gleamed at its tip.

With his back to the lamps, Sidian's countenance was shadowed as he looked Raine up and down. "Get on the bed."

Raine shook with nervous excitement as he laid back on their four-poster bed. The cotton linens were soft and clean, smelling of spring from their time hanging on the clothesline outside. He rested his head on a pillow near the headboard and looked to his mate for approval.

Sidian said nothing as he walked to a chest in the corner of their room. He remained fully clothed, dress shoes clicking sharply against the floor as he moved.

Raine's cock begged to be stroked. He clenched his fists at his sides and ignored the urge. The last time his mate was in a mood like this and Raine touched himself without explicit instruction, Sidian had pulled a pair of black diamond handcuffs out of their closet and made Raine feel the full repercussions of his impatience.

Glass vials clinked. Raine's cock wept as his heart raced. He knew what Sidian was grabbing, and his body's response was as eager as a cat in heat. Or a dragon, for that matter.

"Catch." The smoky command was followed by a small, soaring vial. Raine caught it on instinct, surprised he managed any coordination in his state. Sidian stood at the foot of the bed, surveying Raine with hooded eyes. "Prepare yourself."

Raine sucked in a breath, gripping the vial harder. "P-Prepare myself?"

He'd never ... That was to say, Sidian always slicked his entrance. His mate enjoyed touching him there, employing fingers and sometimes tongue before fucking him mercilessly.

Sidian watched him silently, a hint of challenge in his stare. He'd picked up on Raine's uncertainty and was deliberately ignoring it.

Raine drew a breath and unstoppered the vial. Oil spilled out and pooled on his abdomen. The heady scent of cinnamon and vanilla wafted through the air. A mutual favorite. He coated his fingers and reached down. His knees bent as he spread his thighs.

The oil was cool and slippery against his tightly budded entrance. A wave of scorching lust rocked him. He gasped, lips parting as Sidian's desire crashed through him like a riptide. It gave him the courage to slip a digit inside. Raine's body was tighter than a fist, muscles clenching hotly around his finger.

He looked up, panting at the wildfire raging in his belly. Sidian's expression was no longer schooled to cool indifference. No. His mate's visage was stark with hunger. A ravenous wolf mid-winter. Raine moaned, pushing deeper into his hole.

His flesh gave reluctantly. Squeezing so tight, Raine preened. He knew the exquisite pleasure his mate took from their couplings. He savored the wrecked wonder on Sidian's face every time he sunk into him. His mate's huge cock entering his small, slick hole was heaven on the verge of torment, for both of them.

Raine moaned again as he added another finger. His cock wept as he imagined that impossible pressure encompassing his mate, the sheer bliss he gave Sidian with his body. Loud, uneven breaths sawed the air. Raine thought it was himself until he glanced at Sidian, two slick fingers buried deep in his hole.

His mate had unlaced his breeches. The dusky tip of his cock peeked out from a fist as he stroked himself, long and slow, eyes fixed on Raine like he would die if he looked away. "Another," he ordered huskily.

Raine swallowed hard, the tie around his neck more constricting than a collar. With shameless alacrity, he scooped some of the spilled oil off his stomach and added a third finger. There was a slight sting, the pressure almost painful. He crooked his fingers, searching. But no matter how he adjusted the angle, he couldn't find his sweet spot.

Sidian's control was masterful. He stroked himself with a measured pace that never quickened, though Raine could feel his desire. Thicker than syrup and so hot, he marveled that his mate hadn't sprouted flames.

Raine wondered if his mate was waiting for him to add a fourth finger when Sidian's hand fell away from his cock. With smooth, unhurried motions, he undressed.

Raine panted, working himself with his fingers as Sidian climbed onto the bed. The mattress dipped with his weight as he knelt between Raine's spread thighs. His callused palms were warm and rough as they cupped Raine's knees. Sidian's gaze lingered on Raine's buried fingers before trailing to his face.

His brown eyes were molten with desire. "You're so fucking gorgeous." Raine gasped, his mate's smoke-laden compliment wrapping around his cock like velvet. Sidian's intense gaze dropped to his erection, rigid and leaking. "So needy."

His focus returned to Raine's hole. "So eager for my cock." Raine moaned a breathy affirmation, and Sidian chuckled darkly. "Remove your fingers. I want to see how well you did."

Raine withdrew, feeling empty and vulnerable as his mate inspected his hole. Sidian's palms squeezed his knees before dropping away.

"Not bad for a first try," Sidian purred. "But you need more oil."

Raine's muscles twitched and bunched as Sidian swiped a hand over his abdomen, gathering the oil there. He was careful about it, ensuring he didn't so much as brush Raine's throbbing cock. Raine whimpered a protest. Sidian chuckled at the sound before inserting his own fingers into Raine's hole.

Raine moaned, back arching as Sidian expertly prepared him. His mate was in the mood to tease, his strokes light and evasive, never brushing against the tiny bundle of nerves that made Raine see stars.

"Please," Raine begged, knowing it was useless. His knuckles were white where he bunched the sheets at his sides with his fists.

"Please, what?" Sidian stared at him from between his thighs, his blue-black hair falling to one side. "Tell me what you need."

"You." Raine's voice was thin and breathless. Desperate. "Fuck me. Please, Sidian."

Sidian groaned and twisted his fingers viciously. "You want to feel my cock breaking into your tight body? Want me to fuck your pretty hole until you're slick and full with my cum?"

"Yes," Raine sobbed, his hips canting upward as he fucked himself on his mate's hand.

His hole was abruptly empty. Before Raine could whimper at the loss, Sidian yanked him downward with a bruising grip around his hips. The blunt head of Sidian's cock pushed at his entrance. Raine hissed, then moaned as his flesh yielded to his mate's thick, hard shaft.

Sidian sheathed himself fully, then paused. Eyes of liquid mercury met velvet brown. Sidian's face was a mask of unbearable rapture as he waited for Raine's body to adjust. But Raine was too hot and aching. He needed Sidian to pound into him more than he needed his next breath.

He lifted himself up and wrapped his arms around Sidian's neck. Their mouths met in a hot, plundering kiss. Sidian's frame was as tense as marble, muscles locked and rigid as he mastered his desire to fuck Raine senseless.

Raine would have none of that. Sidian was masterful in his self-control. But Raine was masterful in snapping that control. He sucked Sidian's tongue into his mouth and tasted the lingering sweetness of cake icing as he lifted his ass and thrust down, fucking himself on his mate's cock.

He swallowed Sidian's shaky groan as the grip on his hips grew painful. The broad shoulders beneath Raine's hands were taut and trembling. He lifted his hips and bore down again, seating his mate fully inside him.

Sidian's mouth tore away on a ragged gasp. Cupping the smooth globes of Raine's bottom, he snapped his hips forward, driving his cock exquisitely deep.

It was pleasure and pain and utterly mind-numbing.

Sidian's cock sank deeper as he guided Raine backward and covered his body with his own. Raine's lips parted on a breathless gasp as Sidian fisted his cravat with a brutal hand and pounded into his hole with unrestrained ferocity.

Raine moaned, slack-mouthed and eyes glazed. Above him, Sidian was tight-lipped and unblinking as he drank in Raine's every reaction. He tugged the cravat harder, until Raine could barely breathe. He grew lightheaded, and his cock pulsed between them, achingly sensitized.

Spots danced in Raine's vision, and the cravat loosened. Raine gulped air, then gasped as his mate's thrusts became wild and punishing, almost cruel. Stretching Raine's hole to the limit over and over.

Sidian's cock dragged against Raine's sweet spot, setting off spine-melting fireworks. Raine arched off the bed, his arms cinching around Sidian's neck for purchase as white-hot rapture overtook him. Sidian reached between their bodies and wrapped a fist around Raine's erection. It was embarrassingly slick, dripping with desire. Sidian's hips moved in sync with his hand, fucking Raine's hole while fisting his cock. The pleasure was too much to endure. Raine was going to shatter like blown glass, explode in a cloud of ash and embers.

"Look at me," Sidian rasped. The edge of need bleeding into his demand made it no less authoritative or compelling.

Raine peeled open his eyes, which he hadn't realized were shut. Sidian scrutinized Raine's face as he filled him with a slow, intentional thrust. His cock crammed against Raine's sweet spot and stayed there. Raine's features wrenched with delicious agony and Sidian moaned, experiencing reciprocal ecstasy through their bond.

"Fuck, Raine," Sidian hissed. A prayer. A curse.

As Sidian withdrew, their bond opened further. Raine felt the searing heat of his own body, the silken squeeze of his hole. The unearthly bliss of sinking into pure heaven as Sidian pushed back inside him.

"So fucking greedy," Sidian gritted. Without warning, he slammed into Raine's sweet spot. They both moaned. "Do you like it when I fuck you sore? Like feeling me stretch your pretty hole?"

Fuck. As Sidian spoke, Raine became acutely aware of how swollen and tender his hole was. Sidian fucked him deep and slow, as if reveling in the way Raine stretched around his cock. Raine's hole clenched and fluttered as Sidian grinded into his sweet spot over and over. Long, lazy strokes that turned Raine molten. He whimpered and sobbed, clinging to Sidian as an orgasm burst through him like a geyser, coating Sidian's hand where it gripped him.

A low, hoarse groan tickled Raine's ear as a second orgasm ripped through him. Sidian's cum flooded his hole, slicking him with his spend as he fucked out the final throes of their climax.

Raine closed his eyes, savoring the strong, steady beat of his mate's heart against his ear. They were naked, limbs intertwined beneath a pile of sheets and blankets. He nuzzled his face deeper into Sidian's chest and hummed in pleasure as his mate began to massage his back.

After their fierce lovemaking, they'd shared a bath. The lamps had burnt out while they lingered in the water. Now, their only light source emanated from the corner hearth, where a crackling fire licked logs into coals.

"Why are you so fearful of Betony and Lorrivare discovering that you're their offspring?"

Raine's back stiffened. Sidian continued his slow, lazy massage. As if he hadn't just snuffed Raine's cozy afterglow like an icy draft winking out a candle.

"I'm not afraid," he said tersely.

"Oh?" Irony dripped like poison from Sidian's utterance.

Raine lifted his head to scowl at him. "I haven't been hiding from them like some frightened rabbit."

Sidian arched a raven brow, exuding skepticism. Blankets bunched around Raine's waist as he sat upright and faced Sidian fully.

"I just don't fucking *like* them," he snapped. Bitterness, black and sticky like tar, coated his throat and tongue. "My father died saving them. And for what? They've done nothing but dishonor his sacrifice since. They destroyed his home, killing over a hundred men. They're self-centered, ungrateful brutes. I wish my father had let them fucking rot. All of them combined aren't worth half of him."

Silence yawned like a chasm. A log popped loudly in the fire as Raine struggled to calm his racing pulse.

"We have already been through this," Sidian said patiently. "Fresh out of the Cavern, they were unstable and ignorant of human society."

"That doesn't excuse their actions."

"They didn't know—"

"They didn't *ask*." Raine's silver eyes flashed.

Sidian straightened, his broad shoulders squaring. "Neither did I," he said coldly. "I am guilty of atrocities. Of mistakes I cannot reverse. The only reason I stopped hunting and slaughtering dragons was you."

Raine swallowed against a sudden tightness in his throat. "That's different."

"How." It wasn't a question, but a demand. "How can you blame them and forgive me? Forgive Nyx? Hell, forgive your father, whose illustrious career of savaging dragons was so celebrated that he became a legend for it?"

"Because I love you," Raine spat. "And because I know you, heart and soul. And like my father and Nyx, you changed as soon as you knew better. You are the best fucking thing in my life, and I'm not going to listen to you act like that's not true. To hell with your mistakes, Sidian. My life began anew the moment I saw you. I like to think it works the opposite way, too. That maybe our love remade you, as well."

Sidian's expression softened. Eyes like melted chocolate sucked Raine inside, bathing him in dark decadence. Raine shivered as a callused finger tucked an errant lock of hair behind his ear. "You are my heart," Sidian murmured. "Your love didn't remake me, Raine. It made me, period."

He opened his mouth. Closed it. "Oh."

"You met me at my worst and loved me when I didn't deserve it. You met your parents at their worst, as well." Raine's lungs swelled a protest. Sidian shushed him with a look. "The circumstances aren't identical, but they are similar enough that I know something else is at play here. You do not blame Betony's storm for your father's death. You do not hate them for their mistakes. So, I ask you again. Why are you so fearful of Betony and Lorrivare discovering that you are theirs?"

Raine sighed and tugged the blankets more securely around his waist. Of course, his mate saw through his bullshit. Their bond was more intimate than anything he could have imagined. It left no room for bluster.

"Because they don't like *me*," he mumbled to his lap, twisting the sheets with his confession.

"Raine."

His hackles rose at the tenderness in Sidian's voice. Whatever his mate had to say, Raine didn't want to hear it. He looked up and wasn't surprised at the excruciatingly tender expression on Sidian's face. But Raine wasn't looking for pity or reassurance.

"No, Sidian. Whatever you're going to say—*don't*. Betony disowned me. Right before the Nine recaptured her storm, remember? And you know what? Good riddance."

"That was ill-done of her," Sidian said carefully, as if choosing his words. "She was out of her mind with paranoia and fear when she said that. Betony has since apologized to you. Formally and sincerely."

Raine snorted. "Yeah, she did. *After* I transformed."

Sidian's tone gentled further. "Your disowning was never valid. And what's more, Betony revoked the sentiment the very next day. I promise that your parents will not only like you. They will love you. All they need is a chance."

"Betony and Lorrivare have never once speculated that I'm their son," Raine said slowly, enunciating each syllable. "Whenever they address me, I'm just the ill-mannered upstart gatekeeping them from their *precious* young. Nevermind that I could easily *be* one of theirs. Nevermind that I *am*. Their refusal to so much as consider the possibility tells me everything I need to know about how welcome that news would be."

Sidian's brows knitted as Raine spoke. He was full-on frowning by the time Raine finished. "Has it occurred to you that they might think such speculation would be unwelcomed by *you?*"

Raine scoffed. "They don't give a flying fuck about offending me, so I don't see how that would stop them." Before Sidian could scrounge up more feeble excuses for Betony and Lorrivare's attitude towards him, Raine said, "The issue is moot. As you've already pointed out, a process of elimination will reveal me as their third child. I'm over it."

"Come here." Sidian leaned back against the pillows at the head of their bed and opened his arms.

While their topic had agitated Raine, he didn't think he would ever be so irritated as to deny himself an embrace with Sidian. Tawny gold met sun-kissed alabaster as their chests aligned. Raine buried his face in the crook of Sidian's neck, inhaling the uniquely sweet scent that sang to his soul. Sidian's arms wrapped around him and squeezed.

Raine didn't care what Betony or Lorrivare thought of him. The only person who mattered was his mate. He hummed his approval as Sidian smoothed a hand down his back. Sidian's chest shook on a silent laugh as Raine's cock hardened between their stomachs.

"I am attempting to console you," Sidian announced gravely.

Raine lifted his head and met his mate's deadpan stare. "Console me with your cock," he purred.

With a low growl that electrified Raine's core, Sidian flipped him onto his back and proceeded to do just that.

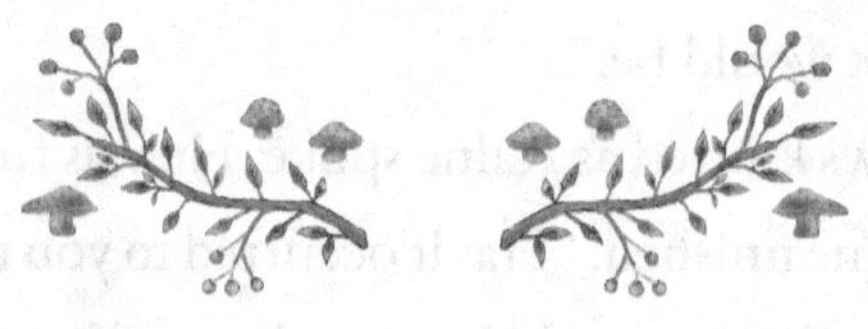

Raine jolted to awareness, blinking in confusion. Sidian stirred next to him, muttering something incoherent into his pillow before burrowing deeper under the covers.

Raine frowned, uncertain what had awoken him so abruptly. A series of firm knocks rapped against the entrance to their living quarters, and Raine groaned before slipping out of bed. His ass was deliciously sore as he padded across the stone floor and threw on a silk robe to shield his nakedness.

Hoping it wasn't Wylan telling him the lumber they'd purchased was going to be delayed another month, he moved through the sitting room. The first rays of dawn faintly illuminated a pair of well-worn sofas and the coffee table littered with Raine's wallpaper designs and sample rolls.

Whoever it was began knocking a third time just as he threw open the door. And froze.

Betony's fist dropped like a stone. She was wan, her silvery purple hair unkempt about her shoulders as though she'd just rolled out of bed after a restless sleep.

"Raine." Her tone was so surprised, he wondered if she'd knocked on his door by mistake.

"Betony," he replied dryly. "May I help you with something?"

He knew she would find out eventually, but she couldn't know this soon. It had to be a separate matter that brought her here, though he couldn't imagine what. Betony had never graced his private chambers with a visit.

Betony brought her hands together, wringing them nervously. "No. Yes. That is." She stopped and appeared to collect herself before meeting his gaze steadily. "I do not wish to impose, but there's something I would say."

Raine nodded encouragingly, hoping it was brief. His feet were cold against the chilly floor, and he wanted to sneak a cuddle with Sidian before the day began in earnest.

She drew a breath. "I realize Lorrivare and I haven't made the best impression. If you do not care to become better acquainted with us, I will understand." Tears glimmered in her pale eyes. The merest drop of purple was all that kept them from being as silver as his own. "But I have loved you since the day I felt you come into existence. A small, dancing flame ensconced in shell inside my body. And I would be honored if we could start over."

She wiped at her face impatiently, but it was useless. Her eyes were faucets. Rivulets ran down either cheek.

Panic ballooned in Raine's chest. He was used to Betony being an abrasive, self-centered shrew. Not this sad, humble watering pot of vulnerability. "I, um. Where's Lorrivare?" he asked, hearing the desperation in his voice.

Betony wiped at her face, and the tears weren't immediately replaced. Raine relaxed the smallest bit. "He told me to give you time. That I should wait for you to come to us. But I couldn't help it." Damn it all to fucking hell, the woman began to cry again. Raine was rapidly coming to miss the prickly, rude version of Betony he was more familiar with. "I had to see you. And make sure you knew you were loved and welcomed by us."

He almost hissed as her uncanny phrasing pierced him. "Thank you," he said haltingly. "I will keep that in mind."

Without another word, he shut the door in her face. His heart raced in his chest as if he'd been under attack. He turned around and nearly leapt out of skin.

Sidian stood there, hair mussed, robe enticingly askew, and a stern look on his face as he crossed his arms and glared.

"What?" Raine demanded. He tried to retreat to their bedchamber. Sidian blocked him. Raine rolled his eyes. "You can't force me to talk to her."

Sidian's brows raised as if to say, *Wanna bet*?

A frisson of excitement shot down their bond before Raine could prevent it, and he blushed.

Sidian's eyes narrowed consideringly. "She made an effort to reach out to you. And whether you realize it or not, you've been as approachable as a thorn bush where they are concerned. It took great courage and love for her to do that."

Raine shifted on his feet, which had chilled to ice. Sidian's words pricked him with uncertainty and guilt. Because the more he thought about it, the more he saw the truth. Raine had done everything possible to rub Betony and Lorrivare the wrong way, then blamed them for their strained association.

"Go. Talk to her." Sidian leaned forward and whispered in his ear, "I'll wrestle you tonight. Whoever wins gets to do whatever they want to the other."

If dragons weren't impervious to flames, Raine would have spontaneously combusted at the heat spiraling through him.

In a flash, he was out the door and halfway down the hallway.

"Betony, wait." She paused and turned, waiting as he caught up to her. Her gaze was cautious with hope. "I would like to begin again, too." With a shock, Raine realized he meant it. "How about we start with breakfast?"

Her answering smile was dazzling. "Now?"

"Now," Raine said firmly. He offered his arm, a thoughtlessly human gesture, then braced himself for censure.

Instead, she took it, smile widening. "I would love to."

AFTERWORD

I'm so sad to conclude this series. I don't want to leave Valdenia (as evinced by my two-part epilogue, heh heh). I hope you enjoyed Raine and Sidian's adventure as much as I did!

There are so many scenes I had to edit out. Otherwise, the story would have been egregiously long. There was a very cute scene when Raine fell asleep on Sidian in the bath (during their first night at Roke Manor). And an amusing morning-after scene where Aly and Rosa teased Raine mercilessly (after his consummation). The Dappled War Horse of Doom made an appearance at Nyx's wedding, too! Ha! So much fun.

I might clean up those scenes and make them "bonus" content on my website (:

Thank you so much for coming on this journey. This duology was very much a passion project. Actually, MM is a passion for me, in general. I can't wait to share my next one. Stay tuned!

ABOUT THE AUTHOR

Misu Loy published her first novel in April of 2023. With dozens of characters inside her head—all clamoring for the spotlight—it's safe to say, many more books are forthcoming.

Romance is the genre she lives and breathes. Readers should anticipate lots of slow burn stories with enemies-to-lovers dynamics. Those are Misu's favorite kinds of stories—and thus, her passion.

When Misu isn't working her day job or writing love stories, she's usually walking her doggos, reading fiction, or pestering her spouse and family to go to the park or play Scrabble with her.

Visit <u>www.MisuLoy.com</u> to connect with Misu or see what she's up to.